I *didn't do anything u* *Until I knew wh*  the
"Our men .... w
best."

The poem grew louder in the room, its meaning still eluding the man in the chair.

Before the cut of the knife, they had bled him more, hoping to cure him, they claimed. He fought them, even broke one doctor's nose when they attempted to hook him up to the wires that shook three teeth loose when the current flew. Different men beat him in varying fashions, until they finally delivered chains to his room. The food and water dwindled, and he was left with only damp bowls and the memories of spaetzel and beer to water his tongue.

The orderly with the new scar on his cheek smiled wider with each visit. *The things he and the doctors did to him. God would never approve.* The man thought even the devil would cringe at the atrocities he witnessed.

The pain sharpened, hitting something deep inside of him. Changing him. His thoughts swam, and he felt himself drown. He watched them sink in his mind, losing clarity, until he forgot for a moment where he was. His anger dissipated, as did his thoughts of his people coming to retrieve him. Every image tilted out of focus, just enough so names and faces swirled in agony.

He sobbed as he realized he now couldn't recall his home, his daughter's face. Only snowcaps remained in his head. The sensation of the doctor pushing that tool into his skull, twisting and turning, grew and dimmed until he could sense his home once more.

The blade had finally pierced his soul.

FEAR THE REAPER

BY DAVID SIMMS

DEDICATION

Thanks to Marty Seibel and the Black Raven Paranormal family. Special thanks to the Odd Stones Alliance for continued motivation (Cecilia, Olivia, Shawna, Renee, and Karen). Of course, thanks to Trudi and Sawyer, who allow me to disappear into the cave to write my stories.

PROLOGUE

When a man plays God, the glint of the devil shines in his eyes.

The moment they dragged the man into the room, he knew the fight was over. He had been there before. Never strapped down into the chair, but he had been there viewing patients. The doctor had warned him, a few times, but his morals finally surfaced. He thought he could do it their way. He believed in the cause. The money. He didn't fear them until it was too late.

"The worst is only as good as the best."

The doctor loved his poems. Godawful and written as if the devil himself had guided his hands as he composed the vile rhymes. He had sung them to the patients during their treatments, as if he was convincing them of their lot in life, their abomination to the nation.

Just as the man sang to him now.

"Defectives will only breed defectives."

The patient struggled, his arms bound tight in leather straps, his head bound in a steel band. The doctor removed the leukotome, slickened with fluids of various hues. He only knew the tool's name as the doctor had been explaining the procedure repeatedly to the others in the room. A nurse, the vicious one, and the man in the fancy suit understood it all. Words uttered meant not for him—a creature lesser than something they stepped on, said the doctor. The long silver instrument resembled a hammer claw at one end, a long shaft stretching into a point that would soon enter him again.

The man's thoughts rambled down numbing arms and legs, believing his body to be severed from his mind. He felt little below his neck. His cheek tickled as a tear rolled over it, convinced his body was ready to die.

He strained with both arms to flinch, twitch, anything, yet both disobeyed him, remaining motionless save for the clenching of his fingers.

He couldn't die. Not yet. After everything he accomplished to get here, to set up a life for his people, good people, he'd fight dying with all his strength. He believed in a second life, but feared an eternal darkness.

Why can't he simply free me? The battle has been over for days now.

He could barely see the room anymore, the doctor, blind to his hell, even though he had only been in the chair for minutes. At least he could bask in his memories with lucidity.

Please God.

I didn't do anything wrong. I did what I was told.

Until I knew what they did here.

"Our men ... women ... blest. Best ... breed only ... the best."

The poem grew louder in the room, its meaning still eluding the man in the chair.

Before the cut of the knife, they had bled him more, hoping to cure him, they claimed. Purify him, they swore, despite noting he had come from a land they had approved. He fought them, even broke one doctor's nose when they attempted to hook him up to the wires that shook three teeth loose when the current flew. Different men beat him in varying fashions, until they finally delivered chains to his room. The food and water dwindled, and he was left with only damp bowls and the memories of spaetzel and beer to water his tongue.

The orderly with the new scar on his cheek smiled wider with each visit. *The things he and the doctors did to him. God would never approve.* The man thought even the devil would cringe at the atrocities he witnessed.

The pain of the doctor's tool yanked him back to the present. Through the remnants of his remaining vision, he saw the man push and twist the metal.

The pain sharpened, hitting something deep inside of him. Changing him. His thoughts swam, and he felt himself drown. He watched them sink in his mind, losing clarity, until he forgot for a moment where he was. His anger dissipated, as did his thoughts of his people coming to retrieve him. Every image tilted out of focus, just enough so names and faces swirled in agony.

He sobbed as he realized he now couldn't recall his home, his daughter's face. Only snowcaps remained in his head. The sensation of the doctor pushing that tool into his skull, twisting and turning, grew and dimmed until he could sense his home once more.

The blade had finally pierced his soul.

The doctor sang the final line of the poem heard so often in this building.

"For the best will only breed the best."

When he woke to the sensation of being lifted from the chair, he heard a faint voice. The doctor's? Possibly the nurse's or one from the offices in New York? Strong arms dragged him towards the door.

He strained with his one good eye, vision melting into a kaleidoscopic stew, as they moved him down the walkway amongst the sighing willows and heaving oaks above him. He sensed nobody around him in the dark. Once the moon rose, all others must have been back where they belonged.

The faint glow illuminated the path. The same path that he had discovered only two nights ago. The one that changed his mind. That altered his destiny and nearly brought God back into his soul.

When they cranked the huge metal door open, the last bit of his reality died.

He screamed into the abyss as they slammed the door behind him.

1

Samuel Taylor knew he couldn't outrun the dead. Two souls would forever claw at his back, longer if he wished to defy God in his work. He felt his flesh grow cold when he recalled leaving the two bodies behind, many miles back.

He should have been breathing in the splendor of the Blue Ridge Mountains as the train crossed into the Shenandoah Valley of Virginia. Instead, he spent the two-thousand-plus miles of his trip focusing not on talking to the two women near him, but praying the new job would somehow redeem him. He prayed to no one that he survived at least until his own ghosts buried him.

One female sat across from him in the riding car, a tall, slender beauty with hazel eyes. She deflected his many glances while perusing a worn copy of H.G. Wells' *The Time Machine*, keeping her eyes on the pages. Her skin appeared to glow, a pale olive tint which drew his thoughts back to the women he had first experienced overseas in the war. He attempted not to look, but even in her long dress, her lithe figure drew him to her.

The other woman sat next to him. His wife kept her hand on his, as he ached to wish her away, yet he knew he couldn't.

She had been dead for over two years. He knew he could never outrun her.

She would never let him forget what he did, even if she were only a figment of his broken psyche. The other ghost thankfully remained at bay, until the depths of sleep bound him.

Fear should have overtaken him, but the absence of it frightened him even more. She simply wouldn't let him go.

Her specter followed him from San Francisco to Chicago on the Pullman cars of the Pacific Railway and now from Richmond to Augusta. She had made sleeping in the horrid trap of a bed manageable, keeping his anxiety at bay while relaxing every inch of him in post-coital bliss.

Ever since her passing, she had only appeared intermittently, seemingly when his life had hit a crossroads. Terror had gripped him the first night she decided to visit him, the night he had accepted the Society's offer. She had appeared in his apartment, their apartment, just as he had been nodding off to sleep. He began to doubt his sanity in that moment when he saw her, but grief buried logic in less than a heartbeat. A sad comfort washed over him when her eyes connected with his, as he convinced himself it had to be a dream—until she reached out and gripped his hand in a cool but soft embrace.

Comfort froze over as he attempted to bolt from the bed, yet found his muscles disobeying. Sam felt his heart halt as she leaned in to kiss him, lips warm but not fully tangible on his. Paralyzed by his own fear, he allowed her to take him that night as he shivered and cried for her loss, until she left him bathed in sweat, fully spent. He had been trying to figure out why she came to him ever since, but had thrown his energy into work to both escape and pray what he did back in San Francisco never happened again to anyone else.

The following morning, he refused to think about the visit, or the sex, afraid she must have come for a reason. His training in psychology suggested the traumas he'd survived had finally murdered his sanity. He couldn't her face then, and couldn't now.

The chill on his face grew as she gazed at him with a look he knew held more love than what they had known during their life together. Something else grew within that look, something which made him refuse to face her. She was attempting to communicate with him, a message she felt he needed to hear, but he insisted on blocking out anything he could feel.

As the wheels of the Pullman car hummed on the tracks beneath, his body vibrated with a soothing sensation, much like the feeling the medication gave him. The physician who had found Sam sitting on the window sill of the hospital with one leg dangling six stories above the cobblestone street in San Francisco had prescribed him laudanum, simply to keep him alive. Yet Sam had kicked that crutch out from under him weeks ago—and stumbled like every man should in his situation. Each night on the rails, the rocking from the wind lulled him into sleep, reminding him he had a mission and another family, awaiting him in a new home.

A new life.

Now he found himself smiling at the living woman just a few feet away from the one whose life had departed, hoping to connect with her gaze, hoping for a diversion from his past realities. Yet still she focused on the pages of her book, possibly aware of him yet not acknowledging it. He would never think himself handsome enough to turn any woman's head, but felt himself drawn to her nevertheless. Ever since she had boarded in Richmond, the pages before her eyes seemed to block out her world. Why he wished for her to meet his own eyes, he couldn't decipher. He hadn't been with a woman since Miriam and still railed against anything more than polite conversation with anyone. Still, he found himself looking, admiring her hazel eyes and long neck above a soft blue dress, all while telling himself to focus elsewhere.

He dropped his eyes to the burgundy carpet strip running the length of the car. *How many couples had walked that distance to begin a vacation or new life? How many walked it to escape their own ghosts, both real and imagined?*

It only reminded him of the death he left behind in San Francisco.

The train had coursed through the Crozet tunnel, the chiseled path which finally allowed rail travel through the formidable mountain range from the Virginia coast and Richmond to the Shenandoah Valley. While he knew on most levels he should have been admiring the sights, the forever views of the mountains and valleys which he would now call home, he couldn't. Sam only knew how to focus on the task at hand.

He had to keep that focus. It pushed his pain behind the wall.

The new job. They had been grooming him for something like this for over a year. Now without a wife or child, he had leap-frogged to the top of their list. His work made him the prime candidate, as his product would help the movement which had sent him here.

With nothing to tie him down, he had jumped at the chance. He had only one stipulation, one which they agreed to without hesitation. His mother and brother would accompany him, transported from his home state of New Jersey, to live out their lives far away from the memories of his pain and a chance for them to escape a world in which neither ever truly felt home.

Samuel refused the windows and the grandeur beyond the glass, focusing instead on the other travelers, wondering if any of the folks might receive his treatment at the facility.

The sensation of his wife staring through his eyes into his past deeds unsettled him. It stirred the memories of what had happened the prior night in the sleeping car, just as it had many nights before. Each time she had shown herself to him, attempted to offer a sign, he always denied her.

The psychologist felt the pressure grow on the back of his hand as the train rounded the bend, exposing its interior to the bleeding colors of the sunset over the Allegheny Range, which lay in the shadows of the massive Appalachians. Something else existed in those shadows, painted with deep purple and crimson brushes, something he couldn't pinpoint. Many in the passenger car whistled or gasped at the spectacle fanning out for miles in either direction. Most city folk had never traveled this far into the state. For most, Richmond was Virginia, along with the towns surrounding Washington and the beaches where even those hit by the Depression sunbathed and wished away their troubles. Over the past seventeen years, he had witnessed nature's most beautiful and horrific scenery, from the California coast dotted with crimson redwoods to the fields of France, which held their own hues of that color in the soil and the soaked uniforms of his friends.

Giving in to the touch of his wife's hand, he finally allowed himself to look, to take in the scenery, the palette of resonant colors in the valley. His bones ached from the many days of travel, the nights in the cramped bunks on which so many travelers spent too much of their dwindling savings. He wondered why they sent him three thousand miles to continue the movement. Virginia didn't have the allure of California, New York, or even D.C.

What he saw wasn't what the tourists saw, what the businessmen, Roosevelt, and the WPA and CCC saw.

The rails brought them to the outskirts of the town which he would call home. He felt a weight in his chest as he focused on what lay beneath the bleeding sky.

Sam saw a pall cast on this future, his supposed salvation from the blood of his past.

Buildings, a series of connected structures A series of burgundy and ivory structures huddled together like the spinal ridge of a sleeping beast, looming ahead on a foothill signaling the entrance to the town. His wife's pressure increased on his hand. He refused to allow her concern to register.

Cloaked in the shadows of the setting sun, the town suggested anything but home to Samuel. Then again, he reminded himself, home for him died two years ago. The loss of two hearts had left him more alone than he ever knew was possible, and the soft touch on his flesh wouldn't allow him to forget. For nearly twenty-two months he had been living as if he had crawled into his own casket, simply awaiting the first shovelful of dirt to hit.

The hospital where he had accepted a position reached north and south along the boundary of the town, set back at viewing distance from Route 11, the main highway of western Virginia. Only from the rail line could the grand facility be seen in its entirety. It reminded him of the plantations in the Old South or the sprawling campuses of New England's Ivy League schools.

That's where he would perform that damned test. He knew it would cause suffering, but he prayed it would also end much more. As his mind catalogued the list of diseases, which he knew the facility would help end, both mental and physical, his wife's and son's faces filled his memory. That's why he took the job. If people passed his goddamn test, they might find happiness. If they failed, at least they wouldn't experience pain as he felt.

He could only aid the mental portion of the sad equations, but if he could help one person from feeling the emptiness which bored through his soul, it would be worth the years of effort. Regardless, the job at Western Valley Hospital and its new facility gave him a purpose, and a reason to emerge from his self-imposed crypt.

His ex-wife squeezed again, this time stealing a bit of his attention. Sam partly turned to her. Her faded but loving face drew him deep, but something in her gaze frightened him. He remembered the stories whispered about the Society but felt his test, his determination, would overcome all. They wanted what he wanted. A better, healthier world. Despite her expression, he allowed himself to smile. He squeezed back, hoping it wasn't all in his imagination.

The train pulled into the station just a half mile beyond the hospital where he planned on spending the remainder of his days. The shadows thrown by the buildings had not lifted, even though he could sense the sunshine the valley was afforded both sides as the mountains parted.

For the briefest of moments, he shivered. When he turned his gaze away from that beauty and memory, he hoped one last time to make eye contact with the tall woman with olive skin.

But she had disappeared, along with everyone else in his car.

2

"Do you think this one will work out?"

From one of the windows in the main building, a man looked out at the incoming train and smiled. "I've researched him," said the hospital superintendent. "He's perfect, for what we're doing. He's tasted both sides of the coin before."

The other man stared past him, past the train. "I hope you're right, sir. The suits writing the checks won't wait forever for this movement to gain traction here in the States."

The superintendent nodded, aware of the ramifications. Yet he reigned supreme over his kingdom, which sprawled over five acres in the valley's biggest city. "He will be better. He has to be."

The Society didn't give two-way tickets. Both men knew this well.

The doctor prayed that he had made the right choices about his new staff. Western Valley had bestowed on him a gift, an allowance to realize his dream and his theories that he knew would make this country better, stronger, for what lay ahead. He knew a storm was brewing overseas and that America needed to be rescued from its own filth. The aftermath of 1929 had left many of the States in disarray and most in power hadn't had the balls to cull the wheat from the shit, to excise the nightmares from the dreams.

Those who came before him had laid the groundwork, just as the tracks he watched had allowed the oncoming train to deliver these people here to realize decades of theory.

"What about the rest? His family? You're sure they'll be enough?" He continued to stare through the window. The doctor wondered where the man's loyalty resided.

"They are all he has left in this world. He wouldn't jeopardize anything."

The superintendent smiled, inhaling the smooth air of the mountains. "Perfect." America would grow strong once again and he would help infuse society with the vaccine to bring color back to its cheeks, muscle back to its bones. The other countries would follow suit, maybe even the one holdout.

This building would be his church. His flock would rise to his ideals and those of the many who supported his efforts. Those who fell would know they were sacrificing for their country.

With a nod, the other man left. The superintendent didn't wish to know where he went next, or what he would do. All that mattered was the movement.

3

Sam stood on the depot stairs and awaited his ride. Before he left Richmond, he had received a telegram that a car would be at the station to bring him to the house where his family would be. He had sent for them a few weeks before he knew he would arrive, but couldn't coordinate it any better. Some ghosts still needed to be packed away in San Francisco.

The cool mountain air brushed against his face. It stirred him from the stupor he had grown used to during the past two years. Virginia smelled pure to him, much different than San Francisco, which would always carry a taint for him.

He feared for them back in New Jersey as neither of them had worked and with the rations running low, he could not count on anyone to ensure their safety. His new employers had followed through on their word and packed up his family's belongings and shipped them ahead.

As the platform began to empty, Sam looked for the woman from the train. Nothing. Families met, and businessmen headed home or to hotels. He had no clue what he would say to her anyway, as she seemed content to avoid him and fall into her book.

When the cream-colored Auburn rolled up in front of him and the smiling driver relieved him of his four suitcases, Samuel allowed himself to collapse somewhat, sprawling inside on the soft leather seats. He did miss his mother, and his brother. Two thousand miles had made it simple for him to build a wall to block out emotion, to drown him. For several months, it had felt good to be submerged.

"Would you like a tour of the town or just to head to your

new home?" The driver appeared to be in his mid-teens, if that. His cap, pulled low, prohibited Sam from examining the man's face, yet the slight build suggested he had yet to reach maturity.

As he hopped into the car, Sam noticed the boy favoring his left leg.

"You bang yourself on my bags? I'm sure they could break a bone."

The boy's hands shook on the wheel. "So, is it the grand tour of your new town or straight to your family?" His voice stiffened.

Samuel rolled the choices around his mind for a moment, thinking of how long it had been since he had seen his mother and brother. *Not since the funerals,* he recalled.

"Care to choose for me?" When the boy shook his head, Sam added, "Give it your best tour, I guess."

They rolled out of the depot and around the corner. A beautiful main street greeted him in a bevy of sunburst colors.

"My god, this is gorgeous. Hey. I'm sorry if my luggage clipped you. I don't want to have you limping to school tomorrow."

"I. Don't. Limp," the boy said, with a bite Sam knew was too defensive.

As he slid into the middle of the seat and watched the heart of the town roll on by, Sam felt fissures cleave the structure he spent two years constructing within him. He wondered how it would feel to be held once again, to feel family from more than six feet away.

The boy drove up and down the hilly route through town, spitting out random facts in a stiff voice. Sam hoped he hadn't insulted the boy by asking about the injury.

"You know, this town has been here since the 1740's. Was a real hot spot in the Civil War, but Augusta is best known for its arts. Creative as heck, so open to all kinds of people, all music and entertainment."

"That's great," Sam replied. "I could use some good music. Got any suggestions?"

The boy's hands rapped on the wheel in an offbeat rhythm. "Jazz is in the park and at the Mockingbird Café. Classical piano and orchestra performances occur most weekends. I can send you the newspaper with the times."

Sam leaned forward, gazing into the sky which had eased into a burned-orange glow. "What about blues?"

He might as well have put a gun to the boy's head.

"That's ... not something I'm familiar with." His voice choked on every word. His eyes burned into the road ahead.

"You *are* hurt, aren't you?" Sam tapped the boy's shoulder. "The blues are rumored to have innate healing powers. I think you'd love them."

The driver only shook his head and sped up. When they arrived at the house a few minutes later, no other words had passed between the two.

The boy carried each bag to the stoop, walking carefully with each step. His limp could not be disguised. Sam thought better of asking again or offering an aspirin. He offered the boy a quarter for his troubles, but the driver muttered something and shook off the money. *Who would decline money during these times?*

"I'm okay," he said in a steadier voice. "I don't limp. Please don't say anything."

Sam stood on the porch confused by the teen, who only took off after being appeased by the psychologist's nod. *Why would he tell anyone? And why would that worry the young man? Loss of business, likely.*

The town of Augusta just might help him find the human within himself again. Though he wondered if the boy noticed that he left a key piece of baggage standing on the platform, one which had turned from him and stared back at the building which would one day reunite him with her.

4

The man in the dark gray suit walked up to the train depot as the sun began to fall upon the small city where his assignment had led him.

In the four years since the onset of the Depression, he had felt himself change quite a bit. Gone was the young man who wished to become a true 'G-man' upstate for J. Edgar Hoover, and who ached for the high school girlfriend he had returned to after two years in the war.

Rather, he felt now as if he had never left. They had taught him the enemy now resided on American soil and just by existing here, was chipping away at true American values piece by small piece.

"Hey," the other man on the platform, a deeply-tanned Native American, said. "Know if I missed the train?" He appeared out of breath. "My truck fell apart and I know the train was due in twenty minutes ago."

The pale agent tipped his hat in reply. "Waiting for someone?"

Would the brown-skinner have said anything to the new doctor? No matter. No one listened to the half-breeds the Valley still held in its land.

Without sound, the man had approached the homeless man, who no doubt had been begging homebound passengers for work in their homes—or even more contemptuous, change from the wallets of the hard-working tax-payers. His bosses would be pleased with this one. Maybe, just maybe, change could occur.

The Native American smiled. "Definitely. Gotta make sure the fresh faces know the scene, know where to go, and where not to." He nodded down the track to the hospital, his smile fading.

The pale man gazed around the station. After the psychologist had left and the train had departed, most of the passengers had also disappeared.

"I understand. We have to keep the town pure," he said, reaching into his pocket and fingering the blade he acquired in the war. "Waiting for family?" The man felt his stomach churn while looking at the hulking Indian. *The doctor had plenty of work to do here.*

The native grinned. "My niece." He stood straight, his pride showing in a stature well over six foot, a few inches more than the man who appraised him. "She's coming here for a new beginning."

"This town is becoming the face for the new movement," the other replied, smiling.

The bigger man leaned over the iron railing, looking east and west at the tracks. "New movement?" He laughed. "She's going to kill me if I missed her. That little fireball will burn my tail if she has to walk all the way to my place tonight."

Probably to some hovel covered in filth and booze, the agent thought.

"Movement," the Indian continued. "We definitely need something after that crash. The entire valley has been a mess since. Hell, the whole country needs a kick in the ass."

"I couldn't agree with you more." *The country needed to become lighter in the coming months. The new laws got the ball running, but not fast enough.*

The Indian regarded him with curiosity. "You waiting for someone, too?"

"Sure am," he replied. "Found them. I'll be meeting plenty in the coming days."

"I just hope the train I missed wasn't hers. She's leaving hell to come here. You know, the American Dream and all that. We all deserve it."

The agent smiled. "We all deserve something." He clenched

his muscles while examining the ugliness of this man, who didn't deserve the same as him. The white-hot anger within him burned.

"Here's to America." The tall Indian lifted his hand.

The agent pulled his own hand from his pocket—together with his favorite tool. "America."

Five minutes later, the platform stood bare as an engine grumbled in the direction of the facility.

5

"You're home!" His mother gripped him tight and squeezed him as only an Irish-German mother could.

"This isn't home," Sam replied, his hands clenched despite sensing that the remainder of his body had melted in her embrace. Two years without human touch went against all the psychology he had learned, yet still, that wall within him stood tall. "Not yet."

His brother stood off to the side of the foyer in the Victorian house on Beverly Street, which connected the main street with Alextine, the main entrance for the hospital. He remained rooted in place, yet swayed from side to side, hands twitching, ready to speak. *Typical adolescent.*

"And how are you, little man?" Sam reached out to shake his hand, and then pulled him into a brotherly hug.

The boy backed off, shaking off Sam's hold.

"I'm not little," he signed. "I'm almost twelve now and," he said, straightening, "I've been the man of the house for almost two years. When you were away."

The comment stung, as Sam had never wanted to leave his family in New Jersey; but when an institution like Stanford called, and Johns Hopkins didn't, you went where the opportunities lay. There were cousins and uncles nearby to assist, but he had known he was leaving when his mother and brother needed him.

"I needed to go, you know that," Sam signed. He had learned and taught his brother the manual sign language before sending him off to school in Carteret. At least the boy had mastered lip reading, for the people who couldn't converse with him. Sam knew there were no schools for the deaf nearby, but before he obtained his doctorate in psychology, the family couldn't afford anything other than a tutor, one of Sam's closest friends. "Hey, have you seen the new school yet?"

The hands crossed at the arms and locked for a moment. *Pissed off again,* Sam thought. He felt the boy's face would remain in angst mode no matter what emotion roiled through his mind.

"What?" He held out his hands and made sure his lips could be read. "It's the best school for deaf students in the country—the whole, entire USA."

His brother's arms unfolded like knives. "I don't want to be a freak. I'm tired of kids talking shit about me." Sam made sure his mother didn't catch the vulgarity. He never taught her much beyond the basic signs. "A whole school for freaks? Now they also have blind kids there. Everyone in the whole town will know where the freak show is."

And being picked on daily is better? Sam bit his tongue, struggling for the right, disarming words.

His mother shrugged, as if she had the motion perfected. "He just sat at home and read all those Tarzan books you sent him. I think he'd rather live in the jungle than go to school."

"Damn straight I would!" Colin signed. "Or in Pellucidar, or on the moon!"

"Colin Frances Taylor!" His mother both signed and yelled at him. "Not under my roof will you speak that way."

The boy shivered when she approached and signed something Samuel missed. Must have been a variation on a vulgarity he had learned at school.

"I'm sorry," he said to her, head hung low. He turned quickly to Sam, "Did you bring any others? New comics?"

"Maybe," he replied, moving his hands to mimic a southern drawl. "If you have a good first week and actually *try* to get along with your classmates and teachers, some might appear in your room."

"But," he signed, almost stomping his foot in frustration. "I *hate* this. I hate school. I hate moving. I hate the south."

"Um … have you seen the southern girls yet? Over *half* of

the school is female. Do you know what that means?" The result was immediate. Colin's stance softened, hands relaxed. *Girls always worked, no matter what the age.* His brother had such a crush on Same's sisters in law.

"I don't know southern words yet."

Sam almost stopped himself, but the older brother instinct took over. "It means that the gorgeous blind girls won't be able to see how ugly you are." He punched his brother in the arm, which elicited a grin. God, how he missed real family. Maybe this time, it would work.

"But they'll still be able to smell the bullshit coming out of your mouth, so the kids will suffer if you visit," the younger brother retorted.

"Touché," Sam said. "Touché."

"Dinner will be ready an hour," his mother said. "Go change and settle a bit. I've been fighting off your brother over the ham ever since this afternoon."

6

Sam unpacked in the master bedroom on the second floor and found himself checking the corners of his sight for signs of Miriam. Exhausted, he wished only to be alone but had grown used to her presence since right before he left California. He simply took in the expanse of the room, much bigger than his university rooms in Stanford or crowded apartment in Manhattan, which they had moved to soon after getting married.

Dejarnette had sent him a letter informing him of the 'borrowed' home in which he and his family would be living, his as long as he stayed on as an employee of Western Valley. He took the news with a grain of salt, happy to be away from the memories of San Francisco and the lean years in New York prior to his invitation.

Anything for job and family, he reminded himself. *Say it enough and it begins to sound true.*

He had cringed at the narrow stairwell leading up to his room, thankful it opened into a large room. He knew most psychologists carried mental baggage, trauma, even a phobia or two, and his time in the trenches during the war had branded a sizable one in his psyche.

The nights spent in the muddy fissures in France while bodies fell from the field above, next to, or onto him, left him with a case of claustrophobia. He fought outside treatment for it, believing it would prohibit the best job offers. Still, it clutched at him nightly, repeated in dreams of suffocation and paralysis in tunnels and muck, until Miriam came for him. The night in the train caused his heart to clench the tightest, yet she soothed him in a manner which likely would have frightened him, if the anxiety allowed the thoughts to materialize in his feverish head.

The furnishings upstairs were sparse, a sizable dresser with attached mirror at the foot of the bed. He refused to look at himself, knowing he might look years beyond his thirty-three. Hopefully, Augusta would do him well and roll back the clock, now that mountains on all sides boxed out the past.

The bed itself, a four-poster sans canopy, stretched to king-size length to accommodate his six-foot plus height. He smiled, thinking he never stretched out in full anymore. Most mornings, he found himself crumpled into a ball or knot of tightened muscles. Thankfully, the upstairs room had one of the modern plumbing designs. He despised having to walk far to piss in the middle of the night. San Francisco had spoiled him, especially the posh housing at Stanford. Here, he had his own bathroom, right beyond the night table. *Things were looking up,* he mused.

A large window gaped into the backyard, complete with a tire swing and box garden ready for his brother and mother to keep themselves busy.

He nearly gasped as the view enveloped him. He pressed his palms against the cool window and then pushed open the windows. Beyond the oaks and maples bordering his house from the neighbors stood a panorama of beauty. This being a clear day, he swore he could see for close to fifty miles to the west. The mountains rose out of the valley in a sheen of autumn hues. His eyes shut out a burgeoning tear, before the curtain of brown and black ridges shut out the memories of what had occurred in the delivery room at Stanford Memorial.

And what he did.

"Samuel," a voice broke through from somewhere below. "Dinner."

God, how he missed hearing a female in the house, one who wished to see him. He only hoped she and his brother could get used to southern living. From what he had seen so far, he didn't think that would be much of a problem. So far, life appeared much slower. Peaceful. His soul needed to drink that in.

A drumming sounded on the walls from below. Another rhythm answered it from the bedroom next to his. He smiled. It was his mom's code to Colin to come and eat. The kid had never responded to her that fast, as far as Sam could recall. Rapid footsteps on the stairs followed.

It felt good to be home, even if home had changed states.

"This is much, much better than the crud they set us up with at the university," he said, knifing into a slice of country ham." Sam grinned at his mother, his plate already half-empty.

"It's too salty," Colin signed.

"He hasn't taken to all of the down-home cooking—yet," his mother said. "But put some sausage gravy and biscuits in front of him and his hands will be too busy to speak a word for days." They had been in the house for a week before he had arrived, decorating the house and moving in several decades of life accumulations.

Sam laughed. Food had always been the family's weak spot. Coming from Germany as a teenage girl and raised in a neighborhood in New York City rife with Irish cooks, Bridget Taylor—née Hermann—had no chance of escaping a destiny as a kitchen goddess. Her culinary skills blossomed despite working in a textiles mill, having to take care of three younger siblings while both mother and father fought a combined five-jobs struggle to keep a one-bedroom apartment in Brooklyn and food on the table. She married one of her coworker's brothers who managed to steal her across the river, where she cooked all day, conjuring up shepherd's pie and stews to match her brats and spaetzle.

Sam placed a forkful of the ham in his mouth and let it melt. True, it was salty, but it rivaled any other meal she had ever cooked for him. The meat fell apart on his tongue, almost more succulent than most steaks he had eaten, even the best in New York.

"Let me know what you think about the rest, too," she said. "I've been busy these past few weeks awaiting your homecoming."

"Mom, this isn't home." Yet something stirred inside of him that belied his words.

She pushed more vegetables his way, along with fresh grits and biscuits. "Cobbler's on the way. And this *is* home—now."

She didn't receive flak from Colin, who usually had something to say about any big change in their lives. "Losing someone can break a person, I know that firsthand. When your father died, I didn't want for a man's touch for over a decade."

"Mother," he cried through a full mouth. "Please. I don't want to know this." He hadn't even considered another woman, despite being surrounded by a city full of women in the Golden Gate metropolis. Miriam still filled his heart, despite her betrayal. He forgave her many months ago, hoping she would stop visiting if he let go of the anger.

She smiled. "I could always embarrass you, Samuel Coleridge Taylor. Simple as pie."

Unlike many boys, Sam had embraced his name. His father, worked to an early death in the building of the New York City subway system, always managed to bring him to the library on weekends. The man carried copies of his favorite books with him always, often stating they brought him peace when he felt trapped in the claustrophobic tubes. He named his first son after the poet, more for what the man wrote about than for the sheer lyricism of his poetry alone. He told Samuel that *Kubla Khan* spoke to him of connecting to the universe, and of how artists of all types were slaves to their muses. The man pushed his son to follow any dream he could imagine, whether it be psychology, music, or baseball. After a string of bruises and black eyes, Sam knew he would never play for the Yankees, and until he entered college, the son would never touch a guitar.

"What I meant, son," she said refilling her own plate, "is that it's been two years. You moved us down here with you for a reason. She's gone. Despite what we thought about it all. It ... well ... that too, is gone," she sighed.

"Mom, please don't. Maybe some other time, but not tonight." He wiped his mouth and crumpled the napkin in his left hand. He felt the back of his neck tingle with the familiar nails of anxiety. "I've got to meet with the new boss tomorrow. He's paying for this dinner, this house, this new beginning. We'll have time to talk—just not now. Please?"

She examined him eye to eye before replying. "Just think of what she would want from you. Imagine if she were here, right here, right now. Would she want you to move on with your life - or live in such an arrested state of grief?"

Mom, if you only knew ...

The trio finished dinner in relative silence. His mother didn't push him, sensing his exhaustion, allowing him to exhale for the first time in months. The tension hung overhead but didn't tighten.

He wouldn't let it this time.

As Samuel climbed the stairs, he questioned his sanity, something he did ever since she first appeared. Was his wife truly visiting him? Or had he finally lost his battle with what happened that night in the hospital room?

As he entered the bedroom, he scanned it to ensure he was alone. Tonight, of all nights, he needed total rest. He had heard the stories about the hospital superintendent: the good and the bad, the innovations in mental health, the point man for the new movement in the country. Sam had to be at his best for the new day. First impressions meant everything.

The blankets remained unruffled by any unseen visitor. He lay down on the bed and felt himself passing out without having time to undress. Dreams assailed him about the new job, wondering how he'd fare, knowing little other than his test, but also if he could handle what the society, government, and Dejarnette expected him to do.

Sleep held him in a deep embrace until after one A.M., when he sensed her again.

7

He awoke in a dreamlike state, not sure which world laid claim to his mind. A certain weight tugged him to his right, suggesting a light being had crawled under the covers with him. He wondered half-heartedly where the family cat was. He whispered, but Shade didn't offer a purr in return.

A finger traced the line of his cheek, chilling his flesh. He settled back into the pillow, resigned that this would be a true visit—or simply another painful dream. Either way, he would accept it. He missed her, plain and simple. Any touch would be welcome.

Maybe one day he would discover if she was real, or if his psyche broke that night in San Francisco.

Until then, he would enjoy what he could of the moment, and of her.

He allowed her to undress him, as his eyes attempted to focus on her. Her smooth hands removed his shirt and trousers, socks and underwear, all without effort or restraint from him. Even after all this time, he could not deny her. When he lay naked, she hovered over him and mouthed something to him. Like the previous times, he could not discern any of her words. Her voice never sounded above a soft rustling, as of a wind through the windows. Like the other times, he didn't care.

Samuel let the incoming moonlight do its work and bathe her in silhouette. Her body remained just as it had on their wedding night; not as it had been on their final night together. She had been a tall woman, buxom in shape, always garnering attention from his peers and neighbors. He placed his hands around her waist, feeling her skin—cool but not cold. She had bucked the

1920's ultrathin look of the flappers and had felt comfortable in her natural shape, where large breasts led to a flat but soft belly. Her thighs held the shape most men would kill for, not like those of the poster girls he could not understand. A woman had to look like a woman—not a string of bones with tits and pallid white skin.

All the more reason why he would love her until he joined her in the next world.

She took him in her hands and loved him in ways she never had during the nine years they were married. He wondered if angels on the other side gave lessons. He also wondered if memories took on their own lives and amplified the realities they masked. For tonight, he didn't care. Her body sung translucence as she rode him, her thighs almost completely real as they clenched him tight. She threw her head back and yelled something he couldn't hear, entangling her fingers in his chest hair. The sensations he felt within her rivaled the first time he was with her

His hands rose to her breasts and found them to be as real as every other fiber of her being. The more he caressed, the more she bucked and undulated her wide hips. The more she bucked, the quicker his blood pulsed. He bit his lip, partially to hold back, but also to convince himself that what happened was real. Just as real as when she showed herself in his Pullman bed the previous night, or the night he accepted the position which would take him back east.

She found his eyes in a deep gaze. Like a piece of driftwood on the shore, he lost the battle against the tide and felt her pulling him deep into her being. Within seconds, he emptied into her and watched the face he had loved for over a decade break into a curious smile.

She mouthed something else. He swore he recognized the shapes without sounds.

Thank you. We miss you.

Before the startling words could fully register, she pushed him back against the pillow and stood. Against the pale light which surrounded her in a pearl-colored aura, she faded, not blinking out like the other nights, but as if timed by an hourglass.

He watched through sleepy eyes as her form winnowed away.

My god, he breathed. Had he truly lost his mind?

Sleep claimed him before she disappeared. His last thought was that she had yet another message for him, one that he still refused to hear.

8

Morning came without further dreams for Samuel. He dressed himself for the first day of the job in silence. Southern culture tended to be different, looking more relaxed while feeling just as formal. Weather in October down in the Shenandoah Valley moved quicker than a man in a barrel full of rattlers. He winced at his mental attempt to be southern and prayed he didn't say anything so stupid in the company of the hospital staff.

Still, he went by the weather forecast in the morning paper, which called for mid-sixties, chilly for the locals but comfortable for him. He picked a light gray linen suit, double-breasted in northern style, and debated on the hat. Far from being a fashion plate, he had always relied on the tried and true fedora. Nowadays, gangster affiliation was tied to his choice, but he figured on not many Valley folk being up on the organized crime getups.

He grabbed his only hat, the faded gray fedora. When it was perched on his head, he often imagined himself to be one of the pulp detectives in the comics he bought for his brother. Hopefully, after a paycheck or two, he would be able to afford a more regional wardrobe—although he doubted he would enjoy it.

Nobody spoke much at breakfast, which included Colin's signing. Maybe, he thought, they could sense the stress he felt about the new life. Or perhaps one of them heard sounds, or felt vibrations from his ethereal coupling with his dead wife—but he fervently hoped not

"Did someone die this morning and not tell me?"

His mother tossed her fork down from the flapjacks she had

been toying with on her plate, rose, and walked into the kitchen to start her cleanup.

"Asshole," signed his brother. "The last time she had breakfast with you was the day you left with Miriam. She expected three to come home and only one did. The last time someone began a new job was when your father began work on the Grand Central line as foreman. She said he was so excited that day, to be in charge for once, that he lost his food before he left the apartment." He looked his brother in the eye. "Now today, you start a new life and I'm supposed to go to a new school, and you talk dying. Fucking idiot."

For his brother to say that, Samuel knew he had to have hit some buttons.

Also, it forced the twelve-year old to admit he wasn't truly family, not first-generation kin. When the influenza broke out in 1918, it claimed his true mother when he was still glued to her breast—and his father as well. Through some miracle, the infant managed to escape the killer disease's jaws. The source of the boy's deafness couldn't be determined, whether from genetics or his brush with the Spanish Devil.

Bridget had taken him in without batting an eye. So far, she had lost a husband, sister, brother-in-law, daughter-in-law, and grandchild before she was fifty. That was pretty darn common with the war and all, but all of her family had perished stateside. The only one in their bloodline to see the war had been Samuel and he only had to endure six months of it before shipping home. Upon his return, he signed up for college so quick, she had no idea how to deal with it all. She just had his promise that he would give them a life much better than anyone in their family had ever seen before.

For all his training in psychology, Sam thought, he had been a shit to his own family in terms of knowing what they needed from him.

"I'm sorry," Sam said, to which his brother simply pointed in the direction of the kitchen. He hung his head in shame, something now familiar to him. "You're right. She moved all the way here because I asked her and yet I barely gave her the time of day."

Yes, but just hours ago, you fucked the hell out of a wife who you tossed dirt on two years gone. You really are an insensitive prick.

He attempted to stand up straight when he reached the kitchen, but faltered once she turned to him.

"I'm sorry," he said, feeling it did no more good to her than it did to Colin. "My priorities are all askew. I'm supposed to be an expert with people's feelings and such, but I shit on my own folk when they need me most."

For a moment, he thought she was set to hit him for cussing, although he remembered her mouth to be worse than any of the railroad crews around back home. Instead, she simply hugged him.

"You're here for a purpose, Samuel Taylor," she said. "Don't go fooking it up for yourself now." Before he could look astounded, she smiled and planted a kiss on his cheek. "Go! You'll be late for work."

9

Sam had decided when the driver concluded his tour the previous day, that walking to the hospital would be a good, healthy idea. Work was only four blocks away. Half of the country still withered in poverty while FDR's programs still were in diapers, and he was going to waste someone's gas money? Not a chance.

Besides, walking cleared his mind, something he needed when a shitload of mental spiders had left clouds of cobwebs between his ears.

He sauntered down Beverly Street and cut a left onto Augusta, wishing to see what the main drag had to offer. Western Valley lay only a quarter of a mile to the east, facing the rising sun with a bit of swagger and a ton of anxiety.

Funny how you never walk in a straight line when adversity hid in the shadows, he thought. During his short stint in France, he had faced his fear either with bravery or stupidity, when he ran headlong into German machine gun fire. Now, just as he survived everything in the past six months by building a mental wall against everything regarding an emotion, he found himself avoiding a cushy job in a world far, far away from all the pain that lay on the other side of the wall.

The town's namesake street rivaled the classiest of the Old West crossbred with 5th Avenue in New York City. A long stretch of stores of all sorts stole his attention. Massie's department store rose up four stories on the northern side of the street. In the window, he noticed a BB gun that Colin would love to shoot Coke bottles with, and a few hats his mother could wear to church. He smiled at the young girl behind the register and walked past a clothing store with a starchy old man guarding the doorway against God knows what. Next, he strolled past a diner that reeked of southern heaven-on-a-plate, and a drugstore on the corner where he meant to turn back towards the hospital.

"Hello, stranger," said a man turning the store's sign to 'open'.

Samuel eyeballed him in the growing light to ascertain his skin color, but could not tell if the bull of a man had Negro in his blood or was of Mediterranean descent. Neither option mattered to the doctor. Sam fought alongside all races and couldn't give a shit for racism. Besides, San Francisco existed second only to New York as the melting pot for America.

"Care for the morning *Daily News Leader*? Might have the Yankees' score in it for ya."

Sam grinned. "Is my accent that noticeable?" He had never been one to notice regional accents well enough, especially since he spent most of his life above the Mason-Dixon Line. "I don't follow them much. Might have to ask my little brother about them. He's quite the nut about that sport. I'm more of a pigskin fan."

"Well, the Giants might be having a big game, then, this Sunday, I might reckon."

"I figured you'd be more of a Pirates fan, or the Skins. I hear they actually run trains to the games from here, now."

The bullish man leaned against the front window, obscuring his sale sign for Cokes.

"Well, gee mista' Yankee sir," he drawled. "That's gotta cost us redneck folk days of shoveling coal, just to see us some pigskin?" The man almost completed the mockery without cracking a smile.

Sam threw up his hands, half-wondering if the guy was yanking his stones or was going to haul off and slug him right there on the street. He felt his skin redden. "I'm… just … I don't."

"Relax there, Doctor Taylor," said the store owner, slapping a massive hand on Sam's shoulder. "Your mother and brother set me up about you earlier this week. I've been looking forward to having someone new to chew the fat with around here, especially one who enjoys the six strings and a drink."

"Excuse me, sir? I don't understand." Despite his training, he found himself thrown off his game, not knowing how to take this odd man. "You know my family?"

"Eugene Walker," said the man, offering his meaty hand. "Your new neighbor on Beverly. Saw you get in last night, but the living dead often don't take notice of their surroundings much. Your momma invited me and the missus over for dinner tonight, except we'll be bringing the food. Jolene's been teaching that fine woman the ways of southern cooking and man, she's been getting it down pat."

"Samuel Taylor," said the shorter man—one of the few times he could be considered that—"but please, it's Sam to friends. I don't know anyone here except my family." He stood straight and realized he only missed the other man's height by an inch or so. Maybe this guy might be able to point out where he could obtain affordable clothing for men of considerable height. "And if my mother and brother like you, then you're already a friend to me. They've had tough times and I aim to give them a new life down here."

The man's smile wilted just a bit as he pumped Sam's hand one last time. "I'm sure they'll do just fine here."

But the hesitation in his new neighbor's voice registered in Sam's psychologist's mind. "What? Don't tell me they set us up in a bum house. It seemed nice. Is it the deaf school?"

Eugene shook his head. "Nothing of the such," he said, softer. "Nothing of the such at all. Your kin's set up in a fine, fine school with a wonderful reputation. I hear they even helped our boys out with hand codes in the war when all hell was breaking loose. That house? Well, you're situated on one of the nicest streets in town, obviously with some of the nicest neighbors you'll meet in Augusta. Just you focus on that. Okay?"

Samuel balked at the reasoning but decided not to push it. The clock up high on a tower at the far end of the block seemed to touch upon a quarter to eight, fifteen minutes before he was due to sign in at the hospital. "We'll talk tomorrow? Over a drink out back?"

The man's smile returned, but just barely. "Of course. You haven't lived until you got snookered on some homegrown while watching the sun snuggled down into the mountains."

"What time's dinner?" Sam began walking as he asked, almost forgetting his manners.

"Whenever you find yourself home, Dr. Taylor. Time operates differently down here in the Valley, sometimes more so in some places. But we'll be there at six o'clock. Enjoy your new job. By the way, maybe we should listen to my Pirates kick the tar out of your Giants one Sunday afternoon!"

As Sam turned away, he couldn't help but see the man's face turn to a frown.

10

He meandered as he cut down the remainder of the town's namesake street, finding nothing of interest, for him. There existed plenty for his mother here, and a toy shop his brother might be interested in, but little for him until he saw the theater. The Dixie shone bright even with the sign turned off, a sign marking the film he wished to see, something about a giant ape coming to New York City. For a moment, he ached for the theaters back in New York, but then he remembered most of the films he saw there had been with Miriam.

The massive marquee hung over gold-edged doors with red carpet outside. If he could find more gems such as this, he could survive the culture shock. *If only they had good music in this valley*, he mused. Maybe he could start taking Colin to some of the more action-oriented flicks. He smiled at the thought of his brother enjoying a movie with him, even if it wasn't a silent one. If only the job was half as promising as the morning walk.

Time to go, he chided himself. He couldn't afford to be late on the first day, no matter how much he hated change.

Turning the corner, he found himself face to face with the Tower Café. Situated on both the main street and the sloping Coulter Avenue, which headed down towards the police station. Above it, a bridge arched over a small stream of some sort. The café was empty, despite the bright sign outside the open door promoting breakfast specials of bacon omelets and half-stacks of pancakes with actual fruit toppings. His belly rumbled at the imagined sensation of raspberries or blueberries rolling through his mouth as their fresh juice caused his eyes to close in ecstasy, or the salty taste of bacon meshing with smooth eggs and cheese from the dairy cows he had spotted all over the fields in the valley.

This weekend. This weekend I'll bring my family here to celebrate new beginnings.

That's when he noticed the boy. Standing on the opposite corner from whence he had just come, a skittish boy of about preteen age rocked back and forth on his heels as he stared inside at the counter, which should have held numerous customers. With no one to block his view, Sam noticed what the boy saw—a line of soda fountains, an ice maker, and a massive silver steel freezer where he supposed ice cream lay in wait for hungry patrons.

Sam found himself turning back around the corner, facing the boy head on. "You hungry?" He heard that the Depression hadn't hit the Valley nearly has hard as the rest of the state, but he was sure many in town hadn't had a solid meal in months, if not years.

No answer. No reaction.

Samuel jingled some change in his pants' pocket, hoping to get the other's attention. "I'm sure a cone wouldn't be more than a nickel," he said. "Would you like one?" He asked gently as to not spook the boy, who seemed disconnected from any conversation, even one about ice cream. At the same time, Sam wondered why he wasn't in school. During the symposium in San Francisco, they had mentioned conditions like what likely afflicted this boy, and how the new laws would help someone like him. A developmental disorder of some sort.

He felt the chill before the boy fully turned to him and replied.

"My favorite flavor is blue." The rocking had stopped.

Sam took a moment to remember his skills and repeated, "Would you like one?" He held out a nickel.

An icy blank stare through hazel eyes greeted him, but the boy's face twitched with a slight smile. "My favorite flavor is blue." With that, the kid grasped the coin and half-entered the establishment before freezing in place, slapping himself upside the head. "No. No. No," he reprimanded himself. "Momma said no ice. No ice before dinner. No ice before school."

"Where do you go to school?" Sam wondered if Colin's new school had a seat waiting for him, even though the two were obviously in disparate worlds intellectually. Besides, the boy didn't appear to be hard of hearing. The hospital might be able to help him. There were many afflictions that medicine didn't yet understand.

The blank stare returned.

Before Sam could say another word, the boy took off, half-running, half-hopping down the hill before disappearing to the right where blocks of factory buildings stood. Sam noticed that many of them had open apartment windows above them. He hoped the boy ran into one of the nearby houses.

The chill within him remained all the way to the hospital.

11

The first thing Sam noticed about the hospital was the fence. Roughly seven feet high, constructed of wrought iron, with an arrow-tipped edge that curved inwards. For a mental institution, he didn't regard that as highly secure, but then most of the flight risks likely never stepped onto the grounds. Those patients barely experienced sunlight from their cells.

Down Richmond Boulevard itself, the fence curved around the perimeter for as far as he could see in either direction. To the left, the train trestle rose above Route 11 and snaked behind the buildings of the hospital grounds as it drew back to earth. Ahead, he saw the main gate about two hundred feet from where he stood. Weeping willows reached over the fence to welcome him, fronds ushering him onwards as they blocked out the thinner but sturdier oaks and maples which dotted the inner grounds. The scents of the flora filled him with a peace he had never felt in San Francisco. Then again, he mused, fish stink never was one for calming him.

The gate itself stood majestically, rising in an arch high enough to allow cars or trucks of any size to pass through. Above the wrought iron a curve of brick existed with more iron inside to support its shape. At the center of the four-foot-high brick surround hung a black sign—welcoming in nature, he supposed, to put families who were interning their loved ones at ease.

Western Valley Hospital, it said. *Established in 1825.*

A lone guard stood inside a brick and wood gatehouse off to the left, looking about as comfortable as a backed-up outhouse. The stone-faced man within sized up Samuel as the psychologist approached, but allowed his expression to soften when he noticed the suit, hat, and polished shoes.

"Good day," Sam said to the overweight man, noting the starchy navy-blue uniform pulled tight against the aching buttons of his jacket.

"Visit or business?" The gruff voice was clearly meant to rattle visitors, likely accomplishing that on most occasions.

"Doctor Taylor, reporting for duty," Sam said in his best military monotone. "I think Superintendent Dejarnette is expecting me. You know, first day and all that jazz."

If the guard appeared surprised, it must have been on the atomic level, as his face rivaled Mount Rushmore's for expression. He picked up his papers and pretended to look at them.

Any security at a facility of this magnitude would know of any new items on the docket, especially a new staff member that the big guy had specifically hired.

He looked up at Sam and pulled out a ring of keys. The look in his eyes told Sam that this was the point where many felt intimidated. Sam tried not to smile. Maybe the poor guy had been bullied by a wife at home or had his cat piss on his new shoes. Sam always tried to find a reason why people took the negative route in attitude. It kept him sane—somewhat.

With a quick twirl of fingers, two keys emerged from the beefy hand and with a gong-like clank, unlocked the double set of locks in what was likely a decades-old mechanism. The guard checked over his shoulders, before pulling the truck-sized gate wide. He likely felt put off by using such a thing for a man choosing to walk inside; normally, he allowed only the newest automobiles and security trucks to pass while affirming a true sense of power.

Sam's first day likely didn't do much to improve the man's self-esteem.

12

Since no pathway existed on either side of the road leading up the main building, Sam figured there would be no harm in striding right down the middle of the bricked road. It wasn't as if a speeding car would flatten him. He would have a better chance of being bowled by a runaway team of patients playing red rover. Likely, most vehicles which traveled the paved roads within the campus entered through a back gate.

The road itself was constructed of brick and nearly sparkled. He knew the facility carried a great pride and history but didn't think vanity paving would play much of a role in impressing the guests, unless Frank L Baum was to pay a visit.

Then again, after what he learned in the symposium, anything was possible.

The maples poked out between the massive tufts of willows on either side of the drive, almost obscuring the first patients he witnessed on the grounds. A pair in business attire strolled down the left hill towards a gazebo, where another man sat on a wooden bench watching the sun rise above the eastern trees. If they noticed him, they showed no sign. Even though he couldn't see faces from this distance, it didn't take a PhD to understand that each of their expressions lay as flat as a railroad penny.

He wondered how much of what he was expected to do would help these patients, these people. Also, how many he would be allowed to help? What did 'help' mean here anyway? Was it help for the patients, or for the Society he learned from back west?

As he took the first of the white stone steps up to the center building, he heard a distinct rumbling. To the left, the trestle which spanned the still-new state highway shook as the freight train rolled from the city depot to the hospital station. Augusta had long since been a major player in the Shenandoah Valley, becoming the 'breadbasket of the south' in the Civil War. Both Union and Confederate troops had traveled the Pennsylvania corridor, transporting soldiers, weapons, food, and loved ones to safety, from what he had read about the region when deliberating the prospect of the job. *It wasn't as if he had a choice in the matter, though.*

The station grumbled a block behind the main shopping street, perfect for tourists and businessmen, but he assumed the hospital still required its own stop, even though it was less than a mile from the first. If the facility continued its plan, heavy building materials would be needed and so would the easy access it wouldn't have from downtown; this partial depot would be worth its weight in gold.

Samuel found the sound of the train soothing as it pulled in behind the main quartet of buildings. He mused that he could get used to hearing it lull him to sleep when everything else in the world, and beyond, insisted he remain in the land of the awake.

Before he continued up the stairs, he stopped a moment to consider the southern architecture of the main building. Rising three stories high in brick, its main entranceway held three doorways, the middle one being the widest and grandest, replete with brass fittings. A rail-less porch ran almost the full length of the first floor outside the building. It halted twice to allow separate entrances—possibly for servants, he thought, yet in a mental hospital, it tended to be foolish to assume common sense. Above the third floor reached another partial story and perching atop that sat a guardhouse. During the ride into the town, he'd noticed at least two other guardhouses but couldn't ascertain why three were needed, with the amount of tree cover and perimeter fencing. Western Valley wasn't a prison and was never meant to be.

He pulled open the middle door and found himself in a lobby fitting a schizophrenic's imagination, melding the entryway of a plantation in the deeper south with the lobby at Carnegie Hall or another high-class New York venue. Oriental rugs the size of Pullman cars lay atop freshly-polished hardwood floors. A chandelier of crystal beckoned above the flight of broad marble stairs wide enough to haul up one of those same sleeper cars. At the landing, the stairs split left and right in pre-war fashion, suggesting that this building may have originally been intended for the original superintendent.

"Can I help you?"

Samuel hadn't realized he was halfway up the carpeted stairs when he heard the velvet voice, tinged with just a bit of steel. He spun, a little too quickly to appear confident, but then he rarely cared about appearances around women. Especially in the past two years.

The owner of the voice stood tall, almost as tall as his wife, yet with bobbed deep-auburn hair framing a friendly face. Despite the fall weather, she wore a knee-length chestnut skirt with a silk white blouse buttoned high, which did little to hide her high breasts and trim figure.

She held a clipboard in one hand and pen in the other. "Sign in? Physician, caretaker, or visitor?"

He allowed himself a grin. "I guess a little of all. I'm a psychologist, here to report to Dr. Dejarnette."

She half stiffened, half bowed her head in mock salute. "We are in dire need of your type, Mister ..."

"Doctor Taylor," he corrected, feeling a bit ashamed for saying so. He hadn't attended medical school, yet had worked his ass off for the title. He gave up so much just to attain the status which guaranteed him to be off the breadlines and out of the soup kitchens back home. He had left his mother and brother for the opportunity he knew would keep them safe, when the rest of the country had crumbled. "But, please, call me Samuel."

Just as he began to remember what it was like to look into a woman's eyes, just as he had hoped to do the previous day on the train, footsteps sounded behind him.

"Call him by what his mother called him, Doris, Doctor Samuel Coleridge Taylor. Born and bred in that Yankee state of New Jersey."

The psychologist turned to the sound of the voice, strong and tinged with an accent that he knew well, yet which had been Americanized for at least a generation or two. A man stood a few feet behind him, entering from a door at the back of the foyer. At least six-foot-tall and lean, his oval glasses appeared to be ill-fitting for his mostly bald head. A set of gray eyes, unflinching as Carnegie's steel, sized him up—although the smile below suggested he found Samuel completely welcome there.

Always over-thinking whomever you face, Sam chided himself silently. *You analyze most people yourself, even when you know you shouldn't.*

Sam buckled a little inside, having heard the stories about how the south had never given up the ghost on the war between the states, but he figured that just hours from the nation's capital, those sentiments should be far removed. Especially in a town as progressive as Augusta.

"Should I have arrived adorned in a rebel flag instead of suit jacket?" His sarcasm had always been friendly, and usually taken as such.

"Touché, doctor, touché. Doris here is my personal assistant and was also at the San Francisco meetings. Do you recall her?" Almost immediately, the man's balding head reddened, just perceptibly. "Of course, you don't. Forgive me, Samuel. My apologies. Things here have been changing with our new program and bringing on so many new staff ..."

"The building, the influx of patients, the ..." added the striking assistant.

Sam waved his new boss off, not wishing him to feel slighted by the forgetfulness. "Please. It was at the end of the symposium and most of our colleagues didn't even realize what had occurred in my life. You didn't even know me at the time."

The balding man, equal in stature to the psychologist, completed his descent of the stairs and took Sam's hands in his own. "I'm embarrassed. I could recall just about every detail about you from the interviews there, in New York, and from your peers. Hell, I could probably even tell you where you stayed the night in D.C., but ..."

"But nothing," the psychologist said. "How could someone not be a bit forgetful during that time? And Doris, I apologize for not recalling such a lady."

She nodded and at some unnoticed signal from her boss, turned and retreated to her office, hidden behind oaken doors which would have dwarfed even the two tall men.

"Anyway," the superintendent continued. "I am Dr. Joseph Dejarnette and I am proud to have you on board. Your work on the Stanford-Binet test relating to eugenics is known across the country by now."

Now it was Sam's turn to blush. "Please. It was one item designed for one university journal. If it helps just one family, my work will be worthwhile. The influenza disaster affected even my family. It was a release to compose that study and escape into the research."

The man in the vest and starched shirt with bowtie rubbed his eyes behind the smallish glasses. "Praise be," he said. "I lost a few cousins on my wife's side as well. Nearly broke that fine woman. Her sister barely survived."

The two shared a moment of silence, Samuel recalling the second most devastating day in his life, the one on which he lost his aunt. He had cursed himself that day, thinking that if he were a psychiatrist instead, he would have had the medical training to help her more, despite whatever rational thinking and logic spoke to the contrary. Instead, he had designed only a test for intelligence, not for saving lives.

"So," Dejarnette said, clapping his big hands, sending an echo through the hall. "Shall we continue this upstairs in your new office? Or since the southern gods have blessed the day, a tour of the grounds?"

"Sir," he replied. "My bottom's been sitting on trains for God knows how long. Definitely the tour. Please."

13

"This place has history, Dr. Taylor," Dejarnette said. "You like history?"

They walked towards the buildings on the left and right of the administration house first, Sam noting that other than the house, whatever else he saw resembled a run-of-the-mill hospital facility. Boxy in structure, they rose up four floors. Reinforced windows reminded Sam of the tenements in Hell's Kitchen.

"Of course. Isn't that what we're trying to do here? Prevent some horrid diseased histories from repeating? Half of my field is learning the past." He breathed in the clean air tinged with a faint fragrance, a definite change from that of the northeast factories.

"This place was first opened in 1828, even before West Virginia left our boundaries. The true definition of 'asylum'—protection or shelter from danger." He raised his arms up and swung in an exaggerated pirouette. "Look to the east and west. Mountains. The Blue Ridge and Allegheny—utter peacefulness. To the north? Not much other than the only major road to other civilization—and still beautiful. Finally, to the south—enough said there," he spoke with a smile.

"So, for the patients who need the time away from life and to heal," Sam said, "it's wonderful. What about the ones we're here for—the chronics and lifers, with diseases medicine might never cure?"

A sly smile spread across the doctor's face. "Could you think of a better place?"

"Meaning?"

The older man began walking down the brick path which headed down to a stream. "Meaning whatever you want it to mean." He beckoned. "Let me show you what some of our patients have accomplished while staying here."

"Out here under the willow trees?"

"Son, you truly have a northerner's sense of humor. Take a look at these hearths. Barbeques once a week for whoever wishes to feast—constructed completely by patients. That stream you just stepped over—dug out and lined with rocks of exquisite detail—same patients."

Sam felt a bit unnerved, thinking of some of the countries his army fought for over there. *The near enslavement of their people..*

"Relax," Dejarnette laughed. "It's not a chain gang. Everything the patients do here, it's volunteer. They want this place to look better. Hell, we even paid them. The ones who don't want anything to do with it? They can sit on their rumps and watch the others who do. Different therapies for different people. Wait until I show you the farm area and the receipts for how much their crops rake in each season."

"Then what's with the spiked fences? Looks pretty ominous to me."

The man snapped his fingers at Sam. "Bingo. Give that man a Virginia cigar! I hate to prattle on about our history, but you'll hear it from others anyway. Back in the days before Gypsy Hill Park and some of the other developments in town, this *was* the park—at least in the eyes of the townsfolk. Look at the prime picnic areas—the benches, the hearths, the vast lawns with escape from the summer heat. Who wouldn't want to come here on a weekend?"

"You built it to keep them out?"

"Not me," he said waving back at the building. "That happened a long time before I was on board. Most of our patients are pretty fragile. The stigma attached to being here when Johnny and Suzie are playing ball—I don't have to tell you how that would be."

"None of this is to keep the patients *inside* the grounds?"

Dejarnette's mouth crept up into that sly half-smile once again. "*Those* patients are kept inside. We'll get to them later—why ruin the mood already?"

14

Colin Taylor also decided to walk on his first day. His journey was just as brief and like his half-brother, he didn't take the direct route. He sauntered down Augusta to wave to Mr. Walker. *The guy was nice. He didn't treat Colin like a deaf and dumb kid, like everyone did back in Jersey. People here overall were much nicer. If only he could meet more like Gene, who had obviously had his own issues to overcome.*

He also wanted to walk by the Dixie Theater and find out when the films were playing. *Of course, Sam had told him about the crazy new movie about the ape, but to him it sounded like kid stuff. Besides, it was a talkie. Not being able to follow along really bit when you couldn't hear. At least with the older films, the dialogue was put right up there for everyone—deaf or not.*

What he really ached for were the sports reels. He already missed the Yankees and even back home, he could only get to the theater maybe once a month, if his mother could take him. Here, with it only a couple of blocks away, he could walk there—without running into any of the street gangs who would rob him of his nickel and leave him with bruises. *To see Lou Gehrig and Babe Ruth weekly on the screen? Maybe he'd even get into football like Sam—if life was how it seemed here, he was really going to enjoy it.*

Once the adventure of strolling through the downtown with no people present was over, he checked out the clock tower and saw he had ten minutes to get to school. *The first day and all would tough enough—he never recalled an easy day in a classroom—but being late? That would truly bite twice as hard.*

He took off at a gallop, not minding the sweat he'd gather or the muss his hair would become if it caught the wind.

The State School For The Deaf and Blind was straight up the hill, around the corner from his new house, but tucked away in a mass of trees. Big trees. Much bigger than he had ever seen back up north. When he stopped halfway up the hill, he whistled as best he could. *The school was gigantic! This looked more like a college than a place for people like him. How was that possible?* The main building was ivory white, just like where the President lived, and other big buildings spread out left and right—and down another hill was a massive field for sports! *This school, this 'special' school, even had their own sports teams, and nobody here would mock him or trip him or whatever.*

He took the remainder of the hill and darted through the front doors just as the first bells lit up overhead. *They even had bells that lit? Geez, this place killed it.*

A pretty woman inside the double doors stopped him and signed his name, asking if that's who he was.

"Yes ma'am," he answered, his hands unsteady in reply. Sweat nearly dripped to the floor under them.

"Good," she replied. "We start the day off with English. Have you ever read Edgar Rice Burroughs before? I think the teacher is beginning the week off with a story of his."

No way. Colin felt his head spin. *This couldn't be.*

Yeah, he was going to like it here. The north could keep its cruddy self.

15

Sam and Dr. Dejarnette had walked to the far end of the campus before speaking again about anything of worth. The superintendent only wanted to hear about the northern sports, food, and the hideous snowstorms that mostly avoided the valley.

"Things down here tend to hang right about in the middle," he said. "We're not about extremes here—in most ways."

Sam thought back to the symposium, but didn't feel like opening up that can of worms just yet. "Well, I know it barely snows off the mountains and from what I read, even the summers aren't truly *southern*." *All of which soothed him. He sought the easy middle of the road these days.*

Dejarnette moved to the right where a long wall stretched from the back of a white building connected to the main house, all the way across the courtyard to another. It rose over a dozen feet high and would serve better than the spiked fence out front.

Were those bars on the windows?

"This, my dear head doctor, is where we keep some of our clients. They have their own courtyard and gazebo and almost everything the others have, but within closed quarters."

"No barbeque?" Sam couldn't stop the words before they hit his lips.

The superintendent laughed. "Nope, we keep them up on the top shelf with the archery sets."

He took out his own ring of keys and opened the gate under the archway.

"In here," he said, sounding serious and looking that way

for the first time since they shook hands, "is the main reason you're here."

"We need someone like you—*exactly* you, in fact—to tell us how much of what we spoke about in San Francisco is accurate, and how much is pure bullshit."

"For me, I love my patients, but if I can stop mud from spreading its DNA into the next generation, color me guilty." The doctor's face twisted to something Sam couldn't quite read with those words.

"Welcome to the real Western Valley Hospital."

16

After a cursory look at the back buildings which lay compressed between the twin walls that reminded Sam somewhat of the beautiful behemoths in China, the tour circled around the main office wing on the left. A three-fifths near-replica of that building, it stood like a lesser sibling, similar in most respects both inside and out, aside from the grand columns and the stairway. It would be his home on the grounds.

Dejarnette escorted him inside, showing him to the main office on the top floor. Brass railings edged the flights which led up to the second floor yet hugged the walls in tight ascent, a vast departure from the main house. *This was more like their apartment in New York*, Sam thought. Three people would not be able to maneuver side-by-side up these flights, as opposed to the ones leading to the superintendent's office, which could hold an entire rowing team—along with the boat.

At the top of the stairs, Dejarnette produced his keys again, and opened a thick white door. A long corridor opened before them, about five feet across with polished hardwood floors underfoot. Offices with closed doors stood on either side. Samuel counted five on the left side, three on the right, with two obvious closets at either end. The door at the far end of the hallway had something he didn't expect to see—bars covering a paned window, and a series of deadbolts.

Maybe his patients would be rougher than he had imagined.

As he considered this aspect of the new position, he failed to notice Dejarnette opening the door right in the middle of the hall on the right side. He shoved the apparently heavy door inwards and smiled.

"Your new home away from home, Doctor Taylor. I hope it suits the work we aim to accomplish together."

A large desk, probably oak or teak, sat embracing the two far corners on the left. Someone likely had situated it there to take in the view through the several windows across the wall, which overlooked the town and the mountains beyond. An elongated couch did sit flush to the near wall, but Samuel assumed it to be more for decoration than Freudian purpose. A pair of high-backed chairs faced the desk, leather-cushioned with polished wood arms. The walls stood stark in a burgundy tint with a pair of nondescript landscape paintings. He swore the wood still emitted a flavorful scent.

Typical high-end psychologist office, he thought. And smiled.

"Just please let me know what you may need, and we'll do our best to accommodate it." The doctor had been revered as one of the pioneers in the Society, spearheading the movement to erase harmful diseases from spreading across America. Sam wondered why he would be deferring to Sam here. *He surely didn't matter much, did he?*

"I thought I was the one trying to impress here," he replied. "I could be a complete and utter failure at this venture. I hope not, but you've got to admit, this is something a bit new."

Sam felt his back muscles tighten, pulling themselves into horrid knots. *He had left all he knew and felt at home with, to come here. Correction: he had lost most of what he knew and brought what was left, to help him forget what he never would be able to unremember.*

The bespectacled man grinned, at least a little humorously. "Samuel," he said. "You have no idea of how many people are counting on this hospital to succeed. On *you* to succeed. Failure didn't seem to be part of who you were when we chose you. Hopefully, it isn't now. Your test gives us so much validation, so much to help the people believe in us."

He pointed to the bureau behind the desk and strode over to it. "This is a stressful job, I know that, but," he paused. "We have perks." His left hand pulled open a cabinet, revealing a shelf of tumblers and liquids in crystal containers.

For a moment, Sam felt the knots slacken. "Is that ...?"

The man pointed to his lips in a shushing motion. "I won't tell if you don't. Regardless, I have it on the highest authority that Prohibition will be nothing but a failed footnote in history by this time next year."

Sam grinned, but wondered how the man knew. The Society had been known to have fingers in the government pot, but J. Edgar was a bulldog. He only hoped the superintendent was right.

"This here, I believe it is imported directly from the country itself. Where else should Scotch come from anyway? New Jersey," he said with a wink. "I also asked your secretary to fetch a good whiskey or two, along with grade 'A' vermouth. Someone told me you like Manhattans."

Sam smiled. *This man, or his underlings, had done their homework on him.* "True, I do enjoy a nightcap or after-hours drink such as that." *And ever since San Francisco, since that fateful night, he preferred only an open bottle, with the glass still untouched.*

"I have a secretary?"

The other man smiled. The courting had not been necessary; Sam had signed on three thousand miles ago. "A smart one, too. Not like Doris, of course. That lady is my right arm in all matters of organization. But I made sure to cull only the best from Mary Baldwin College for you." His arm stretched out towards the window. The famed all-female school lay somewhere below his reach, in the center of town. "She's not too bad to look at, either."

Sam felt himself removed from that moment of connection with the mention of another woman. *Miriam was still with him, whether he liked it or not. When he would be ready, or if he would ever be ready, to get involved with anyone else, God only knew.*

"Thank you," he managed to say, hands feeling for his pockets. "I'll make sure to meet her before I leave today."

The superintendent waved his hands. "No worries. She'll be bringing up the files for your first interviews shortly."

Sam felt the muscles in his neck tighten once more. His jaw pulled as dryness filled his mouth. "We're starting today? But I haven't prepared ..."

"And what *do* you really need, doctor?" The other man smiled at him as he approached. "Remember," he said slowly. "We send reports to them. Frequently. I figured you would want to jump right in with both feet, without a swimsuit!"

For a moment, Sam knew he would stutter the next words, so he collected himself, forcing down the adrenaline burst. "Of course. I'm ready. I just didn't think it would be today."

Their eyes met.

"Remember, I chose you for a reason. Your test. Your research. You epitomized what we were looking for in a candidate. This hospital will be at the forefront of the movement within months." Dejarnette's soft hands gently shook Sam's. "Relax," he said. "Today will be easy. A breeze like from the Blue Ridge on a soft autumn day."

"When will it get tough?" Sam made sure his voice forced the humor he intended.

A slight pause fell on the other man's lips. "Hopefully, for our sakes, never."

Dejarnette made for the door and smiled, letting Sam know that Ms. Sinclair would be up shortly with the patient files. *Relax,* spoke his eyes. *We're in charge here.*

Sam went to the window behind his new desk and gazed out over the town. *A truly beautiful view,* he thought. *Thank God his office didn't sit on the opposite side of the building. He would likely be staring at the white ward and the dorms behind it.* The city of Augusta lay quietly before his gaze; a southern town in the middle of a valley, which even the Civil War could not destroy. The mountains stood behind it like a curtain which promised to block out the rest of the world. Many peaks nearly touched the rising sun behind them.

He wondered from which one of them it would be best for him to jump.

17

Ten minutes later, a stunning brunette knocked on his open door and introduced herself.

"Gwen Sinclair," she said with the stereotypical Virginia accent, voice lilting just a hair. "My office is on the first floor if you need anything." She stood a solid five-foot ten and sported a long black skirt with a pale blue blouse, a subtle attempt to quiet her appeal.

He shot her a bewildered look. "Don't most secretaries have offices adjacent to their bosses?"

She stared him straight in the eye before answering. "Dr. Taylor, I'll bring you anything you need, type up whatever you wish, even run into town for a sandwich if you so selfishly ask. But I'd rather have a few floors between what you do and what I do. No offense." Her charcoal eyes held something within them Sam couldn't discern. *Scorn, or worse?*

"None taken." *My god,* he thought. The patients he had noticed on the grounds during his tour were nothing but docile people, many of them were slow and depressed but harmless. They must be, if no guards patrolled the grounds and the patients walked free. *But not all of them,* he chided himself, recalling the walls. *There were all degrees of mental illness and he was hired to help stamp out those which plagued this country the most.*

Gwen smiled that tight smile as she awaited his next order.

If he was in the market for a woman, Sam might have started with her, but realized he had little to no skill with the fairer sex. Miriam had been a fluke. She had sought *him* out—courted him when he had no idea of her interest in him. *How would he possibly approach a woman? Was he even appealing?* He doubted this one would consider his query about a date, which for the moment, was perfect for him.

Hell, he was a northerner. Maybe women like her would prefer a mangy dog to his kind, for all he knew. What would the woman on the train think?

Yet she smiled her southern smile, which warmed him almost as much as the drink he would have after the first patient left the office. *Life* was *different here. It sauntered where New York sprinted. People breathed their sentences with a touch of honey, instead of cutting their neighbor's ear with a casual remark.* Yet he wondered what this woman truly thought of him, underneath the sugary voice.

Life would be good for his family here. For a moment, he forgot his profession and wondered how anyone who lived in such a place couldn't be fulfilled and well-adjusted.

As Gwen left, she leaned back into the room. "He's on his way now," she said. "Your patient. Should I slow them down until you're ready?

Sam looked out the windows again and fixated on a peak in the distance. *One that would do the trick, if he ever could get there.*

He shook his head. "Send him in, please."

The door creaked open as a lanky man with close-cropped black hair entered. A pair of orderlies flanked him, escorting with beefy hands on each of the patient's biceps. Shackles held his wrists close together. Chains did the same for his ankles.

Great, Sam thought. *First one is a criminal case from behind the building. A wall guy,* he said to himself, imagining patients attempting to scale the high white structures nightly—as if they were able to break free from their cells.

The patient shuffled to the chair on the left and sat down. "You're not Dejarnette," he said in a thick, refined southern voice.

Samuel leaned back against the front of the desk. "Good

eye, sir. Dr. Samuel Taylor," he said, proffering his hand.

"Stephen McIlveen." The man gave his hand a confused look, but shook it properly. "Well, color me tickled. The superintendent didn't exactly appear to me to be any more useful than stones on a mare."

"Excuse me?"

A sardonic smile flashed over the thirty-something face in front of him. *The man was testing him, as most of the tougher cases did.* "You're obviously not from around here. Richmond?"

Samuel pointed upwards. "Different direction."

"D.C.?"

"Keep going."

The man slapped his hands against his knees. "Well, well. I got myself a Yankee shrink. Ain't I the lucky one?"

The psychologist walked to the other side of the desk and sat in the thick leather chair. "Not going to introduce yourself as to why you're here? Somehow, I don't find you to be the bumpkin you are attempting to emulate."

"Well," the man said. "Dr. Dejarnette just sat in his chair and read my file, just like your predecessor likely did. Why don't you just test me like he did?"

Sam looked out the window, wondering for the first time who he replaced.

My predecessor? Nobody had mentioned a previous psychologist, but obviously the hospital had to have had at least a few. In over a century, there must have been countless therapists to accompany the various doctors, even though he knew that his kind were relatively new to hospitals such as this. *Why didn't the last one work?*

When would Dejarnette introduce him to the rest of the staff?

"What did you think of the guy who preceded me?"

The man chuckled. "Asking a crazy person to assess another psychologist?"

"Sure," Sam replied, curious about why nobody had told him this. He'd been told his position had been brand new, based on his test.

"I don't think he liked it here very much." The man's face

stilled. "From friends around town, I surmised he cared."

"That's a bad thing?" *Psychologists needed to care, at least about the welfare of their patients.*

The man leaned back in his chair. "Anyhow, let's get this over with. I've got a long day of sitting in a shit-stained cell ahead of me."

Sam's gaze focused back on the patient. "I didn't read your file. Yet."

The look of confusion was replaced with one of amusement. "Honestly? I don't take you for a lazy one, so what's the call here. Am I supposed to read it for you?"

"Well, why don't you? Fill me in. What's an obviously clean-cut, educated man doing in my new office, shackled like a common hoodlum?"

While Sam meant the comment to either rattle or relax the man, his words achieved neither. The expression he saw gave no indication of emotion.

"They tend to put you here if you kill someone."

"Oh. So, who did you kill?" Sam's money was on the wife. Domestic violence was still ignored in much of the country, outside of the major cities. Police tended to overlook marital 'issues'—unless it resulted in one of the two not breathing.

"The head of Augusta National Bank."

Well, that was a surprise. He had heard that banks in this town were safe, somehow. Another oddity and a draw for the oasis in the middle of a region beset by poverty.

"You don't strike me as a Dillinger type, so tell me it wasn't a robbery."

The man's expression changed. "You don't read the paper much, do you? 'Local man on killing spree'. It was the talk of the town last month."

"Remember, I wasn't here yet. Quite a ways away and I've been out the loop."

The man's eyebrow raised. "You're serious? For the last thirty days or more?"

"Last month? You've been here that long without a trial?" Dejarnette certainly had influence. He had to give his boss some credit. Sam flipped open the man's file and pulled out the news clipping, which lay just underneath the intake form and some brief notes.

'Restaurant entrepreneur murders bank president, chief financial officer, and own wife in front of family'. *It was the wife. He had that part right.* "So, tell me why you're here and not in Lynchburg, awaiting your last breath?"

McIlveen sat without a twitch, looking straight into Sam's eyes. "She had been systematically sneaking the savings from my restaurant, which was one of the few businesses that thrived in the region. Hell, I had professors from Charlottesville coming to dine nightly on whatever specials I had. While I did that, the bitch had pilfered from the basement safe once a week. She was giving the bank president the cash for an investment in Roanoke, on the speculation that the city would become the next Augusta. Foolish me, I only wanted to make sure my children had a future, just in case this damn country ever drags its ass out of the toilet."

Not tough to decipher, Sam mused. *Bank president makes investment, takes easy money. Takes wife. She leaves McIlveen and no one thinks of the crime.* The guy was snookered without a prayer. No one could sue during this depression. By the time all was settled, his life's dreams would be history.

"So," Sam said, recalling the questions he needed to ask. *Was this man insane or just broken as thousands of others had become in the Crash?* "What did you do when you found out?"

"I did what any husband would do to a wife and mother who had just pissed away her kids' lives for a quick fuck and a hope for an even bigger buck. I walked into the bank office where they both sat and emptied my Colt into them."

"Sounds like a crime of passion to me."

"I reloaded. Twice."

"Got it." *Stephen McIlveen. Murderer, yes. Insane? To be determined.*

"So, do I get to be 'cured' like the others down there, or are you gonna find me competent so I can fry?"

Did Virginia have the electric chair, or would he be hung?

"Did Dr. Dejarnette tell you how you'd be cured?" Samuel

knew about the one procedure, the one that so many had adopted, but that wasn't a 'cure' for the immediate patient.

"Sir," McIlveen said, sitting as still as a corpse. "I don't know what happens in the 'treatment' rooms above his office or in those back buildings, but if it's anything like what the others say they hear, I'll ride the lightning and take my chances that the old man upstairs is a forgiving one."

Sam sighed and wondered what his Binet test would prove in this case. *Was this husband genetically defective or did his wife and the times crush his sanity?* Either way, he conducted the test, which the man sat through and answered every question asked.

At the conclusion of the test, over which he already knew the patient had scored in the highest of percentiles, he asked the question which frightened him. "What did you do to your children? It says here you have a young boy and girl. Are they safe?" Sam's soul couldn't handle harm to a child. Not after his own.

McIlveen guffawed. "I doubt it, considering what I did."

Please don't. Sam felt himself wind into a knot.

"Right before I loaded the guns, I put both on a train to Pittsburgh to go see their grandmother—my mother in law. Don't see how any living creature's safe with that woman."

18

Sam wrote up the report for Dejarnette, before he phoned down to Gwen for the next interview. She informed him that the patient had been in the holding area, waiting for him.

"Is the holding area near your office?" He couldn't resist playing.

He heard a deep inhalation. "Sure, doctor. It's near the other side of my door, outside the locked floor door, which is not even connected to any access to where one would come within ten feet of me, between bars, steel, and a bunch of strong men."

"Figured that," he replied. "Just making sure you're happy down there."

"That's a first. But thank you. Mrs. Bowen is on her way."

After the next interview, with a woman who believed she was fighting for the south in a civil war that never ended—which many in this state believed in the first place—Sam decided it was time to call it a day. *Did he mark her as failing the test, or just as an overly enthusiastic rebel?* After she danced out of the room in the grasp of the orderlies, singing 'Dixie', he shook his head and nearly poured himself a drink. He walked the reports down to Gwen, who filled him in on Western Valley's clerical policies, as well as Dejarnette's.

He walked over to the main house and asked Doris to see if her boss was free.

"No, he's not," she said, looking as if he just asked her to jump on her desk and do the jitterbug for him—naked.

"He's upstairs with a patient and his assistants, but figured you'd be stopping by." She fumbled for a file on her desk and handed it to him. "He wanted you to read through all of this, some of his own notes as well as the confidentiality forms— before you leave."

He looked at her, his own face scrunched up with questions, but decided not to rock the boat on the first day. "Sure thing," he replied. "I wasn't looking to knock off early—just wanted to get the doctor's opinion on a case." The file had to be at least two inches thick.

"I'm sure all you have in the file is just fine, Dr. Taylor. He can make his decision based on this." She took the pad of test results Sam held and placed it in her bin.

"Okay, but …" Samuel bit his tongue again. "Well, is there any way for me to meet the rest of the staff? Doctors? Therapists? Janitors?"

This time, she did smile. "You'll meet everyone in time. Just let it all come to you. We're not going anywhere—and hopefully, you won't either."

He returned the smile and waved the file. "Can I fill these out and read outside? I hear it's supposed to be great for the mentally needy."

She laughed a professional laugh and nodded. "Try the gazebo. It's where I usually have lunch."

19

Sam strode out the front door and over to the cedar-planked structure. The campus lay in a thick carpet of Kentucky grass, reaching out in long blades to the fence's edge. He almost felt bad about walking to where he would sit, knowing his shoes would damage where he stepped. But he missed the nature that the cities of Jersey and San Francisco didn't hold. Too often, he couldn't leave the hospital long enough to travel to the Redwoods or Yosemite. *Work numbed the pain. Solitude left him alone with himself.* His fingernails cut into his palms, reminding himself that this turn would be different.

Immediately, he saw why Doris and the patients enjoyed the gazebo. With his back to the front buildings, he looked out through the trees and saw where downtown began. Above the buildings which had withstood the Civil War attacks, the mountains, the same ones which he earlier contemplated heaving himself off, rose above the stately buildings, stark against the falling sun of afternoon.

He sat upon the bench within and leaned his head back, before opening the olive-green folder. Flipping through the files, he found most of the papers to be typical legal notations which stipulated whatever happens here in the hospital, stays in the hospital.

Of course, he thought. *It wasn't like he would call or write his old army buddy who worked for the Post in D.C.* His reporter friend had saved his ass once and Sam returned the favor several times over during their short time overseas.

But he had a career here and knew his mission would benefit the country.

"Enjoying the first day?"

Sam looked up at the voice, having become completely immersed in the files he was assigned to review, while prepping himself on the formal testing he was to complete the following day. He had not heard the man approaching. His military skills, though recently utilized, seemed to have eroded altogether. "Hello." He visually addressed the visitor as well. A man entered the gazebo, roughly around his mid-forties, decked out in a similar suit as he.

"Let me guess," said the man, sitting on the opposite side without a lunch. "The new head-shrinker?"

"That would be me," Sam replied, wondering whether the man was a patient or doctor. *Sometimes they fit both bills. Western Valley held some esteemed practitioners whose families checked them in to cleanse themselves of alcohol and drug habits.* He extended his hand to receive a firm handshake from the other.

"Fun first day? Any interesting cases?" The man drummed his fingers along the railing, while watching some massive bird swoop in a descending circle in the distance.

"You know I can't discuss that," Sam replied. "Don't want to lose my job and wind up in a Hooverville somewhere miles from here, on the run from lawyers. Not on the first day, anyway."

The man chuckled while pulling a flask from his breast pocket. He tipped it towards Sam, who shook his head. "Doctor Maclin. Jed Maclin, but call me Jed. I'm the neurologist here. I believe I'm supposed to be seeing your patient you had today."

"You mean the southern belle crossed with a rebel guerilla?"

"No," he said. "The first one."

Sam felt his flesh grow a little cold. "But that was simple murder. There wasn't anything to suggest a 'defective' in the case. It was even premeditated."

"So you say," he replied, taking a deep swig from the silver container. "Ask more tomorrow. Dejarnette told me to begin treatment after you tested him."

"But I'm not done. We only began today."

The doctor turned to the psychologist with a staid expression, eyes already glazed over. "So, finish up tomorrow, and then I'll get to work. A man who does what he did, he fits the profile. Too bad he already spilled his seed and contaminated society. See you tomorrow. A pleasure to meet you." He arose and walked back in the direction of the building to the right of the main one. *Maybe that's where the labs were,* Sam wondered. *Or just his office.* Right then, he found himself not caring much.

Still, he fought off a shiver. *Miriam's death propelled him here, but would she approve?* He doubted he even had a choice in his life anymore.

He wondered what his role would be here. They told him to use his tests to determine the validity of each patient, whether or not the law would apply to them; the law which had been deemed constitutional in Virginia and several other states, not to mention becoming legal across Europe. Samuel felt as if he would wind up being judge and jury for his patients, but he prayed it would be in a good way.

With a left hand gripped around his pen so tightly two veins swelled to appear like extra digits, he signed off on his reports and the policies. He reminded himself to pick up a bottle of whiskey on the way home, and then remembered. *Damn prohibition.* He hoped Virginia would be the progressive state it had promised to be. Part of him contemplated walking back to his office to take home the container Dejarnette had left for him. The other part realized that he would likely need it for the following day.

After reading the case notes for the patients he would be seeing during his first few days, he bid farewell to both Gwen and Doris and exited the main gate, where a new guard stood, just as sour-faced as the one in the morning.

His day finally took a turn for the upside the moment he passed through the arch.

20

She stood underneath the fronds of the willow tree, out of sight of the guardhouse, her face pressed into the bars of the iron.

"Can I help you?"

"I doubt it," the woman said. "I'm still on the right side of the fence, aren't I?" She turned to face him and he realized she was the woman from the train, who had refused to look at him. Now she did, and his world upended before his heart realized it should have beat. Somewhere between hazel and dark chocolate, her eyes drew him in, rounder than usual for a woman with such an unusual beauty, but he found them far more alluring than those in the films. Her almost shoulder-length hair curled just a bit, as if it refused to follow a set fashion.

"Are you sure about that?" He regretted the words, but they sped from his mouth faster than his lips could shut. "I mean, one might wonder about someone who stares *into* a mental hospital. Do you know someone inside?"

She turned to him, standing slim but with pert curves rounding out her beige dress, just enough to appeal but also leaving enough to his imagination. "Maybe," she said, her voice light with a lilt he couldn't identify. Possibly New England or second-generation European. "Or maybe I'm wondering why they let me leave?"

He smiled—for the second time that day, a genuine smile. While he still fought a storm of pain inside which he felt would never subside, twice this day something in his new town had surprised him with something that felt too much like happiness. "Well, if you have enough greenbacks, Western Valley does pretty nice things for those who need a respite from the real world."

She turned her slight chin towards the rolling lawns and stream which lay inside the gates. "Too bad we're in a depression. Otherwise, I doubt you'd have room for us all."

His smile remained. Part of him believed she did have someone on the inside, or once did, but knew better than to ask. After the long train ride where she wouldn't even connect a glance with him, he felt it folly to blow a chance now.

A chance for what? What did he expect of her? He could barely handle himself and had to reconnect himself with his family. And he thought he could handle a new female friend?

"I think we could add a few extra cots for those in need. And what would be your reason for being committed?" He dug his nails into his palms, berating himself for his lack of grace in speech.

"Lofty dreams," she replied. "Maybe someone in there could help bring me back to this dismal earth."

"Why would you want to be brought back down to where we lowly folk suffer?"

Those round eyes blinked once, as if his words threw her, but only for a moment. That moment of vulnerability opened the door within him, one which had been locked, bolted, and nailed shut for two years. Only a crack, but sunlight bled through.

"To show people that sometimes darkness brings a fresh morn. To show me that hopes can die, even in a beautiful place such as this."

With that, Sam began to slide down a slope of which he wanted no part; to help her revive some hope, even though he felt none of his own. Maybe her darkness could bring him some morning sun.

"I'm from New Jersey. Nothing much shines there—at least where I grew up. How about you?"

She hesitated, shifting a foot, but only for the briefest of seconds. "Maine," she said. "Portland. Dismal place as well."

He thought she lied well; more of her accent emerged as she relaxed.

"I'm having dinner guests at six," he said, glancing at his

watch, which read a quarter to five.

She straightened. "I have to work tonight. My second job begins at seven."

He blushed, feeling heat roll in a splash from scalp to neck. "I wasn't …"

She began to walk. Her embarrassment wasn't visible, but he felt it just the same, which eased his own. "I only meant conversation, doctor."

"How do you know I'm a doctor?" he asked. The smile returned, but halfway this time.

She spoke with her head still down. "Only visitors and doctors walk out of that gate," she said. "I walk past it every day."

He halted in front of her, hoping she wouldn't swing her purse at his head. "Samuel Coleridge Taylor, psychologist, and I'm pleased to have met you on my first day in town."

Her face wrinkled at his title, obviously not sure how to react. "Ruby Kaminski," she said, standing proud at the sound of her name.

"Polish or Russian?" he asked.

"Why do you wish to know? My family's been here since before the revolution."

"Ours or theirs?"

"The Poles rebelled? They knew how?" She gave him a grin like he was a petulant teen. "Our war. The Russian one was only years ago."

He really began to think she lied well. Her eyes barely flickered, but the trickle of pain in them betrayed her. *Just like him, the train had delivered her from something.* "My mother loves genealogy, so I'm always trying to match names with places. Listen, since we both have somewhere to go, would you walk with me to downtown?"

"I'm already walking," she countered, and she was. "I can't be late."

"That's not an answer," he replied, "So I'll take that as a no and walk home from the other side of the street."

Her soft eyes looked as if they were about to break open. "Don't be silly. There's enough room for both of us."

"Okay then. We walk on the same side, but I won't bother you again."

Her lips moved to say something but halted before sound could emerge. Her feet had little trouble as she took the same turn he did that morning, in reverse, traveling up the hill towards the corner restaurant.

"You work in this place?" Both gazed up at the movie titles, which would not light until the weekend.

"No," she replied, too quickly. "I like the cinema and walk by it—or into it whenever I can."

Samuel felt an electric jolt surge through him. "My little brother and I are headed to see *King Kong* this weekend. Do you like dramatic movies?"

"I was hoping for a 'Three Stooges' film myself." The glint in her eyes chased away the growing shadow.

"Well, we'll be there at the afternoon matinée, just in case you happen to find yourself needing a break from laughing."

"That's your best? To make a woman stop laughing?" That smile again. "Maybe I'll sneak in after my funnies."

"Maybe that would be nice." Sam felt the faint taste of his shoe in his mouth, but hoped her standards were low enough to trip over.

She turned into Panevino's Restaurant right as he was going to ask if she might sit with them during the show. He waved, only to her back, as she hurried on and up the stairs. He wondered if she really did have someone who was inside Western Valley.

After just one day on the job there, he prayed she didn't.

21

Colin found his teacher to be fetching, possibly only a decade or so older than his twelve years. He focused on her hands as she signed comprehension questions from one of his favorite books, *At The Earth's Core*.

"What did the characters learn from the other species in the hollow earth?"

"How did they resolve their problems with communicating to the other species?"

"What *is* their Great Secret?"

He found his hand was raised so much during the class that his fingers went numb. He answered every question she allowed, possibly given more attention since he was new. Normally, he wouldn't 'speak out' in class, especially since in here it meant standing up and signing to the entire class. However, cross a beautiful teacher with an exciting book he never thought he'd see in a school, and off went the chains.

When he was first escorted into the room by the aide, he felt the sweat run down his back in tiny rivers, sure to be noticed by all his classmates. Nine other students sat in a wide semi-circle around the teacher's desk as she read to them. Each of them had their own copy—*how did she get them so many?* he wondered. *Was she also a fan?*

He had walked to the lone empty seat and before he escaped into its depths, she called out to him, both in sign and vocally. His mother had told him they taught sign language and lip reading there, skills he could use in the real world when he became an adventurer.

"Introduce yourself, please." He did.

"Tell the class where you're from." He did and quickly learned the sign for 'damn Yankee'. Instead of being insulted, he felt welcomed, for the first time in a long time. Everyone else asked him what New Jersey was like and if he had met Babe Ruth. He was tempted to lie and appear the big man on campus, but found himself telling only what he had lived. No one seemed to think less of him or mock him.

"Now tell the class why you moved down here. Family?"

He answered again. "My brother got a new job so we didn't have to live in the sewer anymore." A cute blonde looked at him and signed, "Where does he work?"

"The hospital," he replied.

With his words, the teacher halted her questioning. The aide simply left the room.

Colin turned to the girl next to him. "Did I say something wrong?"

"She's afraid of that place. Tells us to stay away at night, and day." The happiness that shone in the girl's face had now dimmed.

He made a silly face. "Ghosts? Monsters like the Mahars?"

"No," she signed closed to the desk. "Real ones. Ones that wear suits and stalk the streets at night."

"Bullshit."

She gasped. He felt himself redden. He had never cursed in front of a girl before, well at least not one who could read his signs. "I'm sorry. I am. I just don't believe that."

He knew he wasn't impressing her anymore, but he couldn't hear this. "My brother has always helped people. He wouldn't bring us to a place like that." Still, he cared about her reaction.

"But you believe in an earth that has creatures living inside of it?"

He had no reply for that.

"That's why Ms. Jones has us work on our 'special skills' every day. She says that if we have talents, that if we fit in and make the hearing people understand we're smart, the men in suits won't bother us."

Colin bit his tongue but felt the sweat on his back turn cold.

22

Colin flew through the rest of the first day, slogging through Algebra and Biology, somehow still smiling as most of his class stayed together when classes changed. He never had a chance to mix with the blind students, even at lunch. Not yet, anyway. His curiosity had been piqued, though. In his new world, he wished to learn about everyone and everything. He had time to remind himself that he'd only been there a few hours and already everything had changed. Each class had opened a new door, widening his eyes and smile even more. When the bell flashed for gym, he knew he had died and gone to heaven.

The gym teacher in shorts and t-shirt lined them up and made them do calisthenics. Colin had hated it back home because someone would always slap the back of his head or mouth foul things about his mother, knowing the teacher could not understand a word of sign. Here, the muscular man 'spoke' to them all in such a way that Colin just knew he was also at least partially deaf. By the man's build, the teen also could tell the teacher played athletics, possibly even on a real team.

He allowed them to run to the field that Colin had had his eyes on ever since entering the gymnasium. The two classes, one a grade level above his, he assumed, raced to the baseball diamond and scrambled for spots on the field or in the batter's box, striking his or her best Babe Ruth or Gehrig stance.

Not Colin. He waited on the mound silently and without a gesture, simply hoping the man would toss him the ball.

The man, obviously an athlete, strode up to Colin and signed, "You think you're a pitcher or something?"

The teen shrunk inwardly but kept his form straight as he

faced the teacher. "Yes, sir. Back home, they let me pitch a few times in class and all the time in the street." *Of course, when he struck out the neighborhood kids, they had been quick to beat the living shit out of him.*

The teacher with an army crew cut gave him a curious look as he held out his hand. "No pitching for you. Not even one."

No, please. It was gym hell all over again.

But the teacher couldn't keep his grin inside.

"Not until you find a glove that fits those big hands of yours."

Colin's smile nearly broke his jaw. He raced around until he found the equipment locker near the dugout. Surprisingly, he found *three* lefty gloves. *There were kids here who were both deaf and left-handed? Screw what the teacher supposedly thought back in class. He was home—finally.*

Minutes later, he winked to the gym teacher and showed him why he stepped up to the mound in the first place.

The first pitch breezed by the batter without him even having moved the bat. Colin felt a rush unlike anything he had felt before that lasted until the last batter.

When the class ended, the man put his arm on Colin's shoulder. "Buddy," he said, and Colin knew he said it not because he forgot his name or didn't care to learn it, but because he did care. "You do know we have a baseball team here? We play other schools."

Colin felt his legs again, turning to jelly. *No way. Get out.* "Real schools? Like hearing schools?"

The man laughed and shook his head. "Some. And some like ours. We even travel to play sometimes. Ever been to Virginia Beach?"

No, this wasn't home, he thought. *Home could never be this amazing.* He felt like he jumped right into one of the Burroughs novels he read. He didn't feel his feet touch the ground for the rest of the day.

23

Ruby had nearly been late for her first shift at Panevino's. The dinner crowd wouldn't be coming for another hour or so, but Antonio always wanted the first dishes to be ready for him to sample before the customers even knew they were hungry.

She had run into the kitchen and pulled on her apron. Her boss, the owner and head chef, had the specials list hanging over the island in the middle of the kitchen where the myriad pots, pans, and utensils hung, chiming discordantly as the rest of the crew flew to their stations.

He had hired her based on her school's recommendation, but still, he didn't trust her yet. She found herself relegated to salad and pasta duty. *Boring, dull, inane duties. The female jobs.* Still, she looked around and reminded herself that no other woman stood in the kitchen. At least it was a job and it got her away from the troubles in D.C. Here, she could start anew and prove her talents to a whole new world, a treasure hidden in the cleavage of two beautiful mountain ranges. They reminded her of home. *A good thing,* she had thought last night, but knew tonight she might cry herself to sleep, thinking of what had come before she crossed the Atlantic.

"Do you think you can cook with the men?" Antonio had stared her down on their first meeting. He hadn't come from Italy any more than she had traveled from Maine, but in this kitchen, they existed as true epicureans carrying no lineage that mattered. Only talent did.

"Best marinara in my class," she had answered. "Second best tortellini, but I knew better."

He smiled but also held a temper underneath, which only a

woman who had known true anger could sense. Antonio knew she would improve his restaurant but would keep her from feeling too confident. He would never flirt with her, not with his wife as the maître d', but it didn't stop him from ogling her and fucking her with his eyes from every corner of the kitchen. This, she could handle, as her life was now behind her, and looks couldn't hurt. Augusta's bosom cradled her, protected her from what she feared most. *That,* she thought as she smiled and mixed up a spinach and radicchio salad, a far cry from the 'down-home' cooking she had been hearing about ever since she arrived the day before, *would keep reality at bay until she decided to face it. If she ever faced it at all.*

She found herself wondering about the man who left the hospital with her. *Was he one of the government types who she read about, who were spreading out across the country, even parts of Europe? No,* she chided herself. *Not every man she met would harbor a deep streak of evil within his being. Some had to be whole, without fissures which collected the pitch, the darkness of a society which had only recently turned from words into actions.*

Was he like the uncle who never showed up at the station last night? Or the man she escaped back home?

No, he was a good man. She felt it within, just like her grandmother had told her she would be able to do. *He would be sitting down to dinner with his wife and kids soon, along with whatever company doctors have, right about the time she would have served her twentieth salad and twentieth bowl of penne—with Antonio's sauce smothering her work.*

Tomorrow, she might look for him, she decided. *Or she might decide to stick to the shadows of her life and hope that nothing found her again.*

24

During dinner, Gene and Eliza Walker talked about the civil war, the town itself, how sports would help bring the economy out of the Depression, and how there just wasn't something right about Europe all these years after the Great War.

"Did you fight in it?" Colin asked. He was a sucker for war novels, but Sam would never tell him the truth, the horrors which lay within the glamour of the Hollywood reels.

The older man simply nodded. "They couldn't figure out what I was, color or nationality, but figured I was good enough to go and get shot at."

Sam knew how that felt, barely ready to finish high school but being told he could go fire weapons to decimate a town—when he couldn't even pass Algebra without his friends helping him. His teachers had stared at him blankly, already treating him as a casualty of war.

"I hear you," he replied, not knowing what else to say, but thinking of all he had heard in San Francisco and New York. *All of the Society would know what to say.* He wondered what they would say if they knew he was having dinner with this man. The man's skin was darker than his, his wife's even more so, but not that much more so than the full-blooded Italians he faced overseas.

"Do you have kids?" Colin still had time to work on his social skills, something he'd never had a chance to do in the regular schools. Sam knew he had gotten a taste of teens who likely accepted him as he was today, and was already addicted to the attention.

Gene and Eliza shared an uneasy glance. He hung his head.

"Nope. Everyone who comes into my shop for ice cream I treat as my own."

Eliza didn't utter a word. She only got up to fetch more food. Sam tucked it away to inquire about some other day.

They dined on a stew recipe Eliza helped spice up, along with sausage gravy with biscuits and an array of vegetables.

"They've been in the kitchen half the day," Gene said, wiping up another piece of his meal with his fourth biscuit of the evening.

"Which is about twice the days you spend in there," his wife said, calling back at him.

"I cook," he said, sounding hurt. "I make a mean sundae!"

Gene held up his plate, appearing as clean as if it was freshly washed. Sam followed suit, knowing if he ever wished to indulge in such a dinner again, he had better show the proper appreciation.

"I'll take that as a thank you," Bridget Taylor said, smiling as she cleaned up the table.

Gene stood up and grabbed his own plate, nearly knocking over the water glasses. "Excuse me, Mrs. Taylor," he said, stammering. "This was the best meal I've had that my wife hasn't cooked in years. The sausage gravy alone would have me proposing to you if I were a lesser man."

She laughed. "My dear, you've been gushing since before you even sat down."

"Well, the aromas came and invaded my humble abode when I first arrived home. That's not fair to do to a man."

Eliza came out of the kitchen, wiping her hands dry. "My poor man. He's been working all day and is assaulted by the food of the gods. Next, he'll complain he can't fit dessert in his full belly."

"Guilty." He hung his head and motioned to Sam. "Come on, doctor. I think we're being exiled onto the back porch where we can languish in our sins."

Sam rose and looked back toward the table where Colin sat. Part of him felt terrible about leaving the boy alone with the women, especially at his age. Then he noticed the book in his hands beneath the cloth. He had been reading nonstop since he came home from school.

As if on cue, he turned to his mother and asked, "May I be excused? I want to finish this story for school tomorrow. Please?"

Bridget and Sam looked to each other, half-smiling, half-amazed. The boy had railed against any type of schoolwork for the past couple of years. The teachers at the school in New Jersey ignored him and didn't notice if he did the work of a Nobel Prize winner or an imbecile, which is how he was treated by most. Bridget waved him on and Sam guessed the boy hardly noticed the men were still present.

They nodded to the women and headed towards the back porch. When Sam had first seen the view from there, he had almost forgotten the pain which assailed him every day. The sheer beauty of the mountains from atop the hill on which his new house sat did more than take his breath away: it numbed his mind to the memories.

"Fall in love yet?" George pulled up a chair on the wooden porch as the men gazed out into the last hurrah of the sunset.

Sam opened his mouth, but nothing emerged. He wished to concur with his new friend but was overcome by the tranquility. The night air chilled his flesh, but in a pleasing manner. The blend of purples and reds soothed his eyes in a way that even the ocean or the Golden Gate had never done.

A clink sounded next to him, pulling him back to earth. Gene had produced a clear bottle filled to the top with a caramel-colored liquid. His other hand held a pair of mason jars.

"I thought you southerners only drank moonshine."

"And I thought you Yankees were supposed to be funny," he said, pouring two fingers in each. "You've never heard of Jack Daniel's?"

"Wasn't that a whiskey made in Tennessee before the prohibition?" He picked up the drink and allowed it entry down his throat. Instant warmth lit a fire through his entire being.

"*Is* a whiskey, my good doctor. *Is*. That damned amendment. It should be gone the way of the dinosaurs—and likely will. If you read into the newspapers, it will be. What did that damn thing accomplish? Creating John Dillinger and a brand-new type of criminal? Smart men who run Washington. Now, when they fix their mistake, do they take ownership for all the damage? Hell no. They'll simply rake in the greenbacks on the liquor tax and hope the people drink themselves back to prosperity."

He tossed back the entire glass.

"I didn't think I'd be breaking the same law twice in one day." Sam sipped his own glass.

Gene turned to the doctor and gripped him with a stare and smile. "And I thought *I* had a perk-filled profession. The good caretaker in his kingdom partakes of the nectar of the gods? I guess when you reside that far up the medical chain, rules don't apply to you. I wonder what else he'll have you do." He regarded Sam with a look the man couldn't decipher. "But enough shop talk. So, tell me, what do you think of our fine city?" He pointed first to the mountains and then back towards Western Valley.

"Pretty ... unique so far. Nothing like the north. Or the west."

The older man laughed. "I've been here since the end of the war. Eliza wanted out of Richmond and so did I. A new beginning, something much deserved after what I saw over there. The Valley, she's beautiful in the way a woman is who barely speaks." He spun his head just to make sure his wife wasn't within earshot. "What I mean is that you can simply enjoy her beauty, without the flaws of society. Mostly." His hand shook slightly as he placed it on the wooden table.

Sam poured another drink for each of them. Condensation clouded his glass, turning the liquid within as clear as his thinking would soon become. "Mostly?"

"We moved here to town after my brother disappeared. He was living close by, in Waynesboro, at one of the factory plants. The man could fix *anything*, which is why he got the job—and kept it. Neither of us dealt well with the shit some of these rebel-thinking rednecks gave us after the war, especially after we saved their asses in the battlefields each day in the war."

"But you're ..."

"Son, I'm Italian. Southern Italian, but still of the boot. Some of us are naturally dark—well, dark compared to those lily-white pasty-faced Irish and German folks who run the country. No offense. I'm still a darkie to most people here."

"None taken." Sam recalled the speeches of Davenport and Grant, who had called for certain purebreds in their plan to make America stronger. He shuddered at those meetings, but thought enough of the rational men existed who only wished to eradicate disease and mental illness—not to mention his prime target, criminal behavior.

Sam believed his test could help prove the existence of those traits. And show that they had nothing to do with race.

"Anyhow, I figured he'd been lynched. Happens all the time down here, if you don't keep to the main roads. Doesn't matter *what* you are in most places in this country, it's *how* you look. And we look colored."

Sam couldn't move his mouth much. *Even in the war, it was country versus country, not man against different shade of man.* Yet he knew racism still raged in the States. "Did you ever find him?"

Gene shook his head. "It didn't matter much at that point. He was dead, somewhere. We came here and knew the town needed a few good businesses. I made some good contacts in the war, who lived in Virginia Military Institute and Fishburne Military. Knew they'd set me up and set the tone for us to live comfortably here. That didn't matter much, either. Augusta's an oasis in a sea of hillbilly. Progressive as all hell here. I could be blue and polka-dotted and the folks here would likely accept us—mostly."

Sam couldn't comprehend the thoughts of the Davenport-Grant '10%' plan. Thankfully, most in the know didn't get behind it, other than in theory. *Gene would have been part of it. So would Sam's brother.* It was then that he realized that night had completely stolen the light from the sky.

Gene swirled his glass. "Well, enough negative. Augusta's survived the Civil War without more than a few scratches, the Crash without a single bank closing, and has been the cultural hub of the region since Lincoln's time. Hell, even the influenza outbreak didn't dent the area much—besides your hospital blaming certain 'folks' for bringing it into town. Those folks were quarantined."

"Let me guess—blacks? Immigrants?" Sam hadn't heard

much about that yet but knew fringe groups put the onus on anyone but the rich lily-whites.

"You'll hear about the mountain folk, both at work and from us regular folk. I'm sure your Dr. Dejarnette will let you work with plenty of them. They've been long accused of everything from bad moonshine and inbreeding to creating diseases and eating babies from neighboring towns."

Sam shivered. "And the truth?"

"They're isolated—they prefer to be. After some of the things they've seen, what I've seen in this country in the four years, I can't say I blame them. They're Depression-proof in their own world."

But many in academia saw them as a blemish to society. Sam hoped that the paranoia after the war and stock market crash would soon settle and allow reason to rise once again.

"Tell me, did your boss decide who the 10 percent will be in this area?"

Sam felt his stomach fall to his socks. "I don't know …"

Gene waved him off. "You forget. It's been in the *New York Times.* Real or not, it's out there. I read—and listen. Live this close to the biggest train depot in the valley and all sorts of people come through. Many like to talk. Especially over a soda or ice cream. When the bartenders disappear, it's the ice cream man who doles out the free therapy. Blend them all together and it's like truth serum."

Sam tried to read the other man. *Gene knew much more about the goings on in the town than he did, at least for now. Something shadowed his soul.* "I really don't know what's happening there yet. I was hired to test people—and help." Yet he could almost hear his words hit the floor with dull thuds as he spoke them. The look in his new friend's eyes reflected his own misgivings about what was truly at stake.

The bigger man got up and clapped his hands. "Like, I said, enough negative. It's your welcome dinner. It's my duty to show you the good side of your new life here. Relax out here in the smooth night and drink up." A big smile broke the tension both men so obviously felt. "I have another gift for you."

Sam finished his own drink, recalling the hell his hometown

had turned into, thanks to the birth of organized crime. "Really? Better than this?" He shook his empty glass.

Gene got up and disappeared into the house. Less than a minute later, he re-emerged with both hands full of what truly intoxicated Samuel.

A beautiful guitar hung from each hand. He offered one to Sam.

"I just happen to have a spare, from when my brother lived with me. It's been a long time since I played with someone else. Ever play the blues?"

"I live it. Every fucking day."

25

Samuel took the long route to work the next morning, with a bit of a headache but not caring one bit. The Martin neck had felt like butter in his hands and even though it had been many months since he had touched a guitar, he picked it up right where he left off, at least in feel. After watching Gene mystify with the blues, a style Sam had listened to but never played, he knew he had left some of his talent in San Francisco. The other man's mastery of the walking bass and little riffs which danced around Sam's humble strumming displayed a world of artistry which he had never known.

He looked forward to returning to it and punching the same ticket his neighbor had, entering a world which would shield him from everything—his wife, his grief, his mission at his job.

Gene had handed him a handful of Bayer tablets before he left for the night, along with the rhubarb pie neither had managed to eat. Both had eased the pain in the morning. He could see himself becoming fast friends with them in the future, especially if more blues and Jack Daniels returned with the music. He truly ached to learn the style which his friend had seemed to simply breathe through his fingers. It lacked the sophistication of jazz or classical, but held a purity, a depth which Sam had never felt before. Of course, his own skills were meager in comparison, so he knew enormous work lay ahead— work he would slave over nightly.

Already, the sun had begun to chase the chill of the night away and even though a slight sense of humidity crept into Sam's clothes, sweat beading and threatening to layer his clothes to his flesh, he didn't care.

He passed the boy again, who once again stood in front of the restaurant. When he asked for a name, he received the same line as the previous day. "My favorite flavor is blue."

"My name is Sam."

The boy halted his rocking, giving his heels a break. "Freddy. My mother calls me Frederick, but my father called me Freddy before he died." The reddish-brown-haired boy smiled at Sam, with brown eyes which connected to the psychologist if only for a moment.

Sam smiled, thinking that on the way home, he would spare the nickel and buy the boy a 'blue' ice or ice cream, whatever that would turn out to be. Maybe he would even talk to the boy's mother.

He wished the guard a good morning, to which he received a simple grunt, and headed straight to his building with a smile still on his face. Gwen awaited him in a stunning navy dress, but he found he only had recollections of Ruby. She might never sit on his porch or grace his bed, but she had discovered a perch in his consciousness that blocked out a beauty such as the one sitting before him. *Still, she blew him off once before. Being polite might not have changed much.*

"What's on the roll for this morning?" He noticed her smile back at him and wondered what she thought about him.

She spread out a trio of files in front of him. "Mr. Painter, Mrs. Rowe, and Mr. McIlveen again. Dr. Dejarnette wishes for you to perform your test on all three this morning, if you could."

"Before the initial interview?" This veered from protocol— but then again, he mused, it was one of the reasons he was sent here. His test, which he helped to create from the dust of the original Stanford-Binet, would hopefully give the Society and Dejarnette what they wanted, to help accumulate the census to further their cause. *It would help,* he had said. *"I could help those who needed the treatment they sought to improve society,"* he mentally repeated the words he had spoken in San Francisco.

Still, Gene's words from last night echoed in his head. *What would his role truly be here?*

"Yes," Gwen replied, not making eye contact. "We're expecting visitors from out of state sometime soon. Maybe this week." She appeared unsettled by that last comment, but Sam couldn't afford it much thought.

"Sure," he replied. "The boss is the boss and that is what I'll do." Of course, he planned on interviewing them anyway, as he needed to do in order to gauge a proper baseline—to ascertain if the test would be accurate. *If it wasn't, then why bother administering it?* His was a purpose that was needed here, to push Western Valley past Lynchburg's asylum and onto par with D.C.—maybe even surpass their progress. Sam wished that his instrument could possibly affect the quality of life of every citizen in America.

Besides, he was looking forward to talking with McIlveen again. Despite his triple murder, he didn't blame the man for what he did. Evil didn't exist within his soul, Sam would bet. A crime of passion and the destruction of a man's purpose in life would break any human. *A criminal who deserved jail, yes, but not the harsh treatment he had heard about in other facilities.*

He slipped the folders under his arm and began the long walk upstairs. "Send them up when you're ready. And Gwen," he said.

"Yes, Doctor?" Her professionalism was in full swing.

"Do you ever listen to the blues?"

The look on her face answered his question. She appeared to be a fine woman, but one who had never been exposed to 'lesser' music, likely only hearing classical and folk styles in her upbringing.

Sam regained his bounce and swung through his door, giddy as a rooster in a hen house with no doors. *Today,* he thought, *he would truly begin his work. Today he would begin his mission here to help society accomplish what it could not on its own.*

If only he had known this before his wife …

The door opened, and a young woman entered, tears streaming down her face.

"Help me," she cried. *Just like his wife did, an hour before she died.*

26

"Sit down, please," Sam said. "Care for a glass of water?" The woman, clad only in a hospital-issue blue gown, gave him a sad smile. "You know they don't allow us real glass. "Never know what we crazies might do with it."

Sam nodded to the orderlies so that they would leave. Even if she had tried an attack, the war had trained him to defend himself against most hand-to-hand attacks. People said the insane could defy laws of human strength when set off, but so could soldiers when a knife threatened to spill their innards all over a muddy trench.

He poured her a full glass from the pitcher behind him and handed it to her. "I'm not 'them'. What do you need help with?"

"That doctor," she whimpered, accentuating each syllable. "He killed my baby."

Maybe the 10% percent rule had begun after all. "Mrs. Rowe, who killed your baby? Why would someone do such a thing?"

"The doctor. The one with the glasses and the strange name. He told me it was better for me. My husband doesn't know where I am."

"Strange name?" Sam felt his head lighten. His flesh turned clammy yet warm.

"He said it so quick and my head's a mess. I don't know. Didn't sound American. Should we have American doctors, with the state of this country now? He told the other two to take care of me. I woke up with these." Sam turned away from the stitches she showed him when she lifted her dress.

He knew the sterilizations would happen, but didn't appreciate the weight of their effect on him. Not after what happened to his wife.

At least Betty Rowe survived her ordeal.

27

"How did you wind up in here again?"

She relented and sank into the couch.

"Isn't it in your files, there?" She knew the deal and didn't appear to wish to waste time.

Sam didn't even bother to open the packet. "Please. I'd prefer your story."

She deflated into her seat. "My doctor, the one who was looking over my pregnancy, he examined me and interviewed me, like I was headed for a job as his nurse. He was all smiles, just like he was with our friends, when he helped them through their terms."

"So?" He was wondering when she broke. *Where was the crack?*

"I filled out the family history and since we're on that damned census thing, I guess they found out somehow."

"Found out what?"

"My grandmother had been in Eastern State in Williamsburg as a teenage girl, after her first baby. Got the blues as women sometimes do. When my ma's sister died in the flu times, grandma couldn't take it and fell asleep in a bathtub of crimson water."

He nodded. Depression had yet to be recognized as a curable disorder and with females, was noted to be inherent and a gateway to other issues.

"The next day, Dr. Baker sends for me and when I arrive at the office, two men are waiting for me. They tell me 'You're going in for a test for the baby.' I ask 'What for? What's wrong?' but they get me into the truck without letting my husband know."

She wrung her hands again like someone doused them in lice. "He was in the factory and never knew. I know they didn't tell him. Otherwise, he'd have come for me, with his gun."

Sam knew what was coming but couldn't stop her. Didn't want to, either. He knew her pain. He wondered if Miriam still felt hers.

"Everything afterwards was a blur. The operating room. That doctor. Falling asleep."

"I woke up and knew he had been inside of me—with those tools of his. All he said was, 'I'm sorry. You lost your baby.' I cried and asked what happened between the tears. He just regarded me like a sick dog that someone should put down."

The words cut deep. Especially after losing his son the way he did. "And that's when you …"

She smiled in a manner that chilled him. "I'm just a dull woman. Why bother removing sharp objects from the table next to the bed? He never saw me pick it up."

Her smile grew, but tears began to form at the corners of her eyes. "Just stood there, jotting down notes, talking like I was already dead to him. He said to the nurse, 'Send the report. Cross her off the list.'

"All I could see was my hand driving that steel into his neck, cutting the life out of *him*."

"But," she continued, her voice lilting in a minor key. "The nurse and assistant saw it all. I did get within six inches of his pasty white flesh, but they managed to restrain me while I howled for my baby.

"'And that's why you can't have one,' he said, and left the room. I've been locked up for the past month. The things they've done to me …"

"If I'm going to help you get back home, I need to ask you some questions first."

He didn't recognize the town on the intake form. *Mountain people. They had told him about those folks and how they bred without thought. Still, they were people. She wouldn't tell him what happened after the baby, but he could guess.*

Her hands shook like mice caught in a trap.

Classic anxiety. She appeared to be wound so tight that a breakdown was almost inevitable. Then again, it would fit, if she truly lost her baby. If Dejarnette truly did sterilize her, this would be normal. He imagined Miriam, if she had lived to see what happened.

"Whatever it takes to get me home, but I still want to kill him," she seethed.

"You do realize that if you threaten someone's life, I have to report it," he replied, feeling the fraud.

"Fine, I don't want to kill him," she said, wringing her hands. "I'll just think happy thoughts about bunnies and birds. Just ask me the questions already."

He reached for the test folder and opened to the first page. "Try to relax, as hard as that seems. Answer as honestly as you can and not as you think you want me to hear."

"If I do, will you get a message to my husband, to at least let him know where I am?"

"I see no problem with that," he said, and believed it. "The first section is with reasoning. Misery is to poverty as happiness is to what?"

"This will help me get home?"

He nodded, hoping he was right.

"Children," she said. "That's my answer."

He continued the test, beginning with more reasoning and logic questions, before spatial, knowledge, working memory, and visual-spatial reasoning. Samuel had spent over two years tweaking the original IQ test before presenting it to the Society. *"With the original, we couldn't decipher if the testee was a genius or imbecile. If he or she had come from a different country than America, he or she would automatically fail, no matter how smart they were."*

He had also mentioned that the truly insane, especially sociopaths, could fake every answer and produce a perfect score, only to go home and slaughter their families without blinking. But this test would spotlight those with violent tendencies and several disabilities and allow them to receive treatment.

By the end of the three-hour session, Betty had nodded off

twice, most likely due to the sedatives the physician had given her.

He dismissed her as she gulped down her third glass of water. She placed it in Sam's hands like a mother returning a toy to a child. "Thank you for treating me like this. I know you'll do the right thing."

"We'll talk again." Sam attempted a smile but failed miserably.

Her smile succeeded, but the watery eyes nullified it. "We won't, but thank you. I know which procedure comes next for me."

Sam regarded her with a bit of confusion and felt confident he would see her again, despite the darkness which seemed to settle over the office. *He needed to talk to Dejarnette.*

The report took over an hour to write, but he told himself it was imperative to submit it to Dejarnette. The truth would likely be ugly, yet he signed on knowing the position would not be all roses and kittens. Her score would place her in the average category, above the 10th percentile, yet her anxiety would have to be noted.

The comment about killing the doctor did not make the cut.

28

Once Sam had listened to a record of his favorite jazz, some of which reached into the blues, he felt comfortable asking Gwen to send up the next patient. *He would hold off on the test for a bit on this one. The initial interview would occur just as he preferred.*

"Oh," Gwen said, without a hint of meaning behind the words. "Dr. Dejarnette would like to speak with you before you leave for the day."

"Sure," he replied, his mood lifting, thinking he could ask about this morning's patient. "Should I ask about what?"

She kept typing whatever report she was working on. "We receive visitors from time to time. Some from the capital, others from the capitol. Other times, they're smart people." She grinned at her pun.

"Great," he said, muttering to himself as he left her office.

He sometimes regretted his role in this scheme of eugenics. He cared about the disease and what killed his wife, what might have caused his brother's condition, what produced H.H. Holmes.

His contribution was meant to help the people of his country—not imprison them. He knew about the sterilizations. The whole country did. Hell, it was front page news in the *Times* back home—but eliminating the spread of disease was one thing. Prohibiting imbeciles from having babies when they couldn't care for themselves—it would help society. Still, discerning who could be helped, and how, was his main drive, and he wouldn't have come if he didn't believe he could fix at least one cog of this screwed-up machine of a nation.

Then why did he feel as if Betty Rowe had gouged out his soul with her story?

29

Theodore Preston entered the office without a word. The averagely-built man looked like he could disappear into any crowd, with average haircut, average features, but determined eyes. Those gray eyes pierced the cloud Sam had been in since Mrs. Rowe had left.

He made a mental note to find her husband in town sometime this week.

"Doctor Taylor," he said, extending his hand. "How are you today?"

"No offense, doctor," the average man replied, "but can we skip the pleasantries? I know what's coming in the next couple of days and know that no matter what I say or do, I won't be leaving this hospital."

Sam opened his file folder and read the admission report, which took about thirty seconds. He called for the orderlies. "We're getting some air and conducting the rest of the interview outside."

"But," one said. "Dr. Dejarnette never ..."

He waved off the bigger man. "The doctor isn't here and he asked me to interview this patient. He didn't specify where. Is this man a danger?"

The two men looked at each other. They had heard of no imminent problems or incidents since the man had been committed.

"Good," Sam said. "You can follow us if you like, but we're headed out to the grounds now."

The average man smiled.

30

"I don't hate her," Theodore said. "I just don't understand why."

Sam and the patient began their walk through the front doors of his office building and took the path down to the stream, under the willows, and then past the back white building which still produced a chill in Sam. Most of the campus still gave off a calming sensation—the effect of its architecture, not the current climate.

They traveled beyond, to where the general rooms lay and a sizable hill rolled over the greens.

"Have you seen the farm yet?" The patient gestured past the hill to an enormous, long structure that would have been found on any pre-depression property in the south or Midwest. Several workers, likely patients, wandered in and out, carrying various bushels, tools, or equipment.

"My God." Sam had never seen such a thing. A whitewashed longhouse loomed ahead that spanned close to the size of a football field, with barn-door-sized openings that might have been garages, if not for the apparent crops being trucked in and out by carts, hands, or tractors.

"Yep," Ted agreed. "Apparently, the first superintendent doctor here thought it to be cost efficient if the patients worked the hospital. Building the structures, tilling the land, providing upkeep like typical servants or farmhands—he thought it was therapeutic. I believe it was, too. You know, he never forced anyone to do this?" The man examined the doctor, likely to gauge who he was dealing with and how deep Sam knew he was buried within the problem.

"He made sure everyone knew it was all volunteer work. No perks, no special treatment and more importantly, no punishment for those who came here simply to get better. He did pay those who worked, though. Hell, even Dejarnette still forks over five bucks a week to those who partake."

Sam had stopped, half staring at the farm building and half bewildered by the patient. "And you know all this because?"

"I teach at Robert E. Lee High School. Taught. U.S. History, obviously. Even if I didn't, my family's lived here since the war. Gives me a leg up on the incoming teachers."

He turned towards the doctor with a look of defeat. "My wife's not from around here. Emigrated from Birmingham to teach at the college. Did so until she realized it was work. Did so until she realized my family had a fat egg in the bank. She didn't understand why I still worked when I didn't have to."

"Why did you?"

"If a man doesn't work, what purpose does he have in this world? She wanted the moon, but I only fed it to her one slice at a time. Depression think, you know?"

Sam nodded his head. *Miriam had wished for him to cash in on his test, to take the money and run, to whisk her away from the dust of academia and all its stuffiness. He wished he had—but would it have changed history?*

At least she cared about him. She cared about their family.

The man ducked under another willow and turned away from the buildings. Sam noticed that the guards had already stopped for a smoke a hundred or so feet behind them. "When she grew weary of the humble life here, beautiful as it is, she begged for a change. For us to leave. I refused. Hell, I told her she could go back to the home of the Crimson Tide—with a divorce."

"The next night, she came into the school where I was working on an article for the school paper. My buddy Carl and I had our ritual each Sunday. We picked a topic, something for the school paper, and usually it got picked up for the town rag as well. We were proud of it."

"Well, that, and a chance to get away from the wives and toss back a few shots of whiskey his family delivered once a month." He smiled, recalling the memories of normalcy. Sam wished that he had brought a flask like Maclin had for this walk.

"Sounds normal to me," the doctor replied, anticipating the killing words.

"But she walked in on a drunken night, dumbfounded as a one-balled bull in an udder-filled pasture. But, she smiled, just fucking smiled, and turned tail. I didn't find her home when I stumbled in around midnight."

"Two men in the sheriff's truck came to the door the next evening and told me I had an appointment here. 'For deviant behavior' they said. 'For displaying behavior of a defective citizen of Virginia.'"

"When I couldn't reply, they shackled me, and I wound up in a cell, I mean hospital room." He stared at the trees which led to a section of the grounds Sam hadn't visited.

"Is that when she accused you?" Sam almost felt the man's pain, but knew to keep his distance. He noticed that the further they moved from the sweet smell of the willows in the front and the west side, the closer he felt to walking in a graveyard. Even the stench of the manure from the fields beyond the longhouse couldn't mask the sense of death. Whether that death was literal or of the soul, he couldn't discern—yet.

"Of sex with another man? With my best bud Carl? Who I grew up playing football and traded stories of screwing any women in college with? Hell, the whole school knew of my reputation growing up."

"But she did so anyway."

"And obviously, it stuck. I was told by the good superintendent that I'm scheduled for the state operation this week. You're just the formality."

Sam tripped over something hard and fell face-first into fresh grass. *At least,* he thought, spitting out a mouthful of blades, *the landing was soft. Otherwise, he would be spending his first paycheck on a dentist bill.*

A hand reached down and Sam gripped it. Theodore pulled him up with ease. He found he liked the man, whether he had been 'deviant' or not. If the teacher had not been locked up, Sam wouldn't mind having a drink with the man. He figured Gene would have enjoyed his company as well.

He brushed loose dirt and grass off his white shirt and gray trousers, not caring much how he would appear to anyone else that day. He doubted the 'important visitors' would be arriving just yet. Sam had met nearly every mover and shaker in the movement and had yet to be intimidated by the suits who talked through money.

"Welcome to the last stop in Western Valley's treatment plan," Theodore said, gesturing to what Sam had tripped over.

Short, thin gravestones lined up in narrow rows atop the hill, which led into a patch of thick woods.

Sam gasped at the sheer number. The gray slate markers laid out flat, about eight inches long, must have been in the hundreds, stretching from where they stood far back into the trees. *True, the hospital had been in existence since 1825, but why so many graves?*

Sam's eyes lost focus as they found a similarity on each stone he noticed. *None had a mark on them. No name graced any stone. Not even a cold date.*

"They don't give us names here," Theodore said. "They call it confidentiality, but I call it like I see it. Most families would want their kin back and buried in family plots, don't you think?"

The psychologist had no answer for that. Again, the words Davenport had spoken in last year's symposium echoed in his head. The words that nearly everyone in attendance had applauded. Sam remembered that his mind had tried to wrap itself around what ten percent would actually be—in this country, in the world. *Ten percent—to begin. Ten percent of the population.* Theories had always been there, but they had always been just that. Theories that rational minds would never act upon.

"I've got to get back to my room, doctor," the average man said. "But thank you for the walk and talk. It's nice to feel human once more." He smiled a thin smile. "Do me a small favor?" When Sam nodded, the man continued. "Go tell her that if anyone could make me turn to a man, it would be her cold, motionless body."

Sam turned to him, shaken from his memory. "A pleasure,"

he managed to say, and meant it. "I'll administer the test tomorrow. Hopefully I can help."

The man gave an odd smile and simply turned away. He walked down the hill and headed back towards the main building, where the two orderlies would be awaiting him.

The psychologist wondered if there was any saving grace within that file back on his desk. *Possibly if he could summon the wife or other teacher into the hospital, he could clarify the man's story and set things right. If he proved that she had lied to get at her husband's money, she might even find herself at the end of a rope in these parts. If someone would believe him.*

But as he descended the same hill, his life at the hospital changed with one sight.

31

His patient from the day before crossed his path, oblivious to the world around him.

"Mr. McIlveen?" Samuel knew before he asked, before reason and logic attempted to fight him. He reached out to stop the man. A dangerous move, especially to a murderer. Yet the man didn't even flinch. He simply halted in mid-step.

"Mr. McIlveen," he whispered, echoing the doctor's words.

"What are you doing here?" He knew that the patient should be within the white walls, secluded from the rest of the population.

"What are you doing here?" Again, the man spoke with a monotone echo.

Then he turned to face Sam.

Beneath both eyes hung thick black bags, bruises swollen as if he had boxed a dozen rounds with the Olympic team. His left eye itself was a reddened mess. Capillaries burst from pupil to edges, rendering half of the eye as crimson as the Alabama football team.

As Sam's legs threatened to lose all bone within his flesh, the stark realization became crystal clear to him.

Someone had given his patient a lobotomy.

32

Sam bolted for the main building, not giving thought to how he appeared to the others. *Hell, most on the grounds were patients.* While he ran, he felt sanity falling from him. Doris greeted him and waved to slow him down, but he barged right into Dejarnette's office.

The bespectacled man turned to him, a full tumbler in his hand. "I'm assuming from your jaunt over from the field that you spoke to Mr. McIlveen."

"Spoke to?" The psychologist heaved a few breaths, attempting to unleash on the other man. "You. They didn't tell me. *Why?*" He felt his fingers curl into fists.

"Here," the director said, handing him the glass. Sam took it and wondered how his hands gripped it without shaking it to the carpet. "Sit down and swallow this."

Sam did, his mind reeling with anger and confusion. The whiskey burned with a smoothness he hadn't felt since France. *Why had he listened to this man? The man had just delivered him from a working tomb and promised him a fresh, waking life here in the middle of beauty.*

"I just interviewed him yesterday," he managed. "He didn't seem …"

"He murdered three people in cold blood. He needed to be 'calmed.' People with the killing gene don't improve. They fester in their dark minds, hair triggers that could snap at any time. Hell, I think many of them actually enjoy it."

"But a crime of passion …"

"He planned it. Angry, yes. Jealous, yes. But he did know

what he was doing—and that's frightening."

"Yet a man who didn't care wouldn't put ..." Sam attempted, and then tried to reel the words back into his mouth.

Dejarnette smiled. "The kids? Yes, he did put them on the train. Very touching. I like kids." He poured Sam another glass and looked towards his telephone. "We're looking for them right now."

Rage filled Sam again. "Why? Do they get lobotomies, too? Violence isn't proven to be genetic."

The man still gazed at the desk, perhaps awaiting the instrument to ring. "We don't know it isn't. Lobotomies? No. I'm not a monster. But you remember the consortium, the Society at Cold Springs Harbor. The directive—the one you signed off on—stated that any measures would be taken to achieve the 10% reduction."

"Have you read the *New York Times* recently?" He reached over and held up a recent copy. "'Sterilization The Ideal Means'." He flipped to the next paper and held it higher, clearer in Sam's line of sight. "'Plan Nation-Wide Eugenics Society'. 'Race Purity is the Aim.' These aren't my words, son. These are the words of the many who are crying for a change."

Sam put down the glass, his entire body shivering. "Doctor, I signed up for helping to stop overpopulation and testing the criminals and psychologically hindered so this wouldn't happen. Not this."

"No? And how did you think the Society was going to achieve this? Talking to the defectives and asking them not to fuck like filthy animals? Not to shit out a dozen imbeciles for America to feed? Teaching the feeble-minded not to do the evil things they do?"

No, he did know what he had signed up for and he did know that it wouldn't be pretty, but he didn't think the people would be like this. He expected animals. But he wanted to help people—not automatically sterilize and lobotomize. *That damned test.*

The patients he interviewed would never be animals.

"I want to help. The directive. Yes, if they're deemed irreparable, if they're truly criminal."

"And McIlveen wasn't one of these?" He slammed down the paper. "This isn't fun, happy work, Sam. You don't think it eats away at everyone here when we perform one of the procedures that changes a life forever? It does—except when they fight us and refuse to see how they're hurting the country and killing their families in the process. In that case, I struggled with the Lord to find mercy."

Sam thought of his brother. *What would Dejarnette wish for him if Sam weren't an employee?* "And what constitutes who's hurting our country?"

"You've seen the reports. Criminal behavior. Psychologically unsound. Deformities. Blindness. Susceptibility to diseases. Seizures. Madness. Should I go on?"

"You forgot deafness." His voice attempted steel but sounded like tin.

"How's Colin enjoying his new school?" The man's smile appeared true, but the implication behind it shone like a blade.

Sam felt his fists grow white. "He loves it. He's a hell of a pitcher. I fought alongside a deaf man in France. His use of signs in combat saved our asses many times. We could learn a lot from them."

"Of course, we could," the doctor replied. "But imagine if we fostered that weakness? Encouraged it?"

"I'm not saying that," Sam stammered. "I just help him make the best of life and he's well above average intelligence. People like him need to know they have a purpose and can help the country."

The doctor refilled his glass, and Sam's. "Not arguing with you there. Just imagine if we allowed deaf couples to breed. Two becomes four; four becomes eight; and so on. We'd have entire towns that couldn't hear an attack coming. You see my point?"

"Are you serious? Even high school students know the tenets of a Punnett square. Recessive genes prevail in only twenty-five percent of each birth—and that's IF both parents display. *Both.* Having one blind parent doesn't mean the family will have a blind child."

"But why chance it? You saw we struggled in the war. Look at history, Sam. The Spartans, Greeks, Romans, Chinese dynasties—all who became world powers—they never let themselves kowtow to the weak. They mercifully dealt with the defectives."

"They butchered their own."

"And ruled their worlds for centuries because of it. But 'butchered', Sam? I don't think so and we don't do that here. None of the countries in the Society do."

"Did you ever stop to think that those world powers eventually succumbed to their own egos? That they thought because of their planning, they were invincible? That was their downfall." Sam saw red so dark it could have burned Rome.

Dejarnette regarded Sam with a look undecipherable to the other man. He pulled out a third paper from his desk. "So, are you telling me that you can't do this job? Or won't?"

"Neither," Sam said. He deflated within, feeling the nails on his coffin pierce his soul. "I knew what my test was for. I just didn't think it would be dealt with like this. I don't want to lose this country. Not after fighting for it."

"Good. I knew I chose wisely. So tomorrow, you'll go back to testing the patients? We have so much work to do and those back in New York are anxious about results."

"They're in New York now?" With each word he heard, he felt himself shrinking a little more.

"Where else would the Carnegies be? The richest of the rich, in the biggest city in the world? Makes sense to me. What else makes sense is that without their money, without the money from the backers we have, all of this just goes away. It goes to other people, and we're stuck back in the footnotes of history. I don't know about you, but I want to change the world—for the better."

Sam went to say something, feeling himself relax, but his voice failed him. *If the Carnegies and other businessmen were powering this movement, he didn't have much choice.*

"Tomorrow I want you to come down to the hospital section of my building. I want you to see what we really do."

"Thank you, but I do have several rounds of testing and scoring. It will have to wait."

"Samuel, I want you to be with us with both feet, soaked to

the gills. Please join me tomorrow. See what your research helps us accomplish."

Sam sensed a refusal would draw something he couldn't afford yet. *Or anytime.* Still, he found himself not replying to the man's request. As he held the other's gaze, he saw that third newspaper rise close to him in Dejarnette's pink hands.

"Remember, please, that I chose you specifically for this hospital. Others petitioned to hire you as well, but I won out. But please don't take that as weakness on my part. I want you to be with me here as we make history. Yet if we fail, we disappoint people who don't take to disappointment well."

He unfolded the paper and ice rained down Sam's neck and back. "I take it that you never saw this edition."

The headline read, 'Nearly 15,000,000 Schoolchildren are Defectives.'

"They know everything about you. Remember that.

"Why don't you go home and have yourself some drinks & come back after you've thought things through. Remember— this is what you signed off on & developed that famous test for— you're a part of this. A crucial part. Keep that in mind.

"Go play yourself a sad song on that new guitar of yours," the doctor said, waiting for the realization to hit Sam. "Maybe your friend can mire you in the mud music. It does stir the soul."

Sam didn't remember shaking Dejarnette's hand or stating that he agreed to visit the doctor's section the following morning. He simply ghosted through the office and past Doris before pausing at the front door. The sun had just begun to crest over the mountains to the west. He was drawn to it without a thought. *The man had him followed. Watched him. Knew about it all.*

When he was halfway to the gates, a noise intruded his mental haze. His eyes opened wider and his head turned to face the railway traveling from town into Western Valley. He shook off the clouds behind them and squinted past the falling red lights beyond him. He noticed it wasn't a complete passenger train, but one of several freight cars, opened at the upper ends like those which brought cattle. He figured the hospital would receive supply cars, but a feeling overtook him. *This train held much more.*

As Sam continued to walk towards the outside world, the train rumbled into the property. He swore to himself as it crawled to a stop just out of view. *Why would it stop here if it wasn't a true cargo line?*

The blood drained from his face as he caught the stare from a strained face within the dark car.

33

"Do you think he'll follow through?"

Dejarnette gripped the phone tight, as he always did when Grant decided to check in on one of his projects. Western Valley and its keeper had been the most promising, outside of Cold Springs Harbor.

"Yes," he said to their benefactor, second only to Carnegie in terms of power, within the States. The man's stare could make any other avert his eyes. "I think he realizes he doesn't have a choice." The keeper watched his new psychologist walk out of his kingdom and head back into town. *Did he notice what was on the train? Did it matter? Sooner rather than later he would know all. Hopefully, he would stay on board when he saw what was behind the curtain.*

"We hope so. He wasn't our first choice, but we trusted your instincts."

Dejarnette felt himself stand up straight. "He created that test, the one that will give us the accurate readings we need for our files." The choice could cement the cause's public impression, or poison it.

"The ones we don't need."

He sighed. "Mr. Grant, we do need them. If this is to go to the next level, we're going to need proof of why we do what we do. This country, our government, won't buy the movement if the data is as gossamer as a drunk spider. We can't go off half-cocked."

"Why not? The world is churning out more mud every day without thought. Why can't we wash that mud back into the ditches, where it belongs?"

"Because people don't get the chair for fucking, even if they're not worthy of breathing. People get the chair for what you and the Society tell us to do." The words sounded sincere, but Dejarnette believed the mission was sound.

"There wouldn't be enough chairs."

Dejarnette poured himself another drink. He ached for the operation the following day. *A little release of the darkness within would let in the light.* "Harry, please. You know who they'd come for—not the shadows in the night."

"Maybe," the disembodied voice said. "Yet they couldn't be too upset about the dogs we're going to be putting down."

"Plenty of dogs you're talking about. If your census people are accurate …"

"They are." The man on the other end of the phone sounded like he could have wielded a reaper's scythe. Yet the doctor knew the nickname the nurses had given him. He had always waved it off as a harmless taunt, but with Eli Whitney's creation so close to Augusta, the comparison rang sound.

"Then we shouldn't have much to worry about—we can simply feed the thoroughbreds."

"Good to hear," Grant said. "I'll tell the others tomorrow, before we decide when to visit. Hopefully your main dog will still be doing his trick when we arrive."

The phone clicked without a farewell. "I hate dogs," Dejarnette said, remembering the mutts his wife always brought home. None of them lasted long. He smiled, wondering how she would feel if she knew many of them were helping his research.

34

Gene Walker woke up from his afternoon nap screaming.
"Honey," Eliza whispered, hugging his trembling body.
"It's okay. You're in the store. You're *safe*."

The flashbacks had been subsiding in recent months. It had been almost a year since his lost weekend. Almost seventeen since the war—and thirteen since his brother's disappearance.

Every day on his lunch break, he flipped the open sign to 'Be right back' while he shut his eyes for a few, checked the inventory in the back, or took a stroll up and down Augusta, enjoying the fresh air. He wasn't prone to true naps, not until the new movement began inside the buildings down the road.

His eyes sprung open like a man whose life was just returned to him. His huge hands nearly broke the arms of the rocking chair in which he sat.

"It's back," he wheezed. "I thought I buried it."

"Honey," Eliza spoke, her voice steady. "You're never going back there. I promise. Dr. Taylor wouldn't allow it."

He turned to her with a look that froze her. "Dear woman, do you honestly think anyone could control that monster inside that hell hole? Sam's got enough to worry about. He just doesn't know it yet."

35

Colin left the school right after he met with the school's principal. His amazing day took a dark, confusing turn before she let him on his way.

"Son, what do you want to do with your life? Become a doctor like your brother, join the army, and work for the government?"

His smile burst from somewhere deep within, a sensation he hadn't experienced much in school.

"Nope. I'm going to be a writer, just like Burroughs, Wells, and Verne. If I have to start off with playing baseball games, I'll do it, but I want it all."

She almost took his hand in her own, but stopped just short. He thought it to be because she wouldn't be able to sign to him. "You do that—but make sure everyone knows how good you are. Make sure they ALL know how worthy you are."

He signed assent and a quick thank you, and then left, wondering what she meant. He caught up with Chloe, the girl he talked to in English class, who lived right down the street from him. Of course, he wanted to learn all about southern girls. What he found was something that would keep him awake most of the week.

Chloe 'spoke' well, having grown up the daughter of a professor at the university in town. Both of her parents had extensive education, her father at UVA and her mother in secretarial college. They managed to teach her to read lips and sound out words that looked authentic. Colin wondered if they sounded as sweet as she looked. With straw-colored hair which flowed down most of her back and eyes that reflected the light like the kaleidoscopes he saw down at Atlantic City, he became enamored immediately.

Chloe, on the other hand, played the aloof card so well, he couldn't figure whether she viewed him as interesting or as a bore. *Maybe she was just doing a favor for the principal.* She told him about the town, the best place to get ice cream (Mr. Walker's store) and the neatest places to play, and most of all, she showed him the library. He nearly peed himself when he saw the size of it. Being in a smaller town, he expected a rinky-dink building. Instead, this stood on the corner of two of Augusta's busiest streets and looked like it could hold a million books.

He made a mental note to come back later that week to get a card and begin some new adventures. But first, he allowed her to take him on a tour of the main streets, up the hill to the beautiful college campus. *All girls*, he mused. *What would a college be like with 100% females?*

"Want to see something really neat?" She mouthed to him but her eyes showed more than a little excitement.

He nodded and attempted a simple "Yes" with his hands but stumbled over his own fingers. The sun had just begun to fade over the tops of the buildings and would bring the first rays of darkness when it dipped behind the mountains bordering the town. *If he was back before sunset, he would be okay.*

Somehow sensing his reticence, she said, "Don't worry, we'll be back before dark. My father would kill me if I was a minute late. He'll kill me for walking with a strange boy just the same!"

Colin smiled and signed that he'd love to meet the man. He followed her as she turned the corner where the police station was being built. The old one still stood down on Richmond Ave, close to the hospital and the interstate. She ran up to a massive opening in the ground and peered over an iron railing. For a moment, Colin felt she might jump into it.

She waved him over and he followed. He looked down where she did, and his mouth dropped. About ten feet across and thirty feet long, a river or strong stream surged below them.

"The construction workers from the CCC found this when they began work on the new station." She turned left and right.

"Come back here on the other side. If the coppers find us near it, they'll fine us and drive us home in their squad car. I'd never be allowed out again."

"Me neither," Colin signed, but knew his brother would never punish adventurism. "Where does it go? Where did it come from?"

She shrugged as they sat down in the shadows on the other side of the railings, away from sight. "Nobody's been able to figure it out yet. Since the mountains are off to the west, and east, it's tough for them to agree. Some think it's a cave river that began deep below the surface and since it disappears, dips again under the rest of the town and into Waynesboro Valley."

"Geez!" he signed, exaggerating his signs. "So, it might come from way below the surface?" His mind rallied to summon up images of Pellucidar and their inner earth people. *Maybe they did exist—or something else like them.*

She seemed to recall the story from class and smiled at him. "There's no way people are in there. Relax there, Sherlock." *Did she also read Arthur Conan Doyle? Was she real?*

"No people are in there."

"How do you know? Are there other openings somewhere?" He could barely sit still.

She shrugged again. "I've heard things. Maybe from places up in the mountains, but those people are full of myths and legends. Some say they bury their dead by dropping them into cavern shafts, thinking that God will accept them back into the earth."

"Wow," Colin replied. "I wish I could get a raft ..."

She slapped his arm. "You'd die! Nobody knows where it opens again—or if it does. Unless you have fish in your genes, give up the idea!"

"Still," he said, feeling a bit deflated. "I want to explore this." Maybe he should tell the principal that an archeologist would be a fine addition to his career choices.

He reached behind him to pick up a slab of wood. Maybe if he saw how fast the river took it, he could work on figuring it out. Just as he lifted it, Chloe gripped both his arms tight and stared into his face.

"Shhh ..." she said. She tilted her head to the street side. Someone had just pulled up in a black Model-A. They approached the downturn of the hill with no lights. *Who drives like that? It's a good thing the cops were nowhere near this place yet. He'd be ticketed in a heartbeat.*

Instead of looking for the police, Colin felt Chloe's fingers dig into his. He huddled into the railing.

A tall man emerged wearing all black, maybe a full suit with matching hat, and crept to the back door which faced them.

This time, when he opened the opposite door, he did look all around to figure if anyone else was around. The only souls there were hidden from view. He reached inside and appeared to struggle with something. Something big.

And alive.

The man in dark clothing, possibly one of the infamous 'men in black' from Hoover's crew, guided another big man from the car and pulled him to a standing position. This man towered over the other but appeared shaky. *Drunk?* Colin wondered. Chloe signed the same thing.

The hulking man dwarfed the other one, but was at the mercy of the man in the dark suit. His speed would easily overwhelm his victim. *Victim.* That's the word which came to Colin's mind, as he felt he was watching a terrible movie.

Chloe's nails in Colin's arm drew blood as the two men turned their way. Colin wished to scream in pain, but held back. Instead, he could only watch as the one man guided the other in dungarees, flannels, and boots towards the railing.

He watched closely to pick up the lip movements of their words, just within comprehension. He could see them just fine, but they wouldn't be able to see Chloe and him unless they came to their side of the railing.

"Just a little more, this way," said the G-man. "Your niece will be waiting for you soon. I think she's just around the corner in the apartments above us, with a friend of my wife."

"She knows someone here?" The bigger man slurred. *Definitely drunk,* Chloe signed.

"And where did she come from? Do you remember now?" The G-man looked agitated.

The bigger man shook his head. "No more bad man. Bad beach."

Colin gripped the girl's arm. *Why did he sound so slow?*

"Where?" The man in dark continued. "I need to know where she works."

"Virginia Beach," said the man, and smiled. "She lives ..." and gestured in a wide arc to nowhere.

"We're done. I'll find her and return you to the mud where you came. We don't have time to listen to animals."

"Where?" Finally, the man appeared a bit concerned.

"Time for a ride. You might enjoy this one. The great gods of the sky are sitting this one out."

With that, he grabbed the front of the man's shirt and pulled. At the same time, he placed his right leg in front of the bigger man's, forming a fulcrum. His other hand reached behind as the man pivoted and shoved him—hard.

With a surprised but garbled howl, the man tumbled over the railing and splashed into the raging waters. Chloe and Colin watched as the man flailed for a second or two before disappearing under the cement opening. He never had a chance.

Chloe didn't scream but she did bolt upright and pulled Colin with her. The man heard the rustling but couldn't see them in the shadows. She took off down the side alley and kept motoring until they hit the dormitories of Mary Baldwin College. They sensed the man pursuing but she knew the shortcuts and with the twists and turns so well, Colin swore that only a local could follow her. *The man would never follow them inside a crowded place like that. But, did he catch a glimpse of either of their faces? If so, they would follow the big man into the dark waters.*

They were safe—for the moment. Still, all Colin could do was see the man's face and hear his sound as he plunged to his death. He wondered now if he still wished to discover where the river emerged.

So much for archaeology.

36

At the same moment her uncle became river debris, Ruby strolled through her new town, thinking about nothing at all. Thoughts of her husband she had left—and him livid—fell away as she left her morning job at the school. Each day, she would begin her day planning the meals for the day at the special school, procuring the ingredients for breakfast, lunch, and dinner. She wondered how much of her food was designed for the brass of the school and how much for the kids who had been shipped there by their families from all over the state.

Did it even matter? They offered her a job, just like Panevino's did. *Two jobs in the middle of a beautiful oasis from the Depression and several hours away from the hell she had endured for five years.* One offered her scraps but at this school, she could rule over the kitchen. Most of her friends at the culinary school couldn't find even one job—and here she was with twice the results. Maybe it was the location and lack of competition. Her boss at the restaurant had asked for an Italian cook and so she became one, despite where she truly hailed from—but the school only wished for a quality recommendation for a piss-poor-paying job.

To her, again, did it matter? She would've plucked chickens to escape the hell Claude had given her. She recalled the man who promised her freedom from the growing oppression in her home country. Yet he had only given her beatings and a daily minefield to maneuver through, while avoiding more pain.

She took the bacon and cheddar croissant from her bag and chewed with a growing smile as she thought of his fatal mistake. Criminally brutal in his admonitions that her cooking that 'European slop' gave him gas, he enrolled her in the state's best culinary program. He wanted the best servant and wife possible.

Prisoner in a gulag, she thought.

He talked her away from her family, what little remained after the civil strife, and off to London with him where he taught as a guest lecturer in her country. "Come to America with me and never fear for your life again," he said.

She could laugh now, knowing that he would never find her. She knew nothing but fear while in his clutches—until she unleashed her dreams in the kitchen. She knew she could make anyone smile with her food. Man or woman, rich or poor, criminal or saint. And he provided all of it, never realizing she'd be strong enough to run.

He did know about her uncle in the mountains, but never cared about her enough to ask where. That thought made the food taste even sweeter in her mouth. The molasses she added to the croissant recipe made the headmaster sit up and ask her to send three more to his office for snacks during the day.

She hoped the kids enjoyed them just as much.

Now as she passed the park, with its little lake and train which chugged in an oval around it, giggling children aboard, she recalled the man from the train.

Maybe she should meet him at the theater this weekend.

If only she could find the kind man who invited her to this town in the cleavage of two inviting mountain ranges. He answered her frantic letters and convinced the restaurant owner to ask her school for a chef looking to relocate. Most of her classmates only ached for the lure of the big cities. *Washington, Charlotte, Norfolk, and Baltimore: bright lights and hope for an end to the downslide to the economy.* Not her. She dreamed of a quiet home in the middle of nowhere. She wished for a restaurant that wouldn't ask where she came from or why she wanted to be in their little town.

But now that she was settling in, she wondered why her only family in this country, however distant he might be, was nowhere to be found. She found his apartment fully stocked with food and his belongings.

At least here in Augusta, peace was the only thing which assailed her.

Still, she worried. She would until the weekend, just three more days away. Part of her would rise above the worry, with a tingling she hadn't known was alive in her for close to a decade.

37

"Are you following me?"

Sam had seen Ruby heading towards the theater when he was on his own detour. Before seeing her, he had only been thinking of more of Tennessee's best in a mason jar and picking some blues for the evening. Yet once he caught a glimpse of her in that form-fitting dress blowing in the autumn breeze, he couldn't help but grin. His gait quickened to catch up to her, surprised at himself, but not minding.

"What?" She appeared truly startled at his voice but softened when she turned to him. "I don't like being scared."

"So, I frighten you?" He flashed his psychologist smile, hoping he seemed foolish enough to keep her attention.

She straightened her dress. "Nothing here frightens me. I'm a little more than the waifs you probably deal with around here, doctor."

He offered surrender with a bowed head and raised hands. "I didn't mean ..."

Ruby took a step forward. "No, I'm sorry. I'm just still looking for my uncle. He never met me at the station two nights ago. I don't like losing family."

"This is prime hunting territory," Sam said. "I hear that some storms catch men off guard, even the hardiest ones. Thankfully, I hear several cabins exist up in the Alleghenies to give shelter."

"Not him," she said. "He's a native. A true native." She appeared uncertain about offering that information, but he had a knack of making people around him feel comfortable enough to open themselves. *Good knack to have in his profession,* he smiled to himself. "I'm not, except by relation; he's the only one I have in the states."

"Have you checked in with his friends? Neighbors?"

She deflated. "Not yet. I've been working too much. I guess I seem like a poor soul, not making time to search and investigate."

"Don't be silly. You've only just arrived. I have my mother and brother in a great house, but still haven't even seen half of it. There might be a carnival of midgets or elephants living in the other half for all I know."

Her face cracked a bit and both eyes met his. "You're pretty good at this doctoring stuff."

"I only fix minds," he said. "I'd be in prison if they let me touch other parts."

She blushed a bit but didn't trip on her words. "I think you'd be fine." Beckoning to the theater sign behind her, she continued. "Are you still going to the show Saturday?"

"I think my brother would murder me a thousand ways to Sunday if I bailed on him now. He's never seen a 'talkie' yet." He looked to the movie poster. "I just hope he understands all of it."

"Is he young?" She found herself scanning the streets. *Could her uncle have had her arrival date wrong?*

"Only in body. He's an old soul, as they say. However, he can't hear. He reads lips from a mile away, which scares me, but is brighter than a supernova."

At that, he witnessed her face light up like the event he just mentioned. "My morning job is at his school. He does go to the school?"

"Yes, yes he does," Sam said. "I'm confused. I thought you worked at the Italian joint?"

"Only in the evenings." Her feet danced a little in unease. "I'm new to this career. They don't pay women much for cooking."

"I'd pay plenty for a meal with you. For your cooking, I mean."

The look in her eyes gave him a start he couldn't explain. *"King Kong* on Saturday?"

"You'll join me?" The excitement in all extremities flared electric in him.

"Sure," she said, a little coy. "Bring your brother. I think the three of us will have a grand time."

His smile lit the way home, his anticipation lifting his feet from the sidewalk the entire way.

Sam would have a bright light to guide him through whatever confronted him at Western Valley for the rest of this week. His beacon would keep his spirits out of the grave—at least until he left her Saturday night.

38

This time, Bridget Taylor cooked dinner on her own for the Walkers and her own brood. Completely Irish-style. *Normally, she wouldn't entertain two nights in a row, but it had been two years since her son was home and longer since she had neighbors, or friends, who wished to spend time with her. She never had time, either, with all the work she had in New Jersey just attempting to keep her family's financial head above water. Now, her returning son had given her a new home and reprieve from working herself to an early grave.*

"Is this legal down here?" Gene joked with her as he piled the Irish stew and sauerkraut onto his plate.

"Only if you don't blow your wife out of the bedroom later," she replied, smiling. She recalled the noisy nights of her husband after her feasts. For once, she didn't feel the empty ache within when she envisioned his face.

"I think he needs no help in that department," Eliza said.

"Hush, woman. If this food brings me to the level of something the navy needs for their next battle, I'll sign up all over again. We'd never lose a battle with my reaction to sauerkraut."

The group laughed together, even Sam, who had been in a fog since his meeting with the strange, beautiful woman on the way home. "Have you been to the Dixie?"

Eliza answered for her husband, who was shoveling food into his mouth. "Of course. We're looking forwards to the talkies even more. They'll keep his big mouth shut and offer some peace to the other patrons."

"Woman," Gene said. "I'm warning you. I'll keep eating all night and you'll find yourself on the moon by morning."

"Where's Colin?"

His mother cocked her head upwards. "He came home right before you did and went right to his room. He claimed an upset belly, so I gave him broth and let him be."

Sam raised his eyebrow. "Did you buy his story?"

She regarded him like he had three ears. "Of course not. But he's adjusting. The school is as overwhelming as the move. Too much change for the boy. I'll talk to him later."

Sam wondered how well he knew his little brother. *Should he toss on his therapist hat here, or give the boy some space?* He attempted to remember himself at the gates of puberty.

"I'll bug him tomorrow if he's still in a funk. Besides, I wanted to visit his school anyway. I hear great things about it." *Especially the food,* he smiled to himself.

39

Gene and Sam sat outside again, gazing into the mountains with a drink in each hand, guitar on their knee. They had been trading licks and Gene had tried to teach Sam some of the latest blues runs he'd picked up in the honkytonks he used to visit.

"What's wrong?" The darker man held a steady, sweet vibrato on the steel as he examined Sam's furrowed brow.

"With my playing?" Sam emptied his drink. "I don't think I have rhythm."

"No, friend. Your light is mixed tonight," he said, staring into his new friend's eyes. "I can tell a few things, even though I have no letters after my name. Something is bright within you that wasn't there, but there's a darkness that's begging to bury the light."

He poured each a new drink.

"Are you sure you didn't study psychology?" Sam managed a smile. "I'm just not sure how to read my new place of employment yet."

"Do you mean the boss or the job?"

"Gotta get back to you on that."

The other man slid down an effortless turnaround on the 12-bar progression. "And the woman?"

Sam's smile faltered. He'd enjoy thoughts of her in the morning again, but he couldn't shake a growing anxiety.

The cloud won out now over the light. "All of them," he replied, curious how Gene knew about his new fancy. "But you don't want to hear it. I don't wish to speak ill of my new home. Maybe I'm overreacting."

Gene stared at Sam for a long time before speaking.

"I'd like to tell you about my weekend in Western Valley and how I saw the devil himself inside those gates."

Neither man played a note or lifted their drinks until the last word dissipated on the night wind.

By the time Gene finished his tale, Sam knew that his life would never be the same if he went back. Yet he had no choice. *The devil indeed lived within and fed his family when they would starve elsewhere.*

Worse yet, he had signed the Faustian contract himself, willingly.

"How much does Eliza know?

The big man lowered his head. "Ever since I began having the nightmares, I had to tell her everything. She still wants kids but we know it's not in God's plan. Not since her own appointment."

Sam's head spun. "Wait—they took her too?"

He nodded. "The following weekend she went, but was home before I had awakened. I would never have known if she hadn't told me."

"But why? Why you?" Sam looked Gene up and down, and then remembered the story about the man's brother. *No.*

"You do know I'm not really Italian, right? You're not a stupid man."

"Then where are you from?" He was shaking; images of Dejarnette cutting open his friend. He couldn't imagine Eliza's face.

"Does it matter?" Gene poured another full glass. "Call me Caribbean. It's close enough. But to them, I'm mud. Close enough to the unmentionable races. I think I wouldn't be here if I didn't own my shop."

"What do you mean?"

"You'll learn."

"Tell me, please."

"No," his friend said. "I can't. I can't prove it, even though I know I'm right. Look within your own soul and you'll know. You know already. You just don't want to. You might have signed up for the good fight, to truly help, but when you work for those who dwell in fire, things turn."

Sam and Gene sat in silence until night stole the remainder of the sun. Both fingered chords on their guitars, but neither sounded a note. Sam felt even if they did, the darkness would squelch it.

All they sounded was the clinking of glasses and the promise to each other that they would keep each other's family safe—and Sam from honoring his contract.

"Gene," he said, his voice as steady as a moth in a firestorm. "Who the *fuck* are they?"

His friend quietly drained his whiskey in one slug. "Ah, shit. You want the good news or the bad?"

Sam's eyes were glued to the visitors who arrived in the dark. "Both."

"They're pissed off and only show up at Christmas."

"What's the good news?"

"They're not on the porch yet."

40

The four men were standing in Sam's backyard, out of the moonlight, under cover of the trees.

The duo on the porch strained their vision to gain a look and as if on cue, the quartet stepped forward two steps, just into the faint illumination. Each stood clad in gray or black trousers and boots. Two wore thick flannels, one with overalls covering the thick body underneath. The third's trench coat reached his toes but hung open, revealing a brightly-colored gingham shirt and burlap slacks. The fourth sported something that P.T Barnum might have seen in his nightmares: a tri-color, striped one-piece suit which appeared to be constructed of potato sacks and curtains. Each stripe held stars, moons, or clown faces.

As Sam registered this image, he shrunk back into his seat, accidentally shifting the chair back with a squeal that brought Gene's hand down on his arm in a grip of iron.

"Don't. Move."

None of the men in the yard flinched, which frightened Sam even more. He allowed himself to find eyes behind the grotesque masks each wore. One appeared stolen from a mannequin with the eyes carved out, another was black leather with slits cut for the mouth, nose, and eyes. The remaining two defied description but Sam knew his mind would review every detail in nightmares for years if he survived the night.

"What do they want?" His voice creaked while his arm muscles tightened so much, his fingers tingled. His left hand began to tap on the railing. A pattering like hail sounded with his nervous twitch.

Gene shot him a dangerous glare and held up a pair of

fingers with the source of the noise clipped between them. Sam's habit of carrying his guitar pick, twirling it, palming it, and tapping when he wasn't near a guitar, always drew looks. This time, he prayed the visitors didn't mind.

They didn't and stood stoic in place, eyes unblinking.

"If we're lucky, you won't find out."

"What about you?" He heard his voice break.

"It's not my house. They're here because of you."

The stare-down lasted another ten minutes, during which Sam felt his bladder cramp in protest, but he felt the fear win out and glue him in place. Besides, he had no faith in his legs to move him into the house.

The pick remained in his grip, softly beating out a rhythm that matched his staccato heartbeat.

Then before he could react, all of them stepped back into the dark and disappeared.

Sam barely made it to the railing to urinate before he ruined a good set of trousers.

41

"Bel-*what*?"

Gene emptied the remainder of his bottle, while making sure the women and Colin hadn't seen what they did. "Honestly, I know it doesn't seem like it, but before last year, I didn't drink—much.

"They're called Belsnicklers. Originated in Germany and settled in Pennsylvania last century."

Sam had his guitar in his lap and had been plucking the same few notes over and over, ever since he zipped his pants and filled his drink with a hand that took over a minute to still. *First the lobotomized patient, now this. What the hell did he agree to down here?*

"So, why Christmas, when they look like cast-offs from Halloween?"

"They descended from Germanic folklore …"

"Now you're a historian? Did you learn that in the islands or at university?"

Gene grinned, knowing it was in jest and to kill the stress. "Neither, Dr. Yankee. Over there, not many of our boys would talk to me and true Negroes didn't trust me, so I was often on my own. To keep myself sane, I talked to a good deal of locals. You'd be amazed at how much they loved talking. Even more, when I was assigned to guarding the POWs, some of them couldn't shut up. During Christmas in 1916, one homesick guy told me the stories. Scary shit."

"So why are they here?"

"Immigration, brother. Old Saint Nick had a counterpart, someone who dealt with the naughty kids. Townsfolk got the nod and dressed up to scare the crap out of them."

"I'll have to tell Colin," Sam said, repeating the phrase on the guitar once again. He hadn't been this unnerved since his first night in the trenches.

"You just might," Gene replied. "The tradition sailed here with them and once the corridor opened during the Civil War, more Germanic peoples took up residence. They're a tough group. If they find the naughty children, they let their switches do the speaking for them—and are often invited into homes. If people guessed who they were, the Belsnicklers removed their masks and were fed. If not, they left, hungry and sober."

Instead of following Sam's gaze into the woods, Gene cast his eyes in a different direction. "Something drew them here tonight. Something got word to them that they needed to step up their game early this year and somehow, they know it's not just kids misbehaving."

"My god. And they're here for Colin?"

"Man, you must be snookered already. Don't you get it? They don't come out this early—ever. They're here for *you*."

"But why? I wasn't bad. I'm here to help people."

"Are you?"

42

D r. Dejarnette put the leash on his French poodle and readied himself for his evening walk. Like Sam, he lived just a few blocks away from the hospital. On some nights, he slept in the guest room adjacent to his office, but lately, he felt the need to be close to his wife. And son.

As close as he could be, anyway.

"Come on, Zoe. Let's get some fresh air." He stood at the front door on Rebecca Street, a quiet few blocks of antebellum houses. Only the most influential of the town and county resided within the environs of the narrow passage where former President and eugenics supporter Woodrow Wilson spent many of his years.

He turned back to the stairwell and called to his wife. She appeared at the railing, soundless, as she had likely imbibed whatever prescription he had given her in the past few months. They locked eyes and although he begged her several times a week to break out of her cloud-riddled mind, she found asylum in that haven.

Maybe she couldn't accept that their son could not find the same peace.

Joseph Dejarnette navigated his pet through the neighborhood. *She was a true creature of habit, despite her obvious intelligence. Always trotted up the one hill towards the Wilson library and back down towards Mary Baldwin College. How he wished he could teach a course there on his research, his work. He ached to share his findings with someone, but the Society wouldn't allow it—yet.*

"Go ahead, girl. Take your time. Daddy needs time to think."
And he did. *Maybe if he propelled his own work like Davenport
did in Cold Spring Harbor, maybe then he would be revered like
the others.* He loved the valley, its beauty and isolation, but it
didn't carry the prestige of New York, San Francisco, or even
Chicago.

Should he walk past Taylor's place again tonight? He worried
he might have scared off the young doctor or worse, turned
him against the movement, which would not sit well with those
above. *So much promise in the man,* he mused, *so much fire,
especially after his losses. Only someone with a burden such as
that could appreciate the work of eugenics like he did.*

Joseph smiled at his purebred— the only type of dog he
would own. The town took care of the strays pretty well, just as
the doctor did with the ones entering his hospital.

Soon, he thought. *Soon the world would be back on track
and America would clean its stables. The Carnegies, Rockefellers,
and such would fund the movement and keep the public in check,
until the time was right to show them how right the Society's
views were. The earth couldn't sustain life the way the world was
headed.*

Zoe tugged at the leash, barking her high-pitched bark as
they turned down Samuel's street. He didn't know of any other
dogs around there, but the county was rife with wild creatures.
Thankfully, none would threaten his safety, unless the game
warden from the CCC in the new park was right about the bears
looking for new sources of food.

Survival of the fittest. He could live with that.

A few minutes later he turned his corner, full of vigor from
the fresh mountain air. Yet as he gazed up at the windows on
the second floor where his son resided, he felt his lungs, and
heart, deflate.

Survival of the fittest, indeed.

43

Sam kept his fork full at breakfast, hoping that by appearing hungry, neither his mother nor brother would expect him to converse much. It was Wednesday, just another couple of days until the end of the week where he could gather himself, take stock in what he had gotten himself into, and determine if he could live like this.

Maybe Gene had been right. The man's words rumbled through his mind all night long, as he told himself he *was* helping people.

"Are you?" His friends had been echoing though his brain ever since he put his head to the pillow. His evening visitor failed to appear and soothe him, just when he needed it the most.

As he walked out the door fifteen minutes early, he turned his head downtown, hoping to catch a glimpse of Ruby before she headed to work at the school. *Maybe he could tell Colin about her and possibly meet her before the film, grease the wheels a bit.*

Was he that much of an idiot? *Be a man and do it yourself,* he chided himself. *Man up when you see her at the movies. If she guns you down, so be it.*

At least he would still have company most nights, although his wife would likely never speak to him.

Had she forgiven him? Or was that the reason she visited—to torment him for what he did?

~*~

"You're early," Dejarnette announced as Sam walked through the superintendent's open door. He hadn't knocked since Doris' desk sat vacant.

"I'm an early riser, especially when I know I'm still learning the ropes." He looked around the large room and realized life would continue to turn into the world of the strange and unexpected.

The doctor gestured around him, obviously distraught. "The visit downstairs will have to wait—we need to game plan for the bigger numbers. Lynchburg & Ohio are pulling ahead— we need to keep pace with Cold Springs."

Two men in dark silk suits sat in the deep armchairs by the fireplace table. "Excuse the doctor," the man on the left said. "I don't know if you recall me."

Sam's breath caught in his throat. *The man who spoke founded the Eugenics Records Office, which held information on nearly every breathing man, woman, and child in the United States. He alone often had say over who could breed and who was deemed unfit.*

"Of course, Mr. Grant. The conference in San Francisco. Your work is the reason this hospital is operating."

"Well," he chuckled. "Thank you for the ego-stroking, Dr. Taylor, but Western Valley's been open since my granddaddy was a child. I like to think my work has simply focused its operation. Don't you agree, Charlie?"

The other man nodded, a gaunt individual who seemed to be examining Sam like a bug under glass. "Possibly. I still think you've got a ways to go here. This is no Cold Spring Harbor."

And it wasn't. The man who spearheaded the Society's movement in practical manners was rumored to have little in the way of personality. He regarded most people as specimens, either acceptable or not, fit to live or not. Sam wondered why a biologist was chosen to operate the laboratory up in New York.

The realization washed over him like a wave of black water. *The patients weren't meant to be viewed as people. By the time they had entered Davenport's environs, their fate had been sealed.*

"Am I interrupting something?" Sam had been handpicked for this position and word had it that he was originally chosen for Cold Spring Harbor. Davenport himself disputed the appointment, stating he wanted nothing to do with a psychology man.

"Not at all," Grant said. He looked over at Dejarnette, who seemed like a child whose parents had invaded his clubhouse. "We wanted to see firsthand what the good doctor was up to and why his numbers hadn't been adding up lately. We just returned from Paris and it seems like some of our League of Nations friends are gaining on us."

"Not good," said Davenport and Dejarnette in unison.

"We wanted to see how your test was working, outside of its vacuum here. How many have you scored so far?"

Warmth spread through Sam's arms and face. "Scored? In which way?"

"To find how many defectives you have around here." He pulled a cigar out of his suit jacket and fired up a match. "From what I hear, it's a hot bed of miscegenation in this fine state. Funny since D.C. is so close."

"And since the Mason-Dixon line is at least a state above us," added Davenport.

Dejarnette jammed his hands in his pockets, obviously wanting his whiskey but fearful of what these two powerhouses would think. "It *is* a progressive state, you know. We have our work cut out for us."

Grant pointed towards the window. "I told you Pennsylvania would have been better. They still fear God over science in that wasteland of a state. Even the Pirates seem to be a bit slow in their step. Sad genes."

Both men chuckled. "Seriously," Davenport said. "You're in the bosom of the civilized south. One railroad enters from the north, and another from the east. Who's going to notice what you do? Other than us?"

Sam ached to jump in but bit his tongue. These men were funded by American gold. "What does Carnegie want? Kellogg?"

Dejarnette looked at him like he had just screwed his sister.

"Son," Grant said, his voice even, "I'm glad you realize where the money train begins. Carnegie wants a 'clean' country. Fuck Kellogg. He just hates the mud people, period. He doesn't care how we do things. He'd toss his money into an outhouse shitter if we told him to do so."

"What do you want *me* to do?" Sam feared speaking more, feared hearing the replies. "I'd rather be sure about my patients *and* the validity of the test. I don't want to make a critical mistake."

"Honestly," Grant said. "The powers that be can't wait and neither can you. You have Lynchburg's Feebleminded Hospital under you and this warm fellow," gesturing to the biologist, "above."

"Okay," Sam managed. "I can test more. It's only Wednesday." He turned to Dejarnette. "How many would be sufficient for you, sir?"

The bespectacled man straightened at the comment directed toward him and cleared his throat. "We've had twenty-seven intakes this past week. Fifty-four are still waiting in the main and white wards. That makes less than a hundred, but there are the towns to the west the police are still searching.

"We can make a hundred by the end of the month."

My god, Sam thought. *It's the 17th of October.* To administer his test properly? There would be no way possible.

Maybe that's the point.

As if reading his mind, Grant said, "Son, we *do* need several accurate readings. For the research. But for the rest, it's merely lip-service. We know what's out there and how many need to be sterilized. How many defectives are killing the country?

"Sweden and France have far less defectives and their numbers are blowing ours out of the water. That can't happen. The *New York Times* has been running the headlines supporting our cause. Of course, that's courtesy of JP Morgan and Carnegie handling the presses, but still ..."

The other man chimed in. "We need the government, and the populace, to buy in here. A little evidence here, a little smooth talking there. When we publish your results, America will have to face its problem head on. And the mud people won't be able to do shit about it."

"We'll make it happen," said Dejarnette. "Won't we, Samuel?"

Sam could barely focus. He noticed that Davenport hadn't stopped staring at him. *The man had to know about his past, his brother. The census reports were almost complete in the metropolitan areas. It was only in the outlying states where things got cloudy with the numbers.*

"Of course."

"Now when we're done here, I want you to prepare for the rest of this week and get your head in its proper place. You're going to need it."

The man turned his stare to Dejarnette. "Is your secretary back yet with the breakfast?"

Dejarnette motioned for them to wait as he opened the office door and smiled. "Sam, will you help Doris out?" Sam saw through the door that a truck with stood outside the front door, with a wheeled cart being carried up the stairs by two brawny men. Their uniforms seemed familiar to him. He had seen them just this morning on his walk.

Christ.

Since it was only up the hill and the institutions often shared staff, the food had come from the school of the deaf and blind. *Colin's school. Ruby's kitchen.* She had likely had the assignment for the special meal, as WVH didn't have its own restaurant. She had likely done so with pride, knowing that her name would be attached to it.

He breathed a sigh of relief that he didn't have to worry about her being tested. *Yet.*

Both he and Doris wheeled in several platters of food. *He could do this,* he encouraged himself. *This was what he trained for—his own test was bought for this purpose. If his soul would allow it.*

He inhaled the fine smells and found himself aching for Ruby. *Two more days. He would have to distract himself from this hell with thoughts of a movie night with her and Colin until then. He could do it. After that, who knew how he would cope? At least his family had a good home, protection.*

He waited until Doris fixed the other men a plate before he sat down with his own, which made his senses tingle, his memory falter.

Then Dejarnette turned to him with a smile.

"By the way, don't worry about your friend's results. That faggot you took for a walk yesterday. We found him dancing from the rafters this morning. Don't feel bad. Your test was only a formality. I informed him myself of the treatment he'd be receiving."

Something broke deep within Sam that he knew would never heal. *That man was sane, not a defective. However, he helped fill the quota and added another soul to Carnegie's list.*

He hung himself? Sam begged his mind to deliver an answer different than the truth.

"Salut!" Davenport said, holding up a glass of wine. "One more 'muddy' closer to my numbers. Personally, I think it's a little unfair with what you're working with down here. Then again, I do have much of New York and New Jersey from which to cull."

The doctor held up a rasher of bacon and let it swing back and forth, grinning into Sam's eyes as it did. Just like it was dancing.

45

Sam spent the remainder of the day reading up on the patients and when he saw the sun begin to cry its bloody red light, he threw the folder he was skimming across the room and ran for the stairs.

The back hills were ablaze in oranges and yellows as he sprinted toward the graveyard. He halted just as he reached a cluster of unmarked stones.

"I'm sorry," he said to no one, heaving, but thinking of the man who chose to take his own life rather than visit the treatment room with Dejarnette.

Sam knew he couldn't wait until Monday to see it for himself.

He didn't know which dorm housed Theodore. The file didn't specify. *Why would it? All that mattered was the score. Data never lied, according to many. Was he, or wasn't he? Was he defective, unfit, or ready to breed in America's name?*

Yet data could always be manipulated.

The long building behind him was closest and biggest. Having not been inside any dorms yet, he figured it would be the best bet. He walked up the hill to the main door, covered in wire mesh and triple locks. *Why? If this was guarded, why lock up the sheep? Theodore hadn't been one of the criminals.* He reached for the door and turned the knob without resistance. *Maybe the locks existed for protection from the others.* He stepped inside a dimly- lit foyer.

"Excuse me, sir. Are you lost?" A tall man clad in a guard uniform rose to meet him, from behind a desk where a battered paperback and newspaper lay. He appeared more confused than alarmed at the unannounced visitor.

"Sorry," Sam leaned in closer to read the man's badge. "Mr. Boggs." He proffered his hand. "Doctor Sam Taylor. I just started on Monday on Dejarnette's team. I'm the psychologist."

"Oh," the older man said, relaxing somewhat. "I make sure the good people stay inside and don't wander during the night."

"Is that usually a problem?" *It wasn't for Ted.*

Boggs shook his head. "Not usually. However," he said with a higher lift to his low, slower voice, "some like to get out and walk at night. You know, ponder why they're here, and think about life and such."

Yeah, I know what you mean.

"So then, why the locks?"

"Just in case. I'm sure you visited the white walls. Ain't much good in there from what I hear. I've never been in there, personally, but the others tell me. Don't want any of them getting in and bothering these folks who need some peace. Sometimes, people just break and need time to put the puzzle pieces back together again. A place like this, it's always been here, at least for the past century."

Sam drew in a deep breath. "Ever hear of someone harming themselves, like last night?"

"I guess you're talking about Ted."

"You knew him?" He couldn't imagine the luck of finding the right dorm on the first try, as they began to walk down the hallway of the first floor.

"Well, we didn't drink beers or anything, but in the week he was here, the guy begged for some kind of normalcy. We talked baseball, football, radio shows. Heck, I let him listen to a few shows with me. I get lonely here, too. Ain't any fun when I'm away from the wife. The radio's a lot like her. It talks and talks and talks and I just sit here without it caring one bit what I say. The only difference? Sometimes I actually care about what this little black box says to me!"

They shared a laugh. "I hear ya, Mr. Boggs."

"Call me Kevin," the guard said. "I asked Ted to do the same." Then he hung his head. "It's so sad. He seemed like he was doing so well. Why would he do something like that?"

"I don't know. In fact, I was out for a walk myself and wanted to see his room."

"Sure thing," Boggs replied but shrunk back a little. "Me, I can't. Not once they're gone. I just can't. Creeps me out."

A tremor rippled down Sam's back. "Do they pass frequently? I don't mean hanging or such, just dying?"

The man stared back at him suddenly without emotion. "Doctor, you'd know better than me. It's like a turnstile in here. I'm just the gatekeeper. This house's keeper, anyway. The main one's in the big house up front. That's why I try not to get to know many of the patients. Some go home; some just go."

The conversation just halted there, as if weighed down by a sack of bad memories.

"Do you mind if I have a look?"

The guard ushered him by without a word, but tipped his cap as if in respect. If the man noticed Sam swiping the second ring of keys from his belt, he didn't let on.

46

The dorm reminded him of Stanford's residence halls, without the full doors, sounds of happy music, and feeling of hope. That and the soft yellow walls lent a feeling of decay to the ambiance, especially in the low light of early evening. He passed a few doors and saw a woman staring back at him through a window in the door. She sat on a cot with a toilet and sink in the room, pictures on the walls. The window was open, and he noticed a similar one, yet smaller, reached up in the back wall, allowing a view into the night.

He waved to her. She didn't return the gesture.

One by one, he passed doors on the left and right. Some held patients. Some held only space. Many slept. A few stood by the windows, front or back. The ones in the front were likely curious as to who would be bothering with them. *Did Dejarnette ever come here? Did he take them himself for treatment?* If so, that would explain their odd expressions. The others simply gazed out into the moonlight, likely wishing they were back home, wondering if a family member or spouse still cared for them.

Four doors from the end on the left, a door hung open. The name or number above the knob had already been removed. With a deep breath, Sam entered. The bed lay bare, as Theodore likely used the sheets for his deed. The pillow was fluffed and in perfect place. Oddly, he found himself sitting down on the mattress and looking around the room.

A few newspaper articles hung on the walls, secured with tape. Yankees scores, news of growing unrest in Germany, and an advertisement for *The Invisible Man,* coming to the Dixie later this month, covered the pale walls.

This man appeared just as Sam had thought. *Normal, at least as normal as he was, or Gene, or any other male in town. Even if the affair with his friend was accurate, he shouldn't have been locked up.* He imagined Theo sitting on the back porch and drinking while he and Gene played their blues, Theo tapping his foot to the rhythm.

He didn't need treatment. He needed a divorce and a doctor who didn't have an agenda and didn't believe anything he heard just to make a name for himself.

The movie advertisement hung askew just a bit, something that didn't fit with the rest. Sam hadn't come there for clues. *Hell, he didn't know why he came at all.* Still, he found himself at the wall and carefully removed the paper.

What he saw written behind it turned his legs to jelly and dropped him to the bed.

"You can't cut the truth out of me. The deeper you dig with your knives, the bloodier your own hands will become. I'll still remain who I know I am."

Underneath that statement, Theo had written in black pen, "Will someone go hug my wife—with an oncoming train? "

Sam felt the tears come with the burst of laughter.

When he collected himself, he left the room and found a maintenance door at the end of the hall. The keys he lifted from Boggs opened the single lock without a sound. Not wishing to land the man in trouble, he left them hanging there.

With shaky steps, he walked into the night and found himself in another field of stones. Much smaller, it still held at least a dozen rows of flat, small, blank stones. He wondered when Theodore's would be placed, if at all.

He walked to the middle of the graveyard, as he looked into the forest beyond the hospital. It stretched likely a hundred yards into the hills, with the highway and north-south railroad beyond it. *His past lay there, somewhere.* Then he turned back to where he worked, but couldn't connect his eyes to the building. *All he could see were the deaths he didn't want to see.*

He never felt himself falling to his knees into the wet ground. Nor did he notice the flood of tears, which had never fallen when he lost his wife and son two years ago.

They simply fell now, and soaked the naked stone upon which he leaned.

47

For the second night in a row, Sam saw his wife. This time, she stood alone ahead of him, facing the main building, tears in her own eyes. He had never told Gene she stood behind the Belsnicklers the previous night. He couldn't bring himself to face it, nor take the chance of his friend thinking he had cracked.

Still, she stood there, just out of reach. Part of him wished for her to come to him right then and there, to take him to her bosom like she had on the train and in his bedroom.

Yet she didn't. She simply stood, watching him.

As he walked towards the front gate, he noticed a line of patients watching him from their windows. In fact, every room on the south side facing the main building now housed a patient and eyes. *Did each room house a patient as he walked the hall?* He doubted it, but if he could see his wife, why not a full slate of aching patients who may or may not have been present in body?

By the time he arrived home, he couldn't remember the walk or how he got there. His mother had a plate made up for him, but he mumbled something he couldn't recall. She simply handed him the supper and he climbed the stairs to the cool embrace of the night.

She was there already, waiting for him in the sheets. When he crawled into her embrace, he wept as she took him deep through the night.

As he faded away, he dreamt of the murdering restaurateur, muttering one word over and over. Something he couldn't understand.

Something about *ashes, ashes.*

48

Sam cruised through a fog during the following two days, avoiding everyone from Gene and Colin to Dejarnette and Gwen. The only conversation he counted on was his daily encounter with the boy whose favorite color was blue. The talk consisted of mostly that line, but over the course of the week, the psychologist wriggled out more information. His name was Tristan, odd for the southern state, but the entire Valley seemed to be a melting pot of cultures, a dumping ground for those who needed solace from the big city depression.

Sam wondered what the boy's parents did and why they allowed him to wander the streets. Treatment for mental health had come quite a way in the past century but the stigma for families still hung overhead like bruised clouds. After the law passed, most hid their 'defectives' or simply sent them away and hoped for the best. Usually, that best was best for the family, not the child.

Tristan had been leaving the morning meetings with a nickel in his hands, just enough for a 'blue' ice at the diner. Gene offered the boy free ice cream from his store, but the kid preferred the berry-flavored ice most days.

"Have a great day, Tristan. Enjoy your blue."

The smallish sprite-like boy nearly danced when that shiny nickel hit his palm, acting as if Santa himself had given him a visit. "Thank you, Mister Sam," he rattled off at a fast clip. "My favorite flavor."

"Be careful walking home. Watch out for bears!" *And Belsnicklers.* The anti-Santas hadn't been back to Sam's yard—yet. However, in a town that held a hospital which decided who should breed and God knows what else, he worried about the kid. He also worried a little about his brother as well.

"Straight home through the Gypsy Hill. Mama says run the path."

Sam smiled as he imagined his whole family walking through the beautiful park. Part of him ached for his wife, and what could've been, but a smaller, growing part of him blossomed in optimism when he thought of Ruby. *The woman might never even give him a date, but he knew he could have something special there, if she allowed him the chance.*

Besides, he mused, *he preferred the touch of a living woman.*

49

Day by day, Sam pored through the files, the ones both sent from the Census office on families who might have moved into the valley, and the ones on families Dejarnette suspected might have mud DNA in their blood.

The man had been sending more trucks into the villages beyond Augusta, to the west where only county land existed. Families residing there rarely attended school unless the clans built an old-fashioned one classroom building and accepted donated textbooks from the Augusta school system, or boxes that 'fell off' the back cars of freight trains. Even those without the opportunity to learn were deemed unfit. Dejarnette had the notion that if the families were bright, they'd have seen their misfortune coming and moved into a more prosperous town and procured better jobs.

Sam guessed the Depression didn't factor into the equation.

He checked off patients by sheer file quality; the easier ones, with criminal backgrounds or obvious disabilities. All the information had been placed in the initial folders—by whom, he had no idea. Just by signing his name, he doomed many to sterilization, but that was Virginia law now, as it had become in twenty-seven states. *If he didn't do it, someone else would. Also, Dejarnette would notice.* Sam focused on whom he could help.

Every couple of hours, the man's threat echoed in Sam's head. Colin's school stood just up the hill. He wondered if any students had been 'treated' yet. *Were they protected by some unspoken code from the director?* Maybe there had been an arrangement made, likely in substantial funds from the wealthier families who kept their children there.

Both days at lunch, he walked the grounds, from the fence in front along the creek to the gazebo—if empty—for lunch, then on to the back hills. Somehow, he wound up standing in the middle of the potter's field. Part of him convinced his trying mind that he stood in front of Theodore's grave, even though no one would tell him, even if he had the courage to inquire. Each moment he breathed, he felt his soul darken just a bit more.

"I'm sorry," he said. He longed to find the man's wife and let her know the result of her game. Maybe he would send Ruby. She seemed to have some fire in her bones and would likely lay a slap to the woman that would rattle her teeth. "I should've talked to the doctor for you and got you out of here." Even as the words fell from lips, he knew they fell with undue weight to the sod above the stones. *The man was doomed before he even stepped foot into the hospital, and knew it. At least in hanging himself, he executed one last act of control over his life.*

From his vantage point, Sam could view many of the patients meandering through the campus. Many appeared happy, talking amongst themselves and planning lunch for the day. Most of them had checked themselves in, and many had paid for their stay with funds stashed from before the crash. That they would be shut in their dorms every night didn't seem to faze any of them.

He wondered how the mood felt within the white-walled courtyard.

As if on cue, his eyes caught sight of McIlveen again. Without thinking, he shoved his hand into his pockets and began fingering the guitar pick Gene had left for him. *Solid tortoiseshell, he claimed.*

Sam walked over to the man, who traveled in a straight line from the gate of the white ward to edge of the main building. *Did he recall any of the procedure and find these boundaries meaningful? Or was something else at play deep within his carved-up psyche?*

Maybe he knew that the man who acted as his god watched from the main building terrace from time to time, and couldn't decide which direction would hurt him less.

"Stephen," Sam called. "Can you hear me?"

The man gazed up at the psychologist and spoke. "What are you doing here?"

Shit. The same old. Why would he think this day would be any different?

"What are you doing here? Do you like the ashes?"

Sam froze, blood failing to circulate to his fingers as they numbed around the pick, still tapping against his leg. "What did you say?"

The man shuffled along but seemed aware of his doctor's presence. "What are you doing here?"

"Stephen, I wish I knew. What did you say?"

"Have you danced in the ashes, doctor?" The words slurred, slowed. The angels dance in the ashes every night. I watch them."

"Where are these ashes? Does it have to do with the train?"

At that, the man's eyes focused, just for the duration of his next words. "The ashes give us the angels who dance in the dust."

Then the man disappeared behind the fog of his severed frontal lobe.

Tonight, Sam said to himself, *he would find the ashes—or the angels.*

50

Friday marked the first time Colin had traveled without his mother or brother, and he felt stoked knowing that the only other adult who knew him was the coach. Even though the seats in the dugout felt harder than cement, he could have been sitting on rusted spikes and still nothing could have dulled the moment for him.

Someone truly wanted to see him play baseball.

The whole school would be on display. Apparently, VSDB, Virginia School For The Deaf and Blind, hadn't had a winning record since they formed the team. This season, they had gotten off to a 2-1 start, enough to garner them an invite to the Roanoke tournament. 'Normal' schools would be there as well and he couldn't wait to show them his stuff. Coach promised he would get the start, his first ever.

He recalled the only other time they had allowed him to pitch, in gym class back in Jersey. The teacher had felt sorry for him and told him he would get to face a few batters until the end of the period. Little did the man know how hard he practiced against the front steps and imagining the whoosh of the bats as they connected with nothing but air. The few neighborhood kids who did play with him knew he had a rocket arm, but still mocked him.

Six batters later, a half-dozen students stood dumbfounded and humiliated by a deaf-and-dumb kid that struck them out. The class cheered him, even the teacher, although he suspected some of the clapping was in jest. Colin had learned to be a master at reading emotions and moods through facial expressions.

It didn't matter much, when they got him on the way home

and kicked his ass from here to Sunday, signing 'asshole' and 'retard' in between punches and kicks. He managed to run home when a squad car pulled up. *No way was he ratting on those guys. It would only guarantee beatings for the remainder of the school year—and beyond.*

He had hidden from his mother for a day until she heard him moaning in the bath. When she saw the purpled, mottled flesh covering much of his body, she had grabbed hold of her husband's rifle and demanded to know who did that to him. She marched to the police station and demanded protection, but they refused, at least until Colin fingered the suspects.

Today would be his day of reckoning.

The two-hour ride crawled by as he stared at the majestic Blue Ridge Mountains to the left. *Maybe life down here would be an oasis from the hell which had been his life.* For a moment, he imagined the inner-world races which might be planning world destruction from deep within those mountains, but then quickly returned to practicing his curveball in his head.

When they first arrived, he felt overwhelmed at the size of the tournament. He disembarked and walked into a stadium that felt nearly as gigantic as where the Yanks played. At least twenty schools had arrived. Only a few were 'special' like his, but all were there to knock the stitches off the ball. Coach lined up his team and had each sign their names and positions. The boys looked mostly like hillbillies, but Coach said that if they won, they would be heading to Virginia Beach, or at the very least, Richmond, to take on more schools. Maybe, if there was an amenable coach in attendance, the team would get to play a regular school.

Colin doubted that scenario, but for once, he allowed himself to dream.

51

The Wildcats took the field against Lynchburg when their turn came. At least a hundred or so fans filled the stands when they warmed up. Colin noticed that the opposing team's shirt only sported the word 'Lynchburg'. *Lynchburg Institute for the Feebleminded* might have lost them a little power as they were announced.

Geez, he thought. *How could any of them feel good about being in a school named that?* It was bad enough being singled out in public school and getting bullied daily, but to be branded with that school's name? Once again, he thanked his luck for Sam getting the job in Augusta.

As he threw the final warmup ball before the first batter approached the plate, the coach strode over to him and signed. "Buddy, I want you to knock the crap out of them. Forget their name. Never mind where they come from or what they might be dealing with. Today, it's all about you and the catcher. See the mitt and imagine every pitch hitting it like a cannonball. Think you can handle that?"

Damn, talk about shaking someone's confidence and hatching the butterflies, the boy thought. *I was okay until you said that!* He signed back, "Is it okay if I run the bases if we win?"

The man took him by the shoulders. "*When* we win. *When.* After the ninth is complete, I don't care if you don a tutu and dance until your little toes break. Now go make your school and your family proud."

Colin Taylor did just that. He just wished that his family could be there, but the train didn't hold enough room.

From the first batter, a tall boy who looked like he wrestled bears daily before eating them, to the bottom of the lineup, a squat pitcher with biceps like bricks, he ran through them like the locomotive which drove them here.

He struck out five in the first three innings and got the other four to pop up or ground out in the infield. By the midpoint of the game, his team had pummeled them to a 5-0 lead. Colin helped his own cause with a couple of hits, a double and single, knocking in three. He wished for a homer like The Babe could manage, but nothing would lessen the moment.

Three and a half innings later, he remained on the mound after the cleanup hitter stood looking at a called third strike, which arced over the plate in a hideous manner that Colin was sure nobody there had ever seen before. *His curveball was his secret weapon. Everyone needed one and he used his with pride.* The catcher, a happy blond-haired boy named Todd, raced to the mound and hugged him, shoving the game ball in his mitt. The rest of the team joined him and knocked him to the ground. For once, he didn't mind being in a pile of excited kids.

This day will be my happiest, he said to himself. *I know it will.*

After watching a couple of regular schools play, the Charlottesville team was scheduled to play VSDB for the section winner.

Yet something was wrong. The team founded by the state university sat in the dugout, dejected. Still, Colin raced out on the field. Coach had told him he'd be playing first base, just like Gehrig. That way, his arm could rest. The god of the Yankees, one of 'murderer's row', was also a lefty and would always be a hero to him.

He stood on the base with a bulge in his jersey. The game ball, the one given to him by the catcher and stated by the coach, hung inside close to his belly. He meant for it to be close to his heart, but figured it would look stupid. *No one would ever separate him from that ball. Ever.*

Yet when nobody cheered for the opposing team, he looked

over at the bench. Only five players sat on it, plus the dejected-looking coach.

His own coach walked over to him and then to the organizers of the tournament. The Charlottesville coach looked like he was ready to take a swing at the other one and nearly did when the judges said something to him that Colin couldn't decipher.

All he managed to figure was the word 'forfeit'.

There would be no game, signed his own coach. The remainder of the Charlottesville special school had failed to show for the game. *But what about playing one of the regular schools?* Many of his team begged for the chance. However, coach just attempted to get all the players off the field and bribed them with ice cream from the train depot.

Before Colin stepped off the base, he stared through the stands. Nearly all the spectators wore expressions of dejection. They had wanted to see the deaf kids play again. *Maybe they were a novelty item to many. He didn't care one bit. He only wished to play more. He'd show them what a real player he was in so many ways.*

And then he saw the one smiling person in the stands. It was the G-man from the other night. *Oh shit*, he thought. *Did the man recognize him?*

That man, clad in the same black suit, stared at Colin. The teen thought he was being paranoid, thinking there was no way it was happening. Maybe he was just impressed with Colin's great pitching effort.

Maybe he was. Many of the spectators had been floored by the deaf kid from Augusta.

But the look in that man's faced told him otherwise. Even from fifty feet away, he could see the darkness in his eyes. The same darkness he imagined was there when the man killed the drunk and tossed him into the river to nowhere.

Somehow, he felt like the man was imagining Colin floating away as well. *Would he be on the same train as their team?* He prayed he would not be, but knew nightmares often became real in this world.

He didn't taste one bite of the ice cream the coach bought for the team. He might as well have been eating glue.

As they headed for the train, the coach kept glancing around, possibly keeping watch for the man in the dark suit. He spoke to the other coach, the one with the half-team, along with the one from Lynchburg. Colin could swear he spotted a tear in his coach's eye.

Why?

When the other players fell asleep on the ride home, Colin kept his own eyes wide open, and not on the setting sun over the mountains on the opposite side of the tracks.

He kept watching for that man, who he was now sure had watched him from the stands the whole time. He was sure that man, or someone with him, had something to do with the forfeit.

Every time he began to doubt this thought, he turned to the back of the long car. About twenty rows back, the truth stared him right in the eyes.

The nightmare rode back home with him, still wearing that same smile.

52

"Is this movie really about a giant ape in New York City?"

Sam shrugged, smiling for the first time in days as they approached the Dixie Theater. Gene had told them it had been standing since 1913 and originally hosted vaudeville acts, in addition to the silent films and newsreels that brought townsfolk up to speed on what was happening 'over there'.

"No," he signed. "It has a little pink unicorn dancing through flowers."

Colin punched his brother in the arm.

"Ow!" *Maybe the kid did have a rocket arm. Maybe he could go somewhere with his baseball skills. Or maybe he just wished the impossible, in a world that wasn't ready to accept people with disabilities just yet.* How he wished he could have been at his brother's game, but a full day away from the testing was forbidden.

Still, Sam smiled. Today was all about escape. Time out with his family was something he missed terribly while out in California. Too bad his mother didn't wish to join them that night. "Too many monsters already in this world," she had said. He wondered what she had meant by that, if she was referring to the new laws. Or maybe it was just the war and what was brewing all over due to the Depression.

Without her, it would be boys' day out.

With that thought, he found himself looking around for the other 'her'.

He craned his neck left and right while he and Colin waited in the long line.

Nothing. Yet.

During the twenty minutes it took for them to reach the usher at the ticket booth, he nearly gave himself whiplash. Maybe she had to work early tonight. Sam figured that the matinée would be prime time for her as the restaurant wouldn't be open for another four hours or so. *Maybe he came on too strong and she felt skittish. With her past, he couldn't blame her.* He wanted to kick himself. As they entered the theater, he smelled the popcorn and the sweet scent of the soda syrup and watched as his brother's eyes popped wide. *It would be a good day regardless of his company.* He put his arm around his companion for the afternoon and walked into the grand theater, right next door to where *Gone With The Wind* was showing.

As he passed over the threshold, his heart jumped a beat.

53

The lights dimmed, and the newsreels began. Sam marveled at the design of the architecture, the ornate columns reaching up to the burgundy-painted ceiling. Balcony seats on either side were afforded to whoever reached them first, not to the rich. In the rear, a typical elevated section lent another ten rows, mostly to young couples and the stray older visiting family, who would see more romance in the seats than on the screen.

The velvet drapes parted to display the highlights of both the Giants and Pittsburgh Pirates, two of the premier football teams in a league that grew steadily each year, much to Sam's pleasure. He preferred the logic and chess-match mentality to other sports, but as the next reel played, the theater hit the roof. In 1933, the Washington Senators had bested the other New York Giants, the team which performed on the baseball diamond in the region. Colin didn't appear the least bit upset that his Yankees hadn't made it to the World Series this year, simply satisfied that the team which played closest to where he lived won the pennant.

In the slim light, Sam strained to see what the boy held in his left hand. It looked like a ball, a baseball. *Could it have been the one he caught during a game back in New York, or was it the one he threw in the game the previous day?* Either way, Sam had a feeling that whoever attempted to separate the two would be met with a black eye.

The crowd quieted as the RKO logo hit the screen and the majestic score filled the ears of the patrons. Sam never even registered the person behind him leaning in to whisper.

"I love monkeys, don't you?"

The silky voice with just the faintest hint of a European accent sent shivers down his back.

He attempted to turn around slowly, with a suave expression on his face, but failed on both accounts. "Ms. Kaminski. I thought you would be watching the film next door?"

"A Civil War romance, against a tale of beauty and beast? Please, Doctor Taylor. A modern woman has modern tastes; the antebellum motif is so passé, don't you think?"

Sam believed he nodded his assent. "Would you care to join us?" Colin turned to her and smiled, nudging his brother.

"I prefer to watch my films alone. You know, lose oneself in the moment and forget where you are for a couple of hours?"

Yet she sat right behind them, leaning forward, her elbows remaining on the back of Sam's seat for the duration of the show.

"Is the Empire State Building really that tall?" Ruby strolled next to Sam as Colin appeared happy enough to find some of his fellow students exiting the show.

"Actually, it looked smaller in the movie. Then again, I'm not used to a humongous man in a gorilla suit hanging off it."

Her smile threw him off his game. "I'm only used to bears and other four-legged creatures."

"They have bears up in Maine?" He studied her face for an indicator of truth. She gave him no clue whatsoever.

"You look like a man who needed to smile and escape for a few hours. Did it help?"

What the hell? Reversing the psychology on him? She had a brain, something that excited something in him, much deeper than usual. *She might be a good cook, but the woman must have lived plenty in her years to have such insight, or was blessed with a gift like he once believed himself to have.*

"A little, I guess." Sam tried to get Colin's attention, but the boy had run ahead towards the park. He smiled as he watched the group of boys following his brother, the obvious leader of the group. *Finally, he fits; finally, he feels comfortable.*

"And yes, we had bears up in Maine, but mostly other creatures. I mostly miss my pot-bellied pig."

"You had a pig as a pet?" *There or in the old country?* He bit his tongue. *Maybe one day, she'd feel comfortable telling him all.* "Where? How?"

"On a farm? And no, we didn't cook him when he passed. I cried like a baby for days. Little Edgar was like a child to me."

He unbit his tongue for a moment and prayed. "Did you and the ex ever …"

"No," she answered curtly, but recovered even faster. With a smile, she gazed into the mountains which peeked over the buildings at the end of the street. "But I might love one or two of my own one day. Just not with that man. We'll see if life decides to give me one."

Thank God you're not on Davenport's list, he thought.

54

They walked through the park with its paved walking loop and pond in the center. Both gazed at the train and Sam imagined both had disparate memories of their rail experiences. Somehow, he doubted her ex's ghost crawled into her bunk and seduced her, or held her hand as she looked at another with wanting eyes. Many nights, he doubted even his did so. His mind could only stand so much before shattering.

The train chugged around the perimeter of the water, with a jovial man acting as conductor. He yanked on the bell which sounded sweet harmonics through Sam's ears as the long line of mini-cars passed, full of children squealing with glee.

"That looks like fun."

"I doubt you'd fit," she replied with a smile and a look in her eyes that melted him.

"My inner child would. Freud says that the child in all of us never fully evolves."

"Isn't that the same man that believes everything is male genitalia?"

Sam's face burned in embarrassment. *This woman was smart.* "Where'd you hear that?" He stumbled over every word as they tumbled from his mouth.

"I read a lot. Women can do that, you know. Some of them actually write books, too."

Now she was playing with him. His face cooled off a bit. "Did you read all the books in Maine?" *Better to fish while laughing*, he thought.

"No sir," she replied, smiling, but folded her hands. "They

only had two books in my library. Small town." She quickened the pace.

"So, Virginia Beach had a bigger and better selection?"

"Much. *The Time Machine* and other books of fancy always pulled me in, away from reality."

Sam locked eyes with her, his chest warming. "Reality is overrated."

They continued on the path for another half hour, past the duck pond where several families tossed feed into the fray of mallards and swans. He learned about her schooling, at an actual college, William and Mary. She said that her ex-husband had 'fixed' her admission, as her schooling and records weren't up to par, or so he told her. Basically, he opened the cage door, allowed her to learn to fly, and so she did, like the canary from the hungry cat. *Stupid man, thinking he could control her with such arrogance.* Miriam never would have put up with that, although she had never asked for college. He encouraged her, but only to find her family had raised her to serve her man, whoever that would be, from birth.

"You do know there are at least a million men who would build castles for a woman like you, someone who can push through everything to achieve every dream, to walk her own path."

Her gaze turned to her shoes.

"I have to go now."

His heart dropped fifty degrees as it sank into his belly.

"Did I say something?"

She stopped and took hold of his arm. "Why are you so worried about offending me?"

He didn't even stop to think of an excuse. All he could process was the smell of the ducks in the pond, the chilled breeze that suggested a cold evening, and the suddenly faraway howls of the children.

"I just want to see you again. There's no other reason."

She slid her hand down to his, finding it clammy, despite the temperature.

"Walk me home after work? You can see me then."

"What time?"

55

After Sam walked Ruby down Augusta Street to Panevino's, his mind swirled in happiness, his gait light and brisk. He found Colin back by the theater, sans his friends.

"Figured you'd be home by now?

He shook his head and signed, "They left a few minutes ago and I saw you coming."

"You waited for me?" *His brother lied worse than Ruby.*

"I didn't want to disturb you and your new girlfriend. She's pretty." Now he knew something was up. Colin, or any boy his age, would never bother with worries such as that. They would either interrupt or go home on their own. *He was developing an allergy to bullshit here in this town.*

He smiled at his younger half-brother, so much like him, so much like a blood brother. "Did someone mess with you?"

Again, the boy shook his head. *Maybe Sam shouldn't have asked that. Yet if someone had, he could turn that poor soul's life into a raging hell. But something had glued the boy to the step.*

It was at that moment Sam looked across the street. Out of the bank alcove emerged a man wearing a dark suit. *Hadn't Sam seen him before somewhere?* He couldn't recall when or where, but something set off bells in his head. The man looked directly at him and ducked between the bank and adjacent building, into a narrow alley.

J. Edgar had begun his teams of government men, 'G-men' as the magazines called them. Men in suits with dark fedoras. Enforcers, usually, they worked the mob sites until prohibition ended and now they delved deeper into the dirty folds of

America. Sam knew of many secrets in the underbelly of society, but none which required agents in a small town in Virginia.

It hit him like a pick axe tied to a sledgehammer.

The hospital. Hoover or someone who hired him wanted to keep tabs on everything going on there. *The Society, perhaps. Everyone who worked there.* Maybe they had been helping with the census and gathering those in the herd who needed Dejarnette's 'treatments'.

Without giving it a thought, Sam burst into a sprint, not caring about what gun the man likely carried. He crossed the street in less than five strides, his long legs covering the gap quicker than most. He had run into machine gun fire before, so this frightened him none.

The man in the suit was gone when he hit the curb.

Sam bolted down the alley. In the daylight, he should have been easy to sight, as only two doors stood—one in either building. Both felt locked to a quick but strong turn from Sam. As he exited the alley, the parallel street to Augusta opened up to the courthouse and police station, with enough open space and people movement for plenty of men to hide.

He considered barging into the police station to make a complaint, but harnessed that anger quickly, recalling what Dejarnette said to him. *The veiled threats. His brother.* He couldn't be there day and night to watch over Colin or his mother. If Sam made an enemy here, he'd be on his own.

Instead, he punched the brick wall of the bank with a reddened fist and knew sometime that night he would be applying ice. Maybe then he would care. At that moment, he could only think of someone wishing his brother harm.

When he returned to the theatre, he saw Colin hadn't moved from where Sam left him. He said, "No worries. I think he was just a bum, possibly waiting for a mark to pass by. I'll talk to the police tomorrow."

He noticed his brother shaking ever so slightly.

"It's okay, Colin. They only go for people with money."

The boy looked up at him with a stare that unnerved him and would be forever in his memory.

"Then why was he at my game today?"

"What did you say?

"And why was he talking to that weird kid who likes the blue ice creams?"

"It's only ices," Sam corrected as his world spun.

His good mood dropped from his heart to his shoes. *Dejarnette had gone too far.*

Sam would confront him on Monday.

Threat or no threat, no one screwed with his family.

56

Despite his better judgment, Sam downed two fingers of whiskey before walking to the restaurant at ten o'clock. There was no way he could let anyone he talked to travel alone anymore. He knew that Hoover's and Grant's men had him by the balls. Sam couldn't protect his family and friends day and night. The others wouldn't harm those close to him, unless Sam gave them reason.

The alcohol kicked in right before Ruby emerged from the restaurant, already in street clothes. Her blue dress highlighted just about every positive feature a woman could have. Her beauty washed away his worries in one quick wave. He knew it would return later that night, but for now, he didn't care. Her smile crushed his stress without a battle.

"We have a changing room on the second floor where they keep supplies. I don't like to walk here in an apron and white slacks. It makes me look like an orderly at your hospital."

He smiled at the joke, but it reminded him of the trouble he would face on Monday.

"Are you okay?" She had been looking at him closely since exiting the building.

"I'm fine," he said, realizing that he would now be lying more than her. "Just thinking about the long week I have ahead of me."

"Samuel," she said, her voice saying his name sending a jolt down his spine. "It's only Saturday. The last time I checked, Sunday still comes before Monday. Therefore, you have one more day to not think about it."

Good luck to that, he thought, but found himself thinking

more about her and how, even after a shift in a hot and sweaty kitchen, she had remained beyond beautiful.

"Come on," she said, hooking his arm in hers. "I'm so tired I'm afraid I have to use you as a crutch." Her touch sent shivers through his limbs.

"Use away," he replied. "It's all part of my job."

She made small talk on the way home, which was four blocks away, west of where he lived and up the hill in the oldest section of town.

"This is me."

"You're a brick building?" He tried a stab at humor, even knowing she sensed something odd from him.

"Sometimes I feel like it," she replied, facing him. "It's only half-full, even less so now that my uncle hasn't been home."

"Are you sure he's not off hunting?"

Her eyes welled up for just a moment. "I hope so. He's had his problems, but he gave me an incredible opportunity. Maybe he was called into work."

"What does he do?"

"He works on the railroads. It used to be mostly immigrants until the CCC came about. Now it's primarily white folk, meaning he's frequently out of work."

"I'm sorry," Sam said, feeling foolish for even replying.

She hung her head but stepped up to Sam. "I'm sure he's fine. Somewhere." Yet her eyes told two stories: one regarding her lie, and the other about him.

"Thank you for the escort. But I had an ulterior motive."

He gulped like a frightened child. "Which is?"

"I had to show you where I lived."

"Why?"

She leaned in quickly and kissed him. *Fast but soft,* he thought before his processing capability faltered and scattered. "I can make dinner for you tomorrow." She pulled away quickly, but not before visions of making love to her that moment flooded his mind. *She smelled of garlic and pasta, but he didn't mind one bit. She tasted of a flower he knew hadn't yet been created. She felt like a soft burst of heat and energy, something he could lie down with and die in her arms without a second thought.*

With that, she turned from him and took to the stairs. At the top, she turned to call to him. "Five p.m. Don't be late."

A herd of wild bears from Maine couldn't make me late, he thought. "Should I bring anything? Wine or something? Iced tea?"

She laughed as she opened the main door. "Just bring yourself and maybe a book you think I'd enjoy. I left most of my life back on the beach."

"I'll bring a wing of my library for you."

Before she closed the door, she smiled and said, "Nope. Pick just one. It will speak volumes, so you won't even have to tell me why."

On the way home, he failed to look even once for a tail. He only had the titles of books he had to choose from swirling around his head. By the time he arrived home, he knew what he would bring her.

He swore he saw something walk from the bushes in his yard into the next. Rather, he saw some 'things'. *Plural.* But if the Belsnicklers had returned, they didn't want his attention tonight. *Nor he theirs.*

They could bring a set of switches to tan his back and bottom like the naughty children they were said to punish, and he wouldn't care. Still, he knew they were capable of much more. He knew they would be back. When that happened, he would have his Luger at the ready.

Santa would come early for them as well.

57

"Surprising. Flowers? Doctor Taylor, I'm shocked at your creativity."

"Tough crowd," he said, smiling. "Didn't I promise you something else, too?" He pulled out his copy of his favorite book and handed it to her.

"A monster book? Is this because of the movie, or something in your personality you're not telling me? Maybe a werewolf?" She wore a long black dress which hugged her body yet showed little flesh. While he wished to see more, he simply found himself happy for the first time in over two years. *Where was her apron? Did she cook without one?* His body didn't mind one bit as electricity coursed through every inch.

He handed her the tulips he had procured from the front yard of Dejarnette's house as he slunk past with a childlike giddiness. *If he couldn't take down the man physically, improvise and take a little satisfaction in minute crimes.*

"*Frankenstein* was penned by a woman. She bucked the system when it was written and bested two men in a bet on who could write the wildest story."

She turned toward the kitchen with the book in hand, eyes glued to the cover. "I've heard of it, obviously, but have only read *Dracula*. Isn't this about a man trying to play God and creating life?"

Sam felt his heart clench. *Dejarnette fit the bill, as did Grant, Davenport, and several others within the circle where he now lived.* "Yes, it is. The doctor found himself in a position much lower than a deity." He waved his hands. "I'll shut my mouth. Think of me when you read it." *Why did he just say such a thing?*

"As the monster? Or the doctor?" Her hazel eyes sparkled as she lit the candles on the dining room table.

She had prepared for them a Marsala sauce over beef and pasta, with fresh vegetables steaming in spices and exotic flavor. "This is amazing," he said, his fork already full with another load of heaven. Did they teach you all of this in school?"

"Not exactly," she said, lowering her gaze for a moment. "Just to get into the school, you had to display exceptional skill. Even more was expected from a woman." She heaped another ladleful onto Sam's plate. "I had to bring a little magic from the old country with me to wow the admissions board."

He nearly choked on the rich sauce. "You mean Maine?"

Her stare bore into him. "You know where I'm from. You've always known, so please don't play coy with me. Not about that, anyway. I escaped one fire to jump into another inferno."

"Romania? Poland? Russian?"

"Does it matter to you?"

He returned the stare. "Yes, it does. I'd love to know every little detail of who you are. Maybe your husband didn't care about the intricacies of what made you the treasure you are to life, but I can see it as if it were as clear as the moon as a starless night."

She processed what he said for a long moment, and then reacted. With laughter. She laughed so hard that Sam believed she might burst an artery.

"Did you practice that line before you arrived?"

She truly knew how to push his buttons. Not even Miriam understood how to crawl under his skin and expose him like this woman. "There's a reason why I'm a psychologist. People pay me to listen, not talk."

"Then I guess you are a success. Are you talented in drawing women out of their shells?"

Sam regarded the glass of wine in front of him and then proceeded to drain it, slowly. "Sometimes men as well. Women are typically tougher. Openings in their souls seem unguarded, yet who they truly are remains a mystery to most men."

"And am I a mystery to you?" She poured herself another glass.

"Well, if you were from Russia, which I don't believe, you

could pass for one of those nesting dolls. You know, the ones which open only to reveal another smaller doll, and so on. Just when you think the peeling of layers is complete, another barrier stands in your way."

"Yet you know how to peel away those layers?"

"I try." Her smile continued to light him from within.

They concluded dinner with small talk, about her homeland—Romania, just as he suspected—books, food, and Virginia. They traded glowing reviews of Augusta, the views from all over the town, the people who were about as different as possible from what both had been used to prior to moving, and finally, losing people.

"What tribe is your uncle part of?"

"Cherokee, at least that's what he tells people."

"Why would he lie?"

"Better clout. White people would likely steer clear of a Cherokee red man. You've heard the legends as a child, haven't you?"

Of course he had, but he also knew the truth. They were a people beaten down by society and humiliated by the government which claimed Indian land for its own. Sam imagined the dorms at the hospital, the white wall, the rooms he had yet to see.

"Is he married?"

"Widowed," she replied. "My mother's sister died five years after she moved here. They met in the war, like so many other couples."

"I'm sorry," he said, thinking of where the man might be right now. "I'd like to think that Natives were treated better out here than in other parts of this country."

She chuckled with a bitterness that suggested she had faced much discrimination. "When even your own country spits on you, how does one keep their spirit alive and kicking? He fought for this country, but was shunned by his peers once the troops returned home. He was run out of Richmond and found solace here. I believe they called him and my aunt 'mud people'."

Sam cringed. *Dejarnette's plan.* The eugenics crew considered any non-Anglo people as a 'mud' race, one whose genes had been tainted by disease and primitive traits. It went far beyond a whites-only ideal. They despised people from many cultures and countries that were just as white as him. He wondered whether the man had something to do with Richmond when he studied there, or if it was simply another eugenicist spreading his poisonous words.

"When my aunt told him she wished to return home with him, he cautioned her. He told her about the trail of tears and extermination of entire tribes. You would think that by now, with the Great War over, American society would learn. It hasn't. He would've fared much better in New York City."

"But this was a new start for them. At least they had that. Was she happy here?"

A tear formed in Ruby's eye, one that he was surprised she allowed to remain. "She loved him. Enough to leave her home, and we applauded her because to stay meant persecution. What did she receive? A filthy disease that wiped out entire towns without discretion. My uncle had to watch her die and they wouldn't allow her into the hospitals. Why? Not because of her nationality, but his."

"Do you blame him for her death?"

She shook her head and a tear dropped to the table. "Of course not. He gave her life when she had nothing to live for, in a country which fell apart daily. She smiled for six years. One there when he courted her, and five in this state."

"I just wish I knew where he was."

Sam decided that he would search the dorms and files the following day, to see if a man fitting his description had been treated. He prayed the uncle truly disappeared on a hunting jaunt that led him astray, yet he knew better. *Either way, the man was in trouble. If Dejarnette had him locked away, Sam had little chance of releasing him.*

"Anyway, enough of this." She rose and waved for him to join her in the kitchen. "Help me clear the table and we'll get ourselves ready for dessert."

"I don't think I can fit anything else in me right about now."

He slipped in behind her and wrapped his arms around her. Initially, she tightened, but quickly softened against him.

"Thank you," he said. "I haven't had a meal like that in ages."

"Your mother doesn't cook?"

"She does, and well, but she doesn't wear kitchen attire like yours. Somehow, I think I could get to liking meals here."

She inched back against him, feeling him grow. "Why is that?"

He shifted, embarrassed, not wanting to push her away. "I think dessert here could get a little more interesting than at home."

With those words, she turned to kiss him quick on the lips, and then pulled away. "I don't have much to offer for dessert," she said, her voice fading with each syllable.

Sam pulled back as well, yet grabbed for her hands. "Ruby, I'm just flirting. I didn't mean anything." He felt the night falling away from him like a boulder rolling off a cliff, down the mountains in the distance.

She turned back to him and stared deep. "You still wear your ring. Why?"

He clenched his hands, forgetting they still held hers. "I'm a widower. It's what we do, I think." His eyes dropped to the pie she had set out on the counter. "I don't know."

"Have you mourned her? Allowed her to be at peace?"

The night in the Pullman car and in his bedroom flashed through his mind. "I have. I don't know if she has, though. Sometimes, I feel like she refuses to accept where she's supposed to be."

The slender hands slipped out of his and picked up the wide blade set next to the dessert. "Sometimes the soul doesn't know what it's supposed to do. Sometimes, it aches to hold on to what it wants rather than follow God's will."

And sometimes, that soul simply loves to screw the hell out of her husband, he thought.

"Are you going to tell me what happened, or is it still raw?" Her eyes begged for understanding and though he felt as if her knife had twisted inside him, he knew that if she was to be a part of his life, he needed to open up and speak for the first time about that night.

"I hear the park is usually quiet this time of night. Care for a stroll while I open a vein?"

58

The sun had bled onto the maples and oaks which guarded the opening of Gypsy Hill Park. As seven o'clock loomed and the first of the church bells sounded behind them, Sam and Ruby found the path which led into the depths of the park. He prayed it would bring him a slice of serenity.

In the middle of the park, a string of benches lay strewn on the horse path where couples often rode on a Friday or Saturday night, as they forgot the depression for an hour. Sam picked one hidden in a copse of drooping branches which still held onto their leaves, despite the threats of frost in the week ahead.

"We were supposed to raise a family in the shadows of the Golden Gate Bridge," he exhaled, leaning back into the hard wood of the bench. The moon strained to break through the deep green above him, but the branches only allowed a slight illumination to touch the couple. "Yeah, I know it sounds shallow, but both of us got caught up in the dream of planting anew on a coast that wasn't our own."

Ruby choked on a laugh. "I know that dream. Tastes pretty bitter now." Yet she squeezed his hand and leaned into him. "Go on, please."

"The people who bought my test, the one which would decide how smart people were, and ultimately, who should be allowed to have a family, sold me on that dream. It wasn't a hard sell. I wanted out of the east and to make a name for myself. Believe me, Ruby, I only wished to help people. My test would help kids in school, let struggling students get the help they needed, and place military folks where they could serve and save lives." He sunk lower. "Or, that's what I convinced myself it was for."

"I went to the conferences, the consortiums. I listened to the pundits speak their bullshit about how the planet couldn't survive if people overpopulated it. They compared America to Rome, Greece, and even the Aztecs. They spoke as if they cared about saving the red, white, and blue dream. I inhaled it all. They were set to pay our way, house, pension, and most of all, my name in the history books."

"Who were *they*?"

He shivered as he recalled the looks on Grant's and Davenport's faces the other day. "You don't want to know. All the big countries are hoping for the same result. It's far from just us. They want humanity to rid itself of its viruses, diseases, blemishes, and whatever else 'they' believe is killing us. Name one of the richest folks in the country and he, or she, is opening the wallet or purse to fund the movement. I think I'd feel safer right now if I worked for John Dillinger."

"What was she like?"

Sam found he couldn't meet her eyes. *He couldn't allow his dead wife's face to materialize in his mind, either. It would break what little resolve he had left.*

"Beautiful, smart, a fighting humanitarian, and from a respected family in New York. All she wished for was a family, while I jumped for the brass ring. She followed me across the country and left her own family back home, willing to do whatever it took to make my dream come true. She was fine with it as long as she got her own child."

"How far along was she?"

He squeezed his eyes shut. Pain blossomed behind them in arrow-like precision. "All the way," he replied in a small voice. "She failed to tell anyone about her condition before getting to full-term. If she did, well, I know why she didn't."

"What was wrong with her? Did you know about it?"

He shook his head. He wondered if it would have made a difference. Her family knew, but thought prayer would change the future. "No, I didn't know about it. She had diabetes. She was a hemophiliac, a bleeder. Three of her five siblings had died during their first years of living—but none of them felt it necessary to let me in on it. Why should they? I wasn't a real doctor, just a damned shrink. What the hell did I know about medicine and health?"

"I'm sure they meant well," Ruby said. "In my town, the mortality rate for infants was too high to even consider. Even with a good doctor with the best training, he couldn't help our people."

Sam recalled the issues of the royal families and all the precautions they had taken—all except the admission that most of them shouldn't have been attempting to procreate in the first place.

Miriam did mean well, he knew that. She loved him and only wanted to give him something, a legacy. Something. If she couldn't realize her dreams by following his, at least she could give him this. She meant well.

"She went into labor four weeks early. Just about two weeks after I discovered her insulin supply. I had never known. If the medical world hadn't made the solution available to the public, I doubt she would've lived that long. Hell, I'm shocked she made it through her teens."

"Should that have saved her?" She had taken hold of him as he hadn't realized his body had been shaking.

"No," he answered in a voice much weaker than he remembered ever sounding. "During delivery, the hemophilia was the last nail in the coffin. Maybe if she never became with child—but she did it for me, for us. No one wants to accept that life shackles our dreams with something like that. Human nature—hell, even animal nature—gives us that survival instinct, to never give up until we know death is imminent. Only humans close their eyes to the inevitable and shut out reality.

"The doctor told me even if he could save her, there would be complications, that she might never leave the hospital. And what does she do? Apologizes to me for doing this, for keeping it all a secret."

"She died looking at me as if I'd hate her for what she did."

"But you'd never …"

He heaved as if every rib stabbed his lungs. "Of course I didn't hate her. She lived fighting the odds and did a hell of a job. Maybe she believed she could give us a child that could live the life she knew she couldn't. She tried. And I just sat there holding her hand."

Ruby kissed him. "She knew. Of course, she knew you loved her. And the baby."

"I don't know," he replied and truly didn't know. *Maybe that's why she visited him.*

"What about the child?"

He finally raised his head to meet her eyes. The overpowering scent of blood and amniotic fluids ignited in his memory. He recalled the urge to choke but the shock of Miriam's last gaze had held him like a noose. He could not recall fainting, but knew it happened after her soul left her body. "The doctor must have delivered him, my son, while she was dying. By the time I realized the nurse had him in her arms, the glance between the doctor and nurse said it all. 'I'm sorry,' was all she could say. Then he was gone."

"So, you never had a moment with him?"

He dropped his gaze again. "He was gone before I could look at him."

His lie sounded as strong as the pain of the memory.

59

Once the moon rose high enough in the park so they could see the path again and both their faces had dried of tears, she rose and pulled him to his feet. They had been talking for hours with only the songs of nature to accompany them, her head against his chest, her legs across his.

"Walk with me," she said, giving him a look he could not decipher.

With each step, he felt the burdens of the past falling away, save for the one he couldn't let go of just yet. *That weight was the one which sent him back home, to accept the position at Western Valley, and to give his family the life he couldn't give himself and those who perished.*

They walked the circuit unencumbered by the horse and buggies, the children playing, and even the creatures who shared the park with the townsfolk of Augusta. It felt as if time and nature took the night off, to give him and Ruby the moments they needed.

She slipped her arm around him as they passed the lake and approached the train tracks. He pulled her tight and inhaled her perfume. He found himself guessing at the exotic fragrance but falling short due to a rising in a certain hormone. Her body felt different from Miriam's, even when she was alive, but it wasn't her form which caused the burning within him. Her eyes, her desire to live and escape an unfair and abusive life, her lips as they comforted him with sympathetic words: all kindled something he had begged life to find for him since he left on the train back to New Jersey.

"I did want to talk to you that day last week, as we traveled here," she said.

"Why didn't you? I felt like a leper sitting across from a princess."

She punched him in the arm and smiled. "Stop. I don't trust anyone. Even you, now. But I'm trying. I know there are good people out there and want them to know me, like my uncle, you, and your brother. Even my boss is a good man underneath it all. But it's tough to block out the scars. Sometimes, they're all I feel."

"Me too," he said. "But scars can be shared. Pain doesn't have to be a solitary affair."

She drew his face close between her two hands. "We can try again."

"Try what?

"A train ride. This time with a happier ending."

60

She led him over to the miniature depot where the engine was parked. The octet of cars trailed from it, under cover of the trees which surrounded the structure and the pond within the tracks. Once there, he let her go, unsure of her true motive. Before the light stole her from view, he witnessed visually what the rest of his body had found so appealing by touch. Her dress hugged her body in a way which accentuated it, hips jutting just enough and breasts protruding so that when she walked, it was nearly impossible for her to not garner attention.

Once at the little house where the engine rested, she beckoned for him to join her. Without a word, he strode over and pressed her onto the grill of the engine, their chests touching in an embrace as her left leg curled up around his ass.

"Please tell me you think no one ever visits the park at night," she breathed as her teeth softly clamped onto his lip.

"Why wouldn't they?" He slipped his hand to her lower back, right above her buttocks, and pulled her against him. "I've only been here a week, but I think I'd like to visit every night."

She smiled and looked him deep in both eyes. "It's been well over a year since I've been in this position."

He pulled back for a second. "A year since you've kissed a man while pressed against a train engine? You've obviously not been living."

She grabbed his bottom though his trousers and squeezed. "Fool," she said, smiling with a look in his eyes he hadn't seen in too long. "Actually, it's been four—since I've done so and wanted to do so."

His look of incredulity amused her, so she kissed him deeper.

"It's been over two years for me, but then again, I haven't wanted to."

The conversation ended as his hand rose to meet her breast, circling it with two fingers and caressing the nipple through the sheer fabric. He leaned further into her as she went with the move, her head tipping back until it touched the cool metal of the train. She pulled him into her as both legs wrapped around his ass, locking him in to where she wanted him. Her tongue found his as their mouths opened and a slight moan escaped her. He sensed a growing heat emanating from her crotch to his as he hardened in full, a sensation unfamiliar to him outside of a dream, or the dreamlike experiences he had been having with his deceased spouse. His hand squeezed harder before feeling her stiffen under his touch.

"Are you sure?" He hadn't met a woman in years and had not encountered one who craved intimacy this much since Miriam first returned to him. Yet he felt it was a matter of necessity for her to move past her past by doing so and he could not deprive her of that therapy.

His hand dropped to her leg just above the knee and he felt her cool flesh. He trailed two fingers along her thigh, slowly, as she uttered a sound he took to mean her assent. For a minute or two he toyed with her, squeezing and stroking her as the flesh grew warmer and he reached where both thighs met. As she squirmed and took hold of him through his pants, he slid those fingers inside her silk underwear and much deeper.

In a flurry of motion, Ruby took him out of his trousers, as he slid her panties off to hang on her left shoe. She briefly connected her gaze to his before allowing him to kiss her deep. When she did, her legs tightened and pulled him forward. He slid inside with ease, causing both to inhale sharp breaths.

He braced himself on the engine and planted his feet in the gravel. If he allowed himself to think, he would have worried about others wandering through the park, or a tail from the hospital. But he didn't. He simply found himself lost in her, feeling her clench him as he sank into her, in what became a steady rhythm. The past two years melted away with each plunge, yet reality threatened with the cold air on him when he withdrew. The dichotomy sent him further into a place outside of his own mind and connecting to hers. Her hands braced herself, pulled him deeper, and wrapped around his neck.

For what seemed like hours they fucked, yet each knew a few more minutes would suffice to end their drought. From her breathing, the hitch here and there, he felt her climax rising, which he swore filled the night air with her scent. He begged his own body to hold back, like he could many times with Miriam in their special encounters. Yet he couldn't. She touched him in a manner he hadn't experienced from any woman before and it turned him on like a pipe. In a moment which dizzied him, he emptied into her, as she nearly pained him with her knotted ankles behind him.

When he felt drained, she bucked a couple of times more against him, unwilling to let him halt the escape into whatever world they had fallen into. She bit against his neck with cool lips, as her body seemed to soften. He listened to her breathing change, from rapid shallow gasps to the deepest of inhalations. For several minutes, they existed as one spent body, leaning into the conductor's seat of the steam engine.

When Sam felt his muscles solidify, they collected themselves and left the park without a word. Sam walked Ruby to her apartment and up the stairs to her uncle's apartment. He wouldn't enter, at least this time, citing that he needed to be home but that the week was long and that he would cook for her the following night. She answered him with a smile, appreciating his foolish gesture and kissing him farewell with another deep, yet much softer, smile.

He walked to his house knowing he said a few words in parting, but couldn't for the life of him remember what they were.

As he lost himself to sleep, he felt alone, yet not for the first time in months. And for that, he allowed a sense of happiness to wash over him. Even the events of the coming day couldn't divert him from the brightness which filled him.

He pretended not to acknowledge the spectral figure watching over him from the chair in the corner.

61

During breakfast on Monday morning, discussion flowed, yet from two of the three participants, words felt forced. Colin eagerly begged Sam to come to his baseball game on Wednesday at the school, where they'd take on the Rebels from Winchester's Day School. The boy appeared to have put his experience with the threatening strange man on the back burner of his mind.

Sam nodded and smiled, his mood torn between knowing what lay ahead at work that day and still floating from his 'train ride' the previous evening. *Of course he would attend the game and finally see his half-brother smiling, fitting in and succeeding.* He wished to joke with the boy but couldn't find the lines.

His mother kept shooting him odd looks as she served up salted ham and eggs with toast. He wondered whether or not she knew he got lucky. The last time he had been with a woman and she had been around, it had been right after the war, when Miriam visited frequently. Part of him wished for her to just ask him about the night and get it over with painlessly. Yet he knew she loved a good game and would smile as he writhed like a bug under glass. Still, to spite her, he kept his mouth shut while grinning with his eyes, until he cleaned his plate and washed it in the sink. "Have a good day," she said without turning to face him, but she tapped Colin on the shoulder.

When he passed by the window, however, she wore a grin that spoke volumes. *She always knows*, he mused. *Always.* Maybe he could bring Ruby by next weekend for Sunday dinner. He watched his brother amble off to school with the same ambivalence he himself carried.

He turned towards the hospital with a knot of giddiness shrouded in dread, as images of Ruby fought with those of what he knew he would find in the treatment room.

When he passed the ice cream shop, the corner stood empty for once.

The blue ice boy had taken the day off.

62

"So, are you in with both feet, or do I have to report to Grant that there's a problem?"

Blood rushed to fill Sam's face. Fear followed up his back and into his neck. "What do you mean?" He had rushed into the main building while feeling his feet glue themselves to the bricks along the way. *The dread had been warranted.*

"Davenport got the impression that you were a bit skittish when they were here. He thought you might bail out on us and do something foolish."

"Such as?" His mind scampered for something to say.

The doctor swirled a spoon in his coffee cup before sipping. "Such as writing a friend who works for the *Washington Post,* or simply quitting?"

The fear boiled over into his cheeks. Sam wished for his guitar pick, but recalled he'd slipped it into his shirt pocket. He remembered seeing the visitors in the foyer as he entered the main building, but had taken them for family members of patients, or salesmen for medical supplies. With a jolt, he recalled the man from the theater who disappeared down the alley.

They were *watching him.*

"Do you really think I'd be that stupid? I designed the damned test and no matter what I intended it to be used for, I'm not so foolish to think that I wouldn't be implicated in whatever happens here."

"Implicated? The country *wants* this movement. Haven't you read the *New York Times*? Hell, we're in a race with most of

Europe and Scandinavia to see who can clean up their country the quickest."

"So why the hell would I want out?" Sam felt confusion muddle with his dread.

Dejarnette strode over to him and clamped his pale hands on Sam's shoulders. "I hope you wouldn't. I *convinced* them you wouldn't. Told them you cared too much about your family to act foolishly." The look in the older man's eyes told Sam what he already knew. When the rubber hit the road, the doctor would not hesitate to sacrifice others to secure the trajectory of his mission.

"Again, why would I do that? Because your views on eugenics are a bit more 'advanced' than mine? I brought my family here to start a new life, where ..."

"Your brother could get an education without being laughed at, and could have a purpose?"

Why did he keep bringing up Colin? To frighten him? To remind him who held the cards? And how did he know about his army buddy at the Post?

"Your new lady friend? She needs someone who can give her a new life, too. I don't think you'd skip out on her, either."

Sam didn't think the man was patronizing him. He simply knew the score. "Then why tell me any of this?"

The older man walked to the back door, one with a steel bolt through it, rather like one would see on a meat locker. "Because, my dear partner, besides helping to test and decide who will grow with this country back to prominence, I need your eyes and mind to tell me what I'm doing right and wrong—downstairs.

"I told you we'd be visiting the meat and potatoes of Western Valley today." As Dejarnette pulled the door wide to reveal a service elevator, a sound emanated as one would hear if he were opening one of Dante's circles. The car appeared big enough inside to hold a gurney or two, and several people. "Sometimes, this is much easier than stairs. Besides, my knees haven't been the same since when I played soccer at university."

He smiled and gestured to Sam. When they were both standing in the center of the car, the doctor punched the yellowed button which began the journey into hell.

63

What Sam saw when the doors opened caused his bladder to nearly empty.

"Oh my god."

"My patients."

Music played in the background, a soundtrack befitting a world in which Dante Alighieri would find himself at home. "Handel," Dejarnette's voice said. "Beautiful, intelligent music. No need for anesthetic when the music overtakes the limbic system.

"I don't understand why you embrace that 'mud music' when you understand they'll never be a part of who America should be.

"Does that lady friend of yours also prefer the darker melodies, or is she a fan of the masters?"

Sam felt for his guitar pick and sought the soothing blues in his mind, yet couldn't find them.

All he could see in those contraptions which only Machiavelli could design were his brother, and his love—trapped.

"Welcome to the heart of Western Valley. This is where the world we know will change, for the better, and to save it."

"No," Sam heard himself say in a voice too small to be his own. "I never wanted this."

Dejarnette smiled and led him into the first room. Sam could see the entire campus from the wide window. "But this is what your test was for; it legitimizes the movement. Separates us from what some call a brutal affair. You've helped. When America asks why, we can show them the evidence, the truth behind the movement. For the masses who want the Depression to end but don't have the balls to do what it takes, we will show them. It's been happening for two decades. Now it's time for it all to come to fruition, before the others claim their stake in history."

"But I didn't do anything," Sam managed. "*You* did."

"Don't worry," spoke a new voice. "Today, you will."

"We'll begin on the top floor, where it all began." Dejarnette said. "By the end, I believe you'll understand why you always knew you were meant to be here. I believe your wife would have been proud."

White tiles covered the floor in the expansive operating room. A trio of reclining medical chairs sat near the far wall where the doctors would perform the sterilization. A pair of women stood at the ready in dress whites, reminding Sam of field nurses when the bloodshed halted for a brief time. These women held none of the same compassion in their eyes as those angels he'd witnessed in France and England. They simply secured the wrists of the patient writhing beneath them.

"Rebecca?" Sam's knees went weak as he recognized the patient he'd interviewed just before the weekend.

She glared at him, the trust she had placed in him shattered as both understood what was about to happen to her.

"She's a defective," Dejarnette said, as if he had just diagnosed polio or influenza. "Her results place her in the promiscuous range."

Sam wished he had something more lethal than a guitar pick in his possession. "The woman was raped by her brother-in-law!"

"So she says," replied the other man who Sam now recognized as Maclin, the doctor he had met in the gazebo. "More likely, she waited for her husband to leave for work and then fucked him like one of their farm animals. But with a lesser pedigree."

"You asshole," he seethed. "Did you examine her? I interviewed and tested her, just as ordered. Did you do your job? *Either* of you?" His fists grew tight as the urge to cause someone to bleed escalated.

"Watch your tongue," Dejarnette said. "I know my job. This

woman could have stopped the action if she were stronger, mentally, if she truly wanted it to stop. Some women in this county are no better bred than the sows in the trough."

"So you're saying that if she was from better stock, this wouldn't have happened?" He couldn't believe his ears. These words, uttered from a man trained at Oxford, held no reason—yet Sam knew the man didn't truly expect them to hold true. They simply fit the agenda. "That she wouldn't have been raped?"

"Finish the preparations," the superintendent said to the nurses. Turning to Sam he said, "Actually, yes. The country's a mess because people who are no better than slack-jawed monkeys can't keep their legs closed. Imagine the poverty level if ten percent of the population was erased. Twenty? Thirty? The possibilities are endless."

"And those who caused the Crash? I guess they don't deserve to be around either?"

"Accidents happen, Samuel," he replied with a withered smile. "Yet most missteps don't cripple the greatest country in the world. It happened because the unfit have been riding the backs of the fitter for too long. Something had to break sometime."

Sam backed against the window and gazed into the tree line. Just beyond it lay Colin's school. *How long would it be before he would be considered 'unfit'? Or was he already?*

"But you entrusted me to test her, to test all of the patients. You asked for my expertise and I expected you to heed my results. You didn't."

The man turned to him as if he was a petulant child, rather than a fellow professional. "I did heed your results. We simply have disparate manners of interpreting them. I trust in your test—it's impeccable and brilliant—yet any instrument is subject to deviation. Wouldn't you agree?"

Sam locked eyes with the patient. *He'd failed her.* "I … that's not relevant here. This woman has a husband and child. She deserves more than one test to determine her fate. She deserves us to discuss it, at the very least."

The doctors picked up the forceps and something which

resembled an aberrant version of a scalpel. They held both in front of the woman, who should have screamed, but didn't. She simply burned Sam with her glare.

She blamed him. After all, he spent much of their session assuring her he would help bring the rapist to justice, after procuring a proper medical exam to prove her story true. He had let her down, even if he had zero control over the situation.

"Is your test reliable, or is it not? Twenty-seven states have the sterilization law on their books now. Many of them will be making their decisions based on it. We can lead the way."

Sam collapsed internally. *He never meant for it to be used this way. Yes, for some population control, to help those seriously impaired from making decisions which might be out of their capability, but not this.* This woman here, she would not only be barren after this day, but would be blamed by her husband and shunned by her community. And his test, the one he finalized a year after Miriam's and his son's death, would be the culprit, on paper.

"Please let me re-test her. You can be witness so you'll trust the validity."

Rebecca's eyes still bored into him. *Never again would she trust him or any other man.*

"Can't you see the purpose here?" Dejarnette stroked her hair. "She may still live a happy life, and won't have to worry about starving children, straying husbands, lining up in soup kitchens just to make ends meet. Her one child will be fine, but if she had a litter of four or five, so typical of her kind, at least one or two would perish due to her negligent parenting.

"Now please have a seat." He waved over the nurses and Dr. Maclin, who had yet to say much to Sam. "This won't take long and it's relatively painless."

Sam stood and made for the door. *He needed to feel Ruby's arms, to give him the false impression that he would be okay after this.*

"Don't." The doctor's words held firm. "You're a part of this and I require you to remain here."

"Is this coming from you? Or Grant?" Sam noticed the

sarcasm ease into his voice.

"Honestly, it's my decision, but remember, you're my guest here in Augusta and your house is provided courtesy of the Society. The remainder of the factors I'll leave you to figure out. I can't physically stop you from leaving, but you're a smart man. I think you'd ace your own test, possibly even top my score."

Sam allowed himself to gaze out the window again. *Was that strange man keeping tabs on the grounds, ready to deal with the doctor if he bolted? Or was he still watching Colin?*

A much darker thought entered his mind. *What if the man wasn't alone here in town and his kind, hired by Grant and the group, sought out victims just like the brown recluse spiders he found in the house—watching and waiting patiently, yet lethal when needed?*

"I'm sorry," he mouthed to the woman. He knew she would be staring at him until it was over. The music belied the moment with a major key melody Sam wished to never hear again.

Dejarnette beckoned for him to sit in one of the arm chairs facing the mirrors. He refused and stood for the duration. His reflection bounced off the trio of glass slabs, distorting his image into several separate faces.

He wondered which one would be his true face.

64

When the procedure was complete only half an hour later, the nurses wheeled Rebecca away on a gurney. The woman appeared to be alive and on course to remaining that way. However, Sam knew that much of her had died in the chair and would never be resuscitated.

"Where will she go now?" he asked the doctor, while keeping his eyes on her. *By now, her anger had no doubt turned to despair. Maybe another day she would burn to kill him again, to wish him dead, but for now, what remained lay still under a slightly bloody sheet.*

Dejarnette smiled and washed his hands in the sink. "I told you, we're not monsters. She'll be home soon. I doubt she'll be dishing out slop for the pigs anytime soon, but she'll be hugging her child and thanking God she is in her own home once again."

Without a husband who would ever believe the truth. Sam decided he would go there himself if he had to—he couldn't be a party to ruining any more of this woman's life than he already had.

After they washed up, Dejarnette placed a hand on Sam's shoulder. "Would you like a drink, or are you ready for the next step?"

Seconds later, the trio stepped into the elevator and dropped to the third floor. With three levels yet to go, Sam wondered how long it would take for his own sanity to crack. *Obviously, that was Dejarnette's intention all along. Break the dog, show him who's boss, just in case.*

Yet the doctor had no idea how strong Sam believed himself to be.

Neither did Sam, until they walked into the treatment room. "I'll take that drink now, please."

65

The soured appearance of the second room they ushered him into set the tone for what was about to occur. The lights hanging in quartets around the larger room cast a pus-colored pall over the bevy of equipment which filled Sam's vision.

He had of course read about these contraptions in journals and knew they were present at the symposium he attended in San Francisco, yet chose not to visit the exhibits. He knew psychology, testing instruments, therapy measures, and research. The only invasive procedure he ever utilized was digging into a patient's mind with words, attempting to discover what festering wounds might exist beneath not the flesh, but the façade of normalcy most people wear.

What stood before him was calculated to shake a person to his or her core.

A pair of deep claw-footed tubs sat in the middle of the left side of the split floor. A spike of ice shot down his spine as he recalled the procedures he witnessed back in San Francisco.

"Hydro-therapy?" His voice sounded far away, a voice not his own.

Two more nurses walked in a pair of women and led them each to a tub. From one hissed steam, while the other bristled with chipped ice.

"Yes," Dejarnette answered. "How familiar are you with the treatment?"

"Not very," he replied, wondering if this replaced the sterilization torture or simply added to it. "Something about the extremes of cold, or hot, having been reported in Sweden as efficacious to stimulate the nerves and halt certain neurons from firing, which might explain schizophrenia or depression."

"Or both. Or violence. Impulsivity. Delayed intellectual growth. The research suggests a ton of possibilities. We want to stay ahead of the curve, hence my own research, here. Thankfully, we have a plethora of patients and maladies to cull from in this hospital." He nodded to the nurses. "What we're attempting just might jumpstart what is dormant in their DNA."

Both women climbed naked into the tubs, obviously sedated. Regardless, the heat in the one and ice in the other left both shaking. Leather straps hung from the sides but weren't necessary. The pair sat and stayed put, as if warned prior to entering the room. One visibly cringed at the burning sensation of the ice while the other embraced the heat as if remembering the comforts of home.

Sam failed to recognize either of them as his patients. "Why haven't I seen these patients before?"

"They've been in the dorms for weeks. Your predecessor diagnosed them and prescribed intensive treatment."

The psychologist's mind spun again, this time with the question he feared now to ask. Before today, he simply didn't care. "Who was my predecessor? What was his name?" He walked up to the edge of the tubs and looked at the thermometers. *110 degrees. 40 degrees.* "Christ! You might cause fibrillation."

Dejarnette shrugged. "They're both healthy and with three doctors on hand, I believe they are in good hands. As for who came before you, does it matter? You're here, he's gone. That man passed through the area, a short-sighted experiment by the Society. You have the opportunity to go down in history, in medical books and journals. Shouldn't that be your focus?"

Sweat and ice washed over Sam as he pondered the question. "Yes, it does matter."

Maclin snapped his fingers. "Okay, ladies, switch."

What? No, they couldn't be serious.

"That could kill them!"

The doctors ignored him as the nurses aided the women out of their respective tubs. "It hasn't yet. I built my research on the backs of that by a couple Swedes and Finns, who swear by temperature shock. The body is made up of electricity. Remember that."

The water splashed across the floor and Sam felt grateful no switches or outlets existed at lower levels of the walls. *Why wasn't this therapy held at ground level? Or in the basement?*

As if reading the man's mind, the other doctor spoke. "We're in direct competition with Lynchburg, Richmond, D.C. and those bastards up in Cold Spring Harbor. When the brass shows up to check on the results, they like bright and sunny, not medieval settings."

"Funny," Sam replied. "I would've thought Torquemada helped design this building. The lighting here brings out the piss yellow in your eyes."

The man clenched his fists but with a nod from his superior, Maclin relaxed. "You're lucky the doc likes you, Yankee."

"Or what?" Sam felt himself aching for a fight he hadn't indulged in since the end of the war. "Gonna give me a bath?"

Dejarnette laughed, causing the other to grin. "I told you he had balls."

"Not if he crawled into that tub of ice," Maclin said. "He'd be wearing them as peas up around his chin."

Normally, Sam would go tit for tat with the jawing, but since Miriam, since he buried himself in the work, he had rarely allowed himself much humor. Only when he fraternized with the other psychologists in one of San Francisco's speakeasies did he relent and uncork his smile.

At all other times, whenever he felt like joking, he saw his wife's face as she breathed her final breath, speaking a last joke which would be his life's punchline.

One woman screamed at the pain and bucked against the nurses. They must have been stronger than most, or the woman drained of energy, as they easily shoved her back down into the ice and fastened the restraints. The other woman, either lost in another world or having already given up on the fight, simply stood and awaited her fate. She passed out upon slipping into the tub.

"Ready for the other half of the shock floor?" Dejarnette held Sam's gaze with his stare. It wasn't a request and Sam knew he had no choice, not at this stage of the game.

He lowered his eyes just a bit but took in his surroundings, just in case. The faint, ugly lighting played on his focus and tempted him to ease up on his paranoia. He fought against it with all he had.

"Have you ever heard of shock treatment?"

This part of the room held the same lighting and feel of the hydro setting, yet gave Sam a sensation of horror he couldn't describe. A reclining chair, like one that would be found in a barber's shop, sat against the window. A patient already lay strapped within and mumbled to himself.

"Randall?" Sam recognized the man from the same day he had interviewed the woman upstairs. A thief, he was caught tearing away down Route 11 with a supply truck originally destined for the men working on Skyline Drive for the CCC. He had lost his business a couple of years prior and the banks had foreclosed on him in Harrisonburg. Without income, his family, like so many others, had been growing thinner by the day.

When Sam interviewed him, he told him that his youngest had just died from malnutrition. No one at the soup kitchens or breadlines would offer free medical care. If he had come to Western Valley, the staff could have offered a crib and treatment. Besides their craze for the eugenics race, the hospital had been about helping the people for nearly a century. Dejarnette couldn't erase that much history and goodwill overnight. Also, the baby was white and from obvious good stock.

"Why are you here and not in the town jail? Sam had asked him, prior to testing the man.

"The sheriff thought I was a danger to society and said Doc here could help my family, if I agreed to a shot or two to help me with my anger."

"Do you have a problem with your anger?" Sam had watched the man fall apart, piece by piece in his office.

"I have a problem with watching my children die."

When pressed, Randall Beech admitted to carrying two firearms on his mission to steal the supply truck. While he didn't kill or harm anyone, it took four policemen to disarm him and pry the cans of food from his jacket. "I would do it again—in a heartbeat—if it meant my family could eat for the next six months.

"But the next time, I'd aim better."

Now he was strapped down with a metal band around his head.

The man's arms and legs were strapped tight as well, using lengths of leather without any steel or iron on them. The same with the trio which held him flat to the table across his chest, waist, and thighs.

"So, Doctor Taylor, are you familiar with any form of this therapy?"

"Therapy? Therapy? More like barbarism. First, that idiot who created this injected our soldiers with malaria in order to cure syphilis and other diseases. He *gave* them the damn disease like they were rats."

Dejarnette washed his hands and instructed a nurse to secure the headpiece, a steel ring with bolts jutting out of it, which reminded Sam of James Whale's *Frankenstein* from two years back. *The sick doctor created life, playing God like this man, yet caused utter chaos.*

"He won the Nobel Prize, you know, so the medical community believed in him."

"Then there were the insulin injections." Sam bristled at this, recalling that if doctors spent more time with diabetic research and treatment than with the 'shocks' they believed would make them famous, maybe his wife would still be alive. *So, fuck them if he felt a little anti shock therapy.*

"But it worked," said Maclin. "He cured them. Schizophrenics!"

Sam punched the wall. "Idiot. You believe what you want to fit your cause. None of that worked. Convulsing scared the shit out of the body and knocked the neurons around, caused some temporary reprieves, and the monkeys shit themselves in glee.

"Sakel and Meduna treated their patients as rats. What really came of it? Did it cure anyone?"

Dejarnette laughed. "Well, Taylor, you've certainly researched this thoroughly, haven't you?" He walked to the other side of the patient and flicked a switch on the silver box, an object the size of a small oven. The air sizzled around the four men and one nurse as they produced a large set of forceps with rubber pads on the ends.

Maclin dabbed the pads in alcohol before placing them on Randall's temples. "I've been corresponding with a doctor in Italy who believes true electricity can help cure all sorts of maladies."

"Is this as safe as the hydro?" The man looked up at him with pleading eyes. Sam knew the man was wondering if he'd been given a death sentence.

"Just watch," said Dejarnette. "Just watch. He'll be as docile as a neutered housecat after dining on a mouse."

"You didn't," Sam said. "Please tell me you didn't."

"He couldn't feed his own kids. Do you want more of his spawn draining our world?"

"He's awake and listening, you sick bastard." Sam reached for the straps.

Maclin's arm slapped him back.

"Imagine how your brother would feel in his position. There's a notion that if enough electricity is charged through the brain, or organs such as ear drums, normalcy could occur. Or, I suppose it could fry them completely and kill the little monkey."

The doctor never saw Sam's fist. Before he hit the ground, the psychologist knew the asshole did witness a red mist flying into his eyes as his nose shattered. He landed against the wall and slid to the ground with a thump.

"Well," the superintendent laughed. "At least I know you'll be sticking around for the rest of the tour. You have no idea how many people have fantasized about doing what you just did." A pair of nurses tended to the injured Maclin, cleaning his face and helping him sit upright.

Sam swung around to him, unappeased. "If you, he, or anyone here ever touches my brother, noses will be the least of your injuries."

"Relax, Samuel." He adjusted the pads and placed his finger on the knob which read from 0 to 220. The psychologist assumed that meant volts, and by way of that, pain. "I gave you my assurance that nothing would happen to your family, especially your brother. I hear he's quite a pitcher. If you're okay with it, I'd love to attend a game."

All Sam could hear was the blood coursing through his ears. His anger peaked just then, as he stared into the doctor's eyes. *There would be no trust there, ever. Any man who devalued life half as much as this man did couldn't be trusted with a dog.*

"I'd appreciate it if you didn't go to his games."

The man sighed. "You don't trust me. I get it. But you will find that I'm not the one to fear. I want only the best for this country. You'll see that the longer you work with me.

"Now watch this."

The sizzle of electricity coursed through the air as Sam's patient lost his soul.

66

"Why is the elevator headed to your office instead of the last treatment room?"

The doctor regarded Sam with a tired gaze. "We nearly electrocuted a man, even though I only wished to cure him of his criminal impulsivity. You splattered the room with my doctor's blood. And lastly, you don't trust me enough to allow me to attend your brother's baseball game. You might be fine, but I need a drink before we proceed any further."

When Sam noticed his hand quivering just a bit, he realized he could benefit from a finger or two of Scotch himself, despite the early hour. Possibly he could take a nap after this last destination and before seeing any patients.

He had to admit, Dejarnette held a certain charisma. While he felt loathing for the man, in addition to the men he worked for, he still found himself talking sports and travel with him. Sam cursed himself for being taken in so easily, especially since he held the psychologist degrees, not this sterile-minded physician. *How did that happen?*

But there was a problem all his magnetic personality couldn't fix: the man didn't like football.

When in university, Sam had learned a valuable lesson from a professor, a man who echoed what his buddy from the war had stated about human thinking.

Football was like chess, despite its brutality. Chance still ruled, as it did in many sports, but with football, still finding its way with the growing league, plans set the stage and the determining factor was execution.

It took an entire team to succeed, to lead to victory. Yet it only required a poor leader to fail—or an opponent who could dissect the other's weaknesses. Maybe Sam's Giants might never reach the championship, but he would one day see them play live. And he would watch his team's quarterback completely take apart the powerhouses of the league, leaving them speechless, even if for one game.

Sometimes, just a moment's misdirection and distraction could alter events just enough to achieve what was necessary for survival.

67

The doors opened to the main building's second floor and immediately, Sam wondered why this wasn't in the basement.

"Because only secrets are in the basements of our lives. What we're doing here, what *they* approve us to do here, is no secret."

"Do you treat down there?"

Dejarnette's face lost all traces of a smile. "In a manner, yes, but I pray you never visit there. Sometimes, a man's inner darkness should remain all his own."

He didn't understand what he saw in this dimmest of rooms. This one held a crimson hue in the bright lights. Maybe it was due to the sunlight reflecting off the red bricks behind the building, or possibly it could be due to the obvious.

The amount of blood on the floor connecting the two men likely explained plenty.

"What in God's name are you doing here?"

This was easily the darkest of the three floors, so far. Surprisingly, thin windows let in shards of light, but the angle prohibited anyone from seeing what occurred on this floor. Two more nurses attended the men on the left side of the room. On the right, a closed door filled Sam's eyes.

What existed there that had to be shut off from view, when all else was in plain sight?

"Samuel," Dejarnette said, gazing at the pair of men, likely in their late thirties, each reclining on a cot within an oval metal tub. "Have you ever wondered what causes anxiety? Depression? Hyperactivity?"

Sam just shook his head. "I don't …"

"Well, I did. I still do. This isn't in many research circles, even in the far reaches of the world of eugenics. Maybe a few rogues have attempted something like we have here, but many of them are myopic and don't believe the ills can be cured."

As Sam approached the men, he saw tubes secured to the left arm of one man and the right of the other. Another led from each opposite arm. Again, both were awake with only classical music acting as anesthetic. Neither patient needed to be strapped down for the procedure. He could see the blood flowing from one man to another—and back again.

A sizable puddle had leaked onto the floor and the sides of the tubs. Maybe the men did put up a fight initially, until they grew weak from blood loss.

"Now," Dejarnette said, "I believe that the answers always lie in the DNA. Our two men here, one suffering from depression, the other from extreme violent fits which nearly killed his family in a drunken rage, hold the key to each other's mirror image of dysfunction."

"What are you talking about?" Sam noticed the navy tattoos on both men. *The doctor was operating on soldiers? Veterans?*

"Before you punch me, they volunteered for this. Of course, it was either this or prison for one of them. I believe if the blood is mixed, the same type, of course, the maladies will cancel each other out, or at least cause milder reactions."

"Are you serious? How many have survived this treatment?"

"We're still learning. It's science, medicine. Growing pains. But it's working, Sam. It's working."

He turned towards the other door, a solemn move. "Yet sometimes, you know—I know you do—that no matter what the treatment, some patients will never improve. The physiologically defective, the true unfit, will never function in society. Some are violent, some unpredictable, and some just don't belong.

"Those specimens require something more intensive. I do believe you spoke to Mr. McIlveen after his procedure? He will never again hurt anyone."

"*No*. You're really performing lobotomies? Here?"

"Walk with me. You'll understand." He turned the door

handle and looked back at Sam. "McIlveen would have killed again. Likely. Many here would turn violent again. This patient in here caused damage to one of my staff when they attempted to detain him. Imagine what he could do to others if cornered?"

"What did he do to get here?"

The doctor shrugged. "We decide who needs treatment. Some are just obvious."

As the door opened, Sam knew that he would never, ever erase this day from his mind. The image had been tattooed on his mind just like the sailor's arms. He broke down when he heard the patient's words, happy to see him.

"You brought me blue?"

68

"My god. He's just a boy. His parents ..."

"Don't know or don't care about him. They leave him to wander the streets every day without supervision. Isn't he a danger?"

The boy struggled playfully against the straps holding him into the upright, padded chair with raised headrest. From ankles to neck, restraints held him back from much other movement. On his forehead was another restraint, yet this time it was also leather, not metal.

No nurse stood nearby, either.

"Dr. Sam," spoke the boy. "You bring me ice? Blue ice. I have nickel for you."

The psychologist's eyes grew hazy as the first of many tears began to form. "But if he were to be placed in a school, like Colin's ..."

"Seriously, Sam? Do you think he could pass your test? To show us he had the capacity to function out there and pull his own weight?"

"But his family could take care of him."

"In ten, twenty years? I doubt it. What happens if he gets angry?"

"But you know that lobotomies are dangerous. One eighth of an inch to the left or right and death occurs, often within minutes."

"Mister Sam?"

The psychologist could only wave to the boy who had brightened his mornings.

Dejarnette shrugged again. He lived like a God in this

hospital. "I know what I'm doing. If the patient is meant to live, he will. If not, it wasn't meant to be."

"Bring me my mama?" The gray eyes began to plead. Even through his simplicity, the boy knew he shouldn't be strapped down.

Sam refused to hand the doctor the little hammer which would drive the sharpened end through the corner of the boy's bright eye, into the frontal lobe of the brain and thereby cause the patient to become docile, compliant, and 'cured'.

If they survived the procedure.

All Sam could hear was the boy's voice when he spoke to him on his first day at this new job. He'd only cared about his blue, his favorite flavor of blue. Sam wondered where the boy's parents were and why they allowed him to roam free in such a town. *Surely, they must have heard of what the hospital did, at least a rumor or two?*

Some people surely shouldn't be allowed to procreate. Only those who would love their children without compunction or condition should be blessed with a child.

Because of their ignorance, their son might would never return home again.

Dejarnette stroked the child's head, ruffling the matted hair. "About how old do you believe this boy to be, Samuel?" He gripped the orbitoclast as if it were a fine pen, possibly one to write his own entry in the history books.

"I don't know," Sam replied. "By the size, facial features, maybe twelve to fourteen. It's hard to tell with his language and behavior."

"Hard to tell indeed. Indulge me this before I conclude. Imagine if you had your way and we enrolled him your brother's school. They do service children of all sorts, all disabilities there, don't they?"

Sam recalled speaking to the headmaster over the phone before agreeing to Colin's program. He assured the psychologist that whatever his brother's ailment, the school could handle him, teach him how to survive and thrive in this harsh world. He regaled Sam with success stories of varying sorts, from boys and girls born without limbs to those both deaf and blind who turned into master seamstresses. Colin would succeed there.

"That they do. Are you telling me you would send him there, instead of this?" His waving hand shook more, unaware that the pick remained between thumb and forefinger, cutting into his flesh.

The doctor looked into the boy's eyes and smiled, receiving a smile in return. "Imagine if I did, and he is already of the hormonal age. What if he crept into a girl's bed and spilled his seed into her, transforming her into a mother? She could be like him, or one without legs to run away or fists to beat him down with. Maybe she could be a genius without sight, who could find her way in some profession."

"They have aides there, orderlies, to watch over their charges."

"You honestly believe lazy men and maids keep a keen eye on those children day and night? They're paid pennies."

"You'll end his life here and now, a preemptive strike?"

"Lobotomies are not fatal. Not always. There are a few overseas who have perfected the treatment, just like I will. I'll even whisper a silent prayer for him, if you like."

"Please don't." *A man who played God, summoning him?* The hypocrisy swirled in Sam's thoughts.

"Does that mean you won't assist me? Do I really need to call in a nurse?" He held back the child's head and whispered something into his ear. Whatever the words were caused the boy to smile. "To hell with them. I've performed enough of these to handle it myself. Screw you, Taylor, for making me seem braver for completing the act of mercy solo."

"How many?" His palm bled. Sam recalled the many flat stones out back.

A shrug. "Enough. Enough have survived, too. Just ask McIlveen."

The boy raised his eyes to Sam. They held only a touch of fear. "Doctor bring me home?"

Never did Sam feel so helpless. *If he halted the procedure, his own family would be at risk.* He knew the doctor would report any mutinous behavior, even if he didn't truly believe the Society would lash out in a mortal manner.

He had failed yet another boy. His wife would not comfort him this night.

"This operation takes only minutes, yet accomplishes so much. A calmer, less aggressive patient he'll be. Maybe he can even walk the streets again when this is over. Your buddy Walker can put him to work in his store. Now watch."

The doctor's hands tightened on the boy's chin and the steel tool. He raised the spiked end and placed it at the edge of the left eye just next to the nose. "Shh… The doctor here will bring you a nice ice when I'm done making you feel better."

Sam choked back emotion. "A blue one."

The boy smiled as the silver pressed into the cavity between the eye and orbital bone. Sam wondered how much strength the other needed to press through. Dejarnette's hand shook four times, rhythmically, as he severed what he believed to be the frontal lobe.

"One day," he said, breathing a bit heavier. "They'll say I perfected this, as well in the cleansing of this country. Just not today."

The boy's eyes began to glaze over as a trickle of blood eased out from the tiny wound.

Sam knew at that moment the doctor had a specific result in mind from the beginning. *He already did perfect the act.*

Somehow, before the tears fell from Sam's own eyes, the boy opened his mouth and looked at the man who was nice to him. *He knew. Despite his lot in life, he knew when life cheated him.*

"Going home now. No ice today. Going home." The boy closed his eyes and would never open them again.

69

Sam didn't remember leaving the building or telling Dejarnette to shove the spike through his anus sideways. He could only remember the dying boy's look as he realized he wouldn't be going home again. He tried to recall Ruby's face as he ran through the front gates, something to help him back from the abyss' edge, yet couldn't.

When he reached the stairs of her building, he collapsed in a pile of tears, heaving. Eventually, she heard him and brought him inside her apartment. Within minutes, the psychologist, father, and brother fell asleep in her arms, his weeping continuing long after his eyes shut.

70

"Should I retrieve him for you?" The man held his fedora tight as both watched the psychologist bolt from the building.

A massive sigh escaped Dejarnette. "No," he said. "Let him be. Even though he thought he knew, he truly didn't. I don't expect him to accept this lightly, but he'll come around. Two of his own deaths nag his soul, mostly due to the cause. The war within him will rage for a while, but I believe he will aid us in changing the world."

Whereas Doctor Taylor nervously fingered a guitar pick, the other man, with even more darkness within him, snapped his fingernails against the stock of his pistol. *The mind redeems itself in various ways,* Dejarnette mused. He only hoped that the hired man would be prudent enough to utilize a quieter instrument out in the streets.

"Do you think he'll do something stupid?"

The doctor watched as his new hire turned down into the heart of downtown, knowing where he was headed. He shook his head in disgust. "He already has, but that's not an issue. He's too smart to be stupid."

"That's what scares me."

"Should I just retrieve the woman?"

The superintendent kicked himself inside. *The guards in the dorm would have to be reprimanded. Possibly a month in the white ward would teach them to keep their wits about them better.* "No. I don't need her."

"Good. I'll be doing her husband a favor."

As Dejarnette noticed the man's lips turn into a smile that was bigger than it should have been, he realized something scared him even more than the doctor's potentially loose lips.

71

The man tracked the woman like a rat in one of the wooden mazes he had studied in the academy. *No matter how intelligent the rodent, it always followed the prescribed path of habit. No matter what the prize at the end, they always failed to grasp what happened next.*

Betty Rowe was easy to trace. Possibly once she hit the mountains, he might have some difficulty, but on the city streets, he could almost hear her squeaking for the cheese.

Dejarnette failed to notify him immediately of her departure, which sent him scurrying to find a trail. What he didn't tell the doctor was that he'd have preferred she have an even longer head start. The hunt always satisfied more when the prey had an advantage.

Even if the old man ordered him to retrieve her for more treatment, something would happen to alter that plan. He didn't work for the hospital, or its leader. His bosses knew who he was and what made him so valuable to the movement. They understood his focus and what fed his fire.

The monkey woman had obviously snuck out where the freight train pulled in to drop off supplies. The doctor swore she had been locked in the ward behind the main building, but maybe she pleasured the guard or something. Maybe she simply snuck out. Most guards knew that the only true dangers lived in the white building and that it was self-secured for the most part.

Where did you think you were headed, slack jaw?

He watched the thirty-three-year-old woman grab some

clothes in a house just three blocks away from the hospital. *Hell, she missed the doc's house by a street.* She dropped her gown in the bushes, not even bothering to hide it well.

Even in a blue dress and flat shoes which would aid her speed, the man felt his adrenaline surge. *He would allow her to run down the main drag. If she was smart, which she wasn't, she wouldn't ask for help. The townspeople knew what she was, and the police would be something she would avoid at all costs. Her people always did—and for good reason.*

The park would be her downfall. The road to her people lay beyond it, just before the hills began. He would take her there.

The blade felt like gold in his jacket pocket.

The scent of the trees filled his nostrils. Used to having to divert all his attention to the chase, he never allowed himself the pleasures of whatever setting the task placed him. Cardinals and warblers sang above him in the oaks and creepers, urging him onward in his mission. He halted by the pond—obviously built for aesthetic reasons—just as his prey did on the opposite side, and turned his head to gaze into the water, fettered by the autumn colors of the leaves drowned within.

Several sets of eyes looked up at him. Fish ranging up to a couple of feet in length swam to where he leaned against the iron railing, likely awaiting bits of bread or feed that the ducks missed. Their tails swished in anticipation, each clamoring for a bite before sinking back into the depths.

I hear you, brethren.

The woman meandered through the couples and families who traipsed through the paths leading around the mile-long park. While much of the country hurt for work, denizens of Augusta enjoyed a reprieve from the Depression. He didn't quite understand why, but the doctor believed it to be the culmination of strong breeding and relocation from the better parts of the country.

She only turned to check on followers twice, but he fit in well, walking beside others along the path, chuckling with children when necessary and proffering a "Good Day" if a pair of ladies smiled his way.

He didn't care if anyone noticed him. In fact, it would be much better if they did. Nobody paid attention to the cordial passersby, but they would take note of someone slinking silently in such a social setting.

As both of them turned right, a sign stated the bandstand would be up ahead. Further right stood the hill which shielded the National Guard armory. Why it was built here, he would never know, but it served a purpose: no one would venture too close to its boundaries. Whispers of weapons more threatening than anyone had witnessed in the newsreels during the war still filled the air. The unrest in Europe had many wondering if the States would take a role in any new conflict. He guessed many of the women walking that day had lost fathers in the big one. Roosevelt promised peace and with the sour taste of Hoover still being spat from citizens' tongues, he hoped fascism and socialism would never infect American shores.

The woman scurried to the edge of the bushes by the bandstand, obviously exhausted by her jaunt. *After all, she was still recovering from the operation. Maybe a few stitches pulled and she bled. Without a coat or bag, she would have to be wary of park-goers. If one saw a bloody patch on her stolen dress, they would hail a policeman without hesitation.*

It wouldn't help either one of their agendas.

Time for play.

"Hello, monkey."

She started at his voice and bolted without turning, an animal with a finely tuned fight-or-flight reflex. He laughed as he stepped around the hedges to face her.

"Get the hell away from me! My husband will kill you!" She jumped the first row of chairs, but tripped into the music stands and tumbled in a heap.

"Monkey jaw, pig toe. Where do you think you're gonna go?"

She held up a stand in defense. He simply smiled and waved to her, trying to appear the friendly citizen. Never did she see him in the hospital, and the sheriff and orderlies had abducted her, not him, but the animal had sensed who he worked for.

"Back to your sty, where your kind fuck in the mud." He picked up one of the fallen chairs. "Do you know who plays here?" *No, of course you don't.* "The Stonewall Brigade Band. Famous in these parts and others. Hell, they even played for presidents." *But you wouldn't know that, would you, swine heart.* "Are you here for the show today? I forgot if it's today or tomorrow night."

"Get. Away. From. Me." Her breath was hurried. *An animal knew when it was cornered and faced death.* Instead of running, she fell against the curtain and trembled, her arms and legs quivering. She reached for a music stand to protect her.

"Did you know the band played here well before the park was built? They played during the Civil War, serenading the Union troops during the holidays as they returned home. I guess pride does die hard, doesn't it?"

He knew she had no weapons on her, as he'd watched her dress in the yard. "Don't be afraid. I'm from the hospital, but I'm here to help you. I hate to see a mother cry. Dr. Dejarnette wanted me to tell you that the baby isn't dead. He only wished to save it through some new procedure." *I told him that your breed wasn't worthy, but he insisted. My god, if you had half a goat's brain, you'd run like hell into a crowd of people. But you're as slow as snot.* "May I sit with you?"

She pulled away slightly, but allowed him to ease her up into one of the band chairs in the back row. "My baby? He's okay? They told me he was dead." *They usually did fall for his smile, both men and ladies. He had perfected the gentlemanly look, as if he were just another businessman looking to make ends meet.*

He brushed the back of her head, pulling her hair away. *Always easy when you played the kid card.* He enjoyed the mental win but would regret the shortened chase.

"You'll see him shortly, probably sooner than expected. Would you like to see your family to tell them? I can give you a ride home, if you like."

She nodded, and then looked up at him, knowing. *Somehow, even the unfit knew. How they knew, he would never understand. Damn primitives.* If he considered her an equal, he would feel sympathy. He did feel a pang, however, just as he had whenever his father had to put down the kittens they always found on the farm. Lesser animals had to be treated as such; he never learned not to cry when an animal passed. This time was no different.

The stiletto slid gently into the base of her brain as he smiled at her, locking her head into the crook of his other arm. He was always surprised at how only a few strong wrist muscles were needed to penetrate such an area. The steel made no sound, nor did it draw any blood. It would upon exit, but he would be careful not to soil his coat. Only a tear wet his sleeve.

She managed a wry grin as she died. Her lips mouthed something with her last breath. *Something about her dead child,* he assumed.

He left her sitting in the chair and placed a newspaper in her hands. *Nobody would notice for hours, maybe not until the band arrived.*

It would be much longer until someone cared.

72

"What happened?" Ruby attempted to elicit a sober answer out of Samuel as he spread out askew on her couch. "Why aren't you at the hospital?"

She ushered him into her apartment when he rang her bell, a bottle of something alcoholic in his hand. *Where he got it, she didn't know. Prohibition was failing, but it was still a crime.* She took it from him and poured it down the sink. *Lord knew he'd had enough already.*

"Gene. He'll be pissed," he mumbled.

"Your friend should be smacked upside the head for giving you this in broad daylight."

He smiled as he looked up at her. "He doesn't know it's gone. Shh …"

He stumbled through her miniature kitchen, upending a chair and tearing a picture off the wall. When he crashed into the stove, she gasped but remembered she had yet to light it. Her night off from Panevino's and she had planned on cooking for herself again.

Night after night, she had set two plates at the small table in the main room. *Her uncle might come home, eventually, if the mountains had not claimed him for their own needs.*

"Go to bed, Samuel." She gripped his arm with the strength she had garnered from two years of cleaning, hanging laundry, and finally performing miracles in iron pans and steel bowls. Her limbs were taut with muscle, a trait for which many men drooled over her and one imprisoned her. *Now there existed one who saw her as a whole and appreciated every aspect of her, more inside than out.*

He mumbled a reply and dropped to the full-size mattress in the master bedroom. She had intended to sleep in the side room made up for him. Never did she expect to take him to bed, not there; she wished to make good with his mother and brother, not to appear a common whore in their eyes.

"What did you say?"

"I didn't save him."

Ice crept down Ruby's arms and up her neck. "Who didn't you save?"

He pulled himself to a kneeling position and made a fist. His eyes wouldn't open when he raised his left arm and began punching the wall behind the bed frame.

"I could've saved him, but I was too fucking important. Too big. Now too little." He began to weep as the paint flecked off the wall and showered his head with a light snow. "I just stood there and watched. I'm not a man."

She sat on the bed and pulled him into her. He collapsed like old newspaper as her arms enveloped him. *What demons did this man hide within his skin?*

"What was his name?" She knew she would get little from him which would be comprehensible until the whiskey left his system.

He shook his head. "Does it even matter? He's gone because I wasn't the man I pretended to be." His fist continued to batter the wall while his other braced him from falling on his face.

"Who was he?"

He turned to her with an angry stare, one she'd faced often with her husband. *He would come home or wait for her to arrive and that face, that face blazing with fury, would signal an eruption. Sometimes she could divert him, sometimes she hid or ran. Most times, though, he made sure she lay trapped in his path of destruction. All because he brought her to America and gave her the freedom to hone her craft—that same craft which finally broke the chains with which he bound her.*

Yet Sam didn't raise a fist. His anger simmered far below the surface. *While she knew he fought in the war and likely knew violence first-hand, it wasn't in his blood. She swore to that notion.*

"The boy today. My boy. My wife. All the others. All that blood. Too much."

Before he could continue or she could delve further, he sank into himself and fell unconscious. It was several hours until she could get him to wake, to tell her about Miriam, his son, and Tristan. He halted before detailing the specifics of what occurred within the main hospital building, but the way he shivered when he recalled the day also frightened her.

The thing which frightened her most was how his eyes kept scouting about the room, as if someone were hiding behind a curtain or door. She didn't take him for one to partake in opiates, but it was obvious he saw something there, or was expecting someone to arrive.

As he faded for good that night, calling his house to say he was sleeping in his office, he told her he needed to see Gene in the morning and he murmured, "The hills. The people of the mountain. Got to help them disappear from him."

Tomorrow she would help him to find some of the answers he sought and uncover whatever haunted him.

As she pulled the shades shut, she swore a huddle of figures stood underneath the streetlamp. Each face hid in shadow, but they appeared too long and grotesque to be human. She prayed it was trick of the light, or lack thereof.

She shut her eyes to all of it, his story, the day, and this night. *This supposed sanctuary seemed to bear more mysteries than all the folktales her folks had spooked her with in the old country. Darkness drew closer to her, just as she was beginning to embrace the light life had finally allowed back in.*

When she let herself see the world again, the shapes outside had vanished. *If she were a shallow woman, she would shut the fabric and blame the night.* Somehow, she knew those who walked by her window would return. *They were signs, and signs in the moonlight were never good for one's soul.*

73

"Where the hell would you even take my car? There are mountains in every direction!"

Gene waved his hands at Sam as if he just said he was running off to join the Ringling Brothers, to be shot out of a circus cannon. Sam felt as if he had said something equally ridiculous—and if that cannon aimed him right at a flaming target.

"There's something I have to do," he managed to say. He had zero confidence he would even find where he aimed to go.

"Do you even remember how to drive a car?" His friend sounded incredulous that the newcomer to the valley would consider traveling into such territory. "If you stall out there, they won't find your bones until spring. You do know that, don't you?"

Sam nearly smiled, thankful that for the first time in two years, he had someone he could call a good friend, someone he felt he could trust. "Tell you what. I'll add you to my will before I leave, if that makes you feel better." He lost any semblance of humor as he recalled what happened inside the hospital's treatment rooms.

Gene led him to the Ford Runabout pickup out front, the key dangling in his right hand. He whistled a soft blues tune, most likely to soothe his nerves. "Hell, *I* don't even drive this baby often. I don't trust other drivers. Ever since the crash, I'm worried about those fools who would throw themselves in front of cars. What morons!"

Sam recalled the chaos of the New York streets when Miriam and he first moved there. "If you thought Richmond was bad, stay out of the northeast. It's perfectly acceptable to operate these things with your eyes closed and mind blank." He couldn't afford a car back then and had only learned when he used the university Studebaker on the winding, hilly streets of northern California.

"Do you want me to join you? It would be helpful, if you're going where I think you're dumb enough to go."

Surprise must have shown on Sam's face as his friend chuckled.

"Fool. I know where you work and yes, I do think your soul is still intact, despite playing for the wrong team. The roads once you leave town aren't exactly big-city quality and signs are as rare as a full set of teeth. If you hit snow, you're a dead man, and so am I if the wife finds out I took your sorry ass out here."

"Do you have a map?"

The bigger man reached into the car, into a slit in the leather cushion. His hand emerged holding a .38. "I have a shotgun in the house too. We'll be needing this more than a map."

"You really think we'll need it?" Sam pulled his own Luger out of his jacket.

"Oh, you're raring to go," Gene said. "And what's with this 'we' talk?"

Sam's head spun with indecision. *He knew he must go where Dejarnette's reach went..*

He exhaled, a sigh accepting his fate, and that of those close to him. "Who's going to mind the store?"

Gene slapped him on the back. "My friend, the most dangerous part of this mission will be in your hands. *You* tell Eliza. The truck will feel a mite lighter without your balls to weigh us down."

74

The two men drove out of Augusta proper by following the main drag, part of Route 11 which would eventually lead to Roanoke. That would happen if they remained on the path more traveled, which stretched out into the morning sun; but instead Gene swung the wheel to the right.

That smooth dirt road reached into flat lands, but also headed up into the heart of the Allegheny Mountains. Sam gazed into the mass of peaks which he had considered ending his life from, just last week. How he could think of such a cowardly act now baffled him. Yet his family and Ruby had seemed so safe, just days ago.

Now, nobody he touched could be considered safe. He felt as if he had stepped out of a bad dream in San Francisco, into something from which he might not be able to wake.

As the town fell into the rearview mirror, the trees engulfed the men and their truck. The road grew thin and the ambient sounds of a bustling morning fell silent. For several minutes, both men sat without speaking, content to contemplate the probable events which would change their lives for better or worse.

"Are you going to speak?" Gene tapped his friend's arm. "Praying for better roads will not work out here."

Sam gulped his emotion down, one he wasn't aware he felt until the other man talked to him. "I wanted to kill him. Yesterday. I wanted to kill both of them."

"Dejarnette?"

Sam pulled his hand into a fist and nearly punched the dashboard. Instead, he slammed it into his thigh. His other hand did the same and rose to grab his hair. He nodded. "He and his other doctor. I haven't felt that urge since the war. Even when I lost *them* two years ago, I felt only numbness. Nothing. But yesterday, I could've taken every sharp object in the building and ripped both men open from chin to balls."

"What did they do?"

"Enough. Enough horrible things—the likes of which I haven't seen since the trenches. Even then, I never wanted to kill any man. I shot my gun plenty then, as we ran for our fucking lives and watched friends get torn in half by machine guns.

"But I never saw where my bullets hit. *If* they hit. I know some hit the Krauts, I'm not stupid, but I never witnessed my own devices end a man's life. Thousands of bullets expended, and I've never known if one killed a son, father, husband, or brother."

Gene looked at some point far off into the road. "I wish I could say the same."

Sam barely heard his words. Normally, he would commiserate and inquire about what plagued his friend's thoughts; but just now, he felt drained and altered by the previous day's events.

"I came here to help," he said in a low tone. "I swear I did. Yesterday I only wanted to end two people's lives, when I saw what they did."

The man placed his hand on Sam's shoulder and squeezed. "Tell me everything. You know my story, but I need to know it all, and you need to spit it out."

When Sam finished several minutes later, both men found further words had vanished.

75

Neither spoke again until Sam thought about the unknowns in the woods and felt unease creep into his being. He wished he were back in town to keep watch on Colin and Ruby.

"Will we be seeing our masked friends again today?"

Sam hadn't been able to get the monstrous masks out of his mind since the other night. Part of it was the images themselves; the rest had to do with the reason they had chosen to visit his house.

Gene tapped on the wheel as he avoided a crater in the road. "I doubt it," he answered in a voice that Sam didn't like. "Like I said, they were early. Too early. The Belsnicklers don't show themselves until Christmas time. Usually the first week of December is when they choose their outfits and masks."

Sam watched the man work the brake and clutch as the road took a sudden rise into the green world before them. *The man had made the sensible choice. Sam would likely have stalled the truck or crashed it already, as the road turned into a series of long switchbacks with the valley falling beneath them.*

"But who are they? Religious zealots? Thugs trying to frighten children and women? Inbred country boys?"

The driver laughed. "How about some, all, or none of the above? It's a German tradition, mostly, that traveled with the immigrants before the Civil War. Hell, I think some of them took the boats over before the flags here turned to stars and stripes. The purists act as the myth states: they're the anti-Santa Claus."

"They give coal?"

"If they're feeling nice. Seriously, they're usually jovial folks in the States, but across the pond, Belsnickel, or Krampus, as he preferred to be called, took his business to the naughty children and introduced them to switches. They learned quickly the benefits of nice over naughty. Some over there still believe the masked men kidnap the bad children and lighten the villages of their troubles."

A plume of smoke rose over the crest of the first peak. *A camp? Small village?*

"Please tell me you're kidding. They didn't really take them, did they?"

The big man stared ahead, focusing on the rough road. "Stories gain power with time, my friend. Who knows what happened in the Bavarian forests? But here, they celebrate the holiday, more often than not. They aim to frighten the children, but their antics can become a game with the adults. They knock on doors during the days prior to Christmas and invite themselves inside. If the family guesses who they are, the Belsnicklers unmask and sometimes give gifts. That is, if the children are good that year."

Sam felt the air chill around him as more plumes rose. When the truck took the turn downwards, he knew it was a place where at least someone lived.

"And if they don't guess?"

"Relax, doctor. They don't leave with body parts. The homeowners simply have to provide dinner and drinks for the crew. Most times, it's become a time of celebrating, though uneasy for many. They don't damage too many kids anymore."

"So why did they visit me? Before Christmas? Was it something about Colin?"

Gene downshifted and held the wheel tight. His eyes squinted to focus on the lack of human activity before him. "No sir. Not at all. With him, the only ones to watch out for work alongside you. Those, and the oddballs who think they're invisible as they slink through the streets in their fedoras."

Dread pressed down on Sam's chest as he recalled the failed chase from outside the movie theater. "You've noticed them? Who are they?"

The man's face darkened with an expression Sam could

not read. "Friend, I'd rather have the Belsnicklers sipping my whiskey in my den any night rather than wonder where those friends of your boss may be on any given day."

He stopped the car just outside what appeared to be a small town. Shacks stood on either side of the road, smoke rising from each, likely from chimneys and stoves.

"I think I'll stay here, but holler if you need a hand."

"What? I don't understand. I don't think these people mind your color. They wouldn't take you for something you're not."

Gene stared ahead, looking at something Sam knew he might never understand. "Maybe, maybe not. Still, if they see one man, they might give you what you're seeking. Two men, one of us might not be going home, maybe even both. They don't trust strangers up here, and shouldn't. You go and look for your answers." He patted Sam's jacket and nodded.

Sam understood and removed the weapon, reluctantly. If they searched him, he might not have a chance to introduce himself with a bullet hole in him.

"Don't worry," his friend said. He slid the three weapons under his seat. "I rarely miss when I need to aim straight."

Sam gave him a half-smile and pushed open the door. He nodded and walked towards the middle of the camp, still not seeing a single person. The clapboard, slat, and partial brick structures reminded him of the Hooverville 'shantytowns' he walked through in New York when he was donating counseling to many of the fallen. These appeared well-built, however, and permanent. The brick would help in the cold mountain winters and the furnaces attached to stoves in the back served as heating. These people exceeded the efforts of those in the Big Apple and in San Francisco by leaps and bounds.

His nostrils flared as he entered the encampment. Sweet and sour mixed with the rank of fresh carcasses. He looked at the tin cooking contraptions which oozed steam and bubbled from their tops and whistled as he passed. Another joined in harmony from the opposite side of the road.

Hanging from one tree was a deer, gutted and skin stretched between a pair of high branches. From another, the reek of smoked meats from another deer and an animal he couldn't identify washed away the blood scent, which always turned his stomach. Everything churned together with a scent he knew too well and hoped it was only from a four-legged creature.

He made it past three shacks before he knew someone was home.

The steel against his neck pricked his skin at the same moment he heard a series of guns being cocked.

76

"I'm not here to hurt anyone," he managed to say as he felt the long blade slide along the back of his neck to touch his throat.

"Oh no," said a gruff voice. "The next thing you'll be telling us is that you don't work for the devils in that hospital."

Shit.

"My name is Sam Taylor. I'm here because of Betty Rowe. I'm trying to help her get back home. She told me she lived out this way."

The blade pressed into his Adam's apple. "You work for the devil."

Gene. Now would be a good time.

"Were you the one who killed my wife?" Those words belonged to a new voice, one who didn't hold the knife yet but by their tone, soon would bring him pain.

"Nobody killed your wife. I just talked to her yesterday. She asked me to find you and tell you about what happened."

A massive man moved into his line of sight. His black hair hung across both eyes but it couldn't hide the hurt and violence within. "You lie. My kin found her late yesterday. Somebody left her like a dog in the park. Left her to rot without a proper burying or blessing."

This couldn't be. Sam recalled her treatment the day before. She might have been operated on, but it wouldn't be fatal. "I don't understand. I talked to her. She told me to find you. I want to help."

The man raised his shotgun. Sam saw deep within both long barrels and felt a fear absent from his life since he last ran across the death fields.

"You want to help? I'll bring you to her and you can ask her how you can help her now."

Without him noticing, the road had filled with people. At least twenty men encircled him, each holding a rifle or hunting knife. Several women and children stood behind them, with many holding a weapon as well.

Sam now hoped Gene would be smart enough to just get the hell out of there.

"Move." The man with the blade at his throat removed it only to press it into his back. They guided him off the road and into a clearing where a makeshift cemetery stood.

Oh no.

He felt the tears before he realized the emotion crippled him. "I'm sorry. I wanted to help."

The big man pressed him down to her grave, marked only by a block of wood with her name carved into it and a smooth stone before it. "Tell her." He sobbed audibly. "Tell her how you're not speaking in the devil's language now."

Sam fought for coherent thought. He knew the wrong words would be the death of him, but at the same time, he knew he truly was to blame. He devised that damn test which helped seal her fate. *But how did she die? And where?*

"Why would I come here if I killed her? Why would I come here unarmed to ask for you?"

The man shrugged ever so slightly and stared at the freshly-turned ground, where the woman he loved would never give her a child or love to him again.

"Leave the man be, please."

Sam turned at the sound of his friend's voice.

Why the hell ...?

"I left my guns in the truck. Go check if you like. This man works at the hospital, but there are many there who don't believe in the demon who runs the hell within it. Listen to him, please."

The villagers surrounded him without sound yet didn't attack.

"You." Betty's husband spoke. "You've given us ammo." He looked him up and down, then back at the truck with the name of Gene's store on the side panel. "We don't take to charity. We paid you back in kind."

"And I thank you for your gifts. My wife cooks the deer into fine steaks whenever you deliver one to my store. She prefers the fowl for her stews, but enjoys all of your kindness."

The man nodded but turned away at the mention of the word 'wife'.

Sam turned to Gene but kept his eyes on the man with the knife, which looked like it could skewer him with ease. "You sell ammunition in a pharmacy?"

Gene shrugged, his eyes feigning innocence. "It's behind the ice cream."

"Oh well, that makes everything just fine then."

"It *is* an 'everything' store, you know." Yet instead of continuing the banter, Gene hardened his stance and placed both hands before him in a placating motion.

"Please listen to this man. I can't help my friends up here if you gut him like the deer you give me."

Sam stared them down, ready to piss himself but refusing to show it.

"If he's truly here to help, then he'll be the one to listen."

Gene moved to Sam's side and pulled him away from the man who held the long blade. "Where can we sit? We'll stay until you know we are far from your enemies. I don't know what we can do to help, but I'll bust my ass to help this man and from what I know of him, God is with him and if he says he tried to save your wife, he did."

They sat inside a large shack, away from the winds, which began to kick up as the weapons lowered. A large woman brought each man a metal cup full of shine, which both Gene and Sam drank in nervous gulps.

"Well buddy, now you know where I get my hootch."

"'Hootch'?"

The bigger man shook his head. "Whiskey, you fool Yankee."

77

Over the course of the next two hours, Sam and Gene sampled more of the villagers' wares, both alcohol and cured meat. Both filled the men with warmth and ease. Betty's husband, Dunn, invited both into his house and sat them on finely-crafted chairs around a round dinner table. The heat from the stove furnace made it so hot that Sam removed his jacket. He felt thankful both men had left their pistols in the truck.

"We had to be careful," Dunn said as he offered more strips of deer to the men. "They keep coming here and to the other towns. They don't consider us mountain folk as humans." He stared at Sam with those words.

"Mister Rowe," he replied with all the respect he could muster, "I'm a psychologist. I help people. I only discovered yesterday what the hospital was doing. I'm not flapping my gums and speaking with the devil's tongue here. It's why I came here today."

Gene patted his knee as if to keep Sam quiet.

"If this man vouches for you, then it's good enough for us. They took Betty from me two weeks ago when I was out hunting. The men were out-waiting a group of deer, trying to get to them before the bobcat or fox chased them off, when someone got off a shot. We knew it was happening again."

"Again?" Sam leaned in closer, feeling sweat bead on his cheek. *These people were anything but 'mud'. The jars of cured meats and harvested grains for breads and other foods showed ingenuity and perseverance, living away from the known in the town below. They chose their lives and made it happen. The selling of the 'hootch' likely netted them enough to build more brick buildings and supplies enough to survive any winter or depression.*

The man stoked the oven with a long iron. Sam knew he wished to drive it through the man who murdered his wife. If he could help this man avenge her, he would. *There just might be a way,* he thought.

"First they put up signs in town offering free 'shots' to help protect the townsfolk through new influenza scares. I didn't know shots came with long talks and scars. Our people ain't slow. We choose to live up here. We've seen what happens when you count on paper to keep you fed and warm. It ain't pretty, what happened to all those city folk, especially the vets who bled for this country.

"Then they listened in the town. They visited the schools, looking for the kids who couldn't read. Kids who had trouble walking right or throwing a ball straight. That blind school has kept the fuckers out of their home, but it won't be long 'til that devil's balls get too big to care."

At the mention of the school, Sam felt for the guitar pick and knew the killing urge would follow. *Dejarnette treated anyone less than him like swine.*

"Go on, please." He drained his cup, not caring that noon still lingered far off in the distance. *The hospital would have to do with a lesser version of him that day.*

"After that, I guess they figured we'd be easy targets. Who would miss the hicks and inbreds? They don't know our ways. They don't know how we marry with the other families and have our own commerce. Most of us go to school. We just don't force the state's ways on our folk.

"One by one, our people would fail to return from school, market, or gathering. Some eventually found their way back. Women who returned were barren. Children had odd scars in places they never should. Men walked without a soul. The sheriff even drove some back to us—in the past. Now nobody returns."

"I'll do what I can. I'll make sure people know," Sam said,

clenching his fist and stabbing the table with his pick, aching for something more lethal. "I have connections. I can make someone listen."

Dunn laughed with tears in his eyes. "Who's gonna give a shit about us?"

"It isn't just you. It's far from just you. America isn't stupid—or full of cowards."

"My people will be watching," he replied. "They always have eyes open. We have kin all over the county and beyond."

The night visitors. Were they from this village?

"I could use more eyes." Sam looked at Gene, who nodded. "If I'm going to go against this devil, I can't do it alone."

"Sir, there ain't only one devil. Just one in this valley. They're springing up from hell all over this land. It ain't a fight easily won—or one a person could win with help."

Sam thought of his mother, Ruby, and Colin. Now he had Gene and Eliza on his team. *All those lives put in jeopardy because of his fight. He never fought for his wife or son, never thought he could help them in their dying moments. That would never happen again.*

As they headed back to the truck, Dunn grabbed Sam by the arm. "When you head back to the devil's lair tomorrow, smell the air by the tracks. Inhale the train as it passes you by, especially when it leaves the grounds. Souls leave a certain tang in the air when they depart the station."

"I will," Sam replied, expecting some superstitious answer. What followed made sense to him and shook him to the marrow.

He didn't hear a word Gene said all the way back into town. Rowe's words haunted him and would until he could find their truth for himself.

78

"You hear me?"

Colin couldn't help but smile at his teacher's words. *Always joking and toying with words, like no one else had ever done with sign language before. And she was so damn pretty.*

He signed "Yes," but focused more on her blue eyes and light brown hair. He thanked God she sat down, so he didn't have to lose focus when her legs walked in front of him.

"I'm serious." He found even her hands sexy. While he liked Chloe, his classmate who witnessed the Indian's murder, he wasn't sure of her feelings. Or if he should like her. With the murder, odd happenings at the baseball game, and with the creepy guy after the movie, he wasn't sure what to feel.

"I know," he replied, attempting his best to be as serious as she. "I need a marketable skill. I need to find my niche. Baseball is my niche."

She shook her head, her face turning to one of frustration. "No! Enough foolery. Baseball won't save your life."

Colin stopped joking. *Why was she being so harsh?* "I like baseball, but I'm not stupid. No one cares to watch a deaf pitcher. Not yet anyway. I want to write."

This time she smiled, yet her eyes still showed something else. "I know you love your stories."

"It's more than that," he countered, wishing to please her. The sun still shone outside the window, even though he sensed a change in the weather. His mother always called him her little barometer, as his head bothered him whenever the New Jersey storms would roll through their area. Storms rarely occurred here, but he suspected they could be fast and deadly anywhere.

"I want to write for the newspapers. Sports, mostly, but I'll take whatever they give me to get a job. Heck, I'll even cover the social events for the rich folk if I have to."

Another smile. This time it was genuine. "Good. That's more like it. I want you to play baseball. I want you to write your stories. The world needs those, but it would truly benefit from your writing in the *Post* or something like that. Don't keep this talent a secret. I won't."

So why did she still look upset? Did Chloe tell her what they saw?

He wanted to, but after the other night, he felt afraid. *Would Sam yell at him? Or would he help him? After all, he chased the weird man down the alley.* His big brother always acted too protective but this time, Colin hoped he would be there if the man returned.

"What's wrong, Ms. Rogers?" He felt a storm coming. This one would be a big one, if his head was correct.

She shook her head and tried to smile again, but failed. She simply looked out the window which overlooked much of downtown. If they had been sitting on the opposite side of the room, his brother's hospital would be highlighted by the fading autumn sun.

"If there's nothing else, I should go. I usually walk Chloe Andrews home."

A tear fell from his teacher's eye.

Oh no. Images of the team who forfeited due to a team member gone missing and the strange man sitting on the train home with Augusta's own champions filled his head.

"She never returned from her break today."

Colin's world broke around him as he watched her lips speak the words he didn't need to hear.

Once a day, the students were given a break from their schedules, for walks, speech therapy, clubs, or just time in the library to relax. Mostly, the teachers hoped the students utilized the time for socialization, an activity most of the deaf and blind avoided.

Even though Colin had been offering to walk the girl home,

he couldn't bring himself to sit across from her in a normal social situation and 'chat'.

Now he might never get that chance.

"Where did she go?" He knew what likely happened, but the words didn't emerge, their reality blocked.

"Colin," his teacher said, slowly but due to her emotion, not his comprehension. "Your brother is a good man. I'm sure of it. I see how he raised you and gave you this new life.

"However, he works for a bad man at a very bad place. They took her."

No. His brother wouldn't work for bad people. He shook his head. *No.*

"I'm sure he didn't know." But Colin could see that she just signed the words. Her face spoke her true feelings. "Most of us don't who is behind the mask until it's too late. That probably happened for your brother. I'm sure he only wants the best for you."

"What did they do to her? What do they do there? Sam said they make people better there. That's his job." Now *he* didn't believe the words he thought and signed, either.

"I don't know, Colin, but for now, I need to show you something. Something you might never need to know. God, I pray you don't, but just in case."

She rose and motioned for him to follow.

"Did you tell her folks yet?" He walked alongside her so he could see her signing.

"No, but the director of the school has called over to the hospital to check. They won't tell us if they have her." She led him down the main hallway and into the stairwell before the gymnasium. "Stay close. You won't be able to see my hands once we're in there."

Colin had a million questions to ask, but the teacher disappeared into the passageway and down the double flight of stairs. A maintenance basement met them, narrow and oppressive with its heat. Faint lighting led the way past massive pipes and something he figured was the boiler or furnace. She twisted and turned like a bloodhound sensing its prize, maneuvering along the walkway. It felt like packed dirt, not even floor beneath them.

Finally, she stopped at the edge of the main plumbing area, in what was likely the center of the school. A doorway emerged in the darkness, nothing really but a slit in the steel walls, behind the array of machinery and pipes. With only the dimmest of illumination, she grabbed for his hand and placed it on a bolt. She pushed his hand and it slid to the right.

With a creak, the door opened before them. Only darkness beckoned ahead.

She reached down and grabbed hold of a lantern. With a quick turn of a wrist, she lit it and in the flickering amber, reached for him again. *He hated the dark. Terribly.* When she pulled him into the blackness, Colin's heart skipped a few beats. The walls slowly closed in on them, as the passageway narrowed to a white point.

Please, just get me out of here, he begged to himself. *I need to find Chloe.*

It smelled like dank pipes and burning oil. Both frightened him, as they signified a possible end to his times with the first girl who ever accepted him for who he was. By the time Ms. Rogers opened a narrow door leading to a thick span of woods just west of the tracks which led out of town, his chest had tied into a slipknot.

"Just in case."

He swallowed, unable to get rid his imagination of worry. "In case of what?"

"This was built back in the Civil War. Both for slaves and soldiers who needed asylum."

"Rebel or Union?"

"Does it matter?"

He shrugged, finally realizing he was crying. *Even if he failed, he would have to at least try and find Chloe, deep within that building which stood like a sleeping monster off to the right.*

79

"Are you sure you want to do this? Kicking the devil in the stones like this?"

Sam smiled the smile of a man on a mission. "He's not the devil. He's simply a man with a Napoleon complex, who thinks he can play God."

Gene didn't return the expression. "I wasn't talking about the doctor. The devil wears many faces. I tell people I'm from the Mediterranean for a reason, you know."

"To save your dark ass?" He hopped from the car, behind the store in the delivery alley. The shadow of the college hid what he took from the back of the truck.

"I grew up reading mythology. Greek, Roman, and other cultures. The nature of evil is that it never lives in just one man. That doesn't feed its power. It spreads like a disease, one that infects whoever it touches.

"Have you read of the hydra? The monster whose head is cut off only to grow two more?"

"Yes," Sam said, feeling the unease his friend intended. "I know the evil doesn't begin or end with Dejarnette. It began long before him and will fester long after someone puts him in the ground."

"Would that be you, friend? You plan to kill the head of the beast?"

Sam laughed without humor. "He is not the head. He just believes he should be. And I'm no killer, despite what I ache to do. I just hope to inform the people about the disease and stop it before it spreads out of control."

"And what if the people believe in the disease?"

"Then we're dead as a nation. I refuse to believe that a country founded on being a patchwork of misfits would take to such a notion."

"Then good luck," Gene said, handing over the Luger. "Stay alive long enough for us to write our own blues."

80

Sam ducked into the store and looked for the telephone. He hoped he could reach his friend, his former trench mate, who owed him as much as Sam owed him back.

He rang the switchboard and prayed whoever picked up cared as much for her family as he did his. *Maybe someone in her bloodline suffered under the reign of the doctor. Maybe a brother or cousin walked some defect or would never read. Possibly he or she would only need glasses to view his or her future mate and that alone would press her to be discreet.*

"Hello," said a sweet yet businesslike voice. "Augusta Bell at your service."

"Washington D.C. please. *The Post,* if you would."

His heart held in his throat as silence boomed back through the earpiece at him. *Did everyone in town work for them?* He crossed his fingers that the Society hadn't infiltrated the private sector yet. *If so, he just sentenced his family to death. At the very least, he might have angered a beast who would bite back with vengeance.*

"*One* moment please. Your name, sir?"

He smiled and squeezed the pick like a lucky penny. "Joe Pavlov."

Another long moment.

"Please hold for the connection. Have a good day, Mr. Pavlov."

"*Washington Post.* How may I direct your call?"

"Bobby Zachary, please. Junior editor."

He heard a series of clicks and felt the anxiety creep back

into his veins. A loud click sent his adrenaline into overdrive.

"Joey Pavlov?" A government-sounding voice filled the line.

"Bobby Gutenberg?" Sam answered just as low.

"Holy shit," the voice said, bursting into laughter. "How the hell are you doing? Where are you? Still on the wrong coast?"

"No, I'm just a few hours from you, but please, call me Joey."

A slight pause sounded on the other end. "Sure thing. Joey. How's life on your end?"

The change in his friend's tone signaled that he understood. When both men were in the war, they often used fake names when on the prowl for female company in the French taverns and towns. Sam joked about his buddy becoming a mistress of William Randolph Hearst, the newspaper magnate. Calling him Gutenberg—the man who invented the printing press—would be a slap to anyone else, thus referring to his friend as a dinosaur and severely old-fashioned hack. However, the man who had protected his blind side on the battlefield time and time again would only smile at the comment.

"Great, Gutenberg. Just swell." Sam hoped the man would realize this was nothing short of pure business this time and had a pencil at the ready. He also hoped that, just like they did over there, his friend would not use his real name. In the war, their mission was to bed any woman who would take them with their fake names and big dreams of the future. This time, the intention was to keep him alive.

He heard a scrabbling—likely fresh blank stationery, and a pencil. "Okay Pavlov, I'm all ears. Tell me about her."

Sam's muscles relaxed, causing him to sink into Gene's office chair, in the back room of the ice cream shop. His legs felt weak and for a moment, he couldn't catch his breath. *If his friend could get just a bit of the word out, especially in the Capitol, maybe someone who could do something would stand up and take notice.*

Maybe, just maybe, they could slay the beast and let Sam and his family, and his new-found love, find safety in this lifetime.

He rambled on, prompted by the only other man on the planet who he fully trusted. Like his false namesake's canine test subjects, he salivated and spat out the story as if his friend had just rang a bell.

A half-hour later, when his story concluded—at least the details Sam knew so far—he heard a whistle and sigh that lasted a bit too long.

Nothing rattled Bobby. The kid grew up in the worst neighborhood in New York City, with gangs ruling his life and nearly ending it several times before his father signed him up for the army.

Although his friend put on a tough face around the newsroom and his army buddies, he lived for his sister and little brother. Every week in the war when mail arrived, his shell broke at the sight of a letter from them, often resulting in laughs or tears, sometimes both at the same time.

Family kept Sam and Bobby bonded and looking out for each other over there and they vowed to stay close once stateside. They did, until Sam lost his own family and cut off communication to nearly everyone who cared for him.

"Listen. If it's too hot for you, I get it. I don't want you to lose your job, or worse."

"Friends over there, family back here. Remember, Pavlov? I promise to talk to my editor before we leave tonight. Nothing scares that ugly motherfucker. He'll eat this story up."

More relief flooded away the adrenaline. "Thanks, Bobby. I owe you."

"Just come and visit me. Take me out so we can find some women with breasts bigger than my pecker and we'll be even."

"Then I'll have to bring you to the toy store again. Some of those dolls there might have an inch on you."

Both men laughed for almost a full minute, mostly to unleash the stress built up inside each of them.

"Good one, Joey."

His voice dropped again. "But listen. I *have* heard whispers about this before. I've just never had enough to go on—yet. You might have given me the editor's job here. More importantly, watch your family. Hug and kiss your mother and give your brother a punch in the arm for me.

"If this is anywhere as big as you or I think it is, we'll either be rich or six feet under come spring. If it's both, make sure they bury me with greenbacks stuffed in my underwear."

"Finally," Sam laughed. "A reason for women to stick around."

They said their goodbyes and Bobby promised to call back after he spoke to his boss. He would call Gene's store directly to avoid suspicion.

With a deep breath, Sam hung up and snuck out the back door. *He needed to get home to his mother and Colin. Maybe he could convince Ruby to move into their guest room until things calmed down.*

Looking both ways, seeing nothing, he crossed the street and jumped into the crowd of college students milling around for lunch. One thought hung in his mind—returning to Western Valley and confronting the man who was ripping apart the countryside with his sadistic agenda.

Maybe he couldn't kill him, but if he could save just one life here, if he could prevent the death of one more person, the risk would be worth nearly anything he could expend.

81

Seated at the front table in Panevino's, the foursome enjoyed their soup and salads while pondering the specials for lunch. Not open to the public until dinner, the restaurant never closed for business meetings and special affairs.

Dejarnette knew that anytime this group visited his favorite establishment, it truly signaled something important.

He turned to see his man walking towards him, briskly but silently entering from the front.

"Was I right?"

The man deflated a bit. Obviously, he was used to breaking his own cases, cracking codes and utilizing the latest surveillance techniques to aid him on the hunt. "Yes, sir. Almost exactly like you predicted."

The doctor looked at his other two companions, Dr. Priddy from Lynchburg and his head surgeon, Dr. Schussler. *Why did Taylor have to dig? Why couldn't he simply enjoy the path to the Nobel Prize with him? If they—no, when they succeeded—the accolades would bury them.*

Yet here, his new hire, his apprentice, sought to halt their progress. Hell, if the news did leak to the masses, maybe they wouldn't *see things the doctor's way. Maybe he would be viewed as a monster.*

He truly felt for the psychologist. Hopefully, he could convince the man from the Society to hold back and let Taylor prove himself, before considering how to kill him.

"Did you take care of the problem?"

The man removed his fedora and sat down to his salad,

the salad which now tasted sour to Dejarnette. "Of course. My companions in D.C. will make sure the doctor's friend sees things our way. I promise."

As his fork jabbed at a cherry tomato, piercing its flesh, the doctor felt a pang of guilt. *He only wished for success and to make the country great again. Death of true Americans should never have to happen, especially when he had to give the order.*

"Problem, Stefan?" The hawkish-looking man often pretended to play team ball, to do what the Society wished, to act as part of one body. But just like him, the leader of the school for the feebleminded donned glasses and appeared nothing like the dream man of the genetically perfect. That and the fact that he was a pompous asshole never failed to rub Dejarnette the wrong way.

"No, of course not," he replied, and wouldn't let on if he were engulfed in flames. These men controlled more of the country than the president. "Just keeping the citizens in the town happy. They don't want to know what's happening—and if they did know, they'd likely shit themselves. Most of them would qualify for treatment in one way or another. The good psychologist's test would catch most of the rest."

The older man narrowed his eyes as he lifted a spoonful of minestrone soup to his thin lips. "My town knows nothing. Stupid mountain southerners. Why don't you just shop at the school next door to you?" He sipped like an elderly man, yet had only just tipped past the age of fifty. "I usually don't have to go far. If they're not already on the grounds, the police or crew simply retrieve who I ask for."

The doctor bristled but clenched hard on his fork so as to not show his frustration. "We're not in the sticks here. These people have civilization, culture."

"For mostly mud folk, maybe."

"We have a reputable college here. Intelligence walks the streets. What the country needs and what we want is already here. It's just mixed in with the shit. Discretion. You should heed it, especially when you're here."

The quartet ordered and ate mostly in silence, save for trite conversation about the food, service, or mild weather.

Dejarnette and his man exchanged glances occasionally during the meal.

"Are you sure?" He mouthed more than enunciated the words as the main entrées arrived. "Yes," came the reply. He wished he could be surer, but they never sent someone less than efficient for him.

"So," Dr. Schussler said, breaking the silence. "Reginald, is it?" He nodded toward the government man who had caught the psychologist breaking the golden confidence, after his return from Monterey, the mud town in the neighboring county.

"Reggie is fine," said the man, resting his fedora on the table. "It's what my mother called me. How's the soup here?"

"Damn good," answered Priddy. "We don't have good Italian food in Lynchburg."

"No good Italians, either," added Schussler.

They laughed openly as Dejarnette called over the waiter. "Soup for me, too. New chef?" The flavor of the thick sauce hung in his mouth as he spoke. He wondered if he could have it delivered to the hospital during work hours.

The dark-haired man with a towel and tray in his hands shook his head but waved for the owner. A taller man resembling the first approached the table. "A problem, doctor?"

"No, no, Julio. We were just talking about the soup and I noticed even the salad had an extra kick to it. Tell me, what can I have my wife do to replicate this?"

The man wrinkled his face a bit, but smiled once he mulled his thoughts over. "First, I shall tell you that the Marsala is my best ever. I think it would be a fine compliment to the soup, or salad."

"You didn't make the soup, did you?" Priddy smiled, poking fun at the man, but quickly caught himself. "I think some veal Marsala would be a great dinner. Perfect to complete a nice lunch."

"I have a new prodigy, so they call her, from the coast. One of the best schools." He inhaled, whistling on the exhale. "It's an experiment, but she's cheap. She follows my recipes to the T."

"Obviously not," Reggie said. "I haven't met a woman who could cook well until today. Is she as beautiful as she is talented?"

Julio stiffened once again. "She's not bad. I keep her away from the main entrées so far, but she might learn from me."

Dejarnette examined the man, then his own hired hand. "Well, one day you'll have to let us meet this fine culinary sweetheart."

"One day," the owner muttered. "For dinner," he clapped his hands. "What shall you have?"

The men discussed the progress of their plans, over two orders of Marsala and a pair of manicotti dishes.

"Are you optimistic about reaching the 10 percent that Grant and Davenport suggested?"

Dejarnette waved him off. "Fuck Davenport. He's a sociopath who treats everyone like a lab rat."

"But his census work," Priddy said. "It's given us so much leeway. Think about it. I know you have. Entire families, catalogued for generations, and they believe it's simply for the good of the country."

Dejarnette poked his veal. "It *is* for the good of the country. I think we're close to the 10 percent in our region. Most of the patients have no idea what's happening. The influenza scare is still in their memories. The shipments still arrive for us and the next phase has begun to take hold."

Priddy grinned at his colleague. "I think we've already hit the second round of the reaping now. It's a little easier down in the Blue Ridges. No one really cares what happens around there and the people are too dumb to notice. The trains come in from Charlotte, Nashville, and elsewhere each month. I've been told that a bonus might be headed my way ... if my percentages top my northern neighbors."

"The hell with you and your numbers. We're trying to qualify our work here, make it replicable instead of blindly force the quantities. If this test can help prove our point, others will follow the lead."

Both Schussler and Priddy chuckled. "And how did you land your fine psychologist again?"

Dejarnette lifted his glass of water, wishing it were his scotch. "Skill and opportunity, my friend. The boy needed salvation and affirmation. He could've languished in obscurity and depression after his loss, or come to work far away from his troubles. The Society simply made the offer for me."

"Why not go to Cold Spring Harbor? Doesn't he come from there?" Reggie looked at Dejarnette, tapping a finger on the table.

"He wanted a home, not a laboratory. He's what we want. He's one of us." The words stung inside him and he prayed that his protégé would realize how foolish what he had done that day could be. *He admired the man's sense of family and heart. He only hoped it wouldn't be his downfall.* "Also, a key string pulled here or there might have convinced him to leave the cold world of research behind." He flashed a smart smile, hoping his unease failed to emerge.

82

When the men had finished their meals and readied themselves for transportation back to the hospital and train station, one lingered behind, excusing himself to use the restroom.

As he emerged, he passed the kitchen. With the men leaving, the staff would work to ready the restaurant for the dinner crowd. The odor of a sumptuous red sauce permeated the air as he breathed in. While the people in the kitchen themselves existed little above the primitive rung on Darwin's scale, they could definitely cook. Part of him hoped he was wrong about his gut feeling; the dining here would soothe his nerves on many a night. He pretended to peruse the artwork adorning the walls near the staircase leading to the second floor of the dining room, until she exited.

"Hello." He smiled at the young beauty who stepped out to help bus the tables.

She returned the smile and went about her business.

"Great soup today."

She halted, and then continued setting the tables around the room. "Thank you. It's a start."

He edged towards the door, making as if he awaited a friend to honk outside. He didn't wish for her to feel uneasy around him. "What's your specialty? I think if it's anything like the soup, or what you did to the salad, you might scare poor Julio out of a job."

The blush filled her olive-tinged face, perfectly formed in a mostly-round shape, yet she held her eyes downward. "My Pomodoro would be the hit of the restaurant, if he allows me to showcase it. I also knock out a special scampi which would surprise most people in this town. I doubt many here have had good seafood—yet."

Her words stuck in his head. Not the words themselves, but how she said them. They reminded him of something he'd suspected earlier when he noticed her walking around town.

"Have you worked here long?"

She examined him, possibly for his motives, but then hung her head again to straighten the table cloth. "A few weeks. I cook breakfast for the blind and deaf school in the mornings, mostly for the staff. Three days a week, Julio is training me to become one of his junior chefs." Even though her eyes wouldn't meet his, the pride in her voice rang strong.

Why waste such time and life?

"Well, I can put in a good word with the owner if you like. Doctor Dejarnette has some strong pull in this town. There's nothing wrong with two great chefs in one restaurant. Think about it."

He left her smiling as he noticed his boss waiting by the car.

"Trying to score a good time with soup lady?"

Reggie smiled. "Not quite, but I have a feeling we'll be seeing more of her soon."

The doctor gave him one of the smiles which signaled that he realized his main man had discovered something else which would help him find success.

"Should I ask?"

"Don't worry," Reggie said, losing his smile as he thought ahead to what would likely have to be done. He also would have to make a call to find out how their other problem fared. "Your exploring friend will likely help solve a few problems."

"Are you coming back to the office with me?"

He shook his head. "Maybe there're a couple of errands I need to run before I join you. I think I might get the recipe from the owner before I return to the land of the mundane."

The doctor smiled again. "Somehow, Reginald, I doubt your life is ever mundane for long."

Very true, my friend, he thought. If his calls revealed what he believed, boredom would not find him for quite a while.

83

Sam burst through the front doors of the main building. Neither Doris nor Gwen met him at the offices, so he walked around Dejarnette's office, frustrated he couldn't punch anyone. Far from a fighter, he still burned to punish the man. He also began to understand the unsettling feeling building underneath his own skin.

He knew his decisions along his life path had led him here. He could tell himself that he was one hundred percent innocent and ignorant of the real nature of the movement. He'd arrived believing his presence and effort could divert the Society's views into something more positive. He felt they would do the right thing, help who needed to be helped, and help build this country into the powerhouse it needed to be, while bending down to embrace those who needed a hand in guiding them towards success. Instead, he deceived him by what he wanted to see, needed to see.

Anxiety built as his flesh crawled with invisible bugs, he dropped into the doctor's immense leather chair to gather his senses. Piles of papers adorned the oaken desk in too-neat stacks, likely left there by Doris. *Maybe she sent out his reports to the Society and to Grant monthly, or maybe he simply called them when news needed to be shared.*

One by one, he found himself digging through the piles and found only his own reports and those of Maclin, the bastard who'd seemed to revel in the barbarity of the treatments he witnessed yesterday.

The drawers were next. He took careful time to examine the scant contents of each. Surprisingly, none of them were locked.

All slid open with ease, but revealed nothing of note.

Except for one. A thin parcel with a stamp he recognized but could not understand. He picked it up and read the return address. *But why? It just didn't make sense.*

He nearly tore it open, but desperately needed to be on the move. Theo's death still plagued him. The man didn't seem to be one to end his life, not before discovering some bit of justice. Defeat had never shown in the man's eyes, even when it had seemed likely he would not leave Western State anytime soon.

He would take Dejarnette apart piece by piece somehow, until he secured peace and safety for his family. For now, he needed to visit the dormitories again. He must have missed something the first time.

As he exited the building, it still stood empty. *Where was everybody? Lunch?* Maybe most employees spent their free time out in the gorgeous grounds. He envisioned his secretary and Dejarnette chatting about him and how he would be the hospital's fool, as it coasted towards a goal he could not see.

The air tasted different on the hospital campus than it did in Monterey, the mountain town whose name he'd learned once he left. Long gone were the maple and meat scents. Here existed sterility, and a smell Sam could only describe as decay.

He walked first to the dormitory he hadn't yet visited. The reason was simple: a good portion of Western Valley still stood as it originally had, a century prior. Built as both a hospital and resting place for those who needed hospice care or recuperation from life itself, usually paid for by the well to do, about half of the patients still fit that bill. Sam wondered how many of them were treated; gently, by Dejarnette, or did any mental frailty place a person on the list?

The Staunton House held these affluent, safe patients, the ones who walked the campus freely and without locks or armed guards. A smiling man dressed in orderly whites, not the guard grays, met him at the front desk.

"Doctor Taylor," he said, nodding in respect. "Can I help you?"

Sam felt a bit put off as he wasn't expecting to be recognized. However, Dejarnette was nothing if not efficient.

"Just concluding my tour," he said. "Somehow, this building never made it onto my list."

The man held a sheaf of papers—likely the meal requirements of the patients instead of security measures. He grinned as he nodded again. "Nobody ever comes here, even the families. They meet their mothers, sisters, daughters, and sons, whoever, out in the front. Nobody wants to be reminded where they really are. Are you here for a look?"

"Sure," Sam said, but he knew nothing would be learned inside these walls.

The man waved him along. "So," he said as the psychologist passed. "Have you been making much headway with the loonies since you've been here?"

Sam nearly spun on the man and launched into him, but held his tongue.

"Of course. The one inside the rooms or the ones running the joint?"

84

He walked up the first flight of stairs and looked down the hallway. For a moment, he thought himself to be back in New York, at the Roosevelt or another high-class hotel. Light fixtures in ornate designs jutted out between rooms and the carpet lay plush in oriental styles. Most doors stood shut, but he found a few unoccupied rooms.

A far cry from where he once walked with Theodore, this wing spoke old money. He pushed open the door and whistled. A full-sized bed faced the double window, giving a gorgeous view of the northern valley. He could imagine how the sun broke into pieces through the panes both at sunrise and sunset. As the buildings faced north and south, no one would feel bereft of such a therapy. The rest of the room filled the profile of a high-class hotel, not an asylum which seemed hell-bent on becoming the poster child for the new eugenics movement.

Shaking his head, he turned and left.

It was time to revisit the true housing.

A new guard stood upright at the desk when Sam approached the westernmost building, just east of the train tracks. The odd, small fortress-like structure stretched into the air just across from them, filling Sam with an unease he couldn't figure.

"Who are you here to see?" The guard's stiff voice took him aback.

"I'm Doctor Taylor." He found himself digging in one pocket for security ID and with the other, pointed at the man. "Nearly all of my patients are in this ward. Superintendent Dejarnette wants me to conduct my therapy both in the office and follow up back where they reside."

"Really?" This time the guard almost smiled. "Somehow, I doubt you'll find much success today."

Son of a bitch. Why do all these guards have such a big balls complex? Sam never made anyone else feel like a lesser man, or woman, so he didn't understand when others let their insecurities overtake them.

He swallowed his pride, despite the anger seething within him from the morning's events, but the call he made to his friend gave him a little swagger.

But when he sauntered past the guard and down the long, dismal hallway, he felt as if he were the castrated one.

The guard looked up as a low roar sounded from outside. He shook his head with a look Sam couldn't figure out. *No point in asking.* He would have better luck with any of the patients, who likely knew volumes more about the goings on than the guard did.

Yet he realized with each progressive step that any revelations would have to wait until another day.

Nearly every room lay empty.

He spent several minutes running up and down the stairs, the halls, searching for his patients whom he'd tested. Only three remained, and seven patients total filled the sixty rooms.

"Where'd they go? What did he do to them?"

The man's face remained stone. "Treated. They left. They always do. One way or another."

"The lucky ones went to work up in the mountains to help out our CCC boys."

"And the others?" Sam recalled the scant details he remembered about the Society's view of the future North America.

"Like I said, one way or another."

85

Reginald saw the teacher leaving the school by the front door and as the sun set, he stood cloaked in shadow. *It truly was a beautiful school. Too bad they wasted it on the defectives. It would be a great school to focus on those headed to college and further the future.*

The beautiful woman would head to the immense staircase which led down into the parking lot and then branched off into two side streets. She surely lived in one of the smaller houses there, or in an apartment on top of one of the many storefronts on Augusta Street.

As he waited near the trees adjacent to the stairs, he smiled. He had no use for defectives, no matter how pretty they might be. Still, he despised violence against women. When he relieved Betty Rowe of her burden, he made sure it was as painless as possible. She likely never even felt the pick.

Yet the plan changed. She began walking towards the dorms. He knew that some advisors lived on campus. *This was not good. He must reach her before clearing the shadows. Over a hundred children and twenty adults, including some strong men, lived in that building.*

Why didn't he know she lived there?

Because he had been enthralled with the woman in the restaurant. A woman who could cook like that, maybe there was a way ... There always was an exception to the rule. Maybe if he met her again.

"Excuse me, Miss?"

The teacher didn't respond in the manner he intended, or

could have predicted.

The blonde's eyes widened when she saw him, and she ran for the front door. A former sprinter for George Washington University, he caught up to her before she reached the light of the entrance.

Why do the stupid ones always run?

"Excuse me! I just needed to ask you a question. I'm not here to harm you."

"Go fuck yourself," she said.

He laughed. "I didn't know deaf people could curse like that."

She slipped one hand into her purse. *Possibly a blackjack or pocketknife.* Another smile.

"I just needed to get a message to the boy, that's all." He tried his hardest to sound sincere. *The message would be for his brother.*

"Call his brother," she said in that imbecile voice. "He's one of you. Pretty simple to get in touch with." She picked up a rock from the ground and tossed it at one of the lower windows. He had to leave before someone came outside.

"Can you bring him outside? Please?" He began walking towards the school in a semi-circle, hoping to cut her off. Just then a car pulled around the corner, a black sedan. She spooked, obviously thinking whoever it was must be a crony of his. It wasn't.

She turned and, in that moment, he moved in and blocked the entrance.

In a flurry of movement, she bolted for the front of the school, hoping to find safe haven within. Whoever drove the car stopped by the dorm, oblivious to the encounter just out of sight. He caught her in less than two seconds. Grabbing her by the arm, he immobilized it as he saw what she had been attempting to recover from her purse.

A .22 pistol.

"Stupid girl. I just wanted you to give the boy a message."

She kicked at his balls, but he deftly turned, taking a painful blow to the knee. "Like you gave to Chloe? Is she in your sick hospital, too? All cut up before she could grow into a woman?"

The man honestly felt confused. *He wouldn't have done that.* "Shh... I didn't take any girl. I don't do that. Someone else might have. Might even have been her parents, hoping she wouldn't spread her deaf legs for someone in your school."

He didn't want to hurt her. Not a woman.

The woman spat at him. "Your kind should be the ones who are sterilized. You're evil." He felt nervous as her voice rose. *So beautiful, almost like the restaurant girl, but she knew what was behind the curtain.*

"I'm not evil," he said, taking hold of her other arm and stepped on one of her feet. "I'm only helping to clean up America. Now I'm going to have to find that kid myself. I really wanted to be home reading tonight. There goes that plan."

Her expression spoke of confusion. He gently turned her with his fingers on her neck. With a flick of his wrist and push of his opposite forearm, he shoved her backwards down the forty mortared stairs which led to the fields. She never screamed.

Since she didn't give up Colin's whereabouts, her fate was one he could accept.

The unfit never failed to surprise him. This one talked like a human.

Yet somehow, even though her fall was without a death wail, the windows above began to light up. Someone had heard the scuffle. He ducked back into the shadows and headed towards the hospital.

86

"So, you're the new lady of the valley?"

Sam and Ruby turned red simultaneously. "Mother. She's just as new as you, almost."

Bridget Taylor fully enjoyed playing with her son, embarrassing him at any turn. "Sorry, Ruby. It's the Irish in our family. We're always picking on one another. Is your family demented as well?"

Ruby turned to the kitchen. "I can help you serve, if you'll let me."

"No, no." Her voice softened. "Samuel told me you're here by yourself. I didn't mean anything. I just was wondering where your family is now."

Ruby put on her best face and lied like Sam knew she could. "They're back in Italy, both parents. I came here for an opportunity I would never have there." *So, a truth wrapped in a lie.*

Gene guided her to a chair in the dining room. "Please. You kiss bureaucratic butt all morning long and then let some chef much less talented than you take credit for your concoctions." He motioned for her to relax next to him.

She brightened at his words. "You've eaten at Panevino's?"

He nodded. "Ever since I've moved here. I heard about the new blood and slipped in last weekend. I think you'll take the town by storm once that fool allows you to shine a little."

She placed her hand on his. "Thank you." *With those eyes,* Sam mused, *it was no wonder she had to flee across the state to escape the husband.*

"Any word on your uncle yet? I can ask the sheriff if you like. He owes me quite a few favors."

Sam could see that her eyes threatened to spill, so he diverted her attention with a whisper. "Dinner should take us until nine. Dessert until you begin to snore." She slugged him in the arm and grinned.

"Thank *you*."

He leaned in and kissed her while the other women were still in the kitchen. "Anything for my lady of the valley. Now when you go in there," he nodded towards the room where the magic happened, "go easy on them. You have a southern woman and an Irish bulldog in there. They know you can run circles around them and will likely carve you into their stew."

"I've dealt with worse back home."

Gene and Sam laughed. "I sure hope you haven't. Good luck."

They took their places on the back porch, guitars in one hand and hootch in the other.

"How are you holding up?" Gene clinked his glass with Sam's. "You've had a hell of a day."

He listened to Sam detail what he'd told his *Post* buddy and the growing oddity that was his workplace and only nodded with each turn of the story. He acted as if he expected every detail.

"Yeah, I'm fine," Sam said. "I'm just worried about Colin and her. Hell, even my mother, but I'd like to see Dejarnette or his goons try to tangle with her."

"Salut." They drank again, looking out into the back yard and seeing nothing but what should be there.

His friend sat up and focused. "Hey. Where is the little man?"

Sam's anxiety kicked up again. *Was his brother home?* He raced inside and burst into the kitchen. "Where's Colin? Why isn't he down here?"

The trio of females looked at him as if he had given *himself* a lobotomy.

His mother stepped forward. "He had baseball practice today, again. I think they're working him too hard, but he likes it."

Relief washed over him, but the anxiety had never fully abated since that night in the hospital room over two years ago. "Is he joining us, or penning letters to his new belle?"

"Well," she said, "after your boss dropped him off, he walked in without uttering a word and headed for his books. At least, I think that's what he did."

The cold turned into an avalanche within his veins. *"Who* dropped him off?"

"Colin said he was your boss, but he didn't stop in. He did say to thank you for cleaning up his office and hoped you had a relaxing afternoon."

My God. How did he find out? "Colin!" He pounded on the wall.

Nothing.

He called again and bounded up the stairs, blood thumping in his chest. He found his little brother stretched out on his bed, without a book in his face. "Are you okay?" The boy stared at the ceiling for several moments before audibly breathing. As he spoke, he still didn't turn to face his brother.

"They took her."

"Who?" But both he and Gene knew the answer. They just needed to hear it before going after him. "What did he do to you?"

The teen finally turned his head and stared at his brother with a hurtful look. "Him? Nothing. He told me he was looking forward to my next baseball game. I told him I should quit since Chloe disappeared, but he told me I'd be a fool to waste such talent."

He returned to staring at the ceiling. "I know she's somewhere at the hospital. Maybe the man doesn't even know it yet. Can you find her?" The pain in his voice brought Sam's heart up to his chin.

"If she's there, buddy, I'll bring her home. The hospital sometimes runs tests on people. I do it, too."

"That's what he said," the boy replied, stiffness entering his hand movements. "He said you invented the test that a doctor might want to use on her. Is that true?" The expression on his brother's face said it all. "If so, please go to hell."

Sam left him up there while Ruby brought him a plate of chicken and potatoes for dinner. He brought her outside to let her know where he was going, despite her protests, but she insisted he return to take her home for the night. She was a bright one, Gene's look said. He couldn't do anything too dumb if his entire family expected him back home and needed him there.

"Do you want me there?" Gene motioned to the car where the three weapons still sat.

"No," Sam said. "I need to find out from him what's true and how much he's yanking my dick. If it's the former, I might have to kill him soon. If it's the latter, I might let you do it."

After Gene promised to watch over the family until he returned, Sam packed the Luger and marched off towards the house where the monster lived.

87

Sam stormed through the streets but didn't run. He needed to keep his head, for now. When he knocked, he sucked in a big breath. The door to the massive Victorian on Beverley Street opened to display a pale but beautiful woman of indeterminate age. She appeared to be under the influence of some substance. Sam suspected opium or laudanum. *Dejarnette likely indulged himself as well.*

She mumbled something, but stepped aside for Sam to enter the house. She wore a flowing gown that had no place in Augusta, or inside a house such as this in October. Possibly she could have waltzed her way into many a man's heart in Paris, but in the land of the southern belles, she looked severely out of place.

"Doctor!" He heard his voice echo off the high walls, covered in artwork he should have known but didn't. A long staircase led up the side of the massive foyer to a landing. The woman turned from him and climbed the steps, obviously uninterested in his visit. A door slammed shut from the second floor, yet he couldn't see who caused the noise.

Who was up there?

"Dr. Taylor," spoke a voice off to the left. The superintendent walked in from the parlor and gestured for Sam to sit. In his arm sat a small dog, most likely a purebred. *Just as he preferred all his company.*

"Stay the fuck away from my family."

"The boy needed a ride home. I just happened to be there." He smiled an innocent smile at his employee. "You raced over here just for that?"

"You know why I'm here. I talked to them."

The man sat and lowered his gaze to the animal. "Yes," he answered. "Of course you did. I heard you were going to do so and after your behavior in the hospital yesterday, I wasn't surprised. I was only saddened."

Saddened? Why? Did he realize how sick he appeared to Sam? "This isn't what I signed up for and you know that. Those people have been brutalized."

"You also went back to the dormitories. Why?"

"To find out why you shipped them out. Where are they? You asked me to test them and I did! Where are they?"

The superintendent only looked at him patiently, as if this were a chess match. "We treat them and they move on, either going home or on to more intensive facilities. Others' conditions deteriorated, and they are now members of the white ward."

"I want to see them."

"Of course. You're my psychologist." The man sounded sincere, almost. "You know I need your help. Without your testing, the work of this place loses all validity."

True, Sam thought, but he burned with his initial purpose.

A serving set sat off to the side, unused. On the platter, next to the creamer, stood a decanter which Sam suspected held a fluid much more potent than tea or coffee.

Dejarnette sighed. Sam wondered if one of them would die before the night was over.

"Who's upstairs?" He asked, not diverted from his mission, but curious if there was someone else in the house.

The man only looked at the ball of white fur—which sat comfortable and content in this madman's hands.

"I'm sorry to hear about your friend. I heard he earned a medal in France. They'll likely give him a superior service."

The world tumbled away from Sam and his legs felt as if someone ripped the bones from within them. "What?" No. I just talked to him ...

The doctor gazed upstairs to ensure his wife had not been eavesdropping. "It's sad, really, to die of a good news tip. My friend in D.C. said he must have been mugged by one of those mud people on the dole. Likely stabbed by a stolen knife behind the *Post*'s building.

"Wait," he inflected a caring note in his voice. "Don't tell me you haven't kept in touch? It's tragic when one of our own is taken." He petted his precious dog, which licked his hand.

Sam leaned into the seat across from him. "How did you do it?" He already figured they'd heard the phone call and didn't care. *If it hit the headlines, even Grant might have to cut him loose, and lives would be saved. Maybe the patients would find real treatment. Most of the country still believed in helping those in need of psychological help, especially after the war.*

The man shrugged, embracing the animal. He refused to meet Sam's eyes. "I'm not a monster, Sam." His voice didn't break, yet it didn't have the steel it usually held, either. "I warned you. I did." He stroked his poodle a bit harder, holding it tighter.

"You killed him." Sam burned to return the deed right then and there. He noticed the heat rising into his neck, across his face. *His buddy, his trench friend who survived racing through razor wire into a blizzard of gunfire time and time again, had been killed by a knife on the street.*

Because of him. *He was the reason Bobby's wife and kids now had nobody.*

"The Society has people who watch. I warned you. Grant doesn't fuck around. The money trail—Carnegie isn't the only one. You know that. Kellogg. Wells. You name the industry and one of its icons funds the movement. Nobody in this country wants us to fall behind the others. Europe wants to bury us. So does Scandinavia. Hell, everyone outside of the mud races wants in and knows it takes greenbacks."

"Money killed your friend. Even if he published the story, it would never have hit the streets. If he brought it to FDR, he likely wouldn't leave the grounds with his job intact. America can't fail, but it's teetering right now. The wallets that are keeping us afloat won't let them win."

The guitar pick Sam gripped dug into his left hand so hard he knew blood, not sweat, flowed into his palms. He wished for the bayonet he ran with in France, although he'd never felt it pierce another's flesh. This night felt like a good time to start. "You are nothing but a little man, a puppet."

Dejarnette ignored the barb, continuing to avoid eye contact. He had no compunctions about watching his patients die as they were 'treated', yet when faced with a supposed equal, he wilted. "You want to kill me. I know that. But like the hydra, another head would only emerge. Trust me on that."

"You don't believe that, do you? I've researched the hell out of you. You *are* eugenics, just as much as Davenport is. You'd never relinquish your hold on Western Valley. Davenport is a sick fuck, but you, you are building your empire here. I'd be killing a king if I chose to—at least someone who thought he was. You killed my friend and that boy—and god knows who else?

"For what?"

The bespectacled man finally looked up and met Sam's eyes. Something cold lived there. "For what? You're not stupid, but you sound like a fucking imbecile now. Maybe dirtying your pecker in that mud woman has diseased your brain."

Dejarnette never saw the fist coming. It broke a tooth, one that would be tough to replace. He spit blood into a handkerchief he pulled from his blazer without disturbing the dog.

"Go ahead. Insult her again and I'll bring down your wife to watch you bleed onto this nice rug."

The man's eyes flittered. "No." He nearly rose but knew he would lose any leverage. Instead, he gathered himself and tried another tactic.

The man beckoned Sam with a shaking hand toward another door. He opened it, displaying a massive office. Shelves of books rose from floor to ceiling, oaken chairs placed in front of a desk which was covered in files. A thick envelope sat on top of a pile.

"Have you ever heard of the Rosicrucians?"

"Don't play dime-store psychologist with me. What the hell are you hiding?" Red filled his vision as he rose to his feet.

Dejarnette stood as well, blocking Sam's way. "They've existed for centuries, steeped in alchemy, and believe in several odd concepts. However, one has eluded many scholars who choose to not see it. The order believes in keeping the population in line with what nature can provide. Do you think this country is providing, given what has happened this century?"

Sam examined the library, sparse, save for the books. *Why did the man have files here at home? Society experiments? Sam knew of talks for measures of eugenics that he had only heard whispers. The package. Stamped with a slew of colored international markings.*

Sam's head spun with the notion that his boss was operating on a belief he had never heard of before this night. *Is this why he was hell bent on the sterilization? The halting of 'lesser' citizens from reproducing, or even living?*

"Who's upstairs? I don't give a shit about some freaks of the occult."

The man stepped back onto the first of the flight of stairs, hands raised. "They believed that to ensure balance in nature, a certain number of people had to be held in check. If tipped, the world would fail and its systems, natural and societal, would crumble."

Blood dripped from the man's mouth as he spoke, yet he made no attempt to staunch its flow. "We have to give the earth the best of what we can offer, not the excrement of our DNA."

"Who. Is. Upstairs?" Sam shoved the man aside without awaiting the answer he knew wouldn't come.

"Wait," the man called in a fractured tone. "Tamara cannot handle another episode. You must leave her. Please leave them alone."

"Them?" Sam burst to the top of the landing. "What the hell are you hiding up here?"

"Stop!" The man's tone changed to one of panic. "If you go further, I cannot guarantee your family's safety."

Sam halted. "You're *threatening* me? My family? I'm supposed to believe anything you say after you had my friend killed today?"

Dejarnette didn't even bother to reach the top of the stairs. "If we keep culling, the ten percent from the bottom will be removed. We need to keep at it. Davenport's doing it, Lucien's reaping his herd down in Lynchburg—successfully yet primitively—and I need to do so also if we're going to rise above the others."

Sam allowed his eyes to peruse the florid walls. A trio of portraits adorned the walls: one of Dejarnette, one of his wife, looking much more alive and beautiful, and a third, of the couple.

A whimper sounded behind the closed door to his left. The echo sounded off the other doors on the second floor. All were shut tight.

He saw his hand grip the knob on the left and turn. *Locked.* A set of double bolts existed above the knob. Sam threw back both and tried the knob once more. It went with the motion of his fist.

From behind him he heard, "Please don't. If you leave now, I promise you will never again need to worry about your brother, or your friend in town."

Sam felt his other hand, the bloodied one with the guitar pick embedded in it, clench and raise towards the doctor. "I've learned how you treat my friends." And he pulled open the door.

The man howled as Sam entered the room, walking towards the son who had likely spent most of his life hidden from the world. *Now he understood. Now, it all made sense.*

When the boy stepped out from behind the dresser, Sam felt his fists fall. Tears soon followed.

He would never forget the boy's face.

88

Sam walked home in a daze, understanding yet not compre-hending. All he knew was that he had to get Ruby out of his godforsaken town. *His family as well.* Images of the Society filled his head. *They formed in Chicago, San Francisco, New York City. Their tendrils crept as far as the money would allow.*

As he turned the corner to find himself on his street, his legs gave out, muscles failing him as the revelation hit home.

Even if they left, the movement would only grow.

Even if he killed Dejarnette, the Society would go on without him. Without either of them.

He could never beat them. He could only escape.

When the superintendent realized Sam had stolen the parcel from his desk, he would soon become an enemy who would make the Kaiser seem like a long-lost brother.

89

After checking in on his mother and Colin, Sam parked himself on the front steps. He nearly reached for the bottle behind the guitar case on the back porch, but wanted to think clearly, no matter how fate appeared to tear at his seams.

Sometime later, a sharp tap on the shoulder nudged him. He shook himself from the thoughts of his warped reality. The smiling face who had loved for thirty-three years looked down at him with a plate of cherry cobbler, his favorite comfort food. She handed it to him and looked down the street before closing the door behind her. She knew, and while she would never voice it, accepted where he would find peace that night.

Before heading to his destination, he walked next door, where he found his neighbor already perched on the stoop. An empty plate sat next to him.

"Your mother scares up some great grub," Gene said, tapping the crumbs.

"She loves making magic in the kitchen more than most women love their husbands," Sam replied, dropping down on the stair below him. "Since she's been a widow for a long time, I think we're either all in trouble or set to battle Taft for this country's girth record."

The neighbor chuckled but raised his eyes to Sam's. "Do you still have a boss? Or will I have to help you get on the lam?"

Sam's hand reached for a glass which wasn't there, so it fondled the tortoiseshell pick again. The guitar would be a suitable intoxicant yet neither his nor his friend's stood nearby. He shook his head. "The bastard's still breathing." He inhaled sharply. "His skeletons outweigh mine, though. By a long shot.

I don't know how to do this. This was a mistake."

"Coming here?"

He tapped the pick on the railing. "I don't know. I just wanted to start over, to give my mother and Colin a life worth living. I wanted to outrun my ghosts."

"Go to her now," Gene said. "I know you're headed there anyway and *you* know she's expecting you. Something tells me she'll be needing you if she stays around here."

"What do you mean?" Yet he knew. *The census. The Society. The past. They couldn't outrun everything.*

A big dark hand rested on his, gripping in friendship but something else. "Go now. I'll keep watch here, best I can. Come back for the game tomorrow. We have a job to do afterwards."

Sam stared at him. "What Rowe said."

His friend nodded.

The night would reveal its secrets to them, secrets that he wished didn't exist.

"After the game, here."

"Comfort yourself tonight, my friend. You need a clear head for this."

As Sam rose to head towards Augusta Street, he wondered if a clear head would be a blessing or a curse during the coming days.

90

Ruby answered the door without question and did not prompt him for explanation. Still, he told her much, especially about the blue boy.

Without much talk at all, she led him first to the kitchen—where she fed him a cup of coffee and a pastry she must have baked while waiting for him—then to the bedroom. She helped him undress, but did little more than kiss him once on the cheek and once more on the lips. The only true help she offered, other than food, was to allow him to spill the events of the night until he dropped, empty, onto the bed.

He fell asleep in her embrace and drifted off deeper into the nightmares of the day. They pulled and picked at him with angry fingers until he broke through to consciousness sometime in the depths of the night.

When he turned from Ruby, Miriam stood at the foot of the bed. As in any marriage holding years of depth, words would never be necessary. She climbed under the sheets and pressed herself to him. Her cool flesh molded to his in a manner he could not remember occurring when she existed in reality.

She didn't require sex that night, yet he would have given her his world. She simply held him as he wept, with the woman he was falling for half a mattress away.

91

Sam vomited as he dressed for work the following morning. *How could he return to his place of work knowing what occurred there daily?*

Thankfully, the vile fluids missed staining his starched shirt and gray trousers. He wiped a speck of white off his left shoe, aware of its intrusion on his appearance.

Was this how Dejarnette viewed the 'unfit' in his world? Blights he must clean up to improve his country? If so, how safe was Colin? Ruby? Hell, even Gene faced the man down once and even though sterilized, the superintendent might now view him as a dangerous extension of Sam.

He couldn't allow any of that to come to fruition. He lived with the guilt that he'd failed his wife and child. Failure to protect his remaining family and new friends would doom him to a deeper, personal hell from which he knew he would not recover.

The October wind brushed his face, softly yet with an occasion bite he swore felt like broken razors on his skin. A far cry from the weather gauntlets he used to face in New Jersey and New York, it still urged him to hurry his step. His brain countered that impulse, wishing to postpone the inevitable, for the confrontation would likely end in disaster, for one man or the other.

The quiet guard, whose name Sam had yet to learn, manned the gate but failed to acknowledge his passing. *Did Dejarnette give him orders not to address him? Possibly the man simply knew the psychologist was now a cog in the devil's machine and accepted, or even now, feared him.*

For a moment, he hesitated before the main building. Half of him wished to let Dejarnette know of what he had stolen from the desk. Even with his friend from the *Post* dead, he could still end the monster's reign here in Virginia. The Society would likely protect the superintendent from prosecution or imprisonment, yet the court of public opinion might skewer him and send the movement underground. During the Depression, the people of America would either fall apart, or draw together and stand up against the few who attempted to force their will on the people. President Roosevelt had given the populace a reason to believe again and Sam knew that hope in these times of Hoovervilles and dust bowls that would foster positivity where it was needed most. The Society only wished to erase the beaten down lands of the country.

With a half-smile, he shook his head and turned to walk into his own office.

Avoiding Dejarnette would be the priority of the day.

"Good morning, Gwen," he said to his secretary, when she failed to raise her head at the sound of his entrance.

She looked up from her typing and report writing, a forced smile worn on a pale expression. "Hi, Doctor Taylor. Excuse my rudeness. Your boss," she said with a tinge of bitterness, "asked for typed copies of all of our reports on patients you've tested so far."

"Why?" *This couldn't be a good thing*, Sam thought. The sour churning in his stomach echoed the sentiment.

She clenched her fingers in long-nailed fists, and then relaxed each one with a deep breath. "I have no idea. Doris delivered the message when I arrived, and she didn't seem to know, either."

"Don't you two share office secrets?" It was a dangerous attempt, but he had to fish for something.

This time, she did offer a smile, an honest one. "Because we're ladies? Maybe we keep more than we share, at least from the men in our lives. Doesn't your lady keep her own skeletons locked away from you, only to rattle the bones with others when you're not around?"

"How'd you know about her?" He felt the anxiety rise in his

veins again. *Had Dejarnette put out feelers on her already?*

Again, the smile. Somewhat sly, it held no apparent malice. "Doctor, you live in Augusta. We're a small town, despite its rich history. If you sneeze at one end of town, three people on the other end reach for a handkerchief. Everyone knows romance. Welcome to the south. I hear she's pretty."

Sam allowed himself a slight reprieve as he returned the smile, reddening at Ruby's mention. "She is."

"Well, maybe one day you'll let us meet her." Again, her expression exposed nothing but the stress of her job.

"Maybe you will," he replied, wishing he could keep Ruby far away from this hell hole forever.

As he turned to head to his office, she called to him. "By the way, Doris told me to relay this to you: when you're finished with today's clients, bring the file Dr. Dejarnette needs to his office."

The bastard did figure it out. Screw him. Leverage was gold in the world. It might also just save a life this time.

92

Sam skirted the main grounds by walking through the willows, purposely avoiding the path which led to the gazebo. The morning chill had lingered, and he pulled his coat tight.

When he had entered his office, a stack of files had stared back at him. Just by glancing, he could tell at least two dozen patients awaited his testing.

His mind had wandered, wondering if Dejarnette aimed to punish him, to break him down like he did his experiments, or if the pressure from up north had just increased. *The goings on in Cold Spring Harbor pushed everyone to the limit. That would inevitably happen, if one allowed a cold machine such as Davenport to set the pace for the rest of the country.* Sam wondered if the man had a psychologist like him in the facility or he simply used his own system to sentence his patients.

When you're at the top of the food chain, you can dictate to the rest of the sharks, Sam thought. *Sooner or later, though, someone will come for you with bigger jaws.* Right now, he knew that if he didn't abide by the Society's wishes, he would be no better off than a gutted swimmer in the Manasquan Sound. Back in 1916, right before he shipped off for France, he tried to help with the hunt for the great white shark which devoured four bathers and chewed on one more. While he never witnessed the monster responsible, he imagined it to be no less methodical and focused than Davenport.

Sam just wished he was there when the man found himself strung up like a prized catch.

He'd nearly flipped open a few folders, just to see how

'disturbed' or 'unfit' these patients would be deemed, but had thought better of it.

Fuck you, Joseph. I'll test when I'm ready and give you results that will grow hair on your own unfit bald head.

He had slammed the door behind him and fought to calm his hammering heart.

As he reached the fence, he dragged his hand along the iron. *Did the townspeople truly wish to picnic within this place? The mentally ill mixed with the sane? If so, who was who?*

The patients merrily traversed the grounds as he walked clockwise towards the tracks. *How many of them truly admitted themselves, to relax and escape the troubles of the times? How many found themselves committed by family members and discovered they were trapped until someone signed them out, freeing them from this prison of beauty where everything that comprised their identity could be cut away in a heartbeat, without consent?*

When he turned northward, he heard the train in the distance. Gene had told him a passenger train rolled through once or twice a day while supply car arrivals occurred more intermittently. He knew most facilities had their own stations, or off-shoot tracks, which would divert freight if it required a lengthy loading. He strained to see the tracks, yet one building blocked his view. *Not a guard house*, he guessed, as it stretched about three times as long and only half as tall.

A factory?

Sam's mind checked off options in his head as he drew nearer. *For what purpose?* Dejarnette did tell him that the patients earned pay for many forms of work on campus. Maybe this was just another way for them to pass the time, building mass production of tools, machinery parts, or rubber for the car manufacturers. Tires, he'd found, were always a growing need.

A faint acrid odor drifted into his nostrils as he drew within a stone's throw of the facility. A pair of chimneys rose from the roof, solidifying his notion of the building's purpose. He found himself increasing his gait, finding the way becoming less traveled yet the grass more yellowed as he left the front portion of the hospital as if others had preceded him. The railroad connected to this, he thought, as he recalled the lush greenery juxtaposed behind the hospital, where the graveyard and white wall waited for many of his patients.

A brick structure stood before him. No windows opened a view to what lay inside, only a thick black door with a bolt lock. He walked to the far side to examine the back; yet more fencing stretched from the building. The wrought iron reached around and into it, stopped, and then continued as if nothing had halted its way in the first place.

One deviation existed in the fence: a door. It too held a lock on it, but the fence was no higher here than anywhere else in its circumference. He peered through the bars and viewed the tracks. *Why would the train halt its travel here? This didn't appear to be a station, yet what did he know about the inner construction of a facility such as this? Why the locks?*

Medicine, he thought. Even in times before the Depression, hospital supplies could turn the most pious man into a criminal if offered the opportunity. Opium, morphine, and methamphetamine were staples in any hospital and since the Crash, carried much more value than cash.

Behind the tracks lay a ravine about forty feet deep, deep enough to deter many would-be intruders. A few hundred feet past the building, the land leveled out once again, but Route 11 shot northbound towards Harrisonburg.

A stench struck him as he pondered whether to enter or not. His brain registered it, tucked deep in his memories, but couldn't place it. This shouldn't have been here, not in this town. Mixed in was something else, something utterly foreign to him.

He reached out to try the lock but found it solid and relatively new. *Why was it necessary with the fence so easily scalable?* The bolt lock felt just as sturdy and recent. Reaching back to age seventeen, he recalled how his regiment blew a German bunker with a couple of Mills bombs, 'Number 5s' to the seasoned soldiers. Bobby and he had been the backups to the bombing team, but when a hidden Maschinengewehr sliced that team in half, they had grabbed up the four grenades and completed the mission. His buddy tossed one through each window slit, while Sam jammed one in the bolt and another in the hinges. When they blew, the massive door shook for a few moments before crashing to the ground. He knew it would take something similar to break into this odd structure.

He smiled when he thought of the solution.

93

Voices sounded behind him. He turned and noticed two orderlies descending the hill from the left dorm. Before he slipped out of sight, his own eyes drifted to the second dorm. *Why hadn't he been inside that building yet? Right, his own patients had been dying. Still, he knew where to head after doing business at the former home of Theodore Preston.*

At the thought of Theo dying because of Dejarnette's plans to be Grant's poster boy, Sam wished the pick he squeezed to be a dagger.

94

"Harris, isn't it?"

The guard at the first dorm smiled at Sam's entrance. "Hey doc. How's it going? Back to see the rest of the gang?"

Good, he thought. *A friendly guard would be more apt to keep his mouth shut when needed. Hopefully. Maybe he'd bring him some of Gene's hootch to him as a gift.*

"Rest? I thought this wing was pretty much deserted the other day."

The man grinned at him and cocked his head. "Geez. They do work you hard here. You only saw the first floor. There are two more. Next-door has four in all."

"Can I see them?"

Again, the guard gave him an odd look. "You're Dejarnette's man, right?" The start of a grin itched the side of his face. "Your predecessor didn't have your balls. Yours might be a little too big for the job."

Great, Sam thought. *There goes the loyalty factor.* "And here I thought you actually liked a Yankee," he said, forcing a smile.

The man stood, folding up the newspaper he was reading. "Whoa. Hold on there. I do like you, bud, but I follow the boss." He leaned in closer. "My sister in law's from up north and I've been asking for a Yankees cap since the fool married her. No offense."

"None taken." Sam felt the tension ease and the opening became as wide as centerfield in his favorite stadium.

"You'd think that for Christmas or my birthday, she could splurge a bit. My brother has a couple of them himself. I'd even take one of those. It's not like they were hit hard by the crash."

"I went to school with a couple of guys who still work at the stadium. Vendors. I'm sure one of them will be able to send me one the next time I call or write home."

"You'd do that?" His face scrunched up. "Sounds like a tit for tat deal. Is it?"

"You're a bright man, for liking a great team and reading people so well. I don't make deals and don't swindle people. I'd just like it if Dejarnette doesn't know how often I'm here or for how long. I'm new and don't want him thinking I don't know what I'm doing. Personally, the more time I spend with the patients, the more I can help."

The man shook his head as if he'd heard it a million times. "I tell him and the others who check on things that I spend more time checking up on the folks that stay here, too." He suddenly looked guilty of something he didn't do. "I mean, I do patrol and watch those people who seem a bit off on different days, but I'm not going to do it all day or night long."

"Are we on the same team here?"

The man's smile said it all. "Go Yankees."

95

The first floor remained mostly empty. None of Sam's test patients occupied any of the rooms. For a moment, he paused at Theo's room. He could imagine the man swinging from the light fixture, a near smile on his face, realizing that even death would be immensely less terrible than the 'treatments' of Dejarnette. For a criminal, Sam might be able to turn a blind eye. But that patient had been innocent, deceived by his own wife. He entered the facility condemned and knew it. At the end of the hallway, Sam used the key Harris handed him and stepped into the stairwell which led to the second and third floors.

He knew that the answers to many questions would be within the walls of the upper rooms. Voices filled the narrow passage as he stepped closer to the door. Sam knew that while many patients talked to themselves, others found comfort in conversing with those in neighboring cells. *Some of these folks likely knew each other, were kin to others here.*

"Why haven't you visited them before?"

Oh, I don't know, Sam thought. *Maybe because a patient of mine hung himself rather than wait for a release he knew would never come. Also, maybe because I discovered that my boss at the job I escaped another nightmare for turned out to be fitted for one of Dante's circles of hell.*

He pushed open the door after turning the bolt. The hallway resembled the one on the first floor—with one difference. Patients filled the rooms from one end to the other. He peered into the first and saw a woman crying on her bed with an open book on her chest. His left foot pointed towards the threshold, yet halted before his shoe made contact with the wood beneath it.

Now is not the time, he reminded himself. He took note of the name on her door, and would ask to see her in a day or two. Despite whatever Dejarnette had said to her, he might be able to release her, if the doctor kept Sam around long enough. What *had* happened to the psychologist before him? Sam had been so wrapped up in himself and new beginnings that he never cared to read previous files or notes from the man.

"They're the 'regulars' up there," Harris said. "Families drop them off for many reasons, the most often being that they're too much trouble. If there's any money in the bank, this is a great solution to their troubles. They stay here until someone signs them out."

"How often is that?" Sam had asked, already guessing the answer.

"If they don't forget about them?" Harris had whistled, appearing sadder than most hospital workers Sam had ever met. "Probably a couple of months, or years. Then they'll try to bring them home again—if the embarrassment isn't too much."

Sam wondered if this woman faced a similar situation as the others he had seen. *Had her husband accused her of infidelity? Disease? Something worse? If so, she would far worse off than Theodore had been. At least men could fight back in court, if the hospital didn't speed them off to the wards first. No judge would entertain the plight of a woman in court.*

He wandered the length of the floor, gazing into every room. Not one of the patients looked familiar to him so he figured all had been evaluated prior to his arrival, by Dejarnette himself or by Sam's predecessor, whoever that may have been.

Once he reached the end, he paused, not knowing if he had the strength to walk the last flight.

"Doctor," the guard had said. *"I can't go up there anymore. I watch the nurses come and go a few times a day but I'm not strong enough. I have two of my own at home."*

Sam had said nothing, already knowing his reaction but

praying he could refrain from displaying it.

A tear spilled from his eye when he saw the first child in the room. Sitting in a crib, the boy reminded Sam of what he imagined his son might have looked like if he'd lived. Sensing the doctor in the room, he turned to face Sam and smiled at him, raising one arm as if asking for help, or possibly just to be held.

Sam's mind faltered as he tried not to witness any more of the horrors of their confinement in the tiny rooms. Encephalitis, Down Syndrome, minor deformities, blindness, etc. They all had their reasons for living on this floor.

The doctor's boy. Jesus.

He bolted down the steps and raced passed Harris, who simply nodded as Sam passed. *Would these children ever see the light of day? Was this Colin's fate if Sam didn't give in to the Society's ways? What would happen to him if Sam failed to return the parcel?*

Screw the bastard. It was his only leverage right now and he didn't even know if it held anything which would save a life. He could only pray to God it did, as he stumbled to the next building, the one for the rich folk.

Was this what he had condemned his own son to? Or were they right and his son had died within an hour of being born?

96

The other dorm, the one Samuel had heard housed the affluent patients in the Shenandoah Valley. Some came from over
Afton Mountain in Charlottesville, wives and children of university staff who came to recuperate from 'stress'. Others chose to
escape reality completely and traveled by rail all the way from
Williamsburg or the beach towns. Within the confines of the iron
fencing, they didn't have to worry about anything, save for planting flowers, woodworking, or the weather.

Many chose to be committed voluntarily. After all, the history
of the hospital promised only the best care in the state and with
enough of a donation, family members could be pampered even
more than at a resort.

Sam wondered if the sterilizations they received were a
welcome relief or a request from those who committed them.
Either way, they would eventually leave, unlike the patients in
the other dorms who would likely only ever be released if their
ashes were taken home.

From the outside, the residential building appeared the same.
Once inside, the stench of money sickened him. A soft green
carpet flowed down the hallway and music poured from a source
he couldn't decipher. *Brahms,* he figured. *Jazz would be more in
vogue, but the doctor would likely prefer the soothing sounds of
the classics. Dejarnette would consider the still-new style to be of
'monkey-jaw' origin. The tribal rhythms and oft-chromatic tones
would irritate the man's sensitive tastes.* Sam wished he could see
the man's face if he ever saw his psychologist prodigy banging out
a 12-bar blues with a man of color, drinking poor man's whiskey.

His smile lasted until he faced the guard. A complete departure from Harris, this towering man wore his uniform like an evening suit, his expression one of severe constipation. Sam imagined the people inside would find him to be reminiscent of their servants back home, which would promote a sense of well-being.

"Doctor," the guard said in a demure voice. "You have a patient in this dormitory?"

Sam felt himself stiffen in a defensive posture. "I'm the chief psychologist at Western Valley. All the patients are technically *my* patients. Dejarnette hired me to test any and all who reside here."

"Except for those who pay not to be disturbed." The smirk on the man's face burned Sam and caused his fists to tighten. "These aren't the criminals or defectives here. Well, at not poor ones." He regarded the doctor like he'd had relations with the superintendent's 'mud people'.

"I'm going for a walk-through." Sam headed directly at the man, daring him to hold his ground. He didn't. He simply retreated against the wall without a sound. "If you have an issue with my tour, call the man and let him you're the one to make a complaint. If one of your charges inside moan or groan due to my intrusion, I give you my word I'll leave without complaint."

The man looked like he couldn't decide whether he'd won or lost the battle.

"Until then, go fuck yourself and go back to being a bell-boy somewhere."

Sam walked from room to room, floor to floor, visiting each patient by introducing himself with a few words or a simple smile. If the guard did call the superintendent, Same might be removed. He knew he tread on thin ice after the confrontation, but still had that one card to play.

All were complaisant until a few realized his job and asked the questions that no one seemed to ever want to ask, or answer.

He couldn't explain to them why they had scars or why their own flesh and blood, or spouses, would sanction their neutering, for a reason which reason knew nothing of, a Pascal quote he once tried on Miriam. Heart had nothing to do with abandoning loved ones here, though.

97

There remained only one place Sam had to visit before he could go home with some semblance of peace in his soul. Within minutes of exiting the dorm through the side door, he found himself standing in the middle of the graveyard.

His consciousness left him briefly as the world spun from under him. When he returned to Augusta, Virginia, he found himself sitting on the soft ground above a fresh grave which was likely Theo's. McIlveen had likely perished by now if more 'treatment' had occurred, especially with the triple murder hanging over his head which would remove any restrictions on what the doctors could do.

Sam watched the tears hit the dirt under him and it wasn't until several minutes later that he realized they were for the life of his son.

Two years ago, he and Miriam wasted away in that hospital room for a period of time which felt like weeks, but which people would later tell him was only fifteen hours. They arrived early, the moment her waters broke. He cursed himself every step of the way, through the cab ride, through the walk to the private operating room they had set up for them.

The bleeding didn't begin until the doctor began the extraction. He had warned her of the risks due to her diabetes, but she refused to take the insulin. *For the baby,* she had said. *It couldn't be good for it.*

She had lost consciousness twice during the delivery. The first time, she appeared petrified. Her eyes darted to him and to the doctor, back to him. Something was wrong, but she couldn't tell whether it was happening to her or the baby. Her fingers gripped his in a clammy vise hold. Her face paled while her deep green eyes dilated. Below her, the doctor would not meet Sam's frightened look. Miriam wouldn't tear her eyes from Sam's, begging him to fix everything and to forgive her for ruining the one moment they would never get to enjoy. After she passed out, the doctor, one of those whom the Society recruited and who knew of the importance of Sam's test, its implications, told the psychologist the truth of the matter.

He had promised himself to be strong, to hold back any anger or grief, until it materialized into the blackest moment of his life. When she awoke, he realized he didn't have to do a thing.

She had known.

The simple expression on her face told him she knew tomorrow would never arrive for her and night would remain for him, until he could one day allow it to fade. They stared eye to eye, passing back and forth the years spent together, without a word. He knew he had been talking during that time, but his words had fallen without meaning to the cold floor. His mind needed to go through the motions and hers likely appreciated the chatter.

When she faded the second time, she would not wake again.

His son was born sometime after the moon stood full outside, actual time disappearing along with the rest of the room, hospital, and city. The second he heard the cry, he felt overcome with a feeling that still haunted him: anger. Why should a child he never held be born, and live, while his love died? The nurse who cleaned the baby shook her head in a manner suggesting the boy would not do well to live. Sam took her expression to mean he would be dead soon after as well, leaving him with nobody to hold for three thousand miles.

While he heard Nathaniel cry, Miriam's choice, he pretended not to hear it. Instead, when the nurse whispered in his ear, she nodded and took the child away. It would be the last time he would ever see his son. That woman, Sanger, even supported what would happen to him. The last image of the baby was the nurse handing him to a pair of nuns at the entrance to the operating room.

Sam would spend much of the past two years mentally flogging himself for allowing one love to die and the other to be taken from him.

What would Colin, or even Tristan, think if their parents, or doctors, made a similar decision? Sam knew he would receive little sympathy.

He pressed his face into the sod, not caring how he would appear to either staff or patients. Once again, he had failed those who had counted on him. The decision to become who he was came to him while still in grade school. Always the ear and voice of reason for so many friends and classmates, he'd realized he had a gift for helping.

Had.

That gift seemed to fade before his eyes that night in San Francisco. *Obviously, his malign influence now spread to others he touched in life.*

A soft cracking sound behind him shook the self-pity from his mind and allowed him to spin to face it. No longer feeling defensive, he only wished to see who would be there, to see who would twist his brain next.

A man in a pumpkin-style mask stood just at the edge of the woods. His clothes were those typical to the villages and small towns which embraced these men. Sam never flinched. Instead, he rose to his feet on half-numbed limbs and approached the grotesque being.

"What do you want?" Sam spoke the words but only air escaped his lips. The man's eyes were barely distinguishable to him in the fading light and would not help him to identify the figure, regardless. Yet the man stood tall and walked in a brisk manner towards Sam.

Without warning, the strangely masked man turned what Sam had deemed a night of memories best lost and forgotten to a frightening vision of the future. The man leaned in and Sam realized what was to happen, pulling him into a world in which he had found himself entrenched, but only now, fully aware.

One word passed his lips, through the burlap material. One word enunciated so well, Sam saw his life change in a heartbeat. He knew it would end just as abruptly if he didn't act that night.

Gene and he must get his mother, Colin, Gene's wife, and Ruby the hell out of town. Now.

A minute later, after the two men stood face-to-face, an understanding passing between them which chilled Sam but ignited a fury within, a slew of lights blossomed in dim lanterns behind the Belsnickler, yards deep in the forest. Even in the daylight, the trees swallowed the sunlight whole and provided cover, and haven, for those who traveled by the trail of darkness.

98

Sam nearly ran down the street as he remembered Colin's game would be starting soon. He had bolted from the hospital without thought to any consequence. *Fuck him,* he thought, wishing the doctor to choke on his own inhumanity. For all he knew, someone would be scoping out his brother now, set to take him into the depths of the superintendent's perverted surgical playground.

He checked the clock on the courthouse tower.

2:15pm. Shit.

The game would be starting in fifteen minutes if the teams arrived on time. He couldn't help but gaze up at the sculpted metal Lady Justice atop the tower of the building. *With the Society's hold strong in town, could there be any justice? Not likely,* he thought. *Not with Dejarnette running Western Valley and the people of the state unaware of what befell anyone deemed 'unfit' in a madman's world.*

Augusta had survived disasters before. The march of Union soldiers who torched much of the Valley, the destruction of the depot in a deadly train crash. Fires and floods had raged, even a massive sinkhole that swallowed two entire city blocks had threatened the lives of this southern sanctuary; yet it had remained, for the most part, unscathed.

How would the town look when Dejarnette finished his mission? Would there be anyone left who could populate it? Future generations? With the country on edge, salvation from such a man or his superiors felt remote, at best. This oasis between the

*mountain ranges lay like a fawn caught in a cave, simply awaiting
the fatal shot from a hunter.*

Sam turned the corner onto the grounds of the school.
Already the cheers had reached his ears. The irony hit him
immediately and a smile almost hit his lips. *The players whom
the applause was meant for would likely never hear it. Hopefully,
the kids had been watching the stands to see the beaming parents
and classmates who filled the bleachers in front of the field.*
He found himself amazed at the size of the structure, at least
twenty rows deep and close to a hundred feet long. *Maybe
times would change and the zeitgeist would prevail in the favor of
the students marked as* defective *or* unfit. *This wasn't Darwin's
world. Humans adapted to their surroundings and limitations.
The President of the country had just begun to show them that.*

A sinking feeling filled him when he couldn't spot Colin
on the field. He would kill the man who took anyone he loved
away from him, a feeling he had not even felt on the battlefield.
There, he'd doubted himself when presented with face to face
death. Thankfully, he had never watched a soldier die from a
bullet or blade of his own wielding.

Yet now, he knew it did exist in him. He prayed it would
never need to surface, but he wouldn't hesitate to save those
who held his heart. Visions of the doctor and his men dying
under his hand burned in his mind.

Where was the doctor?

Just as anxiety began to speed like fire ants down his arms
and back, he turned to the dugout. The coach hovered over a
child, signing feverishly as the boy shook.

Colin.

Sam ran to where they stood and waved for the man to
notice him. The tall, muscular coach clad in blue and yellow
uniform smiled as he realized who it was. With a fatherly push,
he sent the teen in Sam's direction. When Colin saw his brother,
he sprinted the few yards and landed in his arms.

My God, he thought. The boy had never shown affection
towards him. *Ever.* It had taken long enough for him to accept
Sam's mother as his own, when he found out the truth of what

befell his blood parents.

"Slow down," he signed to the boy, whose hands fluttered like a blazing hummingbird. "I can't understand."

The boy dropped both hands and raised his face to Sam's. Rage and grief filled his expression, along with tears creeping out of each eye.

"She might die." Sam couldn't process such a comment from the boy, who at that moment looked anything but a child from the eyes inward.

"Who?" *Please don't let it be mother or Ruby. Not now. He would gut Dejarnette on the spot.*

The boy turned towards the stands and scanned them from right to left. Sam followed his view. At the end of the top row sat his boss, the monster who would pass judgment on anyone not meeting his standards. He felt his fists tighten and wished his Luger was still in his coat pocket. The man stared back and smiled, but Sam knew he must be boiling over the loss of the package of files.

Yet Colin didn't stop there. He continued to scan the crowd as he gripped the baseball, just like his brother did with the guitar pick—and soon enough, a gun.

"He's not here!" The signing became more rigid and emphatic. "I know he's here. He has to be."

Confused, Sam gripped his brother and stepped between him and the stands. "*Who*? Tell me now. Please."

The boy had been trained to skip between signing and lip-reading so well that he often didn't miss a word. "The man from the theater. He tried to kill Ms. Pritchard last night."

"What? How? Where is she now?" *Please God don't let her be where I fear her to be.*

The boy continued his scanning. Sam sensed that the boy would attack the man head-on if he had a chance. *If the agent was truly from J. Edgar or just a Society hired gun, the boy would not live to attempt a swing. Unless Dejarnette ordered them not to harm him—yet.*

"Colin!" He yelled, hoping his expression and shaking would return the teen to coherence.

"We found her at the bottom of the steps. Someone pushed her."

We? Sam's stomach sank at the thought of a child having to witness something like that. *This school was supposed to be their haven. Despite the onslaught of eugenics all around them, this school was meant to be protected. Otherwise, Dejarnette and his superiors would have closed it down long ago and brought in the children.*

"Can she talk?"

The boy shook his head. "She managed to pull herself up but fell when she saw us. There was blood all in her hair. Her dress was covered in it! She might die."

He pulled the boy closer, purposely shielding him from any others in the stands who might be watching. "Where is she now and what did they say about her condition?"

All at once, the child faded before him and the adult in his eyes spread to his being. "The nurses in the school helped her to the clinic and said it looked bad, but she kept pointing. She talked but I couldn't read any of her words."

Concussion, likely, Sam thought. *Aphasia would rob her of intelligent speech or any other communication, either spoken or signed.*

"They brought in the doctor from downtown. Mr. Zachary, I think his name was. He told them not to move her to the hospital."

There must truly be a god, Sam thought. *If the man in the fedora had attempted to kill her, the physician might as well hand the man a gun if he sent her to Western Valley.*

"Was she able to move?"

This time, his brother only nodded. The shaking had stopped. "Yes, she kept trying to get up, but the doctor looked worried and had three of the nurses hold her down. I don't know who looked more afraid, him or her."

"Sam?"

The voice he heard sounded different than the young man he had left behind two years ago and even from days ago. "Yes?"

"If I have a chance, I'm going to kill him. Chloe disappeared, too."

Fear blossomed in the psychologist. "Don't, Colin. Let Gene and I take care of it. Maybe we can call the sheriff." The look from his brother said it all. While he trusted the two men, the law in town was likely employed by the hospital, or at least paid not to notice. Sam recalled never even seeing the police truck more than once since he arrived. It had likely brought in McIlveen when he murdered the banker and his wife, possibly even making another trip into the village, but with a quiet town such as this, the police tended to act only when necessary. With the CCC and the floods of migrants hitching on trains, jumping off to look for work in this town or neighboring ones, they had their hands full with robbery, violence, and other crimes. A missing deaf girl wouldn't even show up on their bulletin boards, not unless a hefty reward was offered.

Dejarnette would blame the crimes and kidnapping on poor breeding and faulty genes. Sam knew the man was half-correct. Those who had run the country into the crash and depression likely should never have been allowed into power.

He sighed, seeing much of himself in his brother, who truly was only half in blood. Genes did follow people, but so did attitude and drive. Nurture sometimes won out over nature. In this case, it might just get more of his family killed.

"I'm asking you, don't. Not yet, anyway. Please. You need to keep mom safe. There are bad people out there. I'm going to ask Ruby to stay with us, too. That man might have friends in town or be en route from Washington. I'm going to need your eyes and for you to be a man when Gene and I can't be around."

The teen's face softened, but only a bit. "I will, but I still aim to find her and get that bastard for hurting Ms. Pritchard."

"Okay but let me help you. I need to do something tonight with Gene first. Then, I promise you, we'll go after anyone who deserves it."

He looked up at his big brother. "If we do this, are we going to have to leave here?"

Sam felt himself welling up. *Home never stayed put for him.* "Colin, even if we don't do this, we might have to leave. I'm hoping not to, but I don't trust anyone other than Gene in this town. But for now, the best thing you can do is get your ass out there and pitch like it's your one chance to show the world you can play with the all-stars. Not these guys, but players from any school."

Colin stared into his brother's face with a resolve that scared him a little. "I will. Every pitch will be a bullet meant for that asshole G-man." He turned to leave for the mound, before looking back at Sam. "Oh, your boss. He talked to me before we warmed up. He mentioned that during the War, some countries used deaf soldiers to send codes through signs. He told me if I learned some of that stuff, I could really make something of myself. 'Ask your brother about stealing codes, and other things,' he said. Ms. Pritchard said I needed a skill to protect me. Do you think Mr. Dejarnette thinks the same thing?"

Sam found himself mute as he nodded once, watching his brother head to the mound.

99

"Go to my house, right after the game." Sam sat next to Ruby, who came to watch Colin play before her shift at the restaurant.

"Why?" He could tell the fear she displayed, in her dilating eyes and fallen facial muscles, was something she knew too well, more than any woman should. "I have to work. Does this have anything to do with my uncle?"

Sam felt for her, knowing that from the pictures, the man was a native and was likely taken long ago. "I don't know," he said, knowing full well she could tell he was only attempting to comfort her. *She had endured too much in her life already. Because of him, another load now weighed her down.* "I can ask some of my new friends. If anyone would know where he is, they would." Whether he meant the mountain folk or the Belsnicklers, he couldn't tell. The former might still blame him for Betty Rowe's death and the latter—well, no one had been able to figure them out for years.

"I'll go," she said, deflating, and he wondered if her soul died a little more or if it was simply a lessening of stress. "I can handle myself pretty well. If your mother will accept me there, I'll go."

After hearing of her life in Romania, the attacks on her towns and the treatment of women by soldiers, he had little doubt she had some fight in her. He only hoped he never had to witness it. Something in her eyes told him she had already faced violence and come out on top. That only added to why he had begun to fall for her.

As he opened his mouth to speak, she pressed a finger to

the corner of his eye, wiping a tear before it emerged. She then dragged it across his face to press it against her lips.

"I'll do it," she said, her voice steady. "I'll keep your mother safe. Colin, too. Maybe she'll like having me around. *I* like being around."

He choked back what he really wished to say and left it at a nod and smile. She kissed him on the cheek when he rose to find his mother.

"She's always welcome here. No girl should be on her own."

"Thanks, mom."

Bridget gave him another one of her looks; the ones where he could never tell if they were honest or rooted in sarcasm. "She sleeps in your room, of course." A big grin spread across her Irish face. "Before you get your thoughts all stiff and warm, you, my dear, will be downstairs. Sofa or guest room. You choose."

Sam forced a grin he meant, underneath the fear. "I'll see you later, mom."

He stayed for the game, watching his little brother toss eleven strikeouts and hit a couple of doubles, as his school shut out the team from the university school. The boy pitched with a fire Sam had never witnessed before. All the while, he kept an eye on Dejarnette, who appeared rapt with the boy's performance. *Why the mention of the code to Colin? The dig on Sam was clever and expected, but why pretend that a deaf boy, someone he clearly saw as unfit for carrying on the bloodline, could be an effective part of society?* The man would always be an enigma to Sam, at least until he left town—or killed the man.

Why would he keep a child of his own who didn't fit the Society's vision? Did they even know about the boy? After all, Joseph Dejarnette himself bucked the entire image of the ideal man they wished to inherit the earth. Instead of blonde hair and blue eyes, God bestowed upon him a shiny domed head and brown eyes behind glasses. If he was his own patient, he might meet the knife.

When the image of Sam's own son entered his mind, leaving the hospital room in the nun's arms as he refused to even glance at the infant, he felt the shame which plagued him at least once a day. *If he could stop just one of those lives from sorrow, as he failed to do for his own, he might find solace one day.*

Until then, he wondered what it would feel like to watch Dejarnette draw his last breath.

100

"Say no if you like, but I could really use a hand tonight."

"I'm there," Gene replied, hopping up from his porch.

Sam smiled, thankful this new friend behaved like a life-long brother. "But I didn't tell you what or how or where. Or if it was dangerous."

The big man shook his head. "Boy, if you have to explain anything to me at this point, I've really got to wonder about that school that gave you those letters after your name."

"Are we headed to the hospital?"

"Yes."

"Are we going to dig into what that mountain man alluded to and kick over some of the rocks that bastard hides secrets under?"

"Yes again."

Gene clapped his hands and started towards the house. "Then I don't need to know anything else. It's dangerous. Remember, they still have a few pieces of me there already."

Sam cringed, remembering again what his friend had endured. He would be game for anything that would lead to the superintendent's downfall. "How's nine sound to you?"

"Just fine. It'll give me time to find what I need for the job."

"You don't know what the job is yet."

"I know I'll need my gun and a blade in case we meet up with any bad elements."

They shared a smile, knowing the anticipation matched the trepidation inside. Sam just hoped both would return—and with enough to hang Dejarnette.

101

The broken shards of light led the two men through the ravine behind the railroad tracks leading out of town and to the west of the hospital grounds. Neither could afford to carry a lantern. It would be cumbersome on the tricky slope which led down to a creek and back up again through brambles and a maze of trees made slick by the bed of wet leaves. Twice Sam fell and many more times he cursed himself and the path on which fate had led him. *If he broke or even twisted an ankle, the plan would be scrapped and he might never get another chance to enter the factory building.*

"Why is this so important again?" Gene maneuvered the switchbacks and leaf-covered obstacles like a man who grew up in the forest.

"Are you sure you're not part Belsnickeler?" Sam huffed a bit as he had trouble finding his footing—and breath. He never realized how out of shape he'd let himself become until now. He'd thought himself to be proficient in swimming and running, but Gene had told him hiking reminded a person about muscles he never knew he had.

"The package I 'borrowed' from Dejarnette's office means something, but without perspective, I doubt it will reveal what I fear is in that building." He slipped twenty feet from the crest of the hill, becoming aware of a new set of dangers. "If we can bypass the guard up in the tower, I feel this will be easy. Do your part and it might just work without either of us swallowing a bullet."

"Gotcha." The storekeeper reached the top first and signaled his readiness to Sam. With a small bag slung across his back, he strode on, hunched low as to not draw attention—yet.

They chose this path since the freight train that rested at the smaller depot would block out any light and provide cover for them from the rails to the building they targeted. Sam moved to the front of the engine, but Gene signaled for them to slip underneath it and stay in the shadows.

Sam felt his way past the wheels and rolled across the ties to the other rail. When he emerged on the other side, a deeper darkness enveloped him, just as planned. The guard in the tower would not be able to see anything, even if he shone his floodlight their way.

"Be careful. I don't want to deal with Eliza if you get hurt tonight."

His friend merely grinned and disappeared into the darkness ahead. Sam carried his own rucksack and felt his nerves fray just a bit as he crept close to the bolted door of the unknown building.

"Wait for my cue before you kill yourself," Gene whispered back.

Funny, Sam thought. *Real funny.* He was reminded of the run he and his war buddy made on the bunker, way back in 1917. The explosion could be heard for miles. This one could not afford to be heard fifty feet away.

With a strong two-armed grip, he swung the bag he carried over the pointed fence. It landed with little sound. His own hurried breathing drowned out any additional noises. When he hoisted himself over the fence, he made sure not to catch his pants, or more important parts of his body, on the spikes. Once over, he slid down the opposite side and found himself with a clear thirty-foot walk to the building. *Now, if only Gene could manage his end, the mission just might work.*

He stepped in something with the consistency of light snow, yet without the icy chill or wetness.

What the hell?

When they finished, he knew he would have to have a look with a match. The dark side of any government project always sometimes made one feel they just signed a deal at the crossroads.

He dropped his heavy bag at the foot of the door and went to work. Reaching into the cloth knapsack, he withdrew a couple of large fireworks, one rocket and one other which Gene had told him to light and run. He shoved the rocket into the hinges, and what equated to a massive firecracker in the bolt. With a sigh of relief, he placed the two bags of rice against the door, each right in front of the metal. Gene swore to him that a twenty-five-pound sack would absorb the bulk of the sound, and as a helpful byproduct, direct the explosion into the hinge and bolt, hopefully busting both wide open.

He pulled free the box of wood matches and held a pair ready. Deep inhalations steadied him and nearly caused the anxiety to disappear but with each moment, he imagined all the mistakes which could occur before the blast.

As he waited, a red rocket sizzled into the sky on the north side of the grounds. The guard in the tower, likely the only one on duty in Sam's quadrant of the hospital, grabbed his rifle, paced back and forth for a long minute, before deciding to investigate. The man would no doubt suspect bored kids and not pay attention to much else. A second rocket, this time a blue one, ran through the sky in the opposite direction and sent the guard running. On a boring night, he would likely have a ball chasing down the pranking kids who would choose a spot so close to his assigned duty. He would likely put a scare into them before returning to his post, feeling like an effective employee of the Society.

Watching his cues, Sam lit the matches and took cover on the side of the building. He counted the seconds and made it to eight before a dull boom shook the brick structure ever so slightly. The rocket sounded immediately afterwards, more flash than explosion.

He crouched and crept back to the door to inspect the damage. As hoped, the bolt hung askew from the top, fully rendered useless by Gene's suggestion. Sam began mentally thanking his friend right then for stocking just about everything someone in the town could need. He had told Sam he often planned the town's Fourth of July show and often gave the people a smaller red and green light show for Christmas.

When the second bag of rice was removed, Sam felt disappointed at first. The hinge appeared intact. With such a powerful blast, however—half a stick of dynamite, Gene had said—the mechanism would shake free from whatever held it in place. In a moment, he would put the man's words to the test.

A few minutes later, once the stench of gun powder receded, he saw Gene climbing the fence and running up to him.

"Ready?" The man didn't even break a sweat.

"Sure," he said. "Let's see if your stock actually helped us tonight."

Both men braced themselves again the sides of the door and pressed hard before pulling back on the steel latch. It moved slightly, but didn't open. They pulled once more and felt the door give, but not enough. Then Sam stood back a couple of feet and brought his boot down on the hinge. Once, twice, three times he kicked it. A small sound creaked under his foot. Nodding to his friend, they tried once more, together. Each placed a hand on the latch while the other braced against the damaged part of the door.

With a strong two-man pull, the door protested once again, this time with a groan that sounded like it belonged to the giant ape in the film Sam and Colin had seen the previous week. Instead of opening, it simply slid right out of place, nearly collapsing on both of them. They allowed it to lean into them before pivoting it clockwise to stand against the brick.

With a flick of a match, each man stepped into the opening, hoping more explosives did not exist on the other side.

Neither of them said anything for the longest time. They allowed the matches to burn down before lighting new ones.

"What did that Belsnickeler say to you earlier?" Gene's voice no longer sounded like it belonged to a large man.

Sam steadied himself against the nearest wall. "He said just one word. 'Burn.' I didn't understand what the hell he meant—until now."

"My God. Why would they burn all the patients' clothing? Their files? These can't be for what I think them to be."

"Gene," Sam wheezed, feeling the ash burn his lungs. "Tell me I'm wrong and I didn't trip into hell on the way to Virginia."

"They just might be, but I can't believe they'd be used for what it smells like."

"Let's go to the train," Sam said, his voice sounding devoid of life. Both men placed the door back in its proper place and backed away towards the tracks where the freight cars slept for the night.

Gene tapped Sam on the shoulder as they approached the gate to the station. There was no sense in climbing back over the fence when they discovered they could simply walk through the cars to get back home. "You really think that these people here would go that far?"

Sam looked down and saw the Luger in the man's hand. He felt both rage and fear as his legs trembled. The trip had both spooked and repulsed him so far. He could only imagine what being on the grounds did to a man who underwent such treatment.

"You know," he said, breathing heavier, finding a stench growing in his mouth from the night air. "After meeting these people out west, I believed they truly meant to help others from horrible lives. To make sure the population didn't kill the world. Maybe I should be given a lobotomy."

"Shut your mouth, friend. Your wife died and so did your son. You did the best for your family."

"I know."

"No, you don't. You're just a man. You know what else? This shit ain't just happening here. It's everywhere. I hear it's up in Canada, across the pond, up where all the girls have blonde hair and blue eyes, everywhere *except* in that country we kicked the shit out of."

"Do you know what else? When I listened to the radio the other day, a new guitarist played a blazing jazz blues song." Sam could see the bigger man's hands shaking.

"And?" Sam poked around at the ground. "Is he better than us?"

"Just shut your mouth. I'm trying to make a point. Django Reinhardt his name was. French guy. Know what's cool about him? He has only two fingers on his left hand to run about the fretboard. If he were here, that asshole inside would've snipped his balls off. But over there, a prodigy slips through the cracks and becomes a sensation.

"My point, you ask? Not everyone believes in the bullshit that man spouts."

Sam opened his mouth to tell him the truth about the baby, but stepped in the strange substance again. "What *is* this stuff?"

Gene pulled out a match, careful to place the remainder of his fireworks on the ground first. Once he struck it, he exhaled. "Thank god. It's only ash. These freight trains devour tons of coal and what they're doing up in the mountains is they're plowing through bedrock to make room for highways."

"Sounds like you're fishing, there, buddy." Sam dropped to a knee and pressed his hand into the pile. Soft, cool, dry ash met his hand as it sank deep. *Why would they dump it here, inside of the grounds instead of somewhere far removed from civilization?*

Both men walked through the station area, finding at least a dozen small piles of the ash. Sam assumed it came either from the factory building or the trains which stopped at the hospital every couple of days.

"What the hell?" Gene kicked through a knee-high pile and watched it blend into the darkness. "Forget it. Let's just get through the train if we can."

Sam's bad feeling, the one he had since he first saw the building, burrowed into his gut. His eyes followed the glow of the matches and examined the first pile, which he kicked before digging into it. As his hand fished around inside, he felt hard pieces here and there. Gene sat beside him and dug into another.

"What's in here?"

A sound clicked ahead of them. At first, Sam thought it was the guard, or guards, figuring out where the disturbance had originated, but the sound came from their final destination for the evening. *The freight cars.* Something banged on the boards inside, then clicked, and banged once more. Through the slats, something moved. *Cattle? Why would they stop overnight? That couldn't be good for milk, or the beef. If just one died inside, disease could spread within hours and a small fortune could be lost. Nobody would be that stupid in these times.*

Gene hopped up and walked slowly over to the car. His own light dwindled and swayed in a wind he didn't notice. Something attracted him to what moved inside and he pressed the match against the side.

Without warning, two fingers jutted out and snuffed out the flame. Gene fell back on his ass and nearly squealed. The fingers retracted and eyes took their place. Several pairs of eyes. Sam stood up with his fist closed and took a few steps to join his friend.

At first, he swore he saw Colin's face within the train. A00 ringer for Tristan stood next to him. *Couldn't be,* he said to himself. One was safely home and Sam knew the train had arrived hours ago, when he sat next to his brother at dinner. The other boy—well, he had seen him die at the doctor's hands.

No, these boys, maybe girls as well, arrived from some other place. But where? And why would they stop here overnight? Sam's mind put the pieces together quicker than he had wished but he knew the answer before he asked himself. When the mountain folk grew thin and the defectives from the town and those nearby dried up, the supply had to come from somewhere.

Roanoke? Lexington? Charlottesville or further?

"We have to get them out of there," he said. "You know where they're headed. Sooner or later, they'll find themselves here or up on the hill."

Gene pulled at the cargo door only to find another lock. No fireworks he had in his pack would be sufficient to blow the lock. If it failed, it could start a fire and incinerate whoever stood inside.

"Fuck."

As Sam peered inside, a face peered back. "Help me," the boy said in a hoarse voice. "Help." As they held up more matches to the slats in the car, several pairs of eyes reflected at them. The car had been packed tight, so tight that the cargo inside could barely move. Each set of eyes showed the dancing flames.

"Gene, we *did* step into hell. My god, what are these people doing here?"

Sam opened his hand and stared into the mass of ashes. In the middle of one pile lay something which made his heart stop for a moment. It was a pendant. With a couple of fingers, he opened it to find a pair of pictures.

Now he understood the lumps in the piles.

No.

They couldn't be doing this here.

"Gene, this place *is* hell. We have to kill someone."

But his friend didn't answer. Several sets of footsteps did, from behind the fence.

"Run," Sam managed to yell, although he doubted his friend needed prompting. He followed his own advice and watched his feet take three steps before a shot rang out and everything in his world truly did fall to hell.

The last thing he saw was Gene flying through the air, a look of surprise and pain on his face as he tumbled into the ravine. Sam's own pain exploded and drew complete blackness across his vision.

102

Sam woke to the sound of shoes scraping against the floor in a pitch-black room. They sounded muffled at first and he wondered why other people would have brought him to a room without lights.

As he attempted to sit up, he learned fast. His head smashed against something he couldn't see and dropped him to the bottom, his forehead bursting in pain. He balled up his fists and punched at the barrier which held him from escaping. Both bounced painfully back into his face and chest.

He realized then that he lay prone in whatever held him prisoner. His fingers pressed against a thick metal cover and could almost slip through the openings. Whoever designed the device constructed it so that a patient could not catch his, or her, fingers in the mesh, thus giving both protection and frustration. The sounds from outside filtered into his ears as if he had been submerged in the sludge at the bottom of a lake. His head swam, attempting to orient itself, while his hands explored the remainder of the box.

A behavior box? He remotely recalled the barbaric device from an exhibit he saw in New York. Was it at the Smithsonian? *No, that's D.C. he chided himself.* Then where was it? He couldn't recall what had happened to him prior to being placed in it but knew gunshots and pain in his legs had struck, the night before he lost consciousness.

Gene? Was he dead? Sam couldn't remember anything other than the big man running with him, right behind him when all hell broke loose.

The light had been terrible so if a bullet struck him, it would be by chance, not aim. Yet until he could find a way out of the box, he could not even fathom saving his friend. *If that friend still breathed,* he thought.

Behavior box, he wondered again. The one he'd witnessed was built like a coffin yet smaller, meant to be a tight fit. The sides were metal and reinforced with wood or other substances so that when banging on it, no sound would be produced. The patient found himself placed in a position where his or her feet didn't reach the end, so kicking out of the box was stricken from the list of possible escape notions. He or she had to move akin to a worm to shift his head against one end or feet to the other. Rarely did the patient have enough space to punch straight ahead with enough force to make a sound worth hearing.

"Hello?" He screamed but couldn't tell if his voice had been shunted by medication, injection, or simple acoustics from the device. His vocal cords ached as if he had been yelling for hours. *Had he? How long had he been locked away?* Fear assailed him as the thoughts ran through his mind. Not about his own safety but for Colin, his mother, Gene's wife, and Ruby. Gene could take care of himself, or was already dead.

"Hello? Talk to me, you son of a bitch."

Sounds seeped through the cage, yet nothing intelligible reached his ears. *Was Dejarnette standing just outside where he lay? Watching him somehow?* He stretched out his legs and found that feeling had deserted both. Pins and needles replaced the pain he felt from whatever they did to him. *He ached for the pain to return. Without it, he wouldn't be able to stand, to run, when he got out of the box.*

If he got out of it.

When sensation left his shoulders and upper arms, he began to panic. *Would he suffocate in there?* The anxiety he'd battled for most of his life had been kept at bay for years, especially since Miriam. The night terrors he experienced as a child in a miniscule apartment grew when he joined the war. The aftershocks of the time he spent in the trenches shook him awake in soaking sheets for many years. It wasn't until he nearly completed his doctorate that he felt he held the reins on the disorder.

All along, tight places frightened him. First the apartment, then the mud and squeezing between bodies, live and dead, in the tunnels in France, to the boats which funneled him to and from the many battles—all contributed to why he found himself in his profession.

Now he lay in the epitome of claustrophobia, awaiting the final breath, or worse, remaining there for what would seem an eternity.

"Let me out! You sick bastard. I have what you want, so please! Let me out and you can have it back!"

No answer came.

Black surrounded him and held tight, squeezing tighter as the minutes dragged by. Sam tried to keep his breathing steady, deep, but the phobia embraced him with smothering arms. Soon, his bladder begged for release, while his throat burned raw from yelling and the dehydration effects of the anxiety.

Thoughts of Ruby raged through his mind. *Who would be watching her? If Dejarnette captured him, would he go after her next? Someone else?* He figured she had been protected so far due to his connection to her, but now, all bets might be off.

And Gene? Sam never saw the man hit by a bullet or fall to the ground. Then again, from the pain in his leg and head, now beginning to pound, he realized he had been struck at least twice. *If his friend was dead, would anyone come for him?*

Dejarnette had to release him eventually. If the parcel meant that much to him, Sam had hidden it well enough that he doubted they could find it. But they might tear apart his house. Ruby's apartment.

Three people whom he couldn't jeopardize just to play chicken with a madman. Yet if he gave up the location, would the man simply back off and allow him and his family to live in peace?

What felt like another hour had passed. He couldn't tell which ached more, his head or bladder. One would have to be relieved soon. Dejarnette obviously meant to degrade him while locked up, so Sam would defy him and hold on a long as possible.

Where was everyone?

The darkness grew denser in his cage as fatigue began to envelope him. Sleep threatened to creep inside and take him, yet he knew he must listen for anyone who was in the room with him. To sleep might mean to die, or condemn someone he loved to do so.

Yet the blow to his head stole the decision from him within another hour and he found himself dreaming about the train again. Miriam sat next to him while Ruby sat across the row. Both would be his lovers, and both might share the same plane of existence because of him. Images of his wedding, the failed birth, his first kiss with Ruby: all swirled in his thoughts while his subconscious attempted to make sense of why everything had happened. The sex with both women flowed by in his mind, from his house bedroom, to the park, to Ruby's place where Miriam had stood at the foot of the bed smiling at him, to a collage where the two seemed interchangeable and part of him at the same time.

During a dream tryst he was recalling both women lying with him, when a crash shook him. Within the dream, the bedroom door exploded, sending splinters of wood through the air and impaling all of them. Their screams startled him awake to find all was not dark.

"Good. You're still conscious. I didn't want to have Maclin have to inject you with something to make you coherent."

The voice flowed into his ears like rancid honey. He struggled to move, to collect himself before attempting speech.

"Adrenaline?"

"What did he say?" A second voice came from behind the one he recognized.

A shadow moved in front of Sam's eyes, sectionalized like a bee's vision.

"Get me a glass of water."

"Fuck him," said the second. *Maclin?* "He'll talk more dry."

A moment passed in the lightening shadows. A kaleidoscope of black and white formed before his eyes. "Water."

"Get me the glass. Fill it please." With each word, clarity formed in Sam's brain.

"Dejarnette?"

"What's he saying? It sounds like he's chewed up glass."

More sounds of movement in front of his face. A creaking sound burst through his ears. It sounded like a grenade exploding next to his head. He opened his eyes fully and saw the outline of a face a couple of feet away from his. The door in fact did open, which explained the creaking. *The door to his cage.*

"Open your mouth. I don't think you can move, but if you try, I'll let Maclin use his needle on you. Knowing him, it's either heroin or pure adrenaline. With your anxiety, I doubt your heart would appreciate either."

"How?" Sam viewed the vague outline of the man, but the facial features still eluded him.

"I'm a researcher, Dr. Taylor. Did you really think I'd hire you without knowing every detail possible? You have trauma from getting stuck in a cave where your father worked. I believe your mother still had the newspaper clipping when I called her."

"When?" *He called Sam's mother? Why?* He attempted to sit up, but his muscles refused.

"You went for almost two years without speaking to any family, including your mother. Not exactly exemplary behavior for a good son. She spoke highly of you—like all mothers do—and provided me with the necessary background to make my decision complete.

"Your military discharge record was a bit tougher to find. I assume that the war effort left much of the paperwork for many in disarray. However, the week you spent in the hospital in London prior to returning home cemented your Achilles' heel. Everyone has one. I know I do. Maclin here hates the cold, so you'd never see him in Jersey this time of year. The man also can't stand blood. His own, I mean. Isn't that odd for a surgeon? He can dissect all those slack-jawed monkeys with aplomb, but prick his finger with a scalpel and he passes out."

"What heel?" Sam took in the information, hoping he would remember it when he was released. He burned to kill both men. He wondered if he could, up close face to face like that. *His buddies in the army never seemed to hesitate, but would he?*

"You screamed nightly about the trenches. Nightmares of the tight tunnels in France, mud slipping on top of you, the supports slipping which would trap you, essentially drowning you in slop. Claustrophobia is such a childhood phobia, yet it lingers, doesn't it?"

Sam could finally see the smile on the man's face, Dejarnette's glasses reflecting his own frightened face. "And what's yours?"

A bigger grin. "That this country will be overtaken by monkeys and the unfit. I fear people fighting in the streets for food and the nation unable to sustain itself because deviants who should not breed filled the cities with their filthy offspring. This country can only handle so many citizens before the resources run out. It will happen, if we don't do something. The crash will be forgotten as a 'minor' inconvenience of the past."

"Deviants," Sam said. "Like your boy?"

The doctor's eyes blazed. "That boy in the lab was more yours than mine."

They didn't know. They really didn't know. Did anyone?

Sam thought back to the subways of New York and the bustling centers of San Francisco and London. *Dejarnette couldn't be right. Humans would regulate themselves. Historically, they always did. Didn't they? Or was that through disease, warfare, and men like Dejarnette who depopulated their homelands for their beliefs?*

He winked at the man, realizing more words about Joseph's son might end him. *Not yet.*

"That street kid deserved better. America is better than that," he said, and the glass was pressed to his lips. Cold water poured into his mouth, shocking his system for a moment before he swallowed with greed. He begged for his hands to reach up and hold the glass, but the pins and needles had turned to complete numbness. Still, he finished what the doctor gave him.

"Sure it is. That's why we're in the bind that we're in now. That's why the Civil War happened. People care too much about their neighbor and what they think is the right thing to do. The South had strong leaders, but ultimately became too big for its own ambitions. If the north had thought clearly, they would have seen the point. Instead, they fought for ideals, not practicalities.

"Now look at us."

The chill of the fluid woke Sam fully, making him aware of the box, of Dejarnette, and the dark room where they were. "Thank you. Where are we?"

Laughter filled his ears. *How many people did the doctor have with him?*

"Seriously? You couldn't guess? You were a bad boy, Samuel. Where do the bad boys go?" His fingers rolled on the cage top. Sam saw that the lid was honeycombed but open. The main door which locked it tight hung just beyond that. Sensation returned as he pulled himself up.

The white building. They must be in the basement or lower floor. Dejarnette's office did connect the two structures. If he truly was being kept there, nobody would look there. The fear of the violent patients would deter them upon sight.

"Anyway," Dejarnette said. "You have something of mine, and I have something of yours. It's the oldest trade in history. I promise not to harm your little monkey and you will promise to return my parcel. Did you open it?"

"No," he said, partially telling the truth. "I wanted to, but with everything happening so fast, there was no time."

Dejarnette leaned back and examined Sam's expression. "You know what, Jed? I believe the man honestly didn't look at it. Yet."

"You have Ruby" Sam ignored the rest of the conversation and felt his anxiety receding in lieu of rage. "Why? Someone will miss her, at the restaurant, the school." He also thought of Colin's missing friend, hoping she evaded Dejarnette's hand.

"Nobody misses a defective, Sam. Nobody cares about the unfit. It's akin to pulling weeds from a garden. Did you know her husband placed her on the Census for Davenport? I never would've guessed Romania. The girl hides it well. Talented, too. It would be a true shame if you decided to bury me instead of saving her. And then, there's Colin."

"You asshole," Sam seethed. "You *promised* me."

"And I promised him, too. The boy will likely help society in a fine way. I can't let him breed like a dog, but I like him. He's one of the exceptions. Smart, funny, insightful. A much different case than your mud woman. Still, if I don't receive that package, even he's disposable to me. Grant already told me to sterilize, and treat, both."

"In the factory where you found me? What the hell do you do there?"

Maclin laughed behind the superintendent. "Trash gets incinerated."

No. No. No. He didn't want to be right about this. "The car full of people?"

"Mostly mountain folk," Dejarnette said. "Sent from all over for us to test, treat, and 'release.' Western Valley is one of many of its kind now. We're still at the forefront, despite what that sociopath Davenport believes, but we have tons of work to do."

"If I give you the package, will you allow her to leave town? My family? Safely?"

Maclin giggled behind Dejarnette, but the superintendent waved him off. "I keep my promises. You may not like my beliefs and methods, but you're one of us. I don't forget that. This is a strange time for you, Sam. Give it a little time and I know you'll stick by my side."

I'd rather fuck a goat, Sam thought, but kept his mouth shut.

"Where is she now?" He failed to keep the fear from his voice.

Dejarnette leaned into the cage. "Do you like my creation? It's a new take on the Utica Cage. I witnessed one in use in Williamsburg, an actual replica of one from the 1700's. Barbaric, but they do drive the point home. For those who have the cognitive skills, a night in here will cure any ill thoughts, don't you think?"

"*Where is she?*" His throat began to burn again as the pins and needles returned. *In a couple more minutes, he would be able to stand. They might kill him, but he would be able to have a fighting chance.*

"We'll see you soon. I believe you still need time to think this through." Dejarnette got up and shut the honey-combed cover. "How about we talk again tomorrow? I do believe you'll be truly ready for a well-thought-out decision by then."

"No, please," he said, his voice cracking. "I'll take you there now. Just take me out of here and I'll give it to you. Don't leave me in here. Please!"

"Good night, Sam." The solid metal cover shut on him, blacking out the world. *How could he save Ruby and Colin, and his mother, if they wouldn't give him the chance?*

This was a ploy, he realized. *They had to go through their motions. Sam would, too. When the time came, he would emerge from this cage and take care of business. His family and his love would leave town, head somewhere far, far away.*

And he would kill both men. The Society man, too.

He owed all of them plenty.

In less than an hour, he passed out once again and dreamed of death.

103

"Please don't tell me he didn't come home again last night."
"No, and I'm scared. The same thing happened to my uncle and I'm afraid he's rotting somewhere."

Bridget Taylor stared at Ruby with begging eyes. "I won't be mad if he spent the night upstairs with you. I just want to know that he's okay."

Ruby held out a hand to Sam's mother. She surprised herself by keeping it steady. "He didn't. Neither of us would ever in your house."

"It's his house and I'm just a tenant here." Her tears began to flow.

"Please stop," Ruby said, although her worry had reached the critical level. Ever since Sam told her what he found in the mountain town and what he had seen in the hospital, she had feared for him. He didn't strike her as a man who would, or could, sit back and simply accept people being hurt. "I'm sure he and Gene are just stuck somewhere in that town in the hills. They did mention looking for my uncle again. My coworkers at the school tell me that it can be fifty degrees and cool here, while a snow squall can shut down travel entirely on Route 250. They know what they're doing."

"I know I sound like a pathetic histrionic old hag, but he and Colin are all I have. I can't lose them." Bridget accepted Ruby's hand. Maybe one day, she might accept the woman herself. They had gotten along just fine since Sam asked her to stay. The talks they had had both enlightened and relieved her. She discovered that Bridget had never cared much for Miriam."

'There was always something 'above' us in her. She wasn't a

bad person, but I felt she kept pushing Samuel to be something he wasn't, like where he came from was only a starting point, one which he should aspire to rise above. A wife, or husband, should accept his or her spouse for who they are. If not, don't take the sacrament.'

Ruby had nodded. She'd wished she had heeded the same advice, but in her world, women were told who to marry, who to obey, what to do with their lives. That was why she'd accepted her would be husband's offer to give her an opportunity she would never have in her country. *Only a fool would believe a man like that—and she won the blue ribbon.*

"I escaped two bad men before, when nobody thought it was possible." She'd stared Mrs. Taylor down, hoping to make her point.

"Boyfriends? Husbands?" Her wary eyes showed she didn't know what to trust, other than the fact that her son had given Ruby his heart, something he'd imprisoned for too long.

"Add a father to the story and you can understand why I would have swum here if I had to, just to try a new trouble."

Now, Bridget turned back to the dinner on the stove, soup she undoubtedly wished would impress her new boarder.

"Is Colin still in bed?" Ruby turned out of the kitchen to peer up the stairs.

"I think so. Haven't heard him budge in hours, but I know he was up there when I went to remind him about school in an hour."

Ruby slipped on her shoes as the two women danced around what they really meant to say to each other. "Good. I don't want him getting caught up in whatever's really happening down at the hospital. Didn't he say that a girl he knows is missing?"

"His girlfriend, so he says. I believe that's why you're here— to help him realize what his role should be. Sam felt afraid the boy would search for her himself."

Then he would wind up as dead as I believe my uncle to be, Ruby mused. She walked to the front window and peeked out into the street. *Would he be the next to disappear, or would it be her?* No one here knew the training she had received from her brothers and mother back in the village. While still consumed by fear, she felt confident she could at the very least escape a would-be attacker.

"Shouldn't you be packing a bag like Sam asked?" But the older woman only fiddled with her soup.

"And go where? Where should I go with Colin? The Depression is everywhere. What if these people, or the ones who call the shots, decide to prove something to Sam and take it out on someone in this house? I lived nearly thirty years under one roof, adapting to that way of life. Virginia was tough enough for me. It's a good thing they take care of us here."

"That was Sam's point. He doesn't think they're caring for us here. It's more like marking us for the bottom of the barrel. Where's Colin?"

"Upstairs. He's planning his own rescue mission for that girl of his. He doesn't even know about Sam yet."

"I'll walk him to school today."

"Why? He'll be fine. He's fast and smart." She tinkered more with the stove.

"I know the back way. His teacher was almost killed yesterday."

"Maybe."

Ruby understood. *The woman was terrified.* "I was trained back home. I know how to defend myself."

"Against a man?" The look was typical; skeptical, and mocking.

"Especially against a man. Taught by women." When she pulled out the item meant to deter a man into walking, limping, or crawling away, Bridget's mouth hung open.

"Do you still want Colin going alone today?"

The knock at the door shattered a piece of each woman's heart, even before they saw who was standing there.

104

Colin heard the knock-code sent by his mother when the visitor arrived. He looked out the window but couldn't see a car from his vantage point. *Who was there?* He never felt the vibrations of the front door opening last night, but knew Sam had gone out somewhere with Gene. From the looks on his mother's and Ruby's faces, he knew they were worried.

He had his own worries right then. Chloe had been gone for a couple of days now and he knew it couldn't be good. Sam didn't know that he'd 'heard' him talking to Gene the other night. Then he told everyone to stay put and get ready to hop a train to somewhere out of Augusta.

Hell, no, he thought to himself. *Yes, there were bad men in town, some who would like to see him tossed away like garbage. In his school, the word 'defectives' was tossed around quite a bit. He knew he wasn't one. So what if he couldn't hear?*

He had a nasty fastball. His curve wasn't too shaky, either.

Ms. Pritchard had told him about finding his skills for life. *Hopefully, writing would be his key to rising above what people thought he could be.* He noticed the others in the school, the nurses, assistants, and even some teachers, mention the 'unfit'.

Unfit for what?

His school? A regular baseball team? This town?

He also read the lips of those same people who talked about the place where Sam worked. They mentioned a 'devil' and 'evil' in this country which would change everything. He didn't believe in devils and demons, but did know bad people didn't care for him or anyone else in his school. The people in the town were nice, however. They always waved and smiled.

But Chloe was missing and mom had given him the Morse code for 'train'. When Sam had told them that things might get bad for a while, he'd had a feeling they would have to leave. Hopefully, Sam would fix whatever he had to and they could come back soon. Colin didn't want to leave New Jersey at first, either, but he loved Augusta now. Another move could be just as good, or better. He doubted it, though. This was the first time people treated him like he was a real person and not just some deaf kid.

He'd go, but first, he had to find Chloe. He knew that the man with the hat or the guy running the hospital had something to do with her disappearance.

First things first, he thought. Mom wouldn't send a message like that unless something was wrong. She only used it to call him for dinner or to remind him to do his homework or chores.

And she'd signaled it twice.

He popped open the window in his room and stepped out onto the roof. The sloping surface ran around the perimeter of the house and never became too steep, except for near the chimney. As he turned to the right, he saw the drainpipe. The roof remained slick from the night before, so he crawled out on hands and knees. The rough shingles hurt his knees but he knew he had to be quiet. With only about a ten-foot drop, he could've jumped, but if he made a noise loud enough to get the visitor's attention, it might ruin everything. Also, if he turned an ankle, he wouldn't be able to run, or even walk, down the street.

Chloe might need him. He inched to the corner of the house and lowered himself to latch onto the pipe. Back in Jersey, the kids in the apartment buildings used to do this all the time. It was one of the few things he did back there where nobody gave him grief. He wrapped his arms and legs tight and let go of the roof. Even with the cold morning dew on the iron, his hold remained strong and allowed himself to slip slowly to the ground.

When his feet hit the grass, he crept to the window and peeked inside. His mother and Ruby stood in the living room, facing the front door.

The man in the fedora stood only a few feet away from them.

Colin looked towards the hospital and then towards Chloe's house, close to the school.

With a plan in mind, he ran faster than he ever ran before.

105

Sam awoke in the dark some time later, not having any idea how much time had passed. The burning in his bladder had become excruciating, but he would not allow Maclin and Dejarnette humiliate him.

In the dream he was having, a loud sound drummed above him. He assumed that was what had woken him. A black and red eagle flew over his cage, carrying something, an iron cross bent into a shape he couldn't identify.

When he gathered his senses, he recalled where he had seen it before. Fear coursed through his body in a surge of coldness that surpassed the damp chill he'd sustained during his time locked away.

He had seen both symbols on the parcel he had stolen from Dejarnette's home. *But why would he have German correspondence with someone? The man had been born in France and moved to America as a young boy. Surely, he hated the country and all it stood for even more than anyone in this country did.* The German armies had decimated much of the French cities and countryside in their aim to take over Europe.

It just didn't make sense. He would have to read through the document to hope to decipher any connections between Dejarnette and the author of the letter. He only hoped it had been typed in English.

Another hand hit the side of the box. Sam shook but couldn't raise his arms to protect himself from whatever, or whoever, stood outside. Without much noise at all, the lid rose, harsh light pouring inside, blinding him. Someone hit at a second latch and lifted the opening, leaving nothing but dank air between him and freedom.

He strained his eyes, half open, to see who had lifted the top from his prison. No shadows remained in the light, nor did any sound in the room. He felt utterly the cripple as none of his limbs worked.

"Hello? Dejarnette? Joseph?" He wondered if his voice could be heard. All he could hear was a hoarse whisper. *If he couldn't communicate, how would he extricate himself from this box?*

After a few minutes, something scratched along the floor. Hands reached in and grabbed hold of him. *Who would be in here?* He felt someone lift him up and pull him from the cage. *Was it just one person or two?* He weighed close to two hundred-twenty pounds and at six-foot three inches, he knew he wouldn't be easy to maneuver.

The light grew as he felt a colder surface underneath him. The hands released him and disappeared back into the shadows once more. He fought by clenching his eyes tight, and the images pulled into focus. The harsh light had only been two light bulbs hanging from fixtures above his head.

"Help," he managed to say in a voice that resembled his own. "Come back, please." He turned his head to see a trio of figures staring at him. None of them moved towards him. "Please. I need to get to my family. I won't tell." Something about them seemed off, though. Their heads misshapen, bodies askew, not quite the lean outlines of the guards or doctors. Sam wondered how much he had been drugged.

He lifted one hand a few inches, cringing at the pain that receding numbness brought. *How long had he been in there?* His hand waved at the group but they remained steadfast, eyes unblinking. "Why did you let me out if you're not going to help me?"

One by one, they turned to leave the room. *No,* he cried inside. *I can't move yet.* One of them held up a hand, as if to say it would be okay. It was then that Sam knew who had rescued him. *But how had they gotten inside the white building?* He began to cry, finally understanding that he wasn't alone in the fight. *Even if Gene had died, these three, and likely the rest of their kind, also wished for an end to the hospital's reign in the valley.*

"Thank you," he said as the last of the trio disappeared from view.

Minute by minute, he regained more feeling in his limbs. Once he had, he almost wished himself to be numb again. His head, right arm, and both legs ached with bruises. He wondered if one of the blows he sustained had left him with a concussion. As he examined his wounds, he determined nothing was broken, just badly discolored.

Sam crawled on all fours to sit upon another Utica box. As his vision returned, he gazed around the room. Truly white, even on the inside, the paint had faded this lower room. No windows graced the walls, nor did any cabinets, examination tables, or other equipment which would suggest a medical facility.

Three other boxes sat on the floor, including the one which held him prisoner. All of them stretched out on the floor in black wood and metal about seven foot long, two feet across, maybe a few inches more. The lids allowed the examiners to see inside, but not for the patient to view the doctor, unless the top lid had been lifted.

He stumbled on both feet over to his box and looked at the casing. Double latches were built into both lids—akin to his army footlocker, if a rat's cage had been placed inside. His rescuers had busted the outer latches with a tool of some sort, likely a hammer. *Odd,* he thought since none of the four catches appeared to be lockable. From the inside, though, a true lock wouldn't be necessary.

A realization struck him as he gazed into the box. Quickly, he moved to the nearest cage and flipped the latches. Each took considerable strength, likely a sign of his own not fully returned yet.

When he opened it, he fell back to the floor. A man stared back at him. A man whose eyes had lost sight, and life, a least a week or two ago. The body had swelled, diminishing the features almost as much as those of the masked men who had saved him.

Would Dejarnette have left *him* in there long enough to die? *No,* he thought. *The man needed what Sam held in hiding. It meant too much to him.*

Reluctantly, he moved to the other two boxes and checked them. Both lay empty, thankfully, yet reeked of death.

He knew who the corpse was. *Dejarnette was truly a monster.*

Time to leave this tomb, he said to himself. His eyes had fully acclimated to the light and as he looked to the doors, he found two—and a clock on the wall above the inner one.

7:45 A.M.

My god, he whispered. He had been in the box for nearly half a day. That was *if* it was only a day. His belly ached of hunger, but he didn't feel as if he were ready to drop. Still, he could have been in there for longer if drugged. That would have given Dejarnette and his men time to search his house and property. *Shit. His family. If they'd touched any of them …*

He did feel one need which couldn't wait. He raced to the outer door which held a drain at its base and unzipped his denims. He relieved himself for nearly a minute, knowing he could do nothing until he emptied himself. *Now, if only a pitcher of water or faucet was in the room.* His lips chapped, his mouth parched, he knew he wouldn't be able to speak for long without some fluid. *Hell, even a drag of Gene's hootch he got from the mountain folk would suffice for now.*

With his limbs so stiff, had he been in there longer? With the sensory deprivation, he could have been in there for weeks and not remembered. They could have fed him, allowed him to piss, shit, and drink without committing anything to memory. *What else couldn't he remember?*

The sensation of dread and loss weighed on him like a gravestone. *Why had he asked his friend to join him? He might have made a widow of Eliza and lost the only friend he had in this godforsaken town.*

All because of the damned Society. But why did Dejarnette

care so much about that country America had defeated almost two decades ago? The armies had left Berlin in rags with little remaining money and he knew that their depression had rivaled America's.

But he had heard through his army friend—another ghost he added to the list of deaths he had contributed to—that their leader had been growing in power and was pissed about the rest of the world still laughing at them. The reporter suggested that the war had already begun over there once again, and whoever led them wished to wash away all he disapproved of—just like Dejarnette. But nothing in the American newspapers suggested that truth.

Then again, the Society likely suppressed any mention of something that might draw comparison to their efforts. They had spent millions to garner positive press to convince the citizens of this country that their methods and philosophy would lead to the strongest backbone the people ever had, as it removed the blemishes from its 48 states.

He needed to get home. Ruby and Colin were in the crosshairs of Dejarnette and the man, or men, who worked for him. And here he was without a weapon and with only wounded legs to carry him.

The back door led to the courtyard. If he left that way, and patients and guards stood nearby, an alert would sound and he would be dead before he could identify himself.

He turned to the other door, one without a bolt but with a strong double lock. *He needed to pry it open if he were to leave that way.* No tables stood in the room but next to the door hung a series of shelves. Each one held medical supplies. Bandages, gauzes, towels, needles, and bottles of unmarked fluid sat on each, none of which would be of much help. He looked to the opposite side of the door and next to a row of the same supplies sat a silver tray.

On it was a hammer with both sharp and mallet edges, a pair of forceps, and two tools which might just help him escape. He grabbed hold of the scalpel and orbitoclast. One of those would likely help jimmy the locks.

When he tried the first, the scalpel sunk into the lock and with a few twists, it clicked open. It was then that he realized that the lock had likely not been secured. The second lock, however, looked to be a chore for him. The orbitoclast had not likely entered anything but an eye socket and brain before Sam thrust it into this door. He wondered how many men, or women, it had helped kill before he touched it.

After several attempts, the lock snapped inside and Sam heard something hit the floor on the other side. He prayed nobody was in the room or office there.

With a steady, strong pull, he opened the thick door, revealing a short hallway before leading to a set of doors. *My god*, he thought. *Why didn't I realize this?* The white wing was connected to the main building. It made sense as the treatments would likely have first been attempted on the most troublesome, violent patients. Dejarnette's office would be around the corner. So would Maclin's.

He wouldn't have minded if either of them entered the hall right about then. But no one did and only silence greeted him. *Would Doris be there? What day was it? Saturday? Or was it still the work week?* If so, the secretary would likely be arriving any moment. His own secretary normally showed up at 8 am from Monday through Friday. He liked both women and wouldn't want to have to silence either of them by putting them in a closet or something else safe but frightening for them.

He passed Dejarnette's door, which hung open. He peered inside saw no one.

He needed to confront the man. But not until he led his family to safety. Maclin's door, the second on the left, the smaller office about twenty feet down the far hall—a considerable distance from the superintendent's—stood closed. Dejarnette would not wish to have other staff near his own office.

Please, he begged to no one, *don't let the women be there.*

He entered the room with both tools tucked in his jeans, to find the light still unlit. He looked at the clock. *7:49. He still had a few minutes if she arrived on time.*

Sam had a choice now: to leave the building and hope to

sneak by the front guard, or to see if Maclin was there. He had likely been the one to suggest locking him away and he knew that the man had performed the operation on McIlveen.

His shoes made no sound as he stepped across the massive Persian rug laid across the middle of the lobby. Only twenty or so more feet remained when he reached the far hallway. With careful steps, he approached the office and halted.

Music sounded from within. *Bach*, he guessed. *The sharp, angular melodies would be tasteful to this man. Sam liked much of it himself, but could not relax to any of it. This man, however, could likely find solace in the sound of breaking glass.*

Sam steeled himself at the door and placed his hand on the knob.

Are you crazy? he chided himself in silence. *Yes*, he answered. *Yes, I definitely am at the moment. Until I find that everyone I care about in this town is gone from this hell of a place, I wouldn't wish to be anywhere near me.* He looked down and saw that the lobotomy tool was gripped in a reddened hand. No guitar pick would ever feel at home there as this tool did at this moment.

Inhaling deeply, he twisted the knob and burst inside.

"How?" The man had been sitting at his desk but jolted upright at the sight of Sam.

"How am I still alive? Free? Not covered in my own shit?" Sam felt himself unraveling.

Jed Maclin stood and pulled open his desk drawer, and smiled. That motion ended any hope Sam had of keeping his sanity intact for the encounter. He jumped on the desk and pinned the doctor against the wall next to the window. The gun which he had been attempting to reach clattered to the bare floor.

"You're no smarter than your predecessor."

"What do you mean?" *The psychologist before him? But then, why would he have been the first? Sam had just never allowed himself to think it. He created the test which would change the face of mental health, therefore, why would there have been someone before him?*

"The man was a fool, even more so than you. But at least he believed. He knew the monkeys needed their cages, the mud to be washed down the sewers. He wanted the same as we all wanted. You were the only idealistic idiot. And you," he laughed, "were the one who brought the test which hammered the nail into the fate of all your patients. You were just too stupid to see it."

"No, I cared." Sam found his breath labored. *Maybe he couldn't do this.* "No. I came here to fix things. I thought people here did, too."

Still, the man smiled. "You fool. If you leave here without my say-so, your family will be dead by the time you get home."

"Dejarnette knows better. He needs something from me. You know that."

But from the look on Maclin's face—an expression he quickly lost, but not fast enough—Sam realized that the doctor had no idea about the German package.

"They'll shoot you if you try to walk out. Dejarnette himself will be here any moment."

Sam surprised himself by loosening his grip, the one he didn't even realize he had on the man's shirt, which had jabbed his right hand under the jaw, causing Maclin's face to whiten.

The smile returned.

"By the time you think you'd be home, I'll have had your monkey bitch a dozen ways. I know those European women, those gypsy whores, will do anything for a penny. What would yours do to keep herself alive?"

The man's fist shot out before Sam could react. Its impact stole the breath from the psychologist's lungs and caused him to double over. The man attempted to raise a knee into Sam's face, but he dodged it mostly by accident. Another fist landed on the top of his head and dizzied him, but the vision of Ruby dying at this man's hands shook him back to reality. Sam kicked out with his left foot and connected with the man's shin. He pulled back and kicked a second time, landing in the man's kneecap with a sound he hadn't heard since on the battlefield.

The man cried out but raised his fist again. Sam saw that he eyed a letter knife on the desk and had made the mistake of reaching for it. However, when Sam blocked the hand, the man's knee connected with his gut. More breath escaped, and Sam realized that only adrenaline kept him moving. The time in the box had drained him.

Before the doctor could land another blow, no doubt something that would drop Sam to the floor, he reached for the orbitoclast which he realized had dropped onto the desk. The scalpel would have been easier, but Sam felt like he needed something to frighten the man more.

As the man—who when standing was Sam's height and just about his equal in build—saw the tool, he screamed. "Guard!"

Without thinking, Sam's left arm pivoted backwards and drove up into the man's abdomen.

Maclin gasped at the attack, not expecting Sam to truly stab him. Sam had lived all these years proud that nightmares of killing a man up close had never plagued him. *All of that would be in his records. Maybe part of that fucking census that Davenport compiled.*

The man's mouth shot open, likely to draw in a breath and to beg Sam to stop, but the other saw it as another attempt to call for help. A spot of blood trickled out.

Sam's arm pistoned back and drove forward once again, feeling the tool sink to the hilt in the man's chest, through the ribs. Blood poured over his hand in a thick river. He nearly looked down to see if the other could be saved but instead gazed into his eyes. In them, he saw his family, his love, his friends, all dying because this man decided none were worthy of reproducing, of even living. *How dare he decide who Sam had in his life, who loved him? How dare he choose who bore children when this monster here, the one bleeding out in Sam's grasp, did not deserve to even breathe?*

He didn't even notice that his arm continued to drive inwards. It dug, twisted, dug again and he felt the soft tissue inside tear and cause the man to utter sounds he never believed possible.

"Please," Maclin begged as the beginnings of blood formed in bubbles at his lips. "I don't want to die. Please."

He tried to raise his hands to hold onto Sam's, to stop the assault, but only managed to lay one atop the arm which had submerged itself into his belly. Sam knew that the man's heart lay somewhere to the right and turned the long steel pick upwards.

"No," Maclin gurgled. "Get the doctor, please." He wheezed. Sam heard other sounds from within the man's body. "You can't kill me."

Sam halted for a moment, "Why?" A million other questions clamored around his mind, even as the ice pick and half of his fist was inside the man.

"I didn't want to kill anyone. It wasn't me. Dejarnette built the furnace. He called the shots for them. I just. I just ….

"You killed them … just as much as I did."

"No. No," Sam said. "I wanted to save them."

Maclin's eyes blinked. "It's cold. I can't take the cold. Please stop it.

"I can …"

But the man never received the chance to complete the thought. Sam's arm drove up hard and felt a tougher object give way to the sharp tool. *The heart.* As he pierced it, Maclin stared at him with a coward's stare, still begging to live.

He died with his mouth still forming the words he hoped would keep him alive.

106

Sam left the building with his arms still covered in Maclin's blood and crept towards the guard at the front gate. Somehow, he knew that it would be the last time he ever stepped foot on the grounds of Western Valley Hospital.

On the way out, he grabbed one of the doctor's white medical jackets. As enraged as he felt, he knew if caught, there would be no way to save his family. It wouldn't matter who had died at the hands of the doctor. The Society would cover it up and their lawyers would see to it that his story never saw the light of day.

As he approached the guard, he realized only one path lead out of his dilemma. *Stepping onto that path would be like tiptoeing through a minefield for the remainder of his life, but it would be life. His soul would remain intact.*

At the deepest of his core, he knew there existed a good reason why Miriam still saw him, loved him, and why the Belsnicklers had chosen him to help and harass. *Some things just were meant to be.*

The guard never saw Sam walk up behind him. The dolt likely only paid attention to those who walked the path. As Sam had followed the grass and followed the fence instead, the man never even turned his head. He didn't see the fist punch through the open window of the guardhouse and connect with his temple.

Sam walked away as the guard slumped to the floor, his newspaper fluttering over him. The front page told Sam it was Saturday. *Two days solid he had been inside. The rest of the day would not be as simple, but the right path seldom was.*

Right then, his pointed him towards his home with a sour taste in his stomach.

107

When he walked through the door, he understood the source of the feeling. He knew he would not have to call out to either Ruby or Colin. The two women who had meant the most to him in his life so far stood in the living room, awaiting his arrival.

His mother's face streaked in tears. His dead wife simply waited behind her with the saddest look Sam had ever seen. He wished he didn't understand, yet he knew at that moment the reason for her expression.

"Where is she, mom?"

Her face hitched, more tears welling up in both eyes. Miriam cried behind her.

"Where did she go, mother?"

"You do know that he's going to find Colin as well. You didn't stop him. You only pissed him off and possibly made sure he would take out his anger on him."

Sam punched at the wall, cracking the plaster. He seethed, both at her and at Dejarnette. *The man who took Ruby had his orders, and his motivations, but she would still be safe if not for Dejarnette's machinations and his mother's blind love and possible jealousy.*

"That is not fair." She stepped towards her son. He backed up, raising his hands. "Sam."

"Where is he? Is he where we told him to go?" His voice lost all emotion.

She stepped to him again, not backing down. "He left through the window. I think he'll go straight there. Are Gene and Eliza meeting us there?"

"Are you sure he won't be trying to find that girl first? If he does, if he goes anywhere near that school, he might not make to the train."

"You're not listening. The man didn't give me a choice. He told me that if I wanted to live, if I wanted you to live, I had to tell him where Colin was hiding. He said Dr. Dejarnette needed to see him and meet with you."

"And you *believed* him?" Anger coursed through his veins. *He wanted to punch something. Hard.* "Who was he?"

She shook her head. "When I told him that I wouldn't, that I couldn't, that he could kill me before he found out where my son was, he said 'fine, when I do find the boy, I'll make sure to kill him personally in front of you just to prove a point.' I cried and my mind lost it. I scrambled but could only think of one other option."

The walls caved in on Sam. Everything fell in shadows. "No."

"'I'm sorry," she said. "I couldn't let anything happen to either of you. We're family."

His hands slapped the dining room table so hard one of the legs snapped. "You sold her out to save Colin? And yourself? How *dare* you! You know what they'll do to her. I told you, Gene and Eliza told you."

"At least she'll be alive. You don't want a child anyway," she said, attempting to calm him. "Think of the pain it brought you before."

He exploded on her. "But that's *my* choice. It's *her* choice—not *yours!*" He swung his fist again. The family picture of them shattered on the floor.

"I just wanted to keep you two alive. I can't lose anyone else."

"So, you took away the one thing I can't afford to lose? I haven't been happy in two years. You *know* that. You basically signed her death warrant."

Through her tears, she screamed, "I didn't know what to do! You know I don't want her to die. I just want my family to live. I'm sorry." She grabbed for him but he yanked away, refusing to make eye contact with her.

He raced upstairs and pulled out the footlocker he kept in his closet. Two boxes of .22 caliber bullets sat underneath several folders and records he had yet to unpack. He loaded the Luger and pocketed a dozen more rounds.

"I'm sorry," she said when he descended the stairs and paused by the front door. He fought the urge to turn and face her, knowing the love she had for both of her boys. *She had cracked under the pressure like most people would. He hated her now, but hated himself more for putting all of them in this situation.*

"I know," he replied, cracks splintering his words. "But if something happens to her, I don't know how I'm going to live under the same roof as you, knowing you sold her to the wolves." It was cruel, but he felt cruel. *He couldn't relent, not until he knew Colin, Ruby, and Gene were alive. Then he would let his mother know how much she meant to him and how sorry he was for acting the perfect ass.*

"Just get yourself to the train and try to find Eliza and Gene."

He took off with the Luger in his pocket and sprinted towards Dejarnette's house.

Finding the tallest peak would be the final task on his list. It might be the only way he could find solace of heart after all.

108

Running in the opposite direction, Colin found himself on Hilltop Road, nearly out of breath but at the street's apex. Across the road stood Chloe's house, a massive gothic Victorian. He wondered how he could reach her room from the ground. Shimmying down a drainpipe was simple, and mostly safe, yet climbing one took skills he doubted he had.

The flat roof atop the first floor jutted out in a canopy-style wraparound, so if he could reach the second story, he could find her room.

But why not just ring the bell or knock? If the police had been investigating her disappearance, his visit would be welcome. Or would it? A teenage boy from her school, a deaf school, who could communicate only in limited fashion, might not be welcome.

Still, he hadn't raced to her house just to turn around, especially if his own family would be leaving town. *If things with the hospital were getting that dangerous, he had to tell them. It might help. Maybe even Sam could talk to them, make them believe the insanity he had heard about what those people were doing.*

He walked to the thick oaken door and lifted the brass knocker. Letting it bounce twice off the carved frame, he stood back a few feet and crossed his hands behind his back, praying he didn't appear to be a lowlife from the bad side of town.

After half a minute, a gaunt blonde woman answered the door. She looked like she hadn't seen the sun since Bram Stoker's Dracula.

"Hello," he signed. "I'm Colin from Chloe's school and

wanted to know if you needed anything. I've been looking around town for her every day. My brother works at the hospital and he's pretty worried about the things over there. Can I ..."

"No thank you," she signed back to him. "Please leave us alone." The door closed in his face.

Why? He had only come to help.

He had made sure he wore clean trousers with his shoes and an ironed blue shirt. The woman knew sign language but still treated him like crap.

Why?

Her daughter might very well be dead. Hadn't she heard about the missing baseball players from the schools? About what happened to Ms. Pritchard? It wasn't safe. All he wanted was to offer his help. He knew all the places Chloe liked to go, hide, and even her favorite places on the grounds of the school.

Did she not care? Or did she just not care to hear from another deaf person?

He stepped off the porch, contemplating whether to knock again, to give her his last name and Sam's name, just in case. His vision blurred as he thought of Chloe never coming back to school, or if she returned after he and his family left Augusta. He never liked to cry. Even why his father passed away, he waited until everyone fell asleep before allowing himself a moment to let everything out. He didn't feel it was about being manly, but rather a matter of keeping his feelings safe. Years of loss and bullying, loneliness, and hurt did that.

Another tear glazed over his left eye, but not before he noticed something while gazing at the house.

Someone upstairs moved in front of the window.

Someone who waved.

Chloe? What would she be doing home? She went missing. The school said so.

Her beautiful face shone at the window—but hers, too, shone because of the tears which covered it.

Colin needed to get up to talk to her. He doubted she could see his signs from up there. He looked through the lower windows to see if the skeleton mom still watched him, or if there was an equally corpselike father waiting for better company in their parlor. Colin had never been inside such a fancy house before, except when he went to the movies. He wondered if the sets in the films were accurate, or if they made everything seem like a fairy tale.

Nobody moved the drapes inside the house, so he walked away and towards the far end of the street before cutting back after he passed the corner. He snuck close to the corners where the drain was and took some time to quiet his thundering heart. He would need all his strength to climb the dozen or so feet up to the landing where her window was.

He placed one foot on the edge of the porch, to shave off two or three feet from the ascent. With a hand on the railing, he grabbed hold of the pipe with the other. The metal was pebbled in a manner that would aid his grip. He only hoped that his shoes would hold once he began to climb. During the past couple of years, he had been developing his arm muscles with baseball. In the city streets and his bedroom, he busied himself with pushups, pull-ups, and throwing as hard as he could onto the stoop. Now, he would find out if his strength held up to the task.

With a fluid push, he swung his left arm and leg to meet the right ones and embrace the pipe. He didn't slip an inch. *Please let me reach her,* he pleaded with someone above. He had never been sure if a god would allow people to be born with disabilities like his and many worse off than him, but now he hoped everyone else knew better.

He moved up six inches at a time, careful not to move too fast and slip down and break something he would need. It took him nearly ten sweat-filled minutes, but he managed to scale the length of the drain to the landing without disaster. As he pulled himself above it, he swung one leg over, and then another, finally pushing off with both hands to stand on the canopy. Just like in his own home, he knew that one sound which echoed inside the house would doom the rescue.

Resorting to what he thought might work best, he dropped to his hands and knees, and crawled to the window where he'd see Chloe. As he reached it, her face popped up and startled him. If the landing hadn't been flat, he might have fallen off balance and tumbled into the bushes below.

She appeared just as startled to see him up that high.

"Open the window," he signed.

She nodded and lifted the lower section for him. He gripped the edge and motioned for her to step back. After seeing a desk and chair underneath the window, he eased himself inside and dropped into the chair.

"I thought someone had kidnapped you," he said, signing with a look of worry.

"They did." She turned her gaze downward.

"But why?" *Her parents kidnapped her? That didn't make sense.* She came to him and wiped his hands with a towel.

"All the problems in town. Our friends disappearing, Ms. Pritchard falling down the steps, everything. But they heard something else that scared them even more."

"Tell me." He took her face in his hands.

She signed each word slowly, as if it frightened her to sound it out, as if signing it made it too real for her to accept. "They heard about some list that the government is making. They make families write down everyone who is in their house, who they are related to, and what is wrong with them or what they do for a living.

"Our families have to list that they have a deaf kid. Others who have students in our school had to write they have blind kids."

"So?" He wasn't following.

"Dad said that then they'll know who to take to Western Valley. He said they're making sure people come out of there unable to have babies. He said he saw one man's scar, and that guy only wore glasses!"

"No," Colin signed. "My brother tests people there. He only tells the hospital if someone is a criminal, or if they're crazy. That's all they do." Yet something in him spoke a truth he didn't wish to accept.

"So why did you come here?"

Mulling over what she just told him, he stared into her green eyes. "To get you out of here. My family is taking tonight's westbound train. It hits Pittsburgh and then heads to Denver, I think. Come with me, please."

She shook her head. "I can't leave mom and dad. They're trying to save me."

"Remember that guy we saw dump the Indian into the river?"

She nodded, looking at the floor.

"Well, he was the one who pushed Ms. Pritchard down the steps. He stalked me at the baseball game where players went missing. I think he just showed up at my house. Come with us, and when my brother finds a way to shut down the place, we can all come back."

"When would that be?" Her face showed more fear than he expected.

"I don't know. He knows someone at the *Washington Post* who can tell the White House. He knows people in New York. They can help. I even think he made some friends around here."

"Colin," she signed. "People in this town are afraid of that place. They won't help."

"Then we'll have to get out on our own and figure it out without them.

"Are you going to come or not? I've been looking for you for two days now. I care about you."

Tears filled her eyes once more. "Do you swear I'll see them again? They don't know how to protect me."

"Yes," he answered without hesitation, but he knew on some level that he didn't know if any of them would ever be safe, if the man chasing him and others like him worked for people like Dr. Dejarnette. They wouldn't stop until they got what they wanted. He'd read Sam's lips the other night when he told Gene about some 'Society' he had joined in San Francisco. *If it existed out there, and here, where would it not reach with hands which didn't want people like them in this world?*

109

They climbed down the pipe, after Colin told her where they would be heading.

"Trust me," he signed. He then led them to the school, remembering Ms. Pritchard's secret way out.

The school stood only a block away, so it took them two or three minutes to reach the side door. "Wait," he said to her. "That car. I think I've seen it before. Sam's boss was in it a few times. That sick man with the hat drove it."

He peeked around the corner, noting the open classroom window, just in case he had to run at a moment's notice.

"Is that the man who tossed the Indian?"

"I don't know, but I'd bet on it." He pushed her towards the window. "Get inside, please. I'll be right back, I promise." He looked at her hard and stared for a moment. "*If* anything happens, or that man cuts me off from you, run to the hallway by the cafeteria and wait for me there."

"Don't."

"I have to. Wait." Colin craned his neck around the corner. "There's someone else in the car with him. Shit. I'll check it out and I hope I'm wrong. I *really* hope I'm wrong."

110

Once again, Colin crept up to a dangerous place. At least this time, trees gave him cover. If the man wasn't in the car or near the front door, he wouldn't notice Colin. Most likely, the agent had visited the school to pull records of his friends to find out where he might be hiding out.

What's with this guy? Colin thought. *Why did he want Colin so bad? He'd never bothered anyone and Sam would do whatever he could to protect him.*

In the books he read, there was always an evil villain. All the Burroughs stories, Wells books, and the pulp novels he gathered like gold, had a horrid, evil bad guy. They had no real personality, but they didn't seem human, either. This man resembled all of them combined, a killing machine who truly liked to kill. It wasn't reality. Life wasn't a bad book.

But still he lived in Colin's world and threatened to end it without a reason the boy would understand. *Please, Sam*, he begged silently. *Help.*

He moved up to the driver's side of the car—a longer black sedan, likely a Ford—and pressed his face to the window. What he saw inside stopped his heart.

"Ruby?"

He spoke the name, even though he knew it wouldn't sound right. Then he knocked on the glass. *Why was she with this bad man?*

Why wasn't she turning to look at him? Her eyes were shut and she wasn't moving.

Did he knock her out? Or worse?

He banged on the window again. *Nothing.* When he looked closer, he saw no blood on her white dress. No wounds that he could see. *Maybe since he worked for the doctor, he had drugged her so he could also collect Colin.*

All he noticed was a cloth and a long, thin glint of something that reflected the moonlight.

The front door of the school opened and the man with the fedora stepped out, a handful of folders in his hand. He didn't look up to see Colin until he was nearly blocked by a copse of trees. Alarm and recognition registered on the man's face when he noticed the boy.

Shit!

"Goodbye, Ruby. I'll make sure we get you on that train with us. Don't worry. Sam or Gene will come for you."

The man rushed toward him without running. It was as if the guy simply glided on air. *He couldn't be human.*

Thankfully, Colin had the angle on him and ran towards the open school window. As he reached it, he stepped on the ledge and tossed himself inside. Hitting the floor, he skid a couple of feet but was quick to recover and shut the window, throwing the lock. It wouldn't stop the man, but would likely slow him down long enough for Chloe and him to reach where they needed to go.

Right before he jumped, he swore he'd seen another man head for the front door, but with the shadows of the autumn trees, he couldn't make out who it was. *Sam had told him that a bad man usually didn't act alone. If this guy hurt Ruby, he was a coward and would likely use a friend to complete his task.*

Inside the hallways, with school closed for the weekend, only a stray janitor would be present. Even the headmaster would be home, or in the clinic watching over Ms. Pritchard. He was like that, watching out for all his students.

Colin sensed something behind him and saw light enter the classroom which he just exited. *Time wouldn't slow for him and neither would the train. He hoped Chloe would meet him where he asked her to be.* With a quick look behind him, he ran down the opposite hallway, up the stairs, and walked with stealth to the end of the floor, with the hope he could shake the G-man that he knew would be on his heels.

Once on the stairs, still not seeing the man, he stepped carefully down into the hall which led to the cafeteria. He pushed open the door and nearly bumped into the cute blonde who had captured his heart.

"Is he coming?" She signed with calmer motions than he had anticipated.

Colin found his heart beating faster than he wished. Part of him felt fear, for her and his family, but also because he wished to hold her and let her know she would be okay. Somewhere inside of him, he wondered who would really be comforting who.

"Yes. He's just not here yet." He pushed open the door Ms. Pritchard had showed him and pulled her in behind him.

They walked quickly down the same dark path the teacher had taken Colin down earlier that week.

"Stay close, the pipes will burn if you touch them."

She gave him an irritated look. "I'm not dumb, just deaf."

Heat filled his cheeks. "I'm sorry. I'm just worried. We need to get to the train. Everyone else is supposed to be there."

Her face tightened. "What about my family?"

"They kept you locked up. Do you even care about them?"

She hesitated before looking at the floor. "You know I do. I don't want to leave them. They only protect me. Usually too much, but I love them."

Colin sighed. "Then they'll understand if you get out of town for a few days. Things seem like they're about to get worse for a while. More and more students have been disappearing lately."

"I know," she signed. "But I don't want to. I don't want to die. Was that woman in the car dead?"

"No," he answered, hoping he was right. "She's my brother's girlfriend. He'll make sure she's okay. Or Gene will. They just need anyone close to him." With a confidence he knew would dissipate if he didn't act soon, he grabbed hold of her hand. "Come on," he mouthed to her.

They'd hurried around the first corner when the light flickered behind them. Colin turned, slowing down just enough to find a safe nook to duck into without blistering their skin. All around them ran long copper and steel pipes of varying widths.

"He's here," Colin signed.

Colin knew that one slip and his ankle, or more, would be stuck until the broken bone would boil raw. *If he was lucky, that was. If he fell headlong or sideways, he wouldn't have to suffer long.*

He pulled Chloe into the space between two boiler-type cylinders. The light flickered again. And then once more. *The government man was screwing with them,* he thought. *He wanted them to get spooked and do something stupid.*

Like run.

Yet Colin held steady and ducked down, slowly, pulling Chloe down behind him. They waited as shadows shimmered on the walls. The man approached down the walkway and from the vibration of the boards and metal beneath their feet, he walked at a brisk pace.

He was going to head right past them.

Colin looked down the walkway, watching the black boots and trousers swish by without slowing. He hoped he could hold his breath until the man passed by, traveling far enough so that he couldn't hear the exhalation. *One of the downsides to being deaf was not understanding how sound carried. But he refused to feel self-pity.*

He peered out, keeping his head low, hoping the dark would conceal him. The walkway turned left about halfway down, while the straightaway headed further into the depths of the basement level. Ms. Pritchard had led him in the direction that would take them straight to the door that opened to the stairs, leading down to the platform at the tracks.

A short trip, he mused, *but a dangerous one.*

The man continued down the longer route, but would likely double back when he didn't see or hear either of them.

Colin felt the heat bleeding off the pipes around him, sweat running down his face. He wiped it off and foolishly wondered what blood would feel like if the man shot him, or worse, stabbed him.

A tugging behind him reminded him of why he was there in the first place. He turned to face Chloe. She pointed in the direction the man went and signed, "Where?"

He pulled her up with him and signaled to the left. If he remembered correctly, it wouldn't be more than a hundred feet or so. Still, they had witnessed the man killing another. Colin would normally not think a man could end the life of a child, or teen. He sometimes had trouble remembering that his life had just turned a corner from which he could never return.

But the missing students. The baseball team that had to forfeit due to players disappearing. Ms. Pritchard falling—being pushed—down the stairs.

This man would kill them without blinking.

He sucked in a deep breath and yanked Chloe onto the walkway. He signaled for her to wait for him until he saw that the door was in that direction, and unlocked. The last thing he needed was to risk their lives running into a dead end, looking at a padlocked door and seeing the muzzle flash of a pistol, knowing the sound would be imagined yet still thunderous in his mind as it tore into him.

He ran as fast as he could, pretending he was stealing second base. He pictured the catcher grabbing hold of the ball, feeling the one he took from Ms. Pritchard's desk in his jacket pocket, and tore down the straightaway, with the door being the base.

He nearly slid as he approached it. Instead, he skidded just before touching it. He begged for his feet to not have made a noise, as he stood in silence against the door.

Down the hall Chloe waited while he held his breath at the far end, the longest hundred feet he would ever face.

As he stared at her, the man with the fedora stepped into view. Yet instead of the hat, he held a pistol in his hand.

God, no. He stood only a few paces away from her.

If he could only rush the man, bean him with the baseball until he didn't hurt anyone ever again …

He could see Chloe shivering in the spot where they originally hid, cowering back in the dark. Yet it would only be a matter of moments before the man spotted either of them—likely her, unless he provided a distraction.

The baseball.

He pulled it out of his pocket and held it tight. It wasn't the guitar pick his brother held constantly, but he prayed it brought him some luck.

The walkway felt too thin, narrow and barely covered the pipes and array of building innards, so he couldn't sneak up to the man. *If he rushed him, he wouldn't be like the heroes in his books. He would only be the fool, one of the background characters who were always dying some horrible death.*

Colin wouldn't allow that, not with Chloe there and his family awaiting him to escape this damn town. A light flickered somewhere down the hall and off to the right. He knew it had to be something—maybe a guard making the rounds, but it was something.

The man took a few steps in that direction, a few steps past Chloe. Without warning, she bolted from her hiding spot and towards Colin. A heartbeat later, the man spun around and raised his gun.

Colin hoped his instincts were good enough. He sprinted up the catwalk and managed to close the gap to about thirty feet before the gun was trained on him.

Shit. Both he and Chloe would be killed, or at the very least be taken to the hospital, which might be worse. He didn't want that. From Sam's sleepless nights, stories to Gene, and now his disappearance, he knew that place meant suffering.

Thirty feet. He had almost made it.

In an instant, the lights in the halls turned on, blinding the three of them. He took the chance. He had to—there would be no better shot.

He cocked back his left arm and let fly his best fastball. Rarely did he aim high, but he thought back to the days of him pitching against the porch. The ball flew from his hand and just as it closed in on its target, the man turned, ready to block it.

Yet the fastball carried so much velocity, his reflexes couldn't beat its arrival. With a wet smack, it collided with the man's left cheek, stunning him, and he tottered towards the edge of the walkway.

Damn! Colin had hoped for a killing blow, but it only dazed the man. He didn't even drop the guy. However, when Chloe crawled over to him, the man's arm would not hold still. His aim wavered, his entire body shook.

He mouthed something that Colin couldn't decipher, but it must have been something vicious, by the way his body jerked this way and that. Sooner or later, he would regain some balance, his eyesight would focus, and the gun would find them once more.

The lights brightened even more, the man turning his attention to where they originated. A flash followed a second later and he stopped teetering.

Another flash sent him spinning into the railing next to the corner and a blossom of red exploded on his chest. Colin took the shot he had and barreled into him with all the force he could muster, knocking the man over the railing.

With an expression of surprise, the man in the fedora—*the G-man, the killer*— tumbled into the mass of pipes and a wash of steam gushed upwards. In that moment, Colin was thankful he could not hear the man's screams. He couldn't bring himself to look where the body fell.

Gene stepped out of the darkness and grabbed hold of Colin, looking him directly in the eye. "No kid your age should have to do that," he said, Colin reading every word.

He hugged the man and then Chloe. He signed a simple gesture to the big man, who was holding a massive revolver. "Did you come alone? Sam?"

The man's expression turned strange. He shook his head and then said "No."

No to which question? Colin wondered. *Where was his brother?*

"Where do we get out of here?" The man looked nervous as they walked. Colin thought it odd, since they would all be joining each other on the train soon. The man also limped.

The teen ran to the door and shoved it wide. The Virginia sun blazed inward, blinding them all for a minute before they saw the train.

"Aren't you coming?" Colin signed, forgetting Gene didn't understand. Yet the question must have been obvious, for he grabbed the boy's hand and squeezed.

"I'll be there," he said. "First, I have to go fetch a very special passenger." As his face darkened, his eyes turning less than happy, he continued. "Maybe more than one, I pray."

111

The front door to Joseph Dejarnette's house stood ajar.

He knows I'm coming, Samuel thought. *He knows most of what happens in this town.* Someone from the hospital, maybe the guard, or Doris, had called the doctor.

The eight stairs leading to his fate lay painted in white. His limp had nearly disappeared, although the pain lingered.

"It took you long enough. I figured you would have been out of that box hours ago."

"How would I? It was locked."

The man chuckled. "You're a smart man. You seem to find a way to get to where the best place for you is, always."

Sam pulled the Luger. "Where is she?" His arm didn't waver. "Tell me and I promise not to use this."

The doctor regarded his psychologist with a look that bordered on pity. "Sam, why do you love her? You're cut from the finest genes. She ..." he sighed. "She appears nice. However, do you really think she's of your caliber? You couldn't breed with her."

"Fuck you." He cocked the hammer. "If you cut her open ..."

Dejarnette's hand rose in defense. "Relax there, Doctor Taylor. I haven't laid a hand on her. I give you my word."

"Your man took her. He came for either of them and left with her." He waved the pistol in a circle. "If *he* laid a hand on her ..."

Dejarnette slapped the table. "I apologize. I didn't sanction that. I may have asked him to scare a few people, but son, I need you. I wouldn't harm one of your family members—even that gypsy you're laying with, despite what I feel about it. Hell, I'd love to sterilize her, like the law says I can, but nothing more."

Sam looked at him, attempting to believe. "Can you call him back?"

"I'll try. Reggie isn't the flexible type. That's why J. Edgar and the Society chose him for this assignment. However, he is my employee. I'll send the sheriff to find his vehicle and retrieve him."

"I will kill you," Sam said. "I hope you know that."

Dejarnette studied him. "I guess I was off about you. Maybe I do know that now."

A long moment lingered between them.

Sam stared into the man's eyes, just long enough for him to realize what he was going to do.

"No! I told you, I can't retrieve him."

Sam took the first three stairs with a stone expression and mind full of storms. "Then I'll even the playing field." He ascended the rest of the stairs with the gun aimed back at Dejarnette, knowing the man would protect even what he hid from the world.

As he reached the landing, he heard a pair of noises, one from the left room—a bedroom behind a half-closed door—and one from the right, the bedroom which he planned on entering. The sound from the left resembled a shuffle and something else he couldn't decipher. *The wife, likely,* he thought, but couldn't give her much thought. *She surely suffered enough having to live with* him.

The boy sobbed behind the door that Sam meant to shove open.

He couldn't help the thought. *What if it had been ...* He would have been two now, much younger than the boy in the room, but in Sam's mind, the two merged into an image he couldn't separate.

His resolve faltered when he needed it most, yet he fought back the tears. If he had to speak to Dejarnette that moment, his closing throat would disallow any words to emerge.

"Did you watch your son die?" The voice drifted up the stairs and through his haze. The hand which held the gun began to lose feeling as the anger squeezed his fingers tight.

"Or did you simply know it was the right thing to do?"

The anger burned at its target, himself, not the man who taunted him. The moment returned in perfect nuance and colors as he watched the nurse take the baby from his wife's hemorrhaging womb and refused to make eye contact with her, refused to look at what he'd loved for nearly nine months. The nurse gazed upon the infant as if it had been designed by Dante himself. He never even saw what his son looked like.

Why did he do it? Grief or shame? Anger or guilt?

"You believed for nearly two years that you were evil, a bad man, for leaving him to the nurse. Do you ever wonder what she did to him? Suffocation? Or did she just leave him in the place where the Society took all the other defectives?"

Sam lifted the gun, not sure where he was aiming. "He wasn't a defective. He was my son! And I kept my fucking mouth shut." The tears finally won.

"Maybe not," Dejarnette said, suddenly calming. "Maybe there is a place for him. Maybe it wasn't him who killed your wife. She had the disease."

Sam's face and mind twisted around the statement. "How did you know? She didn't tell."

"We knew everything," he replied in a soothing voice. "She ordered the insulin. There's no other use for it. We watched it from start to finish. I'm sorry we couldn't save her."

"You didn't *want* to save her." The gun found its target as Dejarnette climbed the bottom stairs. *God, she was the defective they were hunting all along, not his son. They just assumed it, and he hadn't stopped them. But she wasn't a defective, or an unfit—only in their eyes.*

The man continued to climb the stairs. "She was selfish to go through the pregnancy knowing her weakness. It ended her life, his, and nearly yours. Look at what it did to you. Two years gone from your life."

Sam fingered the trigger, wondering if he could end another life that day. His stomach roiled in nausea at the confluence of events bringing him to the edge of his sanity.

The door his left opened as a small hand wrapped around its edge. "Daa ...?"

The shot rang out before Sam saw the boy's face.

Who kicked him? Did Dejarnette slug him with a bat or chimney iron?

His right arm dropped slack as he felt both knees give from the force of the blow. When he felt the carpet smack him in the face, a second shot buried itself in the wall a foot over his head. A third burned his side. As he fell, he noticed the sunburst splatter of flesh and blood from his shoulder, coloring the wall next to the woman. He knew his side would be leaking soon as well. Since it didn't spin him, he prayed it was just a grazing.

A banshee-like wail followed as Sam watched a frail woman step out of the master bedroom and approach him with a pistol. Her eyes wild, she looked at the open door and waved for the boy to hide back in his room. "Go, Stefan. Go!"

"Tamara," Dejarnette yelled. "Stop it, please! You'll hit the boy."

What happened next startled Sam more than most of what he saw in the war. The woman turned to her husband, forgetting Sam as he bled on the floor, with what he knew now to be a gunshot wound to the shoulder. He wondered if he would be alive long enough to make the train. *He needed to get to Ruby first.*

Dejarnette's eyes went wide as he realized she pointed the gun now at him. "Tamara, no! He wanted to take Stefan. I came to stop him. I protect him, every day."

The gun lay steady in her hands as her mouth trembled. "No, Joseph. You caged him like a circus freak or a pig with a fifth leg. He's not an animal. He's just not what you expected."

Dejarnette raised himself up to face her. "No, he's not," he said in a calm voice. "He's not right and if I brought him to any hospital, you know what they would do."

She wailed again, tossing her head back before steadying her aim. "No! He's our son, but I'm the one who loves him. Not you. He could go to that school up the hill. Maybe to another one. You know you could protect him, but you don't. You're afraid. You're petrified of what people would think. Maybe they'd think that *you* had something wrong with you, and deal with you like you do the others."

He raised a placating hand to her. "No, darling. I'm afraid they wouldn't understand. I can teach him here, away from all those judging eyes. I can raise him like we want. I do love him. I can ..."

"No! You will never let him out of that room. The only reason he's still alive is because you're too much of a coward to end his life like you do to those people in ... there." Her hand waved out towards the window. "You blame me for giving him the bad genes. Maybe it's *you*. Look at you. Bald, glasses, hook nose. You're not one of the 'fit' people your bosses require of this country.

"You, my dear, are unfit. As a father, husband, and walking slug of a man."

"You're my wife! Stop this! I know what's best!"

"Just like that stupid poem you wrote? That one you keep reciting? Singing to the patients and to yourself? It's fucking horrible. *You're* fucking horrible."

With a smile that chilled Sam, she shot her husband in the stomach. He hit the floor holding his gut, beginning to cry as he realized she would kill him in his own house. She took aim again at him but Sam rolled hard into her, his legs clipping hers, sending her headlong into the railing. The back of her head struck the carved oak and bounced off. She dropped next to Sam, likely unconscious.

He tried to stand but a wave of dizziness washed over him. *He needed to get home. He needed to bandage himself and staunch the bleeding that turned the carpet red. Gene would be home. Colin would be there as well. Somehow, they would have Ruby ready to go on the train. They had to.*

When he pulled his thoughts together, he failed to realize that Dejarnette had crawled to where his wife's gun lay. It had slid right to him. Shaking fingers reached for it. Like Sam, he pulled himself to his feet. Instead of shooting Sam, he stumbled to reach the stairs. Using the railing, he lowered himself down step by step until he reached the bottom.

Sam looked at the boy, who had watched the entire scene unfold, and said, "Your mother is fine. She will take care of you and take you away. I promise."

Then he slid himself down the stairs, bumping his ass and back against each one. The pain from his wound knifed into his upper body with each jolt and nearly sent him spiraling into unconsciousness. Yet when he hit bottom, he somehow tangled up his legs with Dejarnette's, sending the man into the den, landing halfway onto one of the high-backed chairs.

Sam knew that only one of them would leave the house that night, and possibly neither.

112

"Are you going to finish what she started?" The man turned to look at him with pleading eyes.

"First, I'm gonna make sure I live long enough to save a few people." Sam ripped drapes from the window and tied off his wounds, hoping they worked. He laughed. "I wonder if you have any clue as to how your patients feel right before you 'treat' them. Somehow, I think you're beginning to understand. Finally."

"I only want to make this world better," Joseph said, heaving. "I care about this world, this country. I want my own family to grow in a safe, powerful country where we don't have to worry about another war."

"You eliminate every breed which doesn't fit your recipe for humanity?"

The man choked, likely in terrible pain. "No. They *all* want that. I just follow their lead. You're part of it, too. You knew what you were signing up for when you came here."

Sam smiled, swallowing his anger. "No. No, I didn't. I didn't know I'd be sentencing them, playing judge and jury with my test. *My* test was meant to identify those who needed more help to live happily, to be successful in life—*not* to give you license to kill them."

"But you can't leave," Dejarnette said, no longer appearing brave. "They will never let you. You don't realize where they are. San Francisco is only part of it. So is Chicago and New York. Hell, we're not the only nation who is part of this project. You don't get to walk away. Even Carnegie himself wouldn't."

Sam's head reeled, knowing the man likely wasn't lying.

"Then the whole fucking world has become an unfit place. And I *am* going to leave. If I find another bullet in my back, so be it, but I'm taking my family with me.

"But first, I have to know something."

Dejarnette sighed. "The package."

He pulled himself into a sitting position, upright as if a hole didn't bore through his belly. Sam tossed him a blanket from a nearby sofa, and then wondered why he offered it. He weighed sitting down or keeping the upper hand by standing.

His legs decided for him, turning to rubber as his vision turned blurry for an instant.

"Bandages in my cabinet," Dejarnette said. "That, with alcohol, will keep you alive until you can get to the hospital."

Sam laughed. There would be no one there to help him except for the nurses. They might not be able to take out the bullet, which likely caused some internal bleeding. He would have to take his chances of surviving until he reached the train with everyone safely onboard.

This wound would be his mountain top.

He arose on shaky limbs and crossed the room to rifle through the massive cedar armoire, and dressed the shoulder wound in sloppy fashion. A clear bottle stood among an array of ointments and medicines. He also noticed a bottle of Bayer Aspirin, vials of morphine, and a glass container of laudanum.

"Try the morphine," Dejarnette said. "It will kill the pain until you get where you want to go."

"No," Sam answered. "I don't do that." But he pocketed two of the vials and the hypodermic which sat atop the alcohol.

He howled when the liquid sunk into the wound in his shoulder and once more when he stripped off his shirt to clean the powder burn from the second shot. *So it did graze him. Thankfully, it didn't bleed much.* He tied a roll of gauze around his ribs to staunch the blood. There might be a cracked rib, but he knew he was lucky. The pain in his shoulder and the fact he still was conscious told him that the slug didn't pierce the clavicle. Still, if it broke the bone and pushed it into a thick enough vein, he could bleed out before returning home.

When he put the shirt back on, he returned to the sofa and

downed four aspirin, dry.

"Why Germans?"

The man gave Sam a wry grin and began the story which would dizzy him more than any bullet. The two of them sat, both bleeding out their genes on a rug woven with more care than the DNA with which the Society wished to populate the world.

The man reached for his cup, likely not all tea. "You read the letter?"

Sam just stared. *Just a letter? Then what was the rest of the package?*

"Their leader now, he understands. Over in the country we decimated, they wish to build a nation full of those of only pure genes. He knows the reason they lost the war, aside from poor planning, was inferior soldiers and officers. The Jews, Russians, and gypsies had polluted their gene pool so much Germany became a whole other entity."

"Like you believe America has become." Sam's mind projected the patients he helped sentence to die, Tristan the blue boy, and Colin. *They would be the first to go in a country like Germany.*

"American *has* become like wartime Germany. You hail from the New York region."

"They're polar opposites."

"No, they're not," he wheezed. "New York City is a cesspool of genes that should have been wiped out a century ago. Immigration killed this land."

"You came from France. You're saying you're part of the problem?"

"The Nordic man is perfect. The Society knows that. The Fuhrer over there realizes that. Maybe with a combined research effort we can prove to the American faithful that what we're doing must be done."

"Blonde hair and blue eyes are recessive traits. Mendel proved it. Even I know that as a psychologist. Traits, both physical and psychological, can be dominant or recessive, depending on the region."

"That's bullshit!" The man attempted to slam his fist into

the arm of the chair. He then looked towards the staircase. *He must truly love both his prisoners in this house,* Sam thought. "They're only recessive because of years of breeding with the wrong people. We evolved from the monkeys who fling their shit. Their relatives still walk the street and start wars, crash the economy, and fuck themselves into seven-child households when they can only afford one.

"Thousands of years of proper breeding led to the Scandinavian people. Northern Europeans. The rest should have been phased out like the dodo and Neanderthal."

Sam laughed again, wondering if he could pull the trigger, if it meant getting his family to a safe place. "You do realize that you'd be dead, too. You don't fit. Hell, *I* don't fit, either. Why did you choose me?"

The man wiped at his face with a bloody handkerchief. "It's not a perfect world, Samuel. It's not a perfect plan. Obviously, we can't have it the way we want it. Not completely. But once the world sees how another country succeeds, grows towards invincibility, they'll finally believe and buy into the Society without allowing their moral compass to blind them."

"And then what? You wipe them out like a species which overstepped its bounds in the food chain?"

The man smiled again, likely still out of breath. "Samuel, you're one of the smartest men I've ever met. You do know that. We show our people this experiment and how it changed life here, improved it. Americans are a prideful people. If they survive this depression, they'll tear the next enemy limb from limb and chew on his heart, simply to preserve what they've built."

"They won't go for it. Every family has a black sheep. Every household has a brother, sister, or child who isn't perfect. They want to be taken care of, to know that this country is there for them, to care for them unconditionally. To care about them."

"But no one cares," Dejarnette wheezed, pulling himself into his chair. "The people want a strong country. Look at history's treatment of the unfit. America needs to bleed out its bad genes."

"We'll see what they say when the people find out that to

make us better, you take away their sons and daughters, cutting or burning them away."

Dejarnette coughed up a fistful of blood. "Let me go see Maclin. If he gets the bullet out, I have blood stored to replace what I've lost. You see? When the world is controlled, there are enough resources to keep the people of this country safe and healthy."

"I haven't seen many healthy people here. Besides, I doubt Maclin will be available tonight or any other night. It might be time to start hiring doctors who aren't sadistic psychopaths. Patients usually prefer breathing doctors, so that could be a problem, too."

If the news surprised Dejarnette, his face didn't display any change of emotion.

Sam couldn't believe he'd killed the man and now sounded like he was bragging. He only wished to frighten the superintendent. *With a gunshot wound in both of them, he shouldn't be talking or doing much of anything other than getting help, getting his family aboard train.* When he took a step closer to the man, he felt his knee give. Not much, but enough to let him know he needed help, fast.

"You killed Maclin?" The doctor looked sorrowful. "Sam, I do care. That man didn't have a humane bone in his body but ..."

"And you *do*?"

"I kept my son. Did you?" Sam recoiled as if from a bite from a rattler. "Do you realize that we figured that if the world keeps populating exponentially like it has in the past century, there won't be enough food, jobs, healthcare, or even prisons to house those who turn to a life of crime just to feed their families? Can you understand that?"

"You're out to help the world now?" Sam wished he could spit on the man but knew he needed every ounce of fluid to stay upright. "The Society have some lofty goals, don't they?"

"They're only trying to stop us from killing ourselves. Think about it. You came from New York. Isn't it a cesspool, overflowing with citizens? Imagine how it will be when the economy recovers."

"*If* it does," Sam replied. In 1933, the New Deal reforms appeared promising—but so did Hoover's plans. "And I'm from New Jersey. There's plenty of open land there." Yet he knew the troubles in the bigger cities. Lying, even to this man, felt wrong.

"And this man, this Hitler, he's also in your game?"

Dejarnette stiffened, either in pride or jealousy. "He will be. Once the funding gets to him. His vision matches ours, but without the restraints.

"Darwin figured out that for a species to survive, the food chain cannot be broken," the man heaved. *The bullet might have shattered an organ.* "If a lion feeds on a gazelle and too many of the pride breed, what will they eat when the supply disappears?"

"There is other prey." *Like humans killed other humans to stay alive.* Thoughts in Sam head began to swirl. *How much was from blood loss and pain, which shot up into his chest with steel daggers, and how much was from the weight of the man's words?*

The doctor shook his head. "You're too smart to believe that. Somewhere in you, you believe me and agree. Why else would you have come here? Why else would you have joined us? You knew enough about what we had planned."

"I didn't plan on killing people." The rage increased with his increasing pain.

Dejarnette looked at him like he would a son. "Maybe not literally, but you knew that by keeping the defectives from being born, you would be helping keep them and their families from lives of pain. Look at me. I can't even show my own son to the public. You think they'd let me keep him if they knew?"

"Bullshit," Sam seethed. "They know everything. You're a society of hypocrites. Even Davenport would turn a blind eye to your boy if he was sure you were doing your job, helping the cause."

The man waved in surrender. "Okay, okay. You're right, but Colin was never in danger. He drew the same protection my son did. Some weren't happy about it, especially in that school, knowing he could taint the image they painted by becoming the next Cy Young, when they're selling headlines to the *New*

York Times hoping to sway the minds of the American people."
He grinned. "Hell, I loved watching that kid pitch. I'll bet he
could join normal high school teams and possibly much more if
he sticks to it. He's got magic in him."

"But you'd still sterilize him," Sam said, tempted more than
ever to break the gun across the other man's nose.

A deep sigh, then a blood-filled cough rattled the man's
lungs. "Maybe, maybe not. There are always exceptions. Look
at me. Hell if I fit the image of the new man the Society wants.
Hypocrites? Definitely. But exceptions always exist. Your
brother's a bright boy. I personally would love to see him go
places. Maybe his kids wouldn't be deaf."

"And your people could be okay with that?"

"Sam," he said, wheezing a bit more. "There's plenty I don't
tell them. I never told them about Ruby. That was Vale's idea. We
call him Reggie—but it doesn't matter. Who knows if that's even
his real name? He has his own agenda when he's not following
their orders. A cop told me about a missing Indian. When I
asked Reggie about it, he only smirked. The man despises all
mud people."

Sam felt the gun rise before he could think. "You bastard.
That was Ruby's uncle. She's been thinking he disappeared—
and now, I'll have to tell her. And you probably helped him to
find out about her past."

"Let it go, Sam. She's already gone by now."

"What do you mean?" His legs turned to boneless
appendages and he dropped into a nearby chair. "Did he …?"
*She was supposed to be out of the city by now, but his mom …
damn her for doing what she did.* "Did you order her dead?"

The man's face turned to one of fear. "Sam," he choked. "I
wouldn't do that. Treat her, yes, but not end her life. Vale was told
to bring her to the hospital and nothing else. However, thanks
to you—and her," he said, nodding upstairs, "I doubt that will
happen tonight. Hopefully, he didn't act on his impulses. Let's
pray she's waiting in one of the dorms."

Sam's Luger shook out of his hand, hitting the floor with a
clank. *No. Gene would find her if he couldn't. But where was his
friend? Dead with a bullet in the grass, or laying in a cell with his*

frontal lobe a stewed mess?

"Don't sentence your family to death like you did your friends."

"Gene?"

The confused expression on the doctor's face told him what he needed to know. "The shopkeeper? He was with you by the train." More fear registered. "My men shot at two others. You were one. They told me they hit the other one, but they never found a body."

Not Gene. Not after asking his friend to help him. He did sentence his friend.

"One last question. Why the furnace?"

Dejarnette shrugged. "We need quicker results. We need to clean up our messes. America can't wait for the defectives to expire on their own. It would take decades; the nation is dying now." He gave Sam a look that showed his intent and disregard for anyone he saw as unfit.

"You know they'll follow you. Wherever you go, they'll go. They don't give up. I didn't."

"Excuse me? Didn't give up on what?"

"Recruiting you. Don't leave. If you do, you'll give up any chance to see him."

The truth gleamed in Dejarnette's eyes like a spear through the heart. Sam nearly asked 'who', but the imminent revelation cracked his mind harder than a shotgun to the skull. The inferno the man's comment ignited would not be quenched, could not. The sounds of the outside world ceased to exist.

Sam gritted his teeth and regretted his decision before his brain even processed the ramifications. *Dejarnette would make sure Grant and even his superiors would find him, to bring him back, if not kill him first. His family wouldn't stand a chance of survival where they were headed if he died.*

He left the house shaking, yet determined. His boss would not be following him.

113

Sam wandered along Main Street towards his house. Despite what his mother had done, he needed her and would force her to join them at the train, even if she fought him.

Every step was an excruciating chore. His side hurt more than the hole in his shoulder, now mostly numb from the shock. The burn marks which tore open just a small wound between his ribs felt like a bayonet piercing his innards with each step.

Would he even make it to the house? He imagined the men from the hospital finding him on the street, either shooting him dead on the spot or taking him back to Western Valley.

After he rested for a few minutes at the corner of Main and Beverley, leaning against a lamppost, he swore he could still see his house. *Maybe the drugs did help. Maybe he would survive the day.* The reek of the blood on his clothes kept him from losing consciousness. Knowing that the dampness of his woolen shirt was colored by the blood of two men propelled him home. He felt shock that no regret or illness befell him after he had murdered them. In its absence, he felt a void where emotion should be, but wasn't. In his experience, only sociopaths felt nothing.

Sam wondered whether the events of the past two years had finally broken his psyche. Yet these men deserved to die, just not by his hands. Dejarnette had warned him, but also tried to kill him. He also symbolized the Society for Eugenics and their plan to 'better' America by cleansing it of anyone they deemed unfit. As long as they held sway over key government figures and those holding the bank accounts, Sam and his family would be looking over their shoulders. Or they would they see him as just a nuisance and wait for him to go away.

He never would. He couldn't.

How many other Western Valleys existed across the country? How many monsters like Dejarnette did the Society utilize to achieve their goals?

Somehow, Sam felt that this monster existed as a unique entity, which was why they'd placed him so far away from the public eye.

Correction: he had *existed.*

When he stepped within sight of the house next to his, a holler broke his daze. A big man came running at him and embraced him, causing him to scream in agony.

"My god, Sam, I'm so sorry. I thought you were dead or locked away in there."

Sam forced himself to focus. "Gene?" He squinted, forcing away his dizziness from the blood less. "Dejarnette told me you were dead."

"Nope," his friend said, shaking his head and smiling. "Took a nasty tumble down that damned ravine, probably fractured my arm, but in the morning, a few of our new friends found me and helped me back here. Good thing, too, since Eliza was set to kill me!"

"What friends?"

Gene relaxed and helped steady Sam. He pointed towards the backyard, where about a half-dozen Belsnicklers stood in full silence and ready for their next task.

"They're on our side?" His friend nodded. "Are you sure?"

"I hope so. They're the only way we're getting to the train. Besides, I think you might feel a certain kinship with one of them."

Instead of delving further into that mystery, he needed to know about what mattered most.

"Colin? Ruby?"

His neighbor studied him with a mixed expression. "Your brother insisted on sitting with your mother and his lady friend. She called for you, you know."

Sam looked away, unable to remove the thought of her betrayal from his mind. She had little to no choice, he knew on many levels, but he couldn't shake the image of her giving up the woman he'd brought to his house for protection. On one hand, he knew she could have delayed the agent. On the other, he realized she could have had a gun in her face or a blade against her throat.

"Soon," he managed, choking half on pain and half on regret.

"She told me," Gene said. "You know she didn't have a choice. If she said nothing, that fucker would likely have killed both right there on the spot."

Sam knew he was right, but couldn't shake the feeling which had plagued him ever since he left the house hours ago. "You didn't answer me," he said. "Ruby. Is she on the train?"

The big man wouldn't meet his eyes. "No, she's not, but will be joining us in Pittsburgh."

Sam fought back the dread that his friend lied. "How? There's only the one train. Where the hell is she?" He wished he had the strength to pummel his friend until the entire story emerged. Instead, he collapsed back onto the porch.

"I saw her not long ago," said Gene, staring into the distance beyond the men. "Now let's get your ass to the train. You're an utter mess."

He waved the men over and they picked him up, placing Sam in a pull cart. "Sorry about the lack of class here, but a car would draw attention down at the tracks." Sam nodded his understanding. "They know the back way."

"Of course." Three of the costumed men guided Sam as he reclined in the cart through a maze of trees on a path that only a native could know existed, and he realized two things. "Rowe?"

"Shh," Gene replied when the men around him continued in silence. "Don't worry about who and what right now. They'll be watching out for visitors at the station and north of the tracks."

Sam wondered if he would ever see Betty's husband without the burlap again. Before he could ask, dizziness claimed him again. The trees passed him by as he attempted to keep track of where the trail led.

"Vale?"

The men continued in silence. Gene looked ahead with Sam

unable to focus on his friend's eyes. The ground felt bumpy under his bruised and torn body. At least in the woods, he could barely smell the blood. Birch and pollen filled his nostrils, canceling out most of the stench, and the memories temporarily. A duffel bag sat next to him on the cart. His friend, or mother, must have packed a fresh shirt and trousers, or more. Hopefully, he could exit the train in clothes without bullet holes.

"Who's Vale?" Sam knew from the flat tone and steady gait that his friend already knew of the man, even if he didn't know the name.

"Dejarnette's man. The guy in the hat."

"Yeah," Gene replied. "That won't be happening." Sam swore he caught a partial smile on the man's face. "Ask your brother about that one. He's going to be a fine man."

"You don't have to tell me that." Sam wondered how they'd found the missing girl, but after giving his addled mind a chance to breathe, he remembered how determined his brother could be. The kid had spent an entire summer working on pinpointing the aim of three separate pitches against the steps of their apartment building back in Jersey, when he burned to be on the school team.

114

Sunlight broke when the men pulled the cart out of the woods. They halted, again without a word, scanning the area for any remainders of Dejarnette's men. All seemed to realize that others would be coming, once word got out about what happened. "They're safe, Gene?" Sam would keep asking until he heard about all of those he cared about, protected—and yet failed.

"They're here," he replied. "They're waiting on the train. I already told you. They're a few cars up. Nobody will be looking for them, so they're safe in the general seating area. In fact, that's probably the safest place for all of them."

Sam felt many hands reach under him and lift. His arms flailed until more hands held them down, placing him inside an open box car. He expected hay or some sort of farm residue on the floor, but only wooden crates stood around them. The Belsnicklers nodded toward the Gene and Sam. The psychologist knew then that they would be protecting Eliza and the rest of the townsfolk until they left the valley. He had heard their kind lived as far north as Pennsylvania, so maybe they would be safe.

"A perfect place for our journey," Gene gestured toward the shadows inside. "If we hear anybody, we have cover." The costumed men slid the door shut, leaving only a crack open for watching during stops.

Gene patted his overcoat. A thick revolver jutted out from it. Sam opened his mouth to ask about the man he feared, but his friend pushed him back against the floor. "Let me check out this hole you have."

"You killed him, didn't you?"

"Does it matter?" Gene pulled off the sopping gauze in a

blinding flash of pain.

Sam nearly screamed, yet bit it back and reached for the parcel he'd told Gene to retrieve from the inside of his guitar case. "You know what they're planning, don't you?"

"I read the letter. Sounds pretty grim. But who's that man Dejarnette is writing? I've never heard of him."

Sam almost howled again as Gene washed the open wounds with a bottle of something. "I have. He's a big fish in a small pond," he said. "Someone the Society believe can test their theories in full. One day, that country will be strong enough to pull that war shit again with someone."

"I know," his buddy said, nodding. "Do you think this man, this Hitler, is someone to worry about?"

Sam recalled the stamp from Berlin, the transferred funds from the Society noted within, the invitation to Dejarnette.

"Only time will tell, bud. By the friends he keeps, it doesn't bode well."

Both settled into a spot in corner, after gathering an armful of empty sacks.

"Do you really think you can get away from them? For good?" Gene looked worried but by now, he'd surely recognized that only the dead were immune from the chase.

"That's why I need to get out of here," Sam replied. "Someone's got to get the word out. They're everywhere, but if the people knew the money makers of this country are in bed with Germany's next Fuhrer and they're fingered, the country could break at the seams."

As Gene leaned back to await the train's departure, he replied. "You know, sometimes a little revolution can be a good thing."

"We'll see," Sam said. "For every Abe Lincoln, there's a Napoleon out there. If Dejarnette's plan catches fire somewhere else, we could all be in trouble."

Gene reached into the bag sitting next to his friend and pulled out a smaller hand gun. "It'll stop the campaign. One mind at a time."

For the next several minutes, they waited. Sam was sure that the sheriff or people from the Society would find them. Each held their gun at the open door, hoping no one was so inclined as to inspect the car once more before departure.

"I've head they have devilish places like Western Valley in Pittsburgh, Chicago, San Francisco. Where are we going to go?"

Sam shook his head. "Somewhere where they'll be safe." He choked on something from deep inside and spat it against the wall. "I'll find a place, don't worry. Mountains feel good right now."

"I'm not worried. Just make sure I know so when I settle with Eliza, we can come join you. Somehow, I don't think it'll be safe here anymore."

Sam wiped the blood from his lips. "When *was* it?"

Right before noon, the whistle sounded and Sam began to feel his world upend one last time. The train started to hitch forward and chugged to life.

He needed Ruby to get him through this ordeal. Why wouldn't she wish to be with him now? Did she fear his presence?

115

"I'm headed to San Francisco, Gene. There's someone waiting for me there. Someone I need to bring home, if he'll have me."

As Sam allowed himself to rest, his mother and Colin safe in a forward passenger car, his friend propped him up against the back wall of the freight car. Breathing pained him. He realized his shoulder wound could kill him if he didn't see a doctor. *Maybe when they stopped in Pittsburgh, he would heal before continuing to the coast.*

"I'm going with you," Gene said, holding a fresh bandage on the wound. The worry in his voice cut through the fog of Sam's thoughts.

He shook his head. "Thank you, friend." He tapped the man on the leg, like the older brother he never had. *If he never saw this friend again, the man would still follow him to the ends of the world. If he ever saw him, he might welcome the company. If he were to ever win this war, he couldn't do it alone.*

The train stopped a few more times before it began its nonstop journey to northern Pennsylvania. Harrisonburg signaled the final loading point for freight as the car rolled to a stop.

Light beamed in as the crack in the slats opened wider. A shadow blocked out Sam's vision, but only for a moment. Gene didn't seem to mind the intrusion. *Maybe he expected it.*

Sam smiled as he watched her step on board.

"Hello," she mouthed. He felt his tension bleed from his knotted muscles.

"Hello," he replied. She moved toward him, her eyes full of sadness, yet also joy that she had found him, alive. "Gene said ..."

"Shh ..." she mouthed at him. He crumbled at the sight of her. She moved within a couple of feet of him but appeared hesitant to draw too close. *Why?*

Gene had not been looking at her. His gaze were cast off into the mountains, his eyes weighed down by something Sam couldn't figure.

As Ruby stood before Sam, returning his smile with the one which he had fallen in love with, another shape formed behind her.

Gene stood up, half awake, and pulled shut the door, bringing darkness back into his world once more. When he stood aside, Miriam joined the other woman's side, a tear forming in her eye.

Yet she wasn't sad. She knew where he was headed and who he was hoping to find.

"Thanks again, friend," he said to the man, who stared with him at the sunlight shining in through the thick slats.

"I think I'll do with the company I have."

"Hitler is beating us at our own game." Dr. Joseph Dejarnette, Staunton, Virginia 1934

"I have studied with interest the laws of several American states concerning prevention of reproduction by people whose progeny would, in all probability, be of no value or be injurious to the racial stock." Adolf Hitler, Berlin (date unknown)

AFTERWORD

The major events in this novel did actually occur in the United States during the 1930s. American eugenics began during the 1880s, spurred on by the work of Sir Francis Galton. Dr. Joseph Dejarnette operated as the superintendent of Western State Hospital in Staunton, Virginia from 1908-1946.

The eugenics movements gained momentum in America during the first half of the 20th century due to the formation of such groups as the Race Betterment Foundation, The Carnegie Institute, The Euthanasia Society of America, The Rockefeller Foundation, The American Breeder's Association, and the Eugenics Records Office.

America's formal obsession with eugenics dimmed when American soldiers discovered the horrors of Auschwitz.

For more information, please check out the following books that were instrumental in my research:

War Against The Weak: Eugenics and America's Campaign to Create a Master Race by Edwin Black.
In The Name Of Eugenics by Daniel Kelves.
The Nazi Connection by Stefan Kuhl
Eugenic Nation: Faults and Frontiers of Better Breeding in Modern America by Alexandra Minna Stern.
Eugenics and Other Evils by G.K. Chesterton
Eugenics: The Science of Human Improvement by Better Breeding by Charles Benedict Davenport

ABOUT THE AUTHOR

David Simms lives in the Shenandoah Valley of Virginia with his wife, son, and animals. He works as a teacher, counselor, music therapist, ghost tour guide, book reviewer, and occasional guitarist in the Slushpile band. *Fear The Reaper* is his second novel.

Curious about other Crossroad Press books?
Stop by our site:
http://store.crossroadpress.com
We offer quality writing
in digital, audio, and print formats.

Enter the code FIRSTBOOK
to get 20% off your first order from our store!
Stop by today!

Made in the USA
Middletown, DE
20 March 2023

27251276R00216